THE
GOAT CASTLE
MURDER
A Novel

Michael Llewellyn

D0861403

Published by Water Street Press
Healdsburg, California

Water Street Press paperback edition published 2016

Designer Credits
Cover art by Robert Bush
Interior design by Typeflow

Produced in the USA

ISBN 978-1-62134-150-5

For Elizabeth Trupin-Pulli.

Acknowledgments

Mississippi hospitality is the stuff of legend, a tradition that I'm pleased to say still flourishes in Natchez. For consenting to interviews, sharing secrets and family letters, and generously opening their historic houses, I must thank Beth Boggess who shared the splendors of Elms Court and showed me Jennie Merrill's playhouse; Margaret Guido of Glenburnie Manor, the scene of Jennie's murder; the late Maggie Burkley; Sissy Dicks; Caroline and Paul Brown Harrington; Mimi Miller; Duncan Morgan of the Historic Natchez Foundation; the late Bob Pully; Lani and Ron Riches, formerly of Monmouth Plantation; Jeanette Feltus of Linden; Anne MacNeil; Becky Spears; Pat Butler; and the research staff of the Judge George W. Armstrong Library. I am especially grateful to the late Sim Callon, whose nonfiction work, The Goat Castle Murder (with Carolyn Vance Smith), was an invaluable research source. In New Orleans, I am indebted to John Anderton, Bethany Bultman, Michael Knight, Ron Marlow, Vincent Miller, Robert Baker Lowe, and Samara Poché. Additional thanks to Adrienne Heuer, Tom Rotella, Ciji Ware, Robert Bush, Lynn Vannucci, and most especially to Mary Lou England, my indefatigable Natchez guide who bought me Krystal hamburgers, picked me a bouquet of Naked Ladies, and introduced me to everyone who mattered.

Prologue

THE BLOOD DRYING under the Mississippi moon was the bluest in Natchez.

She wore a peach silk dressing gown and lay face down alongside a camellia thicket. A bullet had entered above the left breast, another at the back of the neck. Both had passed through the body and left powder marks indicating the killer had fired at close range. One arm was contorted beneath her body; the other was akimbo after she was flung onto the ground like so much rubbish. Her frail flesh was thick with rigor mortis, and she was further violated by the scrutiny of dozens of men carrying flashlights, lanterns and torches.

An erratic trail had frustrated the search party. Two hundred feet of undergrowth, ravine and forest lay between the body and a pool of blood on the open lawn. Scattered widely were the sort of jeweled head combs women had ceased wearing four decades ago, a smashed china lampshade, and a bedroom slipper splattered with blood. More blood smeared the porte-cochère and the house itself, Glenburnie Manor, where the victim lived alone amid forty-five acres of live oak, pecan and pine forest. In twenty-eight years she'd entertained only one caller and had endeavored, with some success, to stop time for him, and for herself as well.

Such eccentricity—and rumors of a great fortune cached in the house—invited the wrong party, and at dawn on August 5, 1932, the rest of the world learned death had come calling on Jane Surget Merrill.

PART ONE

1882–1891

*T*he first European settlement on the lower Mississippi, Natchez has long episodic history marked more by the effects of the tumultuous crop-based economy than by the power and politics of the flags that flew over it. Once cotton ascended its throne, the fortunes it promised attracted a unique society of characters, and they created an architectural legacy unlike any in the South.

Randolph Delehanty
Classic Natchez

I

LIKE MOST YOUNG girls, Jennie Merrill enjoyed being the center of attention. Petite and barely five feet tall, she was not a great beauty but at age eighteen already knew how to showcase her best features and downplay the ordinary. On obvious display were wavy auburn hair, mesmeric brown eyes and lustrous olive complexion, but not so apparent was her less than voluptuous figure with a shortness of leg. Jennie downplayed her physical liabilities beneath a smart traveling costume of rust-colored silk with strategically stationed flounces and furbelows. A high, hard bustle, only now scoring a comeback in New York, left no doubt that she was a lady of fashion.

Certain that she presented an irresistible picture, Jennie graciously returned smiles and nods as she explored the Upper Deck of the Mississippi packet *J. M. White*, unaware that some of her fellow passengers' frank glances and covert whispers were anything but flattering. As confident as she was oblivious, Jennie continued her slow, solitary stroll, pleased when the sweetly pungent river air and spring sunshine vanquished a heavy anxiety that had dogged her for weeks. This newfound invigoration drew her to venture down to the Main Deck, the domain of those less affluent travelers. That this was a mistake became quickly evident when she encountered coarse stares and scornful muttering. Resentment of the richly dressed intruder was driven home when she collided with a tall man who elbowed her purse and sent it spinning across the open deck. Jennie reeled, certain such loutish behavior must be accidental.

"Sir!" she gasped. "My reticule!"

Jennie pretended to fuss with her lacy cuffs while waiting for an apology that never came, insult turning to outrage when the offender blithely strode away and no gentleman rushed to her rescue. She looked about for a deckhand and, seeing none, was dismayed to realize she would have to retrieve the purse herself. Swallowing her annoyance, she picked up the purse, rested a gloved hand on the railing and continued with as much grace as she could muster. To her further shock, she encountered one man after another who neither nodded nor tipped his hat. Accustomed only to private yachts and grandiose Atlantic steamships, she was unfamiliar with riverboat etiquette, but Jennie hardly anticipated such rudeness, especially aboard such a fine vessel. With stained-glass skylights, sumptuous French furnishings and ceiling filigree as intricate as stalactites, the *J.M. White* was the most luxurious steamboat afloat. Although others were newer and faster, her father, Ayres Merrill, was nothing if not pragmatic and, knowing his weak heart was a time bomb, decided if he were to meet his Maker it would be amid the most splendid surroundings available.

Jennie took a deep breath and soldiered on. Near the forward deck, four women hastily bunched heads then lifted their long skirts and made a great show of turning away as she approached. Heat stung her pale cheeks. It was one thing to protect one's hems from squids of tobacco juice, but this was a deliberate affront. She lifted her chin and delivered a polite challenge.

"Good morning, ladies."

Confronted by a quartet of silent, hostile glares, Jennie whirled in disgust, gathered her skirts and flew up the companionway in search of the friendlier Upper Deck. She sought solitude by the stern where she clutched her elbows, alternately annoyed and bewildered by what had happened down below. As was her nature, however, she fretted only briefly before shunting all unpleasantness aside by concentrating on something beautiful.

Natchez.

Jennie was bound for her hometown by her father's decision to return after seven years and, as the great paddlewheel foamed away the final watery miles from New Orleans, she regarded a terrain both welcoming and hostile. To the west, Louisiana unfurled flat like a green scroll, lush lowlands shredded by sandbars vacillating at the whim of wind and tide. On the east bank, the Mississippi side, red-brown bluffs swelled over two hundred feet high, majestic palisades amassed over aeons from gossamer, wind-borne chalk called loess. The bluff was, Jennie recalled, deceptively fragile, its rim ragged from subtropical rains and its base assailed by deadly wicking when the Mississippi River glutted its banks. The watery surplus stole stealthily upward until, like calving icebergs, great chunks of loess swooned and thundered free, commandeering trees, buildings and the occasional human life as they plummeted into the ravenous river.

Situated atop the highest, most vertiginous of these bluffs was Natchez. Founded in 1716, it was the oldest permanent settlement on the Mississippi and only twenty years before it had been dizzy rich from cotton and slavery. Those palmy days were brutally vanquished by civil war and, some claimed, further sabotaged by overweening pride. Now the town with feet of chalk languished and grieved, a bruised magnolia sustained by dreams of lost glory.

"Natchez," Jennie breathed. "Home."

They would arrive tomorrow afternoon, and thoughts of docking there rekindled the old uneasiness. As the sensation deepened, Jennie realized she needed to talk to her father. She'd tell him what happened down below, too, and he'd explain things like always. That is, she thought grimly, if he was feeling better. When they boarded that morning in New Orleans, Merrill had been downright gleeful over their deluxe accommodations and dismissed his daughter's ribbing about the extravagance of two honeymoon suites, one for himself and his valet Caleb and the other for her.

"Is it my fault they're the best staterooms aboard?" he laughed.

Unfortunately, an hour out of port, Merrill grew so fatigued that Jennie had coaxed him into bed, where he perused newspapers until his gentle snoring prompted her ill-advised stroll. Returning to his quarters, she was relieved to find him contentedly studying the dinner menu, but her dark mood soon came rushing back. When Caleb reached for her gloves and purse, Jennie breezed past him and flung them into a chair. The valet stepped away and folded his hands behind his back, the picture of patience as Jennie began pacing the stateroom.

"Good heavens!" her father said. "I haven't seen you in such a state since you were presented to Queen Victoria."

"I'm sorry, Papa, but something dreadful has happened."

"I can see that." Merrill set the menu aside, ready as always to listen to his daughter's problems. "Now then. Suppose you stop wearing a hole in that pretty carpet and come tell your old father all about it."

Jennie perched on the edge of the bed and waved away Caleb's offer of coffee. "I went out for some fresh air and a stroll and was quite enjoying myself until I went below to explore the Main Deck. I hadn't ventured very far before I noticed people seemed to be ignoring me, and after a few minutes some of them actually turned their backs as I approached. It was most unsettling, Papa, and not wanting to think of myself as some sort of pariah I decided I must surely be imagining things, that people couldn't possibly be so rude." Her distress visibly deepened before she continued. "Such wishful thinking ended when a man bumped right into me and sent my purse flying. When he walked away as though nothing untoward had happened, I couldn't help thinking his behavior was intentional."

Merrill pursed his lips as he weighed her comment. "Quite possibly it was, my dear."

Jennie was aghast. "But why would someone deliberately—"

"You should never have left the Upper Deck, Jennie."

"Why not?"

"Because we're back in the South now, and you must remember people in these parts lost everything in the war. *Everything!* To them, anyone fashionably dressed is the enemy, or at least highly suspect, and you should know that class differences here are very different from those in Europe."

Jennie sniffed, only partly mollified. "That's not all that has me so upset, Papa."

"Oh?"

"It's this return to Natchez," she confessed, leaning against the mahogany headboard and tracing an elaborately carved acanthus leaf with her fingertip. "I've felt peculiar all day. Actually, since we left New York."

"I see." Merrill nodded and thought a moment. "What you're feeling is dread, my dear."

Jennie sat back up. "Why, yes! That's exactly it. Dread. But what am I dreading, Papa, and how did you know?"

"I know because you've inherited your mother's uncanny intuition." Merrill waved a hand dismissively. "It's that damned passenger list. With so many people bound for Natchez and everyone checking it to see who's aboard and—"

"What on earth are you talking about?" Jennie pressed.

As he had always done with his favorite child, Merrill sought to buffer life's hard edges.

"I'm afraid Natchez will not be giving us the warmest of welcomes, darling girl. In fact, those rude people are quite likely a taste of what we can expect."

"I don't understand."

Merrill reached for her hand. "You were only a year old when we fled Natchez, so I'm sure you don't remember."

"Not really."

"Did you ever wonder why or ask anyone why we left?"

Jennie thought he really meant *fled*. "I know a little. From Anna Marie."

"What did your sister tell you?"

Jennie's half-remembered memories swooped and settled like flocking birds. "She said it was because you had been on the wrong side during the Civil War."

Merrill chuckled and squeezed her hand. "Trust Anna Marie to muddle the facts. I was on the wrong side for a Southerner, perhaps, but I have always been a Union man despite being born in Mississippi. Your grandfather Frank and great uncle James were Unionists, too, but political loyalties aside, in the Natchez Social Register their blood is the bluest of the blue, and so is yours, my dear."

That was no exaggeration. Jennie Surget Merrill was the great-granddaughter of Pierre Surget, a French *émigré* who had amassed a fortune in farming. Sons Frank and James inherited his Midas touch, acquiring over a hundred thousand acres and thousands of slaves. By 1852, Frank was Mississippi's richest cotton planter and for a wedding present gave his daughter Jane and her husband Ayres Merrill a twenty-nine acre suburban villa called Elms Court. Jane filled it with European furniture and artworks, and, over time, the newlyweds became

Natchez's unassailable golden couple. While the Harvard-educated Merrill built a thriving law practice, Jane presented him with seven offspring, but their familial heaven was smothered by the hell of civil war.

"Natchez was an occupied city when you were born," Merrill continued, "but things were mostly tolerable until I invited General Grant to dinner. Knowing I would be criticized, I tactfully reminded the Old Guard that their ranks included transplanted Northerners, conservative Whigs and a handful of Southerners whose Union loyalty was unshakable. Why, when Natchez named your great uncle James Surget delegate to the 1861 Mississippi Secession Convention, he voted *against* leaving the Union." Merrill took a breath and scratched his muttonchops while weighing his next words. "Once that dinner invitation went out, it came as no surprise that Confederate Natchez, poor as well as rich, was both furious and unforgiving, and you just may have encountered some of these disgruntled folks this afternoon. It's only human nature that their loss and suffering has deepened their reluctance to shed a grudge."

For a long moment, Merrill was lost in painful reminiscence, but he was not a man to leave things unfinished. Indeed, that very trait had driven him back to Natchez one more time.

"Despite that ugly incident and growing criticism, I stayed on and ignored my enemies, foolishly believing friends in high places could protect me, but... Well, one afternoon when I galloped through the gates of Elms Court, my horse stumbled and fell. The bullet that killed poor Balthazar was meant for me."

Jennie was genuinely shocked. "Papa, no!"

"I didn't want your mother to know the truth so I told her only that Balthazar had stumbled and fallen and had to be destroyed when he broke a leg. I don't know if she believed me, but she said nothing when I suggested waiting out the rest of the war in New York. You'll be interested to know it was General Grant who got us safely upriver." He frowned at the recollection then brightened. "Although we were happy in that pretty house on Washington Square, after Lee surrendered I was anxious to come back to Natchez. Your beloved mother refused and the poor thing died of scarlet fever without ever seeing Elms Court again." He rubbed his eyes again as discomfort resonated from a deeper source and his voice turned dark. "When I lost Jane, I didn't think I could continue living. Had it not been for you children I truly believe I would've joined her. I especially needed you, Jennie. You're so very, very like her."

"So you've often said." Jennie's fingers wandered to her throat and stroked her mother's pearls. She was comforted as always when they warmed to her touch.

"After the war, Grant rescued me yet again. As the Great Hero, his fame was at an all-time high and I advised him to exploit such enormous popularity. I supplied legal advice and some valuable New York support, and when he was elected President, he reciprocated with some excellent Washington connections." Merrill leaned forward as Caleb fluffed his pillows. "One business deal alone earned your old father almost two hundred thousand dollars. I must admit it was gratifying, but... Well, something was still missing from our lives."

"Natchez?"

"Natchez," Merrill echoed with a smile and leaned back again. "More specifically, Elms Court."

"But why come back after all that had happened?"

"Because your mother and I met and fell in love in Natchez. For me, she *was* Natchez, and I prayed by returning I could better keep her memory alive. That proved to be true, but, unfortunately, as she feared and predicted, I was thoroughly shunned. Some people even crossed the street when they saw me coming."

"I know the feeling," Jennie muttered, thinking of the four crones who'd turned their backs on her.

Merrill shrugged. "I didn't care what they thought or said about me, but I didn't want the sins of the father to be visited on you children and was heartsick inside. I eventually explained things to the older ones, but you babies were told nothing because I wanted you to know Elms Court only as gracious and beautiful. I tried to do the same for myself, usually by walking the grounds at dusk because twilight blurs the truth. Even though it reminded me of times as lost as the Confederacy itself, my favorite memory was your mother's Ball of a Thousand Candles. It's forever burned into my memory and made me despair of...how did your dear mother put it? Ah, yes. 'Purging the siren Natchez from my blood.' It's something I could never achieve and why should I?" Merrill nodded thanks to Caleb for a fresh handkerchief and dabbed his eyes as he grew wistful. "My beloved Jane always loved drama. How I wished she could have been with us in Brussels, amid all that protocol and royalty."

Because Jennie knew little about her father's lofty business connections, she steered the conversational ship back on course. "Tell me more about your ambassadorship to Belgium. Was this another of President Grant's favors?"

"Indeed, it was." Merrill crumpled the damp handkerchief and tucked it away. "And we'd still be in Brussels if those damned doctors hadn't made me resign. I knew how much you and Anna Marie loved hobnobbing with all those titled folk."

"Not I," Jennie insisted. "Anna Marie was the one who was bound and determined to marry a count. I only wanted to have fun and turn a head or two."

"And, indeed, you did. I'll never forget how you eclipsed everyone at the Belgian court." Merrill chuckled. "And how hard you slapped your brother afterward when Ayres Junior said any young girl could charm that lecherous old reprobate, King Leopold."

"He deserved that slap," Jennie sniffed. "He was always spoiling my fun."

Merrill chuckled again. "Not always, my dear. He was certainly on his best behavior when you were presented to Queen

Victoria. What a glorious day that was! Do you remember how everyone was jockeying for the queen's attention when she suddenly turned to engage you in conversation? I nearly burst with pride. You were only fifteen!"

Jennie's face warmed as thoughts of her brother faded. "How could I ever forget such a moment, or when the British press said the daughter of the former American Ambassador to Belgium received a 'kindly aside from Her Majesty'? That newspaper clipping is one of my most cherished possessions."

"I always wondered what you and the dear lady talked about."

Jennie shrugged. "I was too nervous to remember, but I certainly recall worrying about curtsying in my new dress, and thinking that the queen was even shorter than myself."

"Those were certainly wonderful times." A dull chest pain reminded Merrill of his mortality and he returned to more serious matters. "You're a young woman now, Jennie, and obviously I can no longer protect you from the ugly truth about Natchez. Forgive me for not telling you sooner."

"It's alright," she assured him. "To be honest, I already suspected some of what you've said."

"Smart girl. I'm not surprised."

Jennie was both relieved and disturbed by her father's revelations but wanted to hear no more, at least not now. She retrieved the menu and gave it to him, pleased when he began reading aloud, voice humming with excitement.

"Listen to this, my dear. All provender is from New Orleans. No surprise there, I suppose, but I scarcely realized they would offer fricassee of terrapin, beef ragout, stuffed quail and scalloped oysters." He read further down. "All my favorite Creole dishes, in fact."

Jennie squeezed his hand in gentle protest. Her father had lost a great deal of weight in the past few months, but she knew overindulgence was not the solution. "I'm afraid those are the very things the doctors have warned you to avoid, darling. They're much too rich."

"Bah!" Merrill snorted. "They've taken away everything else, Jennie girl, but I'll be hanged if they'll take the food out of my mouth, too." He waved at his valet. "Call the waiter, Caleb. Tell him we want a taste of everything and that we'll dine in here tonight. Does that suit you, Jennie?"

"Yes, Papa." Jennie retreated to the adjoining stateroom, knowing further protest was useless when she got an empathetic look from Caleb. Like her father's loyal valet, she took some consolation at dinner when Merrill limited himself to small samples of the sumptuous fare. She felt better still when his coloring improved and he began reminiscing about other memorable meals in Paris, New York and, finally, Natchez.

"The food at Elms Court was absolutely sublime," he said, reaching for a Creole meringue. "Your mother was the grandest hostess Natchez had ever seen."

As Merrill's storytelling mood returned full force, Jennie sipped coffee and listened contentedly until her father's strength began to ebb. Another knowing glance from Caleb prompted her to say goodnight.

"It's been a long day, Papa, and I'm suddenly exhausted. But before I say good night, I must tell you how pleased I am that we talked this afternoon. I'm much better prepared to face what awaits us tomorrow in Natchez."

Merrill beamed. "That's my girl. Always remember that we have each other, and that's all we really need." Too tired to lean forward, Merrill waited for Jennie to kiss his whiskered cheek. "Good night, my dear. I could never have made it this far without you. I love you so."

"I love you, too, Papa."

Jennie nodded goodnight to Caleb and slipped into her stateroom, suddenly as weary as she claimed. As she had when they'd boarded that morning, she shook her head at what was dubbed the Cupid Chamber for a carved mahogany tester bed swarming with putti, and as she undressed and crawled beneath the heavy eiderdown quilt, she wondered if she were the only unmarried woman ever to occupy this outrageous wedding bed alone. That was her last thought before, ridiculous or not, the sumptuous mattress seduced her into sweet, dreamless sleep.

BECAUSE HER FATHER remained weak, Jennie spent the next morning reading to him and making small talk while fussing with her needlepoint. When Merrill began to doze after lunch, Caleb tactfully encouraged her to take another stroll.

"The fresh air will do you good, Miss Jennie."

"You're right as always," she whispered, knowing he was suggesting escape from the smell of her father's medicines and thinking yet again that the man was worth his weight in gold. She smiled. "But I think I'll stay in my own neighborhood this time."

Caleb nodded and smiled back. "Yes, ma'am."

Jennie was revitalized by the warm afternoon and gusting river breezes but wisely confined her promenade to the hospitable Upper Deck. She drifted by Spittoon Row with its neat line of cuspidors and a gauntlet of gentlemen admiring her brunette beauty. Jennie was pleased and reassured by an abundance of chivalrous nods as she continued to the fore gallery, the perfect vantage point as the *J. M. White* steamed for the port of Natchez. She found an isolated spot and took a deep breath, filling her lungs with the heavy, fecund air before a man's voice interrupted.

"She's a grand lady, isn't she?"

Still skittish after yesterday's unpleasantness, Jennie ignored the strange comment. After all, she knew no other passengers and didn't believe a perfect stranger would presume to address her.

"Some might even say she's the grandest lady plying the Mississippi." The voice was louder this time, more insistent. To her surprise, Jennie responded, addressing the speaker without looking at him.

"I beg your pardon?"

"This boat, miss. She may have a man's name and be only four years old, but she's already a grand old lady, and a mighty glamorous one, too." Although tempted to look at the speaker, Jennie kept her eyes on the approaching shoreline, close enough now to reveal details along the bluff. "She's the most luxurious steamboat ever built, and I must say I've never seen anything like that dining room!"

Out of the corner of her eye, Jennie watched the man extract a thick notepad from his vest pocket. He chuckled when he remembered his spectacles and read aloud only when they were in place.

"The dining room seats two hundred fifty passengers and has twelve chandeliers. The boat is three hundred twenty-five feet long, with chimneys eighty-one feet tall. Jackstaffs add another twelve feet." He paused and scanned his notes before continuing. "And a five-tone whistle I suspect we'll be hearing any moment." When Jennie remained silent, the young man apologized. "My excitement has made me forget my manners, miss. Forgive me for addressing you without introducing myself." His hat slipped smoothly into his hand, and he bowed. "I'm Stephen Holmes of Natchez."

When Jennie finally faced him, she was disarmed by an engaging smile and inquisitive blue eyes. Holmes was a short, heavyset man with a ruddy, cherubic face making him look even younger than his nineteen years, a disadvantage he sought to overcome, with mixed success, with a thick walrus moustache. His tweed jacket and corduroys had known better days and his crimson cravat was carelessly tied, but Jennie nonetheless recognized the bearing of a gentleman and rewarded him with a smile.

"Mr. Holmes," she said with a brief nod. Remembering her father's cautionary tales, she braced herself for the unknown as she revealed her identity. "I'm Jane Surget Merrill, also of Natchez."

Stephen Holmes bowed again and, when he straightened, the words he spoke flooded her with relief. "An honor, indeed, Miss Merrill. Why, the Surget and Merrill families are older than most anyone in these parts. Your father was the U.S. Ambassador to Belgium, was he not?"

Jennie was more pleased with the man's politeness than his recognition and wondered if his demeanor suggested their generation was less emotional about the war than those who had endured it. She certainly hoped so.

"Yes, sir, he was, but he has retired due to failing health. In fact, it's why we're returning to Natchez."

"I'm sorry to learn he's ill, Miss Merrill. How long have you been away?"

"Seven years. I was born here but raised up North. New York City. We've visited rather infrequently over the years."

"I'm not here all that frequently myself, but I don't believe you'll find much has changed. It's been over seventeen years since the war but, like the rest of the old Confederacy, Natchez is trapped in a time warp. There's a sort of dazed atmosphere about the place. A few people want to get on with things, but for most folks life seems to have ended at Appomattox. They simply can't forget it."

"Or *won't* forget it," Jennie added. She was relieved that her guesswork about Holmes's political loyalties was accurate but hoped she didn't sound bitter. Yesterday's conversation with her father had roused new anger at an old war still wounding her family.

"You look a bit pale, Miss Merrill. Might I help you inside, or get you some water?"

"I'm fine, thank you, sir. The sunshine and cool breeze are all the tonics I need." She fell silent for a moment. "Does your work involve travel?"

"I beg your pardon?"

"You said you weren't in Natchez all that often."

"That's because I prefer the cosmopolitan anonymity of New Orleans to the confining parlors of Natchez and travel the river whenever I can. Mark Twain is my hero, but I'm afraid there's precious little similarity in the style and substance of our writing." He sighed with mock drama. "It's a sad fact I can confirm with a mountain of rejection letters from the New York publishers."

"I'm sorry," Jennie offered, amused in spite of herself. "What sort of things do you write, Mr. Holmes?"

"Mostly public interest items. Fortunately this trip is an assignment paid for by the *Natchez Evening News*. Otherwise, I'd never be able to afford accommodations on the Upper Deck."

That explains the notepad, Jennie thought. "How exciting."

"It is, although I'm afraid my family thoroughly disapproves."

"What would they prefer you to do?" Jennie's face flushed hot. "Please forgive me. I didn't mean to pry into your personal affairs."

"No need to apologize. I admire such frankness, especially from young ladies who don't hesitate before they speak."

Jennie knew he expected her to warm to his confession and perhaps share a confidence, but she did not. Instead she tilted her head back and studied the towering smokestacks, covering her ears too late when the whistle erupted with a deafening stream of steam.

Holmes retreated to safer conversational ground. "Look, Miss Merrill!" he said, pointing off the starboard bow. "There's Natchez! We're home!"

Dead ahead the great river yawned wide, as if taking a restorative breath. In the town's glory days, this treasured stretch of water had teemed with barges, coasting craft and steamboats bearing King Cotton's largesse; today it was a vanquished realm ruled by the *J.M. White* and a scattering of lowly skiffs. As the glamorous steamboat eased toward the landing, Jennie recognized Natchez-under-the-Hill, once the wildest hellhole on the Mississippi, now a harmless shantytown. High above, the town's steeples, domes, cupolas and rooftops drowsed amid bright puffs of dogwood and redbud. Jennie was thrilled to remember the great pillars of Rosalie, the only mansion close to the bluff. Looming like a Greek temple, its splendor reminded her of Elms Court, which in turn prompted thoughts of filial duties.

"Please excuse me, Mr. Holmes. I must see to my father."

Holmes bowed low. "A great pleasure meeting you, Miss Merrill. Perhaps I will see you again."

"Perhaps."

Jennie nodded politely before dodging a man dragging an oversized portmanteau and wading into the swelling crowd. Everyone seemed to have erupted on deck at once, choking the rails with bodies and baggage and making passage difficult for such a small, lone woman. Holmes recognized her dilemma and shoved his way to her rescue.

"Please allow me, Miss Merrill." He took her arm and imposed his considerable bulk between her and the surging masses. Jennie welcomed his aid as Holmes pushed and elbowed a path half the length of the boat to a door marked Cupid Room. "Here we are."

Jennie smiled gratefully. "Thank you."

"At your service, ma'am," Holmes said, fingers grazing the brim of his bowler. "Good day."

"Good day to you, too, sir."

Not until the crowd consumed him did Jennie realize she had not given Stephen Holmes directions to her stateroom.

2

IT WAS NEAR sunset when the chaos of disembarkation subsided and order reclaimed the *J. M. White*. Only then did Ayres Merrill brace himself between a cane and Caleb's arm and creep carefully down the gangway. Although she trusted Caleb implicitly, Jennie followed, monitoring her father's every step. She was distressed by this latest lapse in stamina and, after last evening's revelations, worried that a hostile Natchez might actually worsen his condition.

Two months ago, Jennie had written Eugene and Thelma Roper, Elms Court's longtime caretakers, and instructed them to have the house cleaned and staffed for a late March arrival. She never doubted the colored couple would follow her orders exactly, and sure enough Eugene was waiting dockside in an elegant Victoria polished to perfection. His dark green livery was as impressive as the gleaming leather upholstery and brass lanterns, and he had thoughtfully put the top up for protection against a blinding sun.

"Eugene!" she called. "Here we are!"

"Eugene," Merrill echoed weakly. "All right, then. It's beginning to feel like home."

Once the two servants had assisted her father into the carriage, Jennie climbed in and leaned against his shoulder as they jounced up a steep road gashed into the face of the bluff, leading to Natchez proper. At the top they emerged just ahead of a cloud of dust, and seeing no approaching traffic, Eugene flicked his crop and the coach lurched across Broadway onto State Street.

Jennie patted her father's hand when it crept weakly inside her elbow. "It won't be long now, Papa."

"Mmmm." Merrill coughed softly and nestled against the plush leather upholstery. He closed his eyes, not from illness or fatigue but because he wanted to shut out everything before arriving at his beloved Elms Court. "Tell me when we're home."

"Of course, darling."

He was, Jennie now understood, as apprehensive as she was about returning to the town that had shunned them. She patted his hand while he drowsed but kept herself alert to every passing detail as they clip-clopped along State Street. Downtown was a compact grid roughly seven by seven blocks, dotted with handsome churches and public buildings that seemed overly ambitious until one remembered cotton's vertiginous wealth once bequeathed this town more millionaires than New York. To the left, Jennie glimpsed the landmark gothic spire of St. Mary's Cathedral and the Adams County Courthouse cupola, which her father once criticized as too "meretricious" for the building. It was the first and last time she'd heard the fancy word.

The grand illusion began fading when Jennie noticed that most stores were empty and boarded-up. Weeds sprouted through cracked sidewalks, and lonely dust devils swirled dead leaves through streets in need of a thorough sweeping. Only a scattering of people went about their business, many of them shabbily dressed. A few looked up as the Merrill coach jangled past, but Jennie recognized no one and polite nods were not exchanged. The reporter's comment flooded back.

"A few people want to get on with things," Stephen Holmes had said, "but for most, life seems to have ended at Appomattox."

Jennie was grateful when Eugene turned onto Homochitto Street and left the dusty downtown behind. Buildings were fewer here, replaced by vast estates astounding in both grandeur and sheer numbers. This was Natchez at its most opulent, the glamorous legacy of planters who left their remote Louisiana and Arkansas cotton empires in the care of overseers and slaves and built villas in town to showcase their fabled wealth. As the coach swung onto Kingston Pike, moss-drenched oaks, magnolias and elegant elms pressed in from both sides. In childhood summers, this street had reminded Jennie of an emerald aquarium, but it now loomed empty and lifeless. They passed no other coaches or carts, not even a lone horse and rider, and an odd stillness was broken only by the hollow clop of hooves.

Jennie patted her father's hand again. "We're almost there, Papa," she whispered. "Almost home."

She knew he needed no narration. Even with his eyes closed, Merrill would recognize every bend in the road, every lift and fall of the highway before that final swell up the drive to Elms Court. He peered out as they swept through the gate where his poor horse had been shot from underneath him.

"Look, Papa! There through the trees!" Urgency deepened Jennie's voice to a contralto. "Can you see it?"

Merrill opened his eyes and squinted at a blizzard of blinding dogwoods. He nodded happily. "Yes, my darling. I see it."

As the coach crested a final rise, Elms Court emerged from the deepening dusk and, despite Jennie's misgivings, sent her spirits soaring. Other Natchez homes might be grander or older, but for her none held the magic of this two-story villa hugged by Italianate galleries frothing with cast-iron grape-vines. Elms Court gave the illusion of a house wrapped in lace and, although she wasn't certain it was true, she often told friends in New York and Europe that it boasted more orna-mental ironwork than any other house in Mississippi. She also believed it to be the most beautiful home in Natchez, another claim that went undisputed because it was always delivered with such charming conviction.

"It's even more beautiful than I remember." Jennie sighed, frankly stirred by the pale glow of the house against the rich gloaming.

Merrill nodded at the iron-graced galleries and rallied a weak smile as the Victoria bounced to a halt. "I never thought I'd live to see this place again."

"Nonsense." Jennie kissed his cheek, ignoring a pervasive odor of infirmity. "Elms Court is the only medicine you need."

"Perhaps you're right. Seeing the old place does make me feel stronger."

"Of course it does."

"You're always so sure of things, Jennie dear." Merrill spoke wearily, but paternal pride rang through. "Sometimes you amaze me."

"I get all my confidence from you," she declared. "And despite everything you said yesterday, I've never been as sure of any-thing as your decision to come back here."

Merrill coughed again. "I only wish you had seen Elms Court in the glory days, my dear. It was...beyond beautiful."

"I have no doubt." Jennie didn't remind him they had dis-cussed that matter just last night. Merrill was only fifty-four but had already begun repeating himself. "There's Thelma! And just look at that smile!"

Thelma Roper, a Negress of considerable girth, waddled toward the coach, struggling to conceal her back misery with every difficult step. Because she was genuinely fond of the Merrills, her grin was as real as her pain. "Welcome home, Mr.

Merrill!" she called. She pursed her lips and frowned, pretending not to recognize the other passenger. "Who's that pretty young lady with you? No! That can't be Miss Jennie!"

"Hello, Thelma," Jennie beamed.

"Child!" Thelma threw her arms wide. "You're all grown up!"

Jennie hurried into Thelma's heartfelt embrace, wondering if it would be the only one she would receive in Natchez. Both women wept, and Jennie stood obediently still while Thelma blotted their tears with the hem of her apron.

"It's wonderful to see you, Thelma."

"Mighty good to see you, too, honey." Thelma wrapped a fat arm around Jennie's tiny waist and steered her inside. "You all been gone way too long. Now come on in this house."

"Looks like the Merrills are leaning on the Ropers again." Jennie sighed. "Literally."

Caleb and Eugene braced Merrill between them and helped him upstairs to bed. Jennie followed, grateful as some of the burden slipped from her shoulders to theirs. Once her father was comfortably situated, she went down the hall to the bedroom she'd once shared with sisters Frances and Eustace. She moved slowly and deliberately around the room, touching familiar things to assure herself she was really here. A pair of Old Paris figurines depicting an Oriental prince and princess. An oil lamp with a blue china shade and silver bowl. Her favorite, loved almost as much as her mother's pearls, was a fan signed by singer Jenny Lind, acquired when the Swedish Nightingale entertained Natchez in 1851. Jennie opened the fan and took it to the window to better study its intricate hand-painted interplay of roses and lilies. From there her gaze drifted outside to dusk skies streaked with high-flying amber horsetails, while daffodils down below promised coming warmth.

"Spring," she murmured, untying her bonnet and letting it slip carelessly to the floor. Too tired to retrieve it, she sat on the bed and voiced the question that had hounded her since Merrill announced their return to Natchez. "Where to begin?"

Jennie had come to Mississippi solely to tend to her father's failing health, but things had changed last night, when she heard new tales of Elms Court's glittering balls and soirées. While Merrill's pale face had glowed with the exhilaration of rich memories, Jennie had begun thinking about reviving the villa's glory days, wondering if it might be just the salvation to keep him alive. She would have to ask Thelma, who surely remembered details of the lavish entertainments Merrill so lovingly described.

"Where to begin?" she muttered again, waving the fan in the musty air. Incredibly, some of her mother's perfume lingered. It was lemon verbena, a scent she also wore on occasion.

A gentle voice drifted from the hall. "Miss Jennie?"

"In here, Caleb."

"Mr. Duncan's here to see you."

"Is he now? Well, what a nice surprise. Please tell him I'll be down directly." Jennie rose and smoothed her skirts, then went to the mirror and frowned at her bonnet-flattened hair. "Oh, well. Thank goodness Duncan's just family."

As she fussed with her deflated curls, Jennie considered the correspondence she and her cousin had enjoyed since they were children. Duncan wrote far more often than she, letters so colorful with local gossip that she felt she was witnessing things first hand. Her favorite letter, one she had re-read many times, referred to a New Orleans newspaper clipping with a photo of Jennie in her presentation gown and the news that she had met Queen Victoria. Duncan also revealed that the article had been worn thin from circulation and that all girls her age were jealous of her dress and international status. After her father's confession about the town's hatred, Jennie now saw the letter as hope that Natchez cared more about the Merrills than it pretended. At least those of her generation.

Optimism still danced in her head as she slipped back down the stairs and found Duncan in the parlor. Sitting patiently with hands folded in his lap, he beamed and sprang to his feet the moment he saw her, and she watched, a little awed, as he unfolded a slender physique to tower over her. In the years since they had seen one another, the boy had become a man, just as she had become a woman.

"Hello, Jennie!" The deep voice was another unexpected change.

"Hello, Duncan." She smiled as they enjoyed a brief, chaste embrace before settling onto a velvet settee. "What impeccable timing you have. Father and I only just arrived."

"I know. I was on the bluff, watching for the *J.M. White*. You were so late disembarking I worried you had missed the boat in New Orleans."

Jennie's eyes widened. "Why didn't you come down to the landing to greet us?"

"Your father looked so frail I thought it best to wait."

"But we're family, for heaven's sake!" When Duncan looked abashed, Jennie softened her tone and changed the subject. "How dashing you are in that smart suit!"

"Thank you," he said, color rising, "but I can't be much to look at after all the fashionable gentlemen you saw in Europe. Royalty and nobility and all."

"Nonsense. You're as handsome as any of them. In fact, I always told myself you'd grow up to be the handsomest man in Natchez."

Jennie spoke honestly about her cousin's firm chin and fine cheekbones, his thick, brunette hair and eyes that sparkled with a hint of quandary. Despite his good looks, however, Duncan's physical maturity had outstripped his adolescent ease with women. It was an awkward inequity he tried to hide by appearing reserved.

"And I was right!"

"Thank you again, Jennie, but I always thought you got all the looks in the family."

This was also sincere. Jennie's doll-like beauty had turned heads in the smartest cities in Europe, as well as New York and

Washington. She had inherited her mother's delicate features, an oval face and olive complexion that, like Duncan's, was the legacy of French ancestry. If her radiant brown eyes seemed a bit too large, they were irresistible when leveled full-force. She also had a naturally aloof charm that few could ignore, women as well as men.

Jennie laughed. "Enough of this mutual flattery, Duncan."

"I wasn't flattering you, Jennie. I meant it when — "

"Now, now." She deliberately chattered over his seriousness. "Tell me all about yourself. Your letters have been wonderful, but they didn't prepare me for the man I see now. The changes are a little overwhelming."

"I suppose we've just grown up," Duncan offered simply. "We're no longer children, sneaking away from our brothers and sisters and hiding out in your playhouse."

Jennie immediately recalled the summer of 1872 when Katherine Surget Minor had come calling at Elms Court with her five children. Her son Duncan was ten then, two years older than Jennie, who quickly and deftly manipulated him away from the horde of nosy, noisy siblings and into her secluded playhouse. She was thrilled that an older boy would spend so much time alone with her.

"So much has happened since then," she sighed.

"For you, perhaps, but not us. I'm afraid most everyone here is poor and dreams of the past. They live on memories of what things were like before the war and — "

"I don't want to talk about that awful war!" Jennie snapped, recalling the shabby downtown. "I don't even remember it, for heaven's sake!"

"Oh!" Surprised by the flare of temper, Duncan retreated fast. "I didn't mean to upset you, dear."

Jennie's good mood returned as she patted his arm. "You know, Duncan, your wonderful letters meant so much to me."

"Truly?"

She nodded. "Even though I've spent most of my life away,

Natchez is where I was born and one way or another I suppose it will always be home. I didn't quite realize it until Papa talked about it last night, about Elms Court before you and I were born. He hasn't said so, but I believe he came back to find a peace that has eluded him ever since leaving. I'm suddenly beginning to feel the same way."

"I'm so glad." Duncan's eyes danced but his excitement faded when Jennie's mood clouded again.

"When Papa's health worsened last summer, I was the only one supporting his decision to come here. None of my brothers or sisters wanted anything to do with Natchez."

"Not even Ayres Junior?"

"Him least of all. Well, except for Anna Marie, perhaps, but that's because she married a French nobleman. They're all so horribly spoiled." She considered a moment and tested the waters of local history. "Of course, they could be avoiding the cold shoulder Natchez always shows us Merrills."

Duncan ignored the bait. "I'm afraid we'll seem quite the backwater after all you've seen and done."

"Oh, I don't know about that," Jennie said, disappointed by his feint. "Frankly I'm tired of going back and forth between New York and Newport. Believe me, it's not as glamorous as it sounds."

Duncan chose his words carefully. "You have no idea how happy that makes me, Jennie dearest."

"What a sweet thing to say. I'll be cherishing every kind word I receive, knowing they may be few and far between."

This time Duncan took the lure. "Perhaps that will change in time. Not everyone feels ill-disposed toward the Merrills, and some forgiveness has taken place. My father was a Unionist, too, but we Minors were never shunned like your father."

"Probably because you didn't have General Grant in your house and because the town knows how your poor family suffered during Reconstruction. There were such dreadful stories in your letters, all those hardships and deprivations." She paused. "But I've been doing some serious thinking, cousin dear, and I want to make some changes here. I'd like to..." She looked toward the foyer. "What is it, Caleb?"

The valet stood in the doorway, patiently waiting for a lull in the conversation. "It's your father, Miss Jennie. He's asking for you."

"Please tell him I'll be right up." She faced her cousin, a new weariness vanquishing excitement over plans to revitalize Elms Court. There were so many things she wanted to ask him, but not now. "We must continue our talk later, Duncan. I'm afraid Papa and I are both fatigued from the trip."

Duncan rose with her. "I'm sorry. Perhaps I shouldn't have come over so soon. It's just that I was anxious to see you."

"No need to apologize. It's wonderful to see family. I'll tell Papa you called, and of course you'll give our regards to your mother and the girls." Jennie drifted into the foyer, Duncan dutifully trailing until she paused at the foot of the stairs. "Thank you for coming, cousin dear. It meant a great deal."

"As it means a great deal to have you home where you belong."

Jennie whispered goodnight and hurried up the stairs. Duncan waited until her shadow captured him, darkening his feet before abruptly vanishing. He yearned to be that shadow, a lingering adolescent secret that troubled his soul as he left Elms Court and was swallowed by the night.

3

T HERE WAS NO instant cure but, as Jennie had predicted, Elms Court seemed to be just what her father needed. During the next year, while his health seesawed, she and Caleb stuck by his side until, to old Dr. Henry's astonishment, Merrill began to improve. Still, the physician reminded Jennie that her father's heart could fail at any time and insisted she keep his daily routine simple. It was a big day when they attended their first mass at St. Mary's Cathedral, and another milestone when they took a ride in the country with Duncan at the reins. One September morning, after her father ate a hearty breakfast and seemed especially energetic, Jennie was so encouraged she finally revealed her long-simmering plans for rejuvenating Elms Court. Merrill listened closely, pleased but cautious, and afterwards reminded his Northern-raised daughter that Southerners were quick to forgive but slow to forget, especially when the transgression was so virulent.

"It will be an uphill battle," he warned, "but I want you to know how proud I am that you're taking up such a challenge."

"I'm doing it for you, Father."

"That's very sweet, Jennie, but I'd like to think you're doing it for your mother." Merrill smiled, wondering if Jennie would ever experience a love comparable to what he and Jane had known. "For me, she and this house are one and the same. Your grandfather Frank gave it to us as a wedding present, and with the exception of a few heirlooms, Jane chose every stick of furniture, every piece of china, every painting and lamp to make Elms Court what it is. I see her everywhere, just as I see so much of her in you." Jennie's cheeks grew warm. "My dear, you are so alike that at times it anguishes me to look at you."

"I don't know what to say."

"Say only that you'll proceed with your plan. Make Elms Court glow and sing again. Make it a showcase for Southern hospitality."

"But wasn't Mother a Unionist like you?"

Merrill's response was stunning. "Never."

"But you said that you and Grandfather Frank and Uncle James—"

"Your mother may have been raised in a household sympathetic to the Union, and she may have married a man with Yankee lineage, but Jane Surget was a secessionist and a loyal Confederate. She was very much her own woman, just like yourself."

Jennie was incredulous. Since leaving New York there seemed no end to her father's surprising revelations. Last spring he'd admitted to ending Anna Marie's flirtations with a staff member in Brussels by having the man transferred back to the States, and only yesterday told of a black eye acquired after a drinking bout with King Leopold. "No fisticuffs, mind you. Just a most ungentlemanly tumble down the palace steps." He winked. "Either way I'm glad your mother wasn't there to see it."

Jennie had always deemed her father an unassailable

paragon, an example of everything good and right with the world, and to learn he had such a human side was both disconcerting and endearing. His esteem for her mother touched her especially.

"I wish I remembered her better," she lamented.

"Then remember her with this house, my dear."

Jennie reached across the table and tugged his whiskers, a habit lingering from childhood.

"I'll do it for both of you."

"One more thing. There was something your mother said about the house that I've never forgotten. Her motto of sorts."

"What was it?"

Merrill wistfully recalled the beloved voice. "'Elms Court belongs to its guests.'"

"How charming!"

"You won't forget it then?"

"Never, Papa. I promise."

Later that afternoon, while Merrill dozed and Jennie wandered the deep, sun-splashed gallery, she heard the jangle of harness. She assumed it was Duncan, a steady caller whenever he was home from school in Jackson, but as she shaded her eyes an old, unfamiliar shay crested the drive. The top was folded back to reveal the driver and, although more than a year had elapsed, she recognized Stephen Holmes from the steamboat.

"Good afternoon, Miss Merrill!" he called. "Do you remember me?"

"Of course, Mr. Holmes," she replied cheerily. "Good afternoon."

He reined his horse and leapt to the ground with grace surprising for a man of his heft. A worn derby slipped into his hand as he mounted the first step. "I hope I'm not intruding on any deep, personal reverie."

She returned his smile, knowing he was teasing. "No reverie. I was just enjoying the sunshine and getting a breath of fresh air."

"You're well, I hope." She nodded. "And your father?"

"Much better, thank you. He remains frail but has improved since our return."

"I'm delighted to hear it." Jennie was amused when color rose on Holmes's cherubic cheeks while his bowler danced nervously from one hand to the other. "May I ask you something, Miss Merrill?"

"Please do."

"Well, it's been quite some time, but I was wondering if you saw my article in the *Democrat*."

"About the *J.M. White*? I did indeed." Jennie and her father had discussed the piece at length, both remarking on Holmes's colorful style and vivid attention to detail. "It was kind of you to mention that my father and I were included in the passenger list."

"I suspect it was stale news by the time the story ran. In fact, I'd wager all Natchez knew her prodigal children were back before you cleared the landing."

"Probably," Jennie agreed as a scheme began formulating in the back of her mind. "Would you like to come in, Mr. Holmes?"

"Why, yes. I've heard so much about Elms Court and always wanted to see it."

"Then it's high time we remedied that, sir." Jennie ushered him into the parlor and rang for Caleb. A few moments later, she was serving tea and some of Thelma's delicious sweetmeats.

"Mice candy." Holmes eagerly helped himself to a second piece. "It's a favorite of mine. Mother makes it, too, but her whiskers and tails aren't this long. At least not any more."

"I beg your pardon?"

"She cuts corners where she can," Holmes replied without apology. "I suppose most everyone does these days."

Jennie shifted uncomfortably at his frank appraisal of a splendid French chandelier and pair of Venetian blackamoors standing imperious guard a few feet away.

"Is your mother well, I hope?"

While Holmes nodded and scooped up a third candy mouse, Jennie tried to recall the name of his sister. During her long hours with Duncan, she had picked her cousin's brain in an effort to unravel Natchez's genealogical spider web, ammunition for her upcoming social siege. Extensive intermarriage had made it a daunting endeavor as many people had only one set of grandparents and cousins were related many times over. Finally the name emerged.

"And Margaret?"

"She's well, too, thank you. And a great admirer of yours, I must say."

"But we've never met."

"I showed her an old piece I wrote about your presentation at the Court of St. James. It was in the *New Orleans Picayune*."

"You wrote that!"

"It was part of an article I cobbled together on Southerners in the European courts, and the first time my by-line appeared in that paper. I hope you liked it."

"My cousin sent it to me while we were still abroad," Jennie said, smarting with curiosity. Realization triggered a playfully accusative stare. "Why, shame on you, Mr. Holmes. When we met aboard the steamboat, why didn't you say you had written about me?"

"I doubted you had seen the article, but more importantly such a confession would reveal I knew who you were." Jennie's eyebrows rose. "I checked the passenger list when we boarded in New Orleans. Someone booking both honeymoon suites intrigued me, and you can imagine my surprise when I saw the Merrill name. I was most anxious to get an interview, but you stayed in your cabin until it was too late."

"So that's how you knew I was in that ridiculous Cupid Room?" When Holmes nodded, Jennie second-guessed him again. "And you're here now to ask for that interview?"

"Guilty as charged, Miss Merrill!" Holmes said, grin

broadening. He wanted a fourth candy but resisted for the sake of his waistline. "You'd be doing this poor, humble reporter a great favor."

"Never mind the flattery," Jennie dismissed. "Certainly I should say no, as I said no to reporters in Europe and New York. Proper young ladies don't give interviews. At least we're not supposed to."

Holmes leaned forward, encouraged by her phraseology. "But you'll make an exception for me?"

"No." She gave him a long look before delivering her surprise. "But I'll make an exception for Elms Court."

He frowned. "I'm not sure I understand."

"I'm not one to mince words, Mr. Holmes. No doubt you know that my father and I are considered pariahs in this town because of his Union sympathies."

"I do, indeed, and I thoroughly disapprove." Holmes was sincere in his commiseration. "I say that despite the fact that my father was killed at Shiloh and my mother nurtures deep hatred for all Yankees. When I was old enough to think for myself, I decided such hatred was a waste of time and energy and left for the more enlightened world of New Orleans." He rolled his eyes. "Good heavens, miss! You and I are too young to even remember the war."

Jennie was pleased with his admission. "Quite right. So you should be able to write a fair-minded report on my experiences in Europe and our return here."

Holmes smiled. "In hopes that Natchez will see you and your father in a kinder light, eh?"

Jennie sighed as she acknowledged the transparency of her plan. Playing for public sympathy was scandalous, but she wouldn't allow herself to be bogged down by convention. "Please understand how difficult this conversation is, Mr. Holmes, and that I have no intention of groveling for you or anyone, but, frankly, that's just what I had in mind."

"Splendid!" Holmes boomed. "My New Orleans editor has

been after me to write something along these lines, and it could dovetail nicely with a series I've proposed to the *New York Sun*. One, I might add, in which they have shown great interest."

"What sort of series?"

"The fate of Southern aristocracy after the war. There have been great tragedies, of course, but some great success stories as well. In New Orleans, for example, Samara Poché was one of the most spoiled Creole belles imaginable, but she learned that selling *maman's* famously delicious pralines was preferable to starvation and now has one of the most successful patisseries in the city. Don't look at me like that, Miss Merrill. I'm sure you consider such crass commercialism beneath you but—"

"To the contrary, sir. My look was one of admiration, not admonition. I applaud Mademoiselle Poché's grit and ingenuity. In trying times one does what one must."

He glowed with admiration. "We have something in common with her, you know." Jennie's eyebrows rose. "A strong drive to put the past behind us."

She smiled back. "Indeed."

"Then we can definitely help one another." Holmes lofted his teacup in Jennie's direction. "Quid pro quo, Miss Merrill?"

"Quid pro quo, Mr. Holmes. And please, help yourself to another piece of candy."

4

J ENNIE'S ARRANGEMENT WITH Stephen Holmes amused
her father and horrified her cousin. "You can't be serious!"
Duncan sputtered. "You know very well that ladies don't give
interviews. Why...why, you'll merely provide more ammunition for those who dislike you."

Jennie perched on a crimson silk *méridienne* and fussed with
her skirts, utterly composed while Duncan paced the parlor.
"It's my father they dislike, cousin dear. Not I."

"And what has he to say about this scandalous notion?"

Her reply was not without bite. "Papa lets me make my own
decisions."

"What about the cold shoulder you always get during Mass
and the disapproving looks when we drive down Main Street?"

Jennie's hand waved dismissively. "They were people father's
age, Duncan. I'm only interested in their children. You said
that lots of girls admired the article about Queen Victoria, remember?"

Duncan shrugged. "Mention in a New Orleans paper is much less intimate than an interview."

"I don't see it that way," she said coolly. "Besides, you don't know what Mr. Holmes is going to write."

"Neither do you."

"For your information, he's promised an article emphasizing our family's deep Natchez roots and why we've returned to them."

"And what does he want in return?"

Jennie bristled, resenting both tone and implication. "A story to interest his readers, of course."

"It's an enormous mistake," Duncan persisted. "You've spent very little time in Natchez, Jennie, and you don't understand these people. They'll point to the interview and call it...well, they'll call it common. It will make you more enemies than friends. And speaking of friends, I'd be very careful around Stephen Holmes if I were you."

"For heaven's sake, why?"

"Well, journalists are hardly to be trusted, especially one living in New Orleans. I hear he lives in the French Quarter and is quite the *bon vivant.*"

Jennie glared. "And how do you know such things?"

"It's common knowledge."

Annoyed by Duncan's meddling, Jennie rushed to Holmes's defense. "I've seen several samples of his work and I liked them very much. Besides, why should his private life interest you?"

"It interests me not at all," Duncan replied peevishly, "except in relationship to you."

This was not, Jennie considered, the first time Duncan had exhibited boorish behavior. He often grew sullen when she insisted on needing time for herself, and just last Saturday he had been petulant when she chose reading to her father over a walk with him. Had it been anyone else she would have labeled it jealousy.

"I appreciate your familial concern, cousin dear, but I assure you I know what I'm doing. And for heaven's sake stop pacing before you make me dizzy!" A knock at the front door freed Jennie from Duncan's harangue. She swept into the vestibule, pleased to see Caleb admitting Stephen Holmes. Hoping to further vex Duncan, she greeted her caller with calculated effusiveness. "Mr. Holmes! What a pleasant surprise!"

"Forgive any intrusion, Miss Merrill, but I was on my way to Longwood and thought you might like to accompany me."

"Oh?"

"Mrs. Haller Nutt has also agreed to an interview for the series we discussed." Noticing the tall young man shadowing Jennie, he lowered his voice as though making a confidence. "I thought it would benefit us both if you came along."

"I'm most intrigued, Mr. Holmes. In fact, I...oh, forgive me. May I present my cousin, Duncan Minor? Duncan, this is Stephen Holmes. About whom you have heard so much," she added pointedly.

Stung, Duncan barely muttered, "Mr. Holmes."

"A great pleasure, sir." Holmes smiled at Duncan's antipathy and turned back to Jennie. "Well, Miss Merrill? Shall we have our little adventure?"

"Indeed we shall," Jennie announced, savoring a perverse pleasure as Duncan paled. She turned her back so Caleb might slip a cloak over her shoulders and then shot a parting volley. "Thank you for dropping by, Duncan. I would ask you to come along, but Mr. Holmes's little shay seats only two."

While Duncan paled, Jennie took the startled reporter's arm and flounced from the house. She held tight as Holmes helped her into the small carriage and, as Elms Court faded behind her, she forgot Duncan's unpleasantness and caught some of her rescuer's high spirits. She, too, was excited about seeing Longwood, by far the most exotic of all Natchez estates and one she had secretly yearned to visit. Since Dr. Haller Nutt, its eccentric builder, had been a close friend of her father, Jennie knew its tragic history. Dr. Nutt had expanded the millions left to him by his father—a man who'd introduced the hardy Petit Gulf strain of cotton to the region and was the first to use a steam-powered cotton gin. Building upon his father's innovations and applying his medical degree to plant science, Dr. Nutt had become one of the richest cotton kings in America and, in 1860, decided to build Natchez's grandest home yet. Although Ayres Merrill warned his old friend about the looming war, Nutt began Longwood only to have his Northern brick masons flee to enlist in the Union army before the home was anywhere near habitable. With only the exterior walls completed, Dr. Nutt had slaves finish the basement and moved his family into those eight rooms as war thundered into Mississippi. His claims of Union loyalty and pleas for federal protection were ignored as both armies pillaged his three plantations. Wasted by melancholy and despair, Dr. Nutt succumbed to pneumonia in 1864, leaving his widow Julia and their eight children penniless.

As Holmes cut off the old Woodville Road, Jennie caught occasional glimpses of Longwood through the thickly forested drive. Even unfinished, Nutt's architectural fantasy was stunning. Designed by Philadelphia architect Samuel Sloan, it was a Moorish-Italianate octagon of brick and filigreed wood soaring three stories high. Its 30,000 square feet were crowned with a grandiose oriental onion dome bearing a twenty-three-foot finial. Nothing Jennie had heard or read prepared her for the monumental scale.

"It's like a mirage," she murmured. "At least how I imagine a mirage to be. I mean, how can something like this be right here in Natchez?"

"It's extraordinary all right," Holmes concurred. "It's also magnificent and tragic. A monstrous elegy for the old South. A tombstone for slavery. A monument to megalomania."

Jennie gave him a sidelong glance. "Sounds to me like you've already begun your story."

"Who wouldn't want to write about this?" Holmes slowed the horse as they passed a dried artificial lake, a sad remnant of a lavish garden design that had never materialized. "It's a story begging to be told."

"How is Mrs. Nutt managing?"

"Barely. She divides her time between here and Washington where she's waging an ongoing battle with the Southern Claims Commission."

"The what?"

"The S.C.C. It's an agency that was established by the Federal government for the redress of claims made by Southerners whose property was taken by Union troops. In order to be compensated, they must prove Union loyalty, which is what Mrs. Nutt has been trying so valiantly—and truthfully—to do."

"Why is it difficult? I remember my father saying what a staunch Unionist Dr. Nutt was."

"Sometimes that isn't easy to prove, especially with a claim in excess of a million dollars and a government that doesn't want to cough up the money."

"But there's no denying Dr. Nutt's plantations were destroyed!"

"Nor any denying Union troops burned his crops and his stored cotton and confiscated his shipments, or that Mrs. Nutt opened Longwood as a hospital for Union soldiers. The question is whether she has the documentation to prove it." Holmes clucked at the horse, urging him up the final rise. The house loomed closer now, a gargantuan vision from the Arabian Nights. "Unfortunately, the claims commission often dismisses burned homes and plantations as, how did they put it, 'the fortunes of a war for the public defense' or losses 'due to pillage by unauthorized soldiers.'"

"That's not fair!" Jennie protested, embarrassed when her voice soared high and tinny.

Holmes gave her an avuncular smile. "I'm afraid fairness is an unwelcome stranger when war is involved, Miss Merrill."

Jennie felt dwarfed as they drove past the house, tilting her head for a last look at the dome and finial before trees obscured the view. Once Holmes helped her from the carriage, she walked toward steps leading up to the front door, but he called her back.

"I'm afraid that door has never been used, Miss Merrill." He pointed toward massive brick columns supporting the ground floor. "We enter through there."

Jennie was aghast. "Isn't that the basement?"

"I'm afraid so."

A lone servant admitted them, silently took Holmes's derby and directed them into the next room where Julia Nutt waited in a rocking chair. She was a diminutive woman in black mourning relieved only by an enormous garnet brooch at her throat. Her hair, blonde gone almost white, was pulled behind her head in a severe bun, and she rested her hands atop the curved handle of a Malacca cane.

"Mr. Holmes," she said, glancing at a grandfather clock. "Good. I admire punctuality."

"Good afternoon, Mrs. Nutt. May I present Miss Jennie Merrill of Elms Court?"

Jennie smiled and dropped a quick curtsy, a link to the old days she hoped the elderly lady would appreciate. Mrs. Nutt did not smile, but she nodded approval and gestured toward a settee. Jennie glanced discreetly around the room before taking her seat, noting that the furnishings were expensive if careworn, and not harmonious with such a low ceiling. She felt a bit claustrophobic when she noticed a pier mirror scraping the ceiling.

"You would be Ayres Merrill's daughter."

"Yes, ma'am."

"He was a good friend of my late husband." She glanced wearily about the room. "And one of the few courageous enough to advise against building this place. I believe he was also the one who warned it would become known as Nutt's Folly. Alas, he was right."

"How are things in Washington?" Holmes interjected.

"Another delay, another postponement." Mrs. Nutt sighed. "They continue to question my documentation of our losses. They intend to wage a war of attrition, despite my frequent warnings that my children will take up the cause after I'm gone."

"I much admire your perseverance," Jennie offered.

"Thank you, my dear." Mrs. Nutt craned her neck, peering around them. "Where is that girl with our refreshments?"

Tea was served, and Julia Nutt emerged as a compelling storyteller. For two hours she enthralled Jennie with the tragic saga of Longwood. Holmes took such copious notes he was eventually compelled to write on the back of his paper. He obviously hadn't expected Mrs. Nutt to be so long-winded and looked relieved when she asked if he had any questions.

"Not a one, I'm pleased to report. For the very first time, a subject has anticipated my every question." He smiled. "I do hope my story will advance your cause, Mrs. Nutt."

"I hope so, too." She fussed with a wisp of hair that had worked loose from the fastidious bun. "I worry that I'm running out of energy, but when that happens I simply take a walk upstairs to remember what I'm fighting for. My husband's ambitious dream may never be realized, but neither will it go quietly into the night."

Jennie started to speak, realized her throat was dry from being silent so long and cleared it behind a handkerchief. "Mrs. Nutt, perhaps my father might help. I can make no promises of course, but he was close friends with President Grant and maintains some important connections in Washington."

"I would be most grateful for anything Mr. Merrill might do." Mrs. Nutt neither smiled nor allowed herself a single moment of optimism. "I'm afraid these long years of beating on bureaucratic doors have left my hands all but bloody."

After a respectful moment, Holmes asked, "Might we see the upper part of the house?"

"Certainly," she replied, fatigue marching through her voice. Her painful recitation had taken its toll. "But mind your step. Certain spots are treacherous, in particular those big oval holes in the floor." She dredged a faint laugh from somewhere secret. "After all your fast and furious writing, Mr. Holmes, I'd hate for your story never to see the light of day."

"We'll be careful," he assured her.

Jennie had been staggered by Longwood's extravagant exterior, but awe turned to melancholy as she followed Holmes into the massive unfinished rotunda pierced by dusty streams of sunlight. Two floors of arched brick doorways soared overhead, and through eighty feet of honeycombed pine support beams and scaffolding loomed the great dome.

"It's like a skeleton," Jennie gasped, unaware she was whispering.

"Well put." Holmes took her arm as they negotiated a musty staircase. "Mrs. Nutt was kind enough to let me inspect Sloan's plans. Like the architect himself, they were way ahead of their time." With Jennie safely ensconced on a stretch of sturdy flooring, he pointed to an oval hole in the floor. "That's what Mrs. Nutt was talking about. Skylights. They're in every room. Sloan planned to install mirrors in the dome to catch the sunlight and reflect it down through an ingenious system of indirect lighting. If the sun was strong, there would be light in every one of the thirty-two rooms."

"Thirty-two rooms! Good heavens!"

"Those niches were for statuary, and down there, that huge open space was for a marble staircase. Everything had been specially carved in Italy and it was all confiscated. Mrs. Nutt believes it's in a museum up North, and who's to say she isn't right? Ah! Look there." Holmes pointed to an overturned paint can, its flow forever frozen in time, tools haphazardly tossed about it. "There's proof that the Pennsylvania workmen literally dropped everything and rushed off to enlist in the Union army."

Jennie was speechless as he made more notes. His scratch-ing pen was unduly loud until a faint squeak yanked attention back to the scaffolding. It repeated and then multiplied, louder each time, until a flurry of bats erupted from the dome. Jennie screamed and recoiled from the hideous squeals and flutters, prompting Holmes to hustle her outside and into the carriage.

"We're safe now," he soothed as they wound down Longwood's serpentine drive. He eyed Jennie with concern. "You're still shaking, Miss Merrill."

"Bats terrify me," she confessed. "Once when I was a little girl in church, one flew in the window and brushed my hair. I be-came quite hysterical and screamed so hard they couldn't con-tinue the Mass. Father had to carry me outside."

"Is there anything I can do?"

"Perhaps a drive by the river, Mr. Holmes. I always find it so peaceful."

He flapped the reins and turned right on Providence Road and right again onto Canal Street. A few minutes later they were on Broadway paralleling the river and the crest of the bluffs. He reined up and nodded toward the Mississippi, swol-len now by unusually heavy rains. They were lost in private thoughts until Jennie broke the silence.

"I can't stop thinking about what Mrs. Nutt said about her eight children. It frightened me. There were seven of us, you see, and we could have been in that same awful situation if Father hadn't taken us away. Fate is such a peculiar..." Jennie hunched her shoulders. "How could I feel a chill on such a warm day?"

She turned toward the turgid Mississippi as though seeking something. The smooth, gleaming surface was deceptive, a wa-tery horror of whirlpools and undercurrents awaiting the un-wary. Jennie followed the passage of a mostly submerged tree, a gigantic menace that could cleave the bowels from an unwary riverboat. She squinted at the watery sun dazzle, and when she looked back Holmes saw a face drained of color.

He frowned. "Is something wrong, Miss Merrill?"

"Oh, dear!"

"What is it?"

"I...I'm not quite sure. I think I'd better get home."

Hearing urgency in her voice, Holmes again snapped the reins, and the horse snorted and lurched back onto Broadway. The river fell behind them as they sped toward Orleans Street where Holmes veered recklessly to avoid collision with a milk wagon and clipped a yapping cur beneath the wheels. Jennie screamed and buried her face against his shoulder.

"Hurry, Mr. Holmes! Please hurry!"

As they raced up the drive to Elms Court, Jennie shrank from the house and a near palpable pall. Ignoring Holmes's attempts to help, she sprang from the shay, long skirts snatching at her feet as she raced to the front door. It swung open before she reached it, and Jennie instantly knew Duncan had been waiting all afternoon, just as she knew what he was going to say.

"Caleb has sent for Dr. Henry."

Jennie tore up the stairs, cries for her father rending the oppressive stillness. She paused at the top, cursing her tight stays and struggling for breath. Her chest ached as she reeled down the hall and opened the door to her father's room, heavy now with the fetor of death. Heat flushed her forehead as she approached the pitiful creature in bed. Ayres Merrill's face and arms were yellowish parchment bearing death's indelible scrawl.

Jennie moved slowly, feet as leaden as her heart, and took his wrist. The pulse was so weak it eluded her, and over the next hour, while she and Dr. Henry waited without hope, it slowed and raced as Merrill slipped in and out of consciousness. Twice he awoke in panic and soaked the bed linens with sweat before slipping away again. Just when Jennie thought she would surely lose him, Merrill rallied, confounding the physician by making conversation and even eating a bit of Thelma's rich broth.

"I feel...a little better," he mumbled.

"Don't exert yourself, Ayres," the doctor warned. "This was a very serious attack."

Some of Merrill's old spunk prompted him to test the weary physician. "Think I don't know that, doc?"

Dr. Henry smiled indulgently and took Jennie into the hall, where he whispered the harsh facts. "He may survive the evening, but he most definitely will not last the night. I've given him a strong dose of laudanum to ease his pain. There's nothing anyone can do but pray. Forgive me, but Judith Legér will be delivering her baby any moment, and I must be on my way."

"I understand." Jennie nodded. "Thank you for coming, doctor."

Back in the sick room, Jennie stationed herself by the bed and waited. At one point, her father stirred from his opium dreams and motioned Jennie closer, breathing more labored than ever. Each raw, raspy word was agony for both.

"I'll…I'll see your mother soon," he wheezed with great difficulty. "I'll tell her…your promise."

Jennie saw no salvation in more lies, no purpose in assuring her father he was going to get well. She had never seen death before but knew she faced it now. Merrill dozed again, breathing normal now. His seeming tranquility lulled Jennie toward a sympathetic sleep, but just as she drifted away he awoke, sat up and coughed blood onto his chest. Jennie clung to his hand as he collapsed back against the pillows, his death rattle hurting her heart.

"Father!" Jennie wailed. "Oh, Father!"

Jennie's tears blurred the harsh truth as she fetched a damp cloth from the washbasin and erased the bloody vomit. Her hand trembled terribly as she closed her father's eyes and plumped the pillows as though she might make him more comfortable. Time lapsed as she stroked his lifeless hand until voices outside drove her to dry her tears and kiss him goodbye. When she opened the bedroom door, the pungent odor of death mingling with her lemon verbena made any announcement unnecessary.

"Oh, Miss Jennie!" Thelma cried. "Come here, child!"

Jennie swooned into Thelma's embrace but, after a moment, she pulled away and floated downstairs with Caleb and Duncan close behind. Affronted by the cheery afternoon sunshine flooding the parlor, she told Caleb to close the curtains, and when the room was darkened to her satisfaction she whispered something that sent him back upstairs with the other servants. Then she sank wearily onto the *méridienne* and looked at Duncan.

"Sit with me, cousin."

He perched nervously beside her. "Is there anything I can do?"

She took a deep breath and transformed it into a raw, ragged sigh. "He's gone, Duncan." Another breath and another sigh. "Gone."

"I know. And I'm so sorry that—"

"I'm not," she blurted. Realizing her candor sounded harsh, she said, "I don't think I could've borne much more, sensing his pain and knowing each day might be his last."

"Perhaps it's a blessing then."

She nodded, head wobbling like a marionette. She had never felt so fragile. "Thank God I was there when he died. I don't think I could have endured his dying alone."

"What can I do?" he asked again.

"Send for Cousin James. I suppose. I can't think of anyone I'd rather not see, but I need him to make the funeral arrangements." She paused, sifting through the chaos of her mind. "I've thought of only two things since coming here. Father and I vowed to make Elms Court live again. Now that he's gone, this house is all I have left."

"You have your family, those who love you," Duncan offered.

Jennie didn't seem to hear. "Father shared some important secrets these last few months, including the provisions of his will. He's leaving each of us children thirty thousand dollars."

Duncan was shocked by the indelicate mention of money, but Jennie was forever unpredictable. "Oh?"

"After the funeral I'm going back to New York for a while. I need to...why are you looking at me like that?"

"What about Elms Court and the promise to your father?"

"In time," Jennie said. "I need to make new plans."

"Make them here," Duncan pressed. "I'll help you."

Jennie shook her head. "It's something I can do better from a distance. There's other family business that needs attention. Other obligations, too. Elms Court was not my only promise."

Duncan did not want to hear this. His voice grew low, troubled. "Why are you so determined to leave?"

"Please stop asking questions, Duncan. Obviously I can't think straight just now."

"Which is exactly why you shouldn't be making any important decisions."

"Not so," Jennie insisted. "Frankly I need some time away from..." She looked up, toward her father's bedroom. "From all this."

"But your place is here."

Jennie frowned and saw Duncan as if for the first time. He reminded her of a little boy masquerading in his father's clothes. "What's wrong with you, cousin? You seem to be taking everything I say quite personally."

"It's just that I...well, I don't want you to leave again."

"That's very sweet, Duncan, but I'm sure you'll manage without me. After all, you'll be back in school and—"

"You don't understand," Duncan said, clumsily taking her hand. "All those years when I thought about you and wrote every day, and these past months with you so close and yet so far away..."

Jennie shrank from the unsettling edge in his voice. "Duncan?"

"Only catching a moment here and there. It's nearly driven me mad!"

He tried to kiss her hand, but Jennie recoiled as though scandalized by his touch. She tried to sort through her second shock of the day, but it was too much to fathom.

"What on earth are you talking about?"

Duncan hung his head. "I think you know."

A dull roar numbed her brain as Jennie tried again to right an imploding world. Duncan had been her rock, her salvation during these last difficult months. She had increasingly relied on him as they shared family confidences and coped with impending loss. It was an innocent, natural surrender, never anything more than platonic, and the notion that he envisioned it otherwise was unthinkable.

"You mustn't say such things," she said, rising to pace the dark room.

"I can't help myself, Jennie!" Duncan pursued, showing a kind of mettle hidden before now. "Love doesn't allow one to pick and choose."

"This isn't love!" Jennie cried. "It's…it's betrayal!" She clutched her temples, as though she could purge Duncan's terrible confession. This could not, must not be happening, especially not now when she was fragile to the point of collapse. She swallowed, throat desert dry as she fought a wave of dizziness before delivering her ultimatum. "I want you to leave, Duncan."

"Jennie, I beg you…"

"Please respect my wishes," she interrupted. "I've just lost my father and have no strength left for another shock, least of all from you."

He drew himself up, towering over her small frame. "Why is loving you such a crime?" he demanded, voice hoarse with pain.

"You know why."

"Then say it."

Unable to face or answer him, Jennie walked to the foot of the staircase. She turned her back toward the front door.

"Goodbye, Duncan."

"I'll write you, Jennie."

She took a deep breath. "I won't answer."

"Yes, you will."

Jennie was too drained to respond and prayed for the

crunch of hooves on gravel signaling that Duncan had ridden away. When solitude finally came, she sagged against the banister and surrendered to a fatigue heavier than any she had ever known. She heard and felt nothing, not even when Caleb carried her upstairs where Thelma undressed her and put her to bed. Some time later—Jennie didn't know how long—there were sympathetic murmurs from mostly unfamiliar faces, a dangerous, stormy ride home from the cemetery, and then the long train ride to New York.

There, in her old bedroom facing Washington Square, she awoke as if from a deep sleep. Natchez had come and gone like a half-remembered dream, but where to go now? As Jennie lay still and listened to the sounds of the great city outside her window, she had her answer.

5

ALTHOUGH A SMALL woman, Jennie Merrill radiated the sort of magnetism cultivated and coveted by politicians and entertainers. Because she shone in a crowd, Stephen Holmes had no difficulty spotting her as she trailed the maitre d' through the noisy diners at New York's famed Delmonico's. He rose as she approached his table.

"Miss Merrill!" he beamed, admiring her smart mauve gown and hat with matching ostrich plumes. "How good of you to come."

Jennie returned his smile and slipped into the mahogany chair proferred by the maitre d'. "Please forgive me for being so late. There was a last minute problem at our settlement house down on Mulberry Street."

"Nothing too serious I hope?"

"Far too serious to discuss in a place as gay as this," Jennie insisted.

How could she tell him she had just tended a young mother

whose baby died simply because the air in their tenement was noxious? How could she say she still smelled death along with other odors too indelicate to discuss? She erased disturbing thoughts with a brighter smile and a deft change of subjects.

"Good heavens, how long has it been since we've visited?"

"A bit over eight years," Holmes replied. "I last saw you at your father's funeral in eighty-three."

"September sixteenth to be exact. What I consider a day of great personal epiphany," she confessed. "And one in which you had a hand."

"What do you mean?"

Jennie nodded discreetly toward the hovering waiter. "Shall we discuss it over menus?"

Holmes ordered tea for Jennie, whiskey for himself. "About this epiphany?"

"It began that afternoon you took me to Longwood, an experience that dogs me to this day." The ostrich plumes shivered as she shook her head in sad remembrance. "Poor Julia Nutt. I've always regretted not using father's influence with President Grant to help her."

"His death was beyond your control," Holmes said.

"Which brings me to the second part of the epiphany, my father's passing," Jennie continued. She purposely did not add that the third part was Duncan's profession of love and ongoing avalanche of letters. "I felt as if my lifeline had been cut, just as I believe Mrs. Nutt's terrible dilemma was an omen." She switched abruptly from serious to stern. "Mr. Holmes, please understand what happened that afternoon at Longwood was not something so mundane as a poor little rich girl being upset by poverty and deciding she must help save the world."

"I assure you that never crossed my mind."

Jennie acknowledged his heartfelt sympathy. "Thank you."

"And you came to New York right after your father's funeral?"

"Yes. And without ever giving you the interview we discussed," Jennie apologized. "Again I must ask your forgiveness."

"Not at all. It's perfectly understandable under the circumstances. Besides you've agreed to another."

"Indeed I have." Jennie nodded enthusiastically. "To help the King's Daughters, of course."

"Of course."

Since returning to New York, Jennie had committed herself to a Christian service group founded in 1886 by Margaret McDonald Bottome. Calling themselves the King's Daughters, their ministry in the city's tenements offered support for the aged, handicapped and underprivileged, all three in epidemic abundance as the century drew to a close. Jennie still found time to go to parties, the theater and chic restaurants such as this, but most of her time was devoted to the Daughters. Through them, she had been drawn most strongly to children and young mothers such as the pitiful soul she had just comforted.

"What about yourself, Mr. Holmes? You said you're writing for the *New York Sun* these days, yes?"

"As well as a magazine here and there. I left Natchez not long after you. First back to New Orleans, where I switched back and forth between the *True Delta* and the *Times-Democrat*. I eventually landed an editorship at the *Delta* which, I'm happy to report, sent me into the field." He preened a little. "I've traveled as far as San Francisco and, following in the footsteps of my idol Mr. Twain, visited Honolulu where I met King Kalakaua." He chuckled. "I'm afraid it was nothing like your encounter with Queen Victoria, but it was a royal experience nonetheless."

Jennie, suddenly self-conscious, said nothing.

"I accepted a position with the *Sun* four years ago and began noticing your name in the paper in connection with the King's Daughters. When I read about your work in the tenements, my nose for news immediately began itching."

"So you thought it a good opportunity to get that elusive interview," she teased gently.

"And to see an old acquaintance." When Jennie fell silent again, Holmes said, "The tragedy of the tenements troubles me as well, Miss Merrill. I recall the article stated that you had worked with Jacob Riis."

"Only on a handful of occasions," Jennie amended. "Most of the social organizations overlap, you see, so it was not unlikely that our paths would cross. That reporter made far too much of it, and frankly I think he used Mr. Riis's name to spice up his article. Mr. Riis has received so much publicity since he published *How the Other Half Lives*. I can't remember when photographs created such a firestorm of controversy." The mauve plumes danced again. "New Yorkers can be a terribly jaded lot. Thank goodness he made us see the awful truth. I never dreamed human beings lived like that. In Calcutta, perhaps, but not in New York City."

Holmes had also been disturbed and outraged by Riis's revelations. "I remember reading that Manhattan's East Side has tenements packing immigrants two hundred and ninety thousand to the square mile, the most densely populated spot on earth, including China. London at its worst had only a hundred and seventy-five thousand."

"You know the book quite well."

"I know Mr. Riis well, too," Holmes offered. "I did a story on him three years ago. He was a police reporter writing about our slums with little success until he decided photographs carried far more impact than the printed word. He began prowling the tenements at night, appearing out of nowhere to take pictures with his blinding flash and vanish as fast as he appeared. Those poor souls thought he was some kind of will-o'-the-wisp." The excellent whiskey warmed him to the story. "Since I'd also done a bit of police reporting, Riis asked me to come along. One night I'll never forget, we were somewhere along Bottle Alley when he began shooting. I must confess those bright flashes are startling and, as I soon learned, dangerous as well. Before the night was out, Riis set fire to one of the places he was photographing.

Afterwards, he confessed that this was not the first time and that once he even set his clothes on fire. He was determined to get his terrible subject matter on film, no matter what."

"Good heavens!"

"Happily, his book had precisely the impact he hoped and earned a note from Police Commissioner Roosevelt which I turned into a headline. 'I have read your book, and I have come to help.'"

"I remember it well. Your story was the talk of the town, and I'm embarrassed to admit I didn't notice your byline."

"No matter. What *does* matter is that since becoming President, Mr. Roosevelt has called Riis 'the most useful citizen in New York.'"

"I knew that, too, and it gave me new hope." Jennie frowned, drifting into a private moment tinged with pain. "I've never forgotten those photographs. They're far worse than anything I've seen because Riis ventured into areas much too unsafe for me. People packed thirty to a tiny room with no windows, no ventilation, no sanitary facilities." Prior to her tenement work, a personal baptism by fire, Jennie would never have been so graphic. "What those pictures can't capture, Mr. Holmes, as you surely know, is the foul smells." She shook her head again. "I've been places where I actually couldn't breathe, and sometimes it's so overwhelming I don't think I can continue to..." Her voice trailed off and she waved a gloved hand.

"I admire your work very much, Miss Merrill." Holmes thought of patting her arm, just inches away, but decided it would be indecorous. Instead he asked about other projects.

She demurred. "As I mentioned earlier, I prefer not to discuss certain things over dinner, but you just gave me an idea. Since you were a police reporter, I'd like you to investigate something that has tormented me for some time."

Holmes went immediately on the alert. "Oh?"

Jennie took a deep breath and expelled the words as though they were malignant. "The baby farms. Riis mentioned them in his book, but little has been done to stop something that grows more desperate by the day. A good, strong exposé might get the public angry enough to change that. It will take me a few days, but I'm certain I can make the necessary arrangements."

"I don't remember them, Miss Merrill. Baby farms you say? It sounds disgusting."

Jennie's soft features wrenched as she struggled for composure. She waved her hand again, this time in apology. "Please forgive my comportment, Mr. Holmes. On certain occasions, such as now, I feel a bit overwhelmed. Mrs. Bottome has often warned me not to take things personally and, although I consider that sage advice, I cannot always follow it. My behavior just now was...unbefitting a King's Daughter."

"No sane person could remain unmoved by those inhumane conditions, Miss Merrill, especially when children are involved. I assure you I have shed tears of my own, and I believe the day you feel nothing in the tenements is the day when you are no longer of service there."

Jennie considered his words before continuing. "I've no doubt the experience has changed me, Mr. Holmes, but in which direction I honestly cannot say."

When her tone announced the subject was closed for now, Holmes said, "Well, then. Perhaps I shall tell you about my encounter with King Kalakaua. It's a bit indelicate for mixed company, but I think you'll find it amusing."

It was a random arrow, but it found the target when a faint smile flickered across Jennie's face.

"By all means, tell me about the naughty little Hawaiian king."

6

A FEW BLOCKS NORTH of Delmonico's, a hansom clipped down Broadway, horse strutting as if it knew it was heading for a swanky address. Cones of steam blasted from huge nostrils, and inside the cab Richard Dana and Octavia Dockery shared a lap robe against an early October chill. They chatted incessantly, soft Southern drawls smothered by the din of downtown traffic.

"You really must see the White Mountains of New Hampshire," Richard said, leaning closer so he didn't have to shout. "They absolutely take your breath away, especially this time of year."

Octavia nodded agreement. "I've always said springtime belongs to the South, but New England is the provenance of autumn."

"Spoken like a true poetess."

Octavia smiled. "Frankly, Richard, I think you're smitten more by Amelia Cunningham than those haunting mountains."

His cheeks flushed with the ruddiness unique to youths in their first love. "Oh, Octavia! Who could have imagined I would meet a real-life angel in church, one that would steal my heart under the very eyes of God? And that after only a few months of courtship she would invite me to New Hampshire to meet her family."

"Have you told Amelia how you feel?"

"I wanted to, but I couldn't find the courage until last night after we got off the train."

Octavia felt the warmth of his blush. "Suddenly the words came, right in the middle of Grand Central Station. It was so noisy I had to shout so Amelia could hear and everyone turned to look." He giggled nervously. "Some people actually applauded. Oh, I'm afraid I was a bit outrageous!"

"It sounds terribly romantic to me."

His eyes widened. "But I've never been so bold in my life, Octavia. Just thinking about it gives me the shivers."

"And what did Amelia say?"

Richard grinned. "She shouted back that she loved me, too!"

"I think I'd like Amelia," Octavia smiled. "My goodness, it's all so thrilling!"

Richard grew serious. "But, you know, it's almost too much for me. I...I feel so strange, like I'm not the person experiencing all these emotions. Like they belong to someone else or I've just borrowed them for a while. Does that sound ridiculous?"

"Of course not. It's just all so new that you're feeling a bit overwhelmed. At least I imagine so since I've never been in love myself. I just write about it." Octavia sighed and gestured with mock drama. "Alas! The poor, unenviable lot of a spinster poetess!"

Another giggle from Richard drew a disapproving scowl from the driver. He had been eavesdropping on his passengers' peculiar drawls and high-flown conversation and dismissed them as absurd. Southerners! Who could ever understand them?

Richard roundly ignored the affront. "Look, my dear. There it is!"

Through the left window, as they headed south across Twenty-seventh Street, one building stretched an entire block along Broadway. The name painted most of that length was synonymous with the finest dining in America.

"Delmonico's," Octavia sighed. "I can't believe I've lived in New York all these years and never been here. And to think I'm going to meet your famous cousin as well. It's almost too much excitement for one evening!"

Richard frowned. "Don't be surprised if Charlie asks to draw you," he warned. "I've seen him do it a hundred times. The man simply cannot resist a pretty face."

"I'll bet he won't even notice me. He only draws beautiful rich girls after all."

"You do yourself a great injustice, Octavia. I see how other men look at you."

"Nonsense." Despite her protest, Octavia fussed with the pheasant feathers swirling around a snuff-colored toque and patted her red curls. "Are you sure I look all right?"

"Perfection, as always." Richard looked out the window again as the driver turned left onto Twenty-sixth Street. "Oh dear, I hope you don't mind lines."

"Not when I'm in good company."

Octavia couldn't think of anyone she'd rather tarry with than Richard Dana. They had been introduced just last year by a mutual Mississippi friend when Richard had moved to New York to study music after graduating from Vanderbilt University. Octavia felt an instant kinship springing from more than mutual Southern roots. Richard was barely twenty-one, six years her junior, but the tall, willowy lad exhibited a sensitivity and maturity, albeit sometimes unsettled, well beyond those years. Such traits had always appealed to Octavia, as did a shared passion for the arts, and she cherished hours spent debating music, theater, literature and current events. There was never any romantic spark, especially after Amelia Cunningham arrived in Richard's life, and for that reason he was the only man Octavia felt she could be totally honest with. When she was with him, she disdained all the feminine wiles she had been taught since girlhood, and in return Richard treated her as an equal. Theirs was a special bond few understood and many speculated about, but for them it made perfect sense.

"Stop here, please!" Richard called, ordering the driver to pull up at the end of the line of Delmonico patrons. He helped Octavia from the cab. "We might as well save ourselves the walk from the front door."

"Excellent idea."

Delmonico's was almost as famous for its democratic seating process as its food. Absolutely no one received preferential treatment, including the socially untouchable Astors and Vanderbilts and celebrities like Diamond Jim Brady and Lillian Russell. If you wanted to sample Delmonico's fabled menu you had to wait in line; it was that simple. Octavia and Richard didn't mind, content to enjoy the crisp fall weather and one of the city's best oases for society-watching. Octavia was especially entertained when one disgruntled matron, petulant from waiting, stamped her plump foot and snapped the heel of her shoe. Neither Octavia nor Richard could control their laughter and received a reproachful stare as the woman hobbled awkwardly away. Things moved steadily if a bit slowly, and in twenty minutes they were escorted to a table on the main floor, which was grandly appointed with mirrored walls and a frescoed ceiling. Dozens of mahogany tables gleaming with snowy white tablecloths were tended by a battalion of vigilant waiters.

"Did you see?" Richard whispered as he and Octavia were seated. "Every eye in the place was on you!"

"You're prejudiced!" she hissed back. She had forgotten how sensitive Richard could be and, seeing the hurt in his eyes, she hastily added, "But thank you, sir!"

"There will be a third party," Richard instructed the waiter. "In the meantime, we'd like to...oh, there he is now!"

He waved at a handsome, dark-haired young man threading through the maze of tables, turning as many heads as Octavia but for very different reasons. At twenty-two, Charles Dana Gibson was the town's golden lad of the moment, an artist whose work regularly graced such prestigious publications as *Harper's Monthly, Bazaar* and *The Century*. He had even been awarded a weekly drawing in *Life*. His drawings of society women were all the rage, tempting even the homeliest, most retiring debutantes to seek portraits executed with his flattering magic. All young New York ladies wanted to be Gibson Girls and, Gibson noted with bemusement, some not-so-young ladies as well.

"Richard, my boy!" he cried, pumping his cousin's hand. "Good to see you, as always." His practiced eye darted to Octavia. "And who is this vision of loveliness?"

"Allow me to present Miss Octavia Dockery," Richard said. He smiled but was visibly uncomfortable in the spotlight spilling over from these two beautiful human beings. He coughed to control a stutter. "Octavia, this...this is my cousin, Charles Dana Gibson."

"A great pleasure, Miss Dockery."

"Mr. Gibson," she nodded, relieved that her voice remained steady in the face of celebrity. "Your fame precedes you."

"As yours will no doubt precede you some day," Gibson said, eyes riveted on Octavia as he slipped into a chair beside her. "My dear lady! Please say you will allow me to draw you."

Confidence returning, Richard snickered. "I told you, Octavia!"

Gibson grinned. "What did my mischievous cousin say?"

"That you would ask to draw me," Octavia laughed.

"More than that," Richard interjected. "I also said you couldn't resist a beautiful face."

"He's right," Gibson confessed. "When I see something I

want, I don't hesitate to ask for it." As if to prove his point, he turned to the waiter and said, "We'll start with oysters, my good man. Sherry for you, Miss Dockery?"

Octavia nodded. "Please."

Gibson leaned low and studied her face, partly concealed by the plumed hat. "I swear those glorious red tresses would have inspired Titian himself."

This time Octavia could not stem the heat rising on her cheeks. "Please, Mr. Gibson. You're embarrassing me."

"Then we'll talk about something besides your remarkable beauty," he conceded. "How are things at the conservatory, Richard? I'm so sorry I missed your recital. Do forgive me."

As he often did under unexpected attention, Richard retreated into silence. Familiar with his behavior, Octavia quickly seized the conversational thread. "His recital was a resounding success," she reported. "He played Beethoven and a bit of Liszt. Did you know your talented cousin sings as well as he plays piano? He was just recently a soloist at Christ Episcopal, and I'll tell you something else, Mr. Gibson. Everyone says he has a brilliant career as both singer and concert pianist."

"Splendid, cousin dear! Splendid! I promise I won't miss your next performance." Gibson winked. "If Miss Dockery will agree to pose for me."

Octavia responded with mock sternness. "That's blackmail, sir!"

"Please forgive my little joke." But neither Octavia nor Richard believed he was teasing, especially when he asked if she would prefer being in *Life* or *Bazaar*.

"Really, Mr. Gibson!" she pleaded. "Might we please change the subject?"

Gibson's momentary retreat prompted Richard to rejoin the conversation. "Octavia is a writer, Charles."

"How wonderful! We have writers in our family, too. Did Richard tell you about Richard Henry Dana? He wrote a book many years ago, but, alas, I've forgotten the title."

"Your cousin's book is *Two Years Before the Mast*," Octavia said. "Richard and I read it and discussed it at length, and I believe it's becoming a classic."

Gibson was unabashed. "With all my work, I'm afraid I don't have much time to read, but I would make an exception for something *you* wrote."

Octavia wondered if there was a limit to this young man's brashness but refused to let it undermine her. "I write articles and short essays, Mr. Gibson. Poetry, too. I've been published in a number of magazines as well as the *New York World*."

"Very impressive." Gibson failed to lock eyes and frowned in defeat. "Are you working on anything new?"

"An article on Louisiana." Octavia paused as a waiter delivered drinks and a plate of plump oysters gleaming on ice. She sipped sherry with bitters and delicately forked an oyster. As always, she found the combined tastes exhilarating. "The sugar industry to be precise."

"Do you hail from Louisiana?"

"Arkansas actually. I grew up at Lamartine Plantation. My father moved us to New York when I was twelve."

"Really? How on earth could I have missed you?" A reproachful glare undid his next ploy and he retreated again. "Is this sugar story for the *World*, Miss Dockery?" She nodded. "Perhaps I might be able to do something for you at the *Sun*." He winked at Richard. "Another cousin, also named Charles, was editor. It was some years back, but the Dana name still has influence."

Having endured enough of his bold overtures, Octavia decided to exploit them to her advantage. "I'll make you a deal, Mr. Gibson," she purred. "If you put in a good word for me at the *Sun*, I'll agree to pose for you."

Gibson looked surprised before basking in his own aplomb. "Done!" He nudged Richard. "Where did you find her, my boy? Beauty and brains, too. Now there's a lethal combination!"

The trio dined for over two hours, keeping the waiters bustling to deliver bass in a meunière sauce, rack of lamb,

Maryland terrapin and duckling à l'Alsacienne. Gibson insisted on changing wines with each course and, although Octavia sipped discreetly, she still grew a bit light-headed. It helped that the desserts were fluffy French pastries downed with plenty of ice water. Her corset was so tight by the end of the meal she breathed in short little gasps, but the men didn't notice as they asked permission to discuss family.

"Please do," Octavia insisted, grateful for a respite from the extravagant dinner and Gibson's constant eye. She scanned the noisy room, admiring this lady's hat and that one's brooch, deciding she wouldn't be caught dead in any number of hideous dresses. Only one riveted her attention, a mauve creation on a petite brunette deep in conversation with a dinner partner.

Octavia couldn't help interrupting her companions. "Now there's someone you should draw, Mr. Gibson."

"Who might that be?"

"Over there by the door. That pretty little thing in the mauve dress with the blue roses. Those plumes keep hiding her face, but if you look long enough she'll turn this way and...there! Did you see?"

"My stars, she looks familiar." Richard craned his neck for a better view, catching only glimpses as the Delmonico throngs heaved and meandered. Finally he saw enough to identify her. "Why, that's Jennie Merrill from Natchez."

"An old friend?" Gibson asked.

"A recent acquaintance. I've seen her on a number of occasions and discussed our mutual ties. The houses where we were born in Natchez are across the road from one another."

"How astonishing that your paths crossed in New York," Gibson said.

"Not really," Richard rejoined. "There's a sizable coterie of us Southerners in Manhattan, and we simply introduce everyone to everyone else."

"Which is how we met," Octavia said. "Why didn't you mention her before, Richard? She's lovely."

He looked bewildered. "Didn't I? I thought I did." He entertained another notion and continued, "Miss Jennie told me about working with the King's Daughters, and I seem to recall reading in the paper that she's worked with Jacob Riis as well."

That revelation impressed Gibson. "You know, his book is still causing controversy." He looked at Octavia. "Now that's one I did read. *How the Other Half Lives.*"

"About the tenements," Octavia said. "Those photographs gave me nightmares."

"Indeed." Gibson's interest in poverty evaporated when Jennie stood to leave and surveyed the dining room a final time before she did so. He half-rose from his seat when their eyes briefly locked, then turned to Richard. "Shouldn't you say hello, cousin?"

Never comfortable with crowds, Richard had no desire to leave his sanctuary at the dining table. "She and that man are leaving, Charles, and besides, I'd never catch her in all this confusion."

"Perhaps I can." Gibson sprang to his feet, gave Octavia a polite nod and plunged headlong into the crowd.

Octavia chuckled softly. "Well, Richard, I must say, I've never met a man quite like your cousin."

"I'm sorry, but sometimes...hmmm, sometimes he misbehaves a bit."

"Especially around the female sex, eh? You needn't apologize, dear friend. It was a fascinating evening." She watched Gibson wade determinedly into the throngs and forgot about him. "Natchez, eh? You've told me so much about the place. I wonder if I'll ever see it."

"Maybe I'll take you there after graduation next year."

Although Richard Dana was a man full of surprises and incongruities, this one caught Octavia completely off guard. "Why me? Wouldn't you rather take Amelia?"

"Oh, some day of course, but she spends summers working

on the family farm." He drifted again and continued a bit wist-fully. "Then sometimes I wonder if I'll ever go back to Natchez. I love New York so much. I don't think there's anything I can't find on this marvelous little island."

"Except maybe what's in the White Mountains," Octavia of-fered.

Richard's face resumed the innocent glow from the cab. "If I thought I could live here with Amelia as a wife and have a ca-reer as a soloist or concert pianist, well, it would be an embar-rassment of riches. A man would be blessed to have any one of these things, but more than that? Oh, my! I feel like I would be tempting fate."

"Nonsense. You've been blessed with two absolutely splen-did gifts, and there's no reason why you can't pursue both and some wonderful woman as well."

"I suppose," Richard said slowly. He studied his coffee cup, frowning as if he spied something disagreeable. "But some-times...sometimes it seems a bit...I don't, uh, overwhelming."

Octavia retreated when he suddenly saddened. "Speaking of overwhelming, I've had enough of this noise and cigar smoke. Shall we go?"

"What about Charles?" Richard glanced in Jennie Merrill's direction and saw his cousin disappear in pursuit of mauve os-trich plumes. "Where on earth has he gone?"

"Dearest Richard, did you really think that hopeless Lochinvar would come back?"

"Well, I..."

Octavia smiled and patted his slender pianist's fingers. "I no more thought he'd come back than I thought he'd draw me."

Richard's eyebrows shot up, his face a mask of naiveté. "Really?"

"Really."

7

OLMES WAS AT his desk, ignoring a soggy corned beef sandwich, when he took an urgent phone call from Jennie Merrill. "I know it's lunch time, Mr. Holmes, but can you meet me within the hour? Twenty Washington Square North."

His eyebrows rose. "Do we have a story, Miss Merrill?"

"If we move quickly, I think so. I'll supply details on the way downtown."

After hearing nothing for a month, Holmes had begun to think Jennie had forgotten about the notorious baby farms and was pleased to know she was still passionate about her cause. "I'm on my way!"

He wolfed down his sandwich and rushed to find a hack, relishing the euphoria unique to reporters sensing a good story. At Jennie's address, he told the driver to wait, but as he raced toward the iron gates he was accosted by a beggar. He was about to shoo the woman away when he did a double take.

"Miss Merrill!"

Considering their unusual mission, he certainly hadn't expected fine silks and plumes, but neither had he expected rags. Jennie wore a threadbare gray cloak and skirts and a frayed black hat pulled to her eyebrows. Her scuffed shoes were equally pitiful.

"No sense in attracting undue attention in that neighborhood, eh, Mr. Holmes?" When he continued gaping, she brushed past him. "Hurry now! We've no time to waste!"

"Of course." As he assisted her into the hackney, Holmes thought Jennie looked somehow comelier without her elegant trappings, dark eyes sparkling and face flushed with the spirit of adventure. Then again, he decided that glow could merely be a reflection of fear. Indeed, there was no denying his own feeling of uneasiness as he settled in beside her. "Where are we going?"

She called out just as the driver flapped the reins. "Baxter and Bayard Streets, please."

"You gotta be crazy, lady!" the hack growled over his shoulder. "That's down in The Bend and there's no way I'm gonna drive into that hellhole!"

Holmes was about to reprimand the man for coarse language when Jennie responded coolly. "Then kindly let us out at the corner of Canal and Baxter. I'm down there frequently and can vouch that the intersection is perfectly safe."

Holmes chuckled, impressed. "Obviously you've dealt with this before."

She nodded, impatience growing. "Please hurry, driver. We have an appointment."

The man looked dubious but did as Jennie asked, wondering why someone would venture from Manhattan's smartest address to its absolute worst. Broadway and the Bowery, Canal and Park Streets enclosed The Bend, nicknamed for its diseased heart where Mulberry Street crooked like an elbow. Within those lethal confines were over four thousand apartments, none fit for human habitation, and an erupting immigrant population that eluded the most vigilant census takers. Starvation, disease and murder were the rule, not the exception, and things were at their worst when summer's inferno drove thousands to the rooftops where, desperate for a mere breath of fresh air, many fell or were pushed to their deaths. Frustrated health officials scattered disinfectants through the streets and cellars of Bandit's Roost and Bottle Alley, only to shrug helplessly at the profusion of white mourning badges signaling infant deaths. The place was, as Holmes wrote in his newspaper story, a descent into human degradation and despair only Edgar Allan Poe himself could fathom.

During the ride downtown, Holmes retrieved his new ballpoint pen, positioned it against his notepad and asked for the background information Jennie had promised. "I'll be speaking quite frankly, Mr. Holmes. It's quicker and, I've found, the best way to deal with this sort of unpleasantness."

"Please go on, Miss Merrill."

"Some months ago I befriended a young woman on Bayard Street named Clara Flanagan. It's rare, indeed, to meet anyone in the tenements whose soul isn't completely leached of goodness, but, have mercy, Clara is such a person. She'd just had a second baby and was nursing others for money. Such pitiful wards are called 'pay babies' and, although I was appalled at first, I eventually understood the arrangement. Foundling Asylums are always overwhelmed with abandoned newborns starved for milk. Women like Clara fill that need and are paid for their efforts. Fully half the half million dollars given by the city to the Asylum is earmarked for these wet nurses."

Holmes whistled at the statistic. "That should pay a lot of rents and feed a lot of hungry bodies."

"If only all that money reached its destination," Jennie lamented. "In any case, a while back, Clara told me about a similar source of income derived from babies, something that sickened her. It sickened me as well."

"The baby farms?"

Jennie nodded. "They're run by people who take in anywhere from two to half a dozen babies with the agreement that they'll feed and care for them until they're strong enough to be tended by Asylum nurses. Very few are licensed by the Board of Health, and Clara says almost all are illegally operated by disreputable souls who feed sour milk to the babies and give them paregoric to keep them quiet. When the poor infants die, and they always do, some unqualified medical man signs a certificate stating the cause of death was inanition and that's the end of it."

Holmes was aghast. "But who would believe *none* of those babies could assimilate food?"

"Who is there to question it, Mr. Holmes? Who will file a formal complaint on behalf of dead babies no one wanted in the first place? The practice isn't limited to The Bend either. These terrible places are scattered all over New York, but no one knows how many or even where they are. Jacob Riis said the only complete register is kept by the devil himself."

Holmes's horror deepened as he scribbled away. "This is even more gruesome than I imagined."

"When I questioned Clara further, she agreed to show me such a place on Mulberry Street. We visited after the woman operating it had left, so I was able to confirm the situation." Jennie paused for Holmes to catch up and continued when his pen stopped moving. "I summoned the authorities and the four babies in her care were removed to the Asylum." When his eyebrows rose, Jennie anticipated his question. "Of course, none survived."

"What happened to her?"

Jennie shrugged. "She simply disappeared. There are no secrets in these neighborhoods, Mr. Holmes. I'm quite certain someone warned her before the authorities arrived."

"Is that where we're going now?"

"No. We'll visit the building where Clara lives. A week ago a woman moved in down the hall, and when Clara heard crying babies she went to investigate. The woman, who calls herself Mrs. Posner, is a drunkard who spends most of her time in taverns and actually brags about her baby farm. Like that first woman, Mrs. Posner tried to interest Clara in the same dreadful practice, but she refused and reported the incident to me. Naturally my first thought was our newspaper story. I thought if we could—"

"Please give me another moment, Miss Merrill," Holmes interrupted, glancing up from his work. "You're talking faster than I can write."

"I'm sorry." He was still scribbling away when Jennie called for the driver to stop. "There's Baxter Street. Please pull over to the right."

With The Bend looming dead ahead, the hack was only too happy to discharge his peculiar passengers and hurry back uptown. Holmes felt abandoned as he watched the cab disappear but chided himself when Jennie took his arm and bravely soldiered into the lion's den. Although he had ventured into these slums with Jacob Riis, Holmes had never talked to any of their denizens. That changed when he crossed White Street. Standing at the corner of Baxter and Bayard was a girl who might have been anywhere from fifteen to thirty. She hugged a ragged brown coat close to her thin frame and concealed most of her face with a dirty scarf.

"There's Clara, Mr. Holmes. What a good girl she is!" He was surprised when Jennie embraced the pitiful creature, wondering how she tolerated such powerful body odor. "Why, Clara!" she scolded gently. "Where's your new scarf?"

"Stole, I reckon," Clara muttered. Introduced to Holmes, she nodded but didn't look him in the eye as she indicated an alleyway off Bayard. "It's that way."

"Where's Mrs. Posner?" Jennie asked.

"Some tavern. I reckon she'll be there a while."

"Don't we need someone from the Asylum to take the babies?" Holmes asked.

"Clara and I will take them ourselves," Jennie replied firmly. "The less attention we draw, the better, which is, as I explained earlier, why I wore these clothes."

Holmes cut his eyes toward a mangy gang lolling about the stoop of a derelict building, adding their raggedy stink to a curb overflowing with garbage cans and ash barrels. A few watched suspiciously but said nothing as the odd trio passed. Others watched too, jungle creatures ravenous for fresh prey. Traveling with Riis and a group of able-bodied men is one thing, he thought, but this reckless outing with two females is something else altogether.

"Should we take a policeman along?" he asked warily.

"Absolutely not!" Jennie said. "These people hate the police, don't trust them, and never tell them anything. Surely you've heard stories about the brutality inflicted by the authorities down here."

"It was a foolish question, spoken out of fear," Holmes conceded. He took Jennie's arm and pulled her close before they plunged into the alleyway. "You're not afraid?"

"Always," she confessed without hesitation. "I just pray that the good Lord will be with us, and I suggest you do the same."

As Holmes glanced around, he couldn't help thinking they were entering an area God Himself had long ago forsaken, a thought that somehow intensified the ammoniac stench of urine from a barrel reeking of human waste. He pressed a handkerchief to his nose, noting Jennie had already taken that precaution. Clara had not. About thirty feet in, the alley dog-legged to the left and dead-ended at a four-story structure even more dilapidated than those on the street. Doorways buckled and sagged as though defying the laws of gravity, but the most unsettling experience came when Clara pushed open the door and indicated they should follow her into this vile, black maw.

"Have you matches?" Jennie asked. Holmes grunted no, annoyed at being so ill prepared. "Then take my hand and I'll follow Clara. We have to climb two floors at the end of the hall. Don't touch the walls if you can help it."

Her warning came too late. When Holmes tried to grope his way, he brushed something slimy and foul. The floor was no better, a fetid mixture of unnamable matter alternately sticky and slick. He silently swore with every step and continued the vile odyssey through a darkness so intense his eyes could not adjust. Like Virgil escorting Dante through hell, Clara led Jennie and Holmes up a rickety staircase that creaked alarmingly beneath their combined weight. Mysterious glimmers of light showed the way, but Holmes considered them a mixed blessing as he got a closer look at the wretched surroundings. When his sandwich threatened rebellion, he realized this was far worse than anything he had seen with Riis.

"How can human beings live like this?"

"Clara lives here," Jennie said, tone reprimanding his insensitivity. As they reached the third floor, more inexplicable light glowed, enough to discern another narrow hall with flimsy doors. "Down there, Mr. Holmes! Do you hear it!"

A thin, pitiable cry supported Jennie's claim that human life existed here, however tenuous.

Clara pointed toward the end of the hall. "Hurry!" They unclasped hands and followed the sound. Midway, Holmes coughed and sneezed. Clara turned around and hissed. "You gotta be real quiet now. The man lives in that apartment at the end is plumb crazy and we sure don't want him comin' out here."

Holmes and Jennie obeyed as they followed the pathetic wail. Clara paused before a door, turned to Jennie, who nodded encouragement, and pushed it open. Holmes's gorge rose at the eruption of raw, foul odors, but Clara gamely poked her head inside. After a moment, she slipped into the blackness with Jennie close behind. Holmes lingered in the doorway and tried to absorb the incomparable scene. He heard the mewling again but saw nothing until Clara, using some grotesque sixth sense, found a small candle and matches. A flame flickered across a windowless room measuring five by six feet and throttled by dead air. The bare walls were pocked with malignant mold and years of abuse, and floors were strewn with rags, paper and garbage. A misshapen bucket was the only nod to sanitation, but another corner held something even more unsettling.

Macabre fascination drove Holmes closer. On a small pile of verminous straw lay three tiny bodies wrapped in newspaper. Two were unmoving, he noted, or worse. He watched Jennie and Clara jockey for position as they knelt to inspect the babies. When Jennie stirred the one that was mewing, she triggered an explosion of agonized wails.

"Careful how you pick him up," Clara warned. "Miz Posner beats 'em to keep 'em quiet."

"Oh, dear!" Jennie whispered as rotting newspaper flaked away to reveal the hideous truth. The bruises proved to be too much for Holmes and he backed away, cursing a new wave of nausea. He had retreated only a few steps when he bumped something he smelled before seeing. He spun around to confront a massive, menacing silhouette and wondered if they had roused the neighbor Clara warned about.

"What do you want?" Holmes asked. It was a visceral but inane query, as he knew robbery could be the man's only intent.

The big tough grunted and lunged. He was impossible to dodge in the narrow hallway, and Holmes's frantic scramble propelled him through the flimsy door of another apartment and down another Dantean level. Slits cut into the walls threw pale light onto unspeakable profanity. The room was even filthier than the rest, smothered under straw, garbage and debris, but there was a different odor here, raw and fresh. As Holmes's eyes adjusted to the dimness, he saw the source. Stacked near the door, so close he nearly fell over them, were five bodies of varying size, from toddler to adult, all newly slaughtered, all oozing blood and viscera.

"Good Christ!"

His cry stirred someone else from the dank cave, and he screamed when a shadowy figure sprang up, shrouded in a primordial howl. When Holmes saw the dull gleam of metal, survival instinct succeeded this time and he sidestepped the charge. The man tumbled through the doorway and collided with the lurking tough, locking fast in a battle punctuated by growls more bestial than human. They thrashed and pummeled furiously in a fight lasting just long enough for the thief to wrest away a knife, plunge it into his attacker's gut and twist. The stench and steam of bowels spilled into the hall, and while Holmes held his breath and the women screamed, the thug fled the way he had come.

Time pulsed and wavered in Holmes's mind as he leaned against the sweating wall and shook hard. Somewhere he heard the whimpering of women and a squalling baby and a vaguely familiar voice asking over and over again, "What happened? What happened? What happened?"

Holmes's numbed brain finally surged and once he unraveled the chilling chain of events, he ordered Jennie and Clara to follow him out of the building. When Jennie balked at stepping over the dead man, he took the baby she carried and grabbed her elbow.

"Come with me now! Both of you! And don't look in there!"

He was too late. Jennie paused by the open door just long enough to register the mass carnage and fainted dead away. Holmes miraculously managed to pass the whimpering baby to Clara and catch Jennie before she collapsed onto the eviscerated corpse. His second amazing feat was negotiating the dark, wobbly staircase with an unconscious woman in his arms. Clara trailed, sobbing and coughing as she perched on the now-deserted stoop. The baby was silent and unmoving.

Holmes turned toward her, thinking quickly. "The dead man in the hall, Clara. Was that your crazy neighbor?" She nodded. "Do you know his name?"

"O'Brien. Paddy O'Brien."

"All those bodies in there. Was that his family?" She nodded again and wiped a runny nose on her sleeve. Holmes knew her fear came as much from his questions as what she had seen, and he moved swiftly to calm her. "I'll go to the police later, Clara. Alone. If you help me now, they'll never know you were involved." He touched her arm to reassure her when hope for anonymity dawned in her swollen eyes. "Do you understand me?"

"Yessir."

"Good girl." Holmes shifted Jennie to make her weight more manageable, grateful that she was such a small thing, and hurried from the carnage. Clara and the baby followed him up Baxter Street to Canal where Jennie began coughing, revived in part by sweet, fresh air gusting off the East River. Holmes gently lowered her onto a brick stoop and sat beside her. He beckoned Clara to join them, but she shook her head and began backing away. Knowing she was about to bolt, Holmes grabbed her arm. "Wait, Clara! I need you to tell me what you know about your neighbors. Please. I promise it will help."

The combination of a firm grip and sympathetic tone garnered what the reporter needed to know. Unable to reach pen and paper because he still held on to Jennie, Holmes committed everything possible to memory while Clara sobbed out her story. When he pressed for more details, the girl began repeating herself, and when he relaxed his grip she tore free and fled back into The Bend.

"Oh, dear," Jennie muttered weakly. "And that poor sick baby."

Holmes had noted the infant's lifeless face and quickly changed the subject. "Are you feeling better?"

"Yes, thank you. I apologize for fainting."

"No need to apologize, Miss Merrill. I nearly fainted myself." He helped her to her feet. "Shall we continue down Canal Street and find a hansom?"

"Yes, please." In the safety of the hansom, Jennie brushed

back a sweaty strand of hair and realized she was bareheaded. "My hat!"

"Lost along the way, I'm afraid."

Jennie tugged her coat tighter, sighed and took a deep breath. Then another. "What happened back there, Mr. Holmes?"

"Are you sure you're strong enough to talk about it?"

"Possibly not, but I've learned it's better to face unpleasantness all at once."

"I'm afraid this is more than unpleasant," he cautioned. After a moment, he asked, "How much do you remember?"

She shrugged. "Clara and I heard some noise. A struggle. You screamed."

"I screamed?" That was a detail Holmes didn't recall.

"And there was that fight in the hallway. At first I thought it was you, but there was another man running down the hall. It was so dark..."

"Anything else?"

Jennie took another deep breath and discreetly lowered her voice so the driver couldn't overhear. Holmes wondered whose heartbeat reverberated louder inside the cab, his or hers.

"When...when I looked into that room, there appeared to be a stack of...bodies. And a great deal of...blood."

So she had seen it, Holmes thought. God help her!

"And the man in the hall," she added. "Was he dead, too?"

"Yes."

Jennie paled and crossed herself. "So it's finally come to pass."

"I beg your pardon?"

She didn't seem to hear. "Who was he?"

Holmes leaned against the worn leather seat, reporter's mind sifting through the facts of the puzzle. "As best I can tell, Miss Merrill, someone, maybe one of those hooligans on the stoop, followed us inside to rob us. When he and I struggled, I was shoved through the door to another apartment where I encountered a second man with a knife. He lost his balance when he came after me and tangled with the thug in the hall.

That man killed him and fled." He paused, then added something in hopes Jennie would ask no more questions. "I'll call
the police after I've seen you safely home and tell them all I
know."

They continued uptown, grateful that the boisterous crush
of afternoon traffic made conversation impossible. Both were
lost in their own worlds, Jennie still tingling with mild shock
while Holmes struggled to fathom a madness that had nearly
cost him his life. Neither one saw the driver turn right onto
Broadway and left onto Waverly Place, and Jennie would later
confess to Holmes that she did not remember him helping her
up the steps to her porch.

Moments later, still in the cab, Holmes rushed not to make
a police report but to the *New York Sun*. He spoke to no one
as he hurried to his desk in the busy pressroom, consumed
with reaching his typewriter while details of an explosive
story were fresh in his mind. He had stumbled onto a sensational mass murder that would surely stir outrage throughout
the city, threaten political seats and likely create chaos in the
downtown precincts. While he typed, he occasionally glanced
at the motto of the *Sun's* founder, Charles Dana, which he kept
tucked in his desk drawer: "The *Sun* will study condensation,
clearness, point, and will endeavor to present its daily photograph of the whole world's doings in the most luminous and
lively manner."

Holmes didn't have a photograph but he could supply everything else in abundance since he had witnessed this story
first-hand. Not only that, he thought with satisfaction, but his
reporter's perspicacity had prompted him to question Clara
and glean invaluable details. He now had a story beyond his or
Jennie's wildest hopes, and with luck he could break it before
the police learned of fresh horrors in The Bend.

He wrote feverishly, finishing a first draft in just under an
hour. He read and rewrote, then rewrote again but was still

unsatisfied. He stood and paced, hoping to clear his head; then sat and read his headline aloud for the umpteenth time.

"Driven to Madness by Poverty and Despair, Distraught Father Slays Wife and Four Children!"

Holmes stared at the page until the words blurred, then buried his face in his hands and struggled again to conjure the atrocities he'd seen in that wretched cubicle. Slowly the bloody motes stopped swirling and congealed, and he remembered what he had seen a split second before Paddy O'Brien leapt from the darkness with a knife aimed at his throat. The man had been holding an infant in his arms, tiny throat newly slit and dripping blood. Holmes swallowed bile as he revised his headline, changing "four" to "five."

Then he took the story to his boss.

8

ONCE HOLMES HAD delivered her home, Jennie
couldn't suppress images of the bloodbath in her
brain. She rushed upstairs to her bedroom and blindly paced
until her alarmed housekeeper coaxed out a curt explanation.

"I saw someone murdered, Maggie."

While the bewildered old woman watched, Jennie tore off
her raggedy clothes and hurled them into the hall. Stockings
and underwear followed, then boots, which caromed noisily
off the wall and down the stairs.

"Burn them, Maggie!" Jennie cried, naked and trembling
and consumed by the horrors of the day. "Burn everything and
leave me alone!"

While Maggie rushed to obey, Jennie slammed the door
and staggered into the bathroom, drawing her own bath for
the first time in her life. She lingered in the water after scrub-
bing her skin raw, as though she could eradicate memories as
well as dirt. Then she donned a dressing gown and resumed

pacing, pausing just once to look out on the sunny square busy as usual with nannies and their tiny charges. Those happy, healthy children only reminded Jennie of the hated baby farms and drove her into bed. She drew the covers to her throat and lay paralyzed until shadows crept across her room, stirring only to shield her eyes when blinding sunlight pierced the lace curtains. When the sun finally disappeared across the Hudson River, she crawled from her blanketed cocoon to trim the gas-lights. Night was too evocative of the vile, malodorous black-ness she had barely escaped with her life and she could not abide it. Room aglow, she returned to bed and resumed her odd vigil.

Twice Maggie knocked on the door, once to ask about sup-per and again to inquire if Jennie wanted anything before she retired. Both times she was brusquely dismissed. Jennie didn't have strength for anything but solitude, but just as darkness was intolerable, so was sleep. Her mind was consumed with in-iquitous images she knew would bloom into fierce nightmares, and although insomnia was exhausting, the idea of sleep fright-ened her even more.

Tightening her robe against a deepening chill, Jennie sought her jewelry box, retrieved the heavy gold key nestled against her mother's pearls and knelt by a chest at the foot of the bed. The chest had come from Castile, an indulgence she coaxed from her father during his ambassadorial days. With its heavy leather tooling and metal hardware, it was far too mascu-line for a girl of twelve, but as usual Ayres Merrill acquiesced. Jennie opened the lock and sat back, taking a moment to in-hale a rich, leathery scent and contemplate stacks of letters tied with pale blue ribbons.

There were eight stacks, each representing a year in her life; all were from Duncan Minor.

After fleeing Natchez following her father's funeral, Jennie had been barraged with letters. Duncan wrote once, sometimes twice a day. She had been so distressed by this smothering pursuit that she never opened them and chided herself for not throwing them out. A peculiar amalgam of guilt and instinct had directed her to stash them in the Spanish trunk where they collected for over a year, until New Year's Day, 1885, when she succumbed to curiosity and read the first one. She was repulsed by the gushing, overblown professions of love, but, morbidly intrigued, she read a second and third letter. After a fourth, Jennie could stomach no more and dismissed Duncan's ardor as an adolescent crush spun out of control. She never responded and read no more, but Duncan had never stopped writing.

The following January, 1886, Jennie's inquisitiveness again hounded her to open the second year of letters and, curiosity satisfied after a quick browsing, she put them away again. The ritual repeated itself for two more years, but just when she felt strong enough to swear off her secret addiction, Jennie recognized a marked shift in her cousin's tone. The inflamed passions and flowery poetry of youth abruptly cooled, replaced by simple, mature statements of fact. Instead of addressing her as "precious one" or "my own angel," his greeting was simply "dear cousin Jennie" as it had been when they were children. He no longer pleaded for her to return or begged for a future together. Instead he wrote of quotidian things, about life after graduation from college, at his home, Oakland, and visits to the racetrack. Their family. Natchez. Mississippi.

At some point—Jennie never understood exactly when—she began regarding Duncan differently and questioned her wholesale rejection of this boy who had become a man. He had grown up, that much was evident, but ferocious pride and stubbornness blinded her to critical changes within herself as well. She did, however, know exactly when she decided to respond. It was in June of 1889, when she was twenty-five and Duncan twenty-seven. Jennie was indulging herself at Saratoga's Grand Union Hotel, sharing long, insouciant days with a collection of chic friends when she was suddenly overwhelmed by summery ennui. To her companions' dismay, but not their surprise, she announced she wanted to be alone and excused herself to explore the hotel's famous gardens. The truth was Jennie was lonely and found no real comfort in flowerbeds. Mocked by the bright floral colors, she had retreated to her room, where she sought solace from a most unexpected source—Duncan. For the first time since leaving Natchez, Jennie answered his letters. It was nothing more than a feckless description of the titanic hotel's mile of piazzas and two-hour, eight-course dinners, the endless teas, siestas, concerts, dances and visits to the racetrack, but when she returned to New York his response was waiting. She expected him to tease her for fulfilling his prophecy that she would eventually write, but Duncan's reply was as simple and straightforward as hers. There was no smug I-told-you-so tone, merely a lively account of trips to the Natchez racetrack and his newfound passion for buying and breeding racehorses. He was spending a lot of time in New Orleans, he wrote, and had just purchased a spirited thoroughbred he believe had enormous potential, one he might ultimately race at Saratoga.

Jennie felt both embraced and rejected. Duncan's long years of singing her praises had spoiled her, and when the adulation stopped she wondered how much it mattered. She also asked herself if Duncan had finally bowed to her wishes and stopped loving her. If so, she felt as betrayed as on that day he'd first declared his love. Jennie conceded that she was being unreasonable, that she couldn't have it both ways, but her confusion deepened daily. That same distress drove her to plumb her true feelings for this man.

For another year they continued writing in a platonic vein, and as always Duncan's letters vastly outnumbered hers. To her surprise, they made Jennie nostalgic for Natchez, even when she weighed the great stakes involved. Her work with the King's Daughters remained rewarding, but it had also begun a war of emotional attrition. Instead of finding Christian joy in easing a child's pain or comforting an abandoned wife with hungry mouths to feed, Jennie found herself hurt, even resentful, when those troubles followed her home and invaded her dreams. She repeatedly sought advice from Mrs. Bottome and was told to pray. She prayed to be free of loneliness as well, and when liberation did not come Jennie again sought solace in Duncan's letters. This time she read them from beginning to end. Seen all of a piece, they made her realize that the strange fire which once frightened and repulsed her now suggested warmth and security. They also stirred her heart.

That spring, Jennie sought answers by boldly writing Duncan to ask if he still loved her. His response was what now drove her to rifle for an envelope more recognizable for a tea stain than its May 29, 1891, postmark. It was the only envelope he had ever sent without a letter. Instead, it contained a newspaper clipping entitled "Marriage and Divorce" and included excerpts from an address delivered in New Orleans by one Monsignor Gaetano Squillace. Duncan had marked three sections for Jennie's consideration. Huddled against the trunk, she tucked bare feet beneath her and read them again.

"After showing what was natural marriage, and in what consisted civil marriage, and how carefully in England the latter was guarded, he proceeded to show what a religious marriage was, and stated that while bishops and priests performed the other sacraments of the Church appertaining to their several offices, they did not perform the sacrament of marriage. The ministers of that sacrament were the man and the woman who had made the natural contract of matrimony, and now in the presence of God, and by God's sanction and sanctuary, with most solemn oath pledged themselves forever each to the other as husband and wife."

And, "This brings one at once to the key of Catholic marriage, which is this—that the persons contracting marriage are bound in one bond that cannot be annulled by any earthly power. Their individuality is so blended that they are each the counterpart of the other. That which is lacking in one is supposed to be found in the other; they thus constitute but one moral person."

And finally, "Many are asking, Can the Catholic Church be so cruel as to compel a man and wife to remain married who are incompatible, who from many causes find it impossible to live happily together? The Church answers, this contract was made and sealed in the presence of God; that no power on earth can sever that which God has joined together."

Now, as when she first read them, Jennie dismissed these assertions as high-flown ecclesiastical folderol, but she was searching for a particular line which, as she hoped, brought much-needed inner peace. She read it again, aloud this time.

"'Their individuality is so blended that they are each the counterpart of the other.'"

Jennie tucked the clipping back into the envelope, replaced it in the appropriate stack and went to her secretary. There she wrote the shortest letter of her life, the one Duncan had yearned to receive for eight years. She revived her spirits and burnished her beleaguered soul with every stroke of the pen.

"I'm coming home, dearest Duncan," Jennie wrote. "To Natchez. To Elms Court. To you."

She slipped back into bed, only then noticing fresh sunlight creeping through the curtains. It was dawn and outside Washington Square was stirring to life. She stretched and yawned, surprisingly alert considering she had been awake all night. Knowing Maggie would have risen an hour ago, she pushed a buzzer and was sitting up in bed when the housekeeper rushed to respond.

"Yes, miss?"

"Good morning, Maggie."

"Good morning, miss," Maggie said warily. "Feeling better today, are you?"

"Much better, thank you." Jennie smiled. "I really must apologize for my behavior last night. I'm afraid I wasn't quite myself."

"You worry me sick," Maggie fussed, bustling about to

extinguish the gaslights. "I'm a good Catholic same as yourself, but you shouldn't never go into those awful places downtown. Something terrible was bound to happen and it finally did."

"You needn't worry any more."

"What do you mean, miss?"

"I mean that I'm going to do no more work for the King's Daughters."

Maggie frowned, Gaelic superstitions roused. "Is that why you burned those old clothes?"

"Did I?" Jennie frowned, unable to conjure the memory. Much of yesterday remained a cipher. "I...I suppose so, yes."

"Well, never mind about all that," Maggie said hastily. "Suppose I bring you a cup of tea and then some breakfast."

"Yes, please," Jennie sighed. "That would be nice."

When Maggie returned with breakfast half an hour later, Jennie was fast asleep. The housekeeper drew the draperies and tiptoed out, praying this would not be another unorthodox day. But shortly after two o'clock, Stephen Holmes bounded up the steps of Twenty Washington Square North and leaned on the doorbell until Maggie responded. She was incensed by the insistent ringing but admitted the young man when she recognized him as the one who saw Jennie safely home yesterday. She took his hat but told him he may have come for nothing.

"Miss Jennie's upstairs, sir. She didn't sleep well last night, and I don't know that she's up to receiving visitors."

"Perhaps if you tell her I have some important news," Holmes announced, waving a newspaper with the strong smell of fresh ink. "Very important indeed!"

"I'll tell her, sir, but I can't promise anything more."

While he waited, Holmes took quick inventory of the central hall, parlor and dining room, noting details he'd missed when he brought her home after yesterday's chaos. These were certainly less opulent than the rooms at Elms Court, a bit worn and frayed like the old Merrill/Surget money itself, he thought with a chuckle. He looked up as Jennie's voice floated down the stairs.

"Mr. Holmes," she called. "What's this all-important news?"

"An advance copy of today's *Sun*, Miss Merrill," he called back. "Hot off the presses and hand-delivered just for you!"

Trepidation was evident when she called back. "Is it what I suspect?"

"Please. Come see for yourself."

Holmes couldn't have been more surprised when Jennie descended the stairs in her dressing gown, took the folded paper from him and pointed it toward the parlor.

"Shall we go in?"

"Front page," he blurted, trailing like a puppy unable to contain its enthusiasm. "Just look at those headlines!"

Jennie sat and unfolded the newspaper. The sensational headline was designed to leap off the page at the most casual reader. For her, it needed no such boost.

DISTRAUGHT FATHER SLAYS WIFE, FIVE CHILDREN
DRIVEN TO MADNESS BY POVERTY, DISEASE AND DESPAIR
"Better that I take care of them myself!"
Murderer Killed By Unknown Thug
A New York Sun Exclusive by Stephen Holmes

Holmes paced the room as Jennie read. Her frequent sighs and the occasional, "Oh, my goodness!" revealed exactly where she was in the article. The dreadful facts hastily gleaned from Clara had enabled Holmes to weave the story of a life careening hideously out of control. Paddy O'Brien had emigrated from County Cork, Ireland, six years ago and within a year had married another from the old country and begun a family. While Paddy worked in the sewers, his wife Maureen had five children in as many years while he moved them from place to place, desperate for cheaper rents. A contagious eye disease, gone untreated, had blinded Maureen, making it impossible for her to work, and eventually infected the two youngest children. When poisonous gases in the sewers destroyed Paddy's lungs, he faced the dead end of defeat.

Jennie read aloud. "'Mr. O'Brien's pathetic plight was accidentally discovered when Miss Jennie Merrill of the King's Daughters took this reporter to investigate reports of a so-called 'baby farm' in the wretched tenement where O'Brien and his family resided.'"

Jennie continued silently but read aloud again at the exact moment Holmes expected.

"'Miss Merrill rescued the only surviving infant and along with this reporter made a daring escape from the bloody scene. Her brave actions under the most harrowing and dangerous circumstances surely qualify her for heroism.'"

Jennie looked up for the first time. "I did no such thing, Mr. Holmes. We both know I fainted when I saw those bodies. And you said it was Clara who took the baby."

"Indeed, I did."

"But why—?"

"Because Clara has no interest in being a heroine," Holmes explained, sitting beside her. "In exchange for anonymity, she gave me all the information on poor Mr. O'Brien while you were unconscious. As you said yourself, people in The Bend hate and fear the police, and this way they'll never know Clara was involved."

"How can you be sure?"

"As soon as I filed this story with my editor, I went down to police headquarters on Mulberry Street and told them what had happened. The version you're reading, that is. Then I took them over to Bayard Street where, as I expected, everything was just as we left it."

"No one had called the police?"

"Of course not."

"Dear Lord! All those poor bodies and no one even...?" Jennie sucked her teeth and scanned the article again. "I still don't know what to think. You've made me a heroine when someone else deserves the glory. I don't approve of that." Her tone was less than solicitous.

Holmes was prepared. "Don't underestimate yourself, Miss Merrill. Without your concern for the baby farms, I would never have made that gruesome discovery. Without your help I would never have uncovered such an incredible story."

"I suppose," she conceded.

"There's nothing to suppose. Fate dictated that we get two important stories from your noble mission. This city will reel in shock when people read about the desperation just outside their doorstep. While they're still reeling, I'll hit them with a second story, about the baby farms!"

"That would please me no end." Jennie smiled at Maggie waiting just outside the door. "We'd like some tea now, if you please." When they were alone again, she asked, "Is this the sort of story they call a 'scoop'?"

"Exactly," Holmes grinned. "The sort a reporter dreams about; the kind that falls into his lap when he least expects it."

"Also the sort, I suspect, that earns great notoriety for the writer. Perhaps financial compensation as well."

"It's certainly possible," he said, amused by her bluntness. "I wish you had seen the look on my editor's face when I told him I had actually been at the scene of the crime, and that I was very nearly another of Mr. O'Brien's victims. Oh, I know it sounds crass and uncaring to wrench glory from misery, but it's an occupational hazard."

"Did I look disparaging?"

"A bit perhaps."

"Then I apologize. And I understand better than you might think."

"Oh?"

Jennie's deep breath and subsequent sigh hurt her head, a

reminder of a sleepless night. "I'm sure it's no secret that I was beginning to...to unravel the night we had dinner at Delmonico's. You were not a close friend, yet I told you of my doubts about the King's Daughters. Clearly my work for them has residual effects that can be most distressing, and I have felt for some time that my days there were numbered. Just as you have to be terribly hardened in your work, sometimes so must I."

"If I may return the favor," Holmes interrupted, "perhaps I understand you better than you think. You said something in the cab yesterday that I found very telling. Perhaps you don't remember, but when I told you Mr. O'Brien was dead you said, 'So it's finally come to pass.'"

"I'm afraid I don't remember much about the ride home. What did you think I meant?"

"That you had looked death in the face, and that it was a sign that you must move on."

This time the sigh did not hurt. "It's a relief to admit it," Jennie confessed. "In truth, I don't believe I could go into one of those awful neighborhoods again. Certainly not now."

"My dear Miss Merrill," Holmes said, laughing to lighten the somber mood. "I must tell you that two veteran policemen and one detective were physically ill at the crime scene. One fainted dead away. All things considered, I think you did remarkably well."

Jennie scarcely heard. "I hate feeling defeated."

"You're not defeated, and, again, you're underestimating yourself. You've slaved for the King's Daughters all these years, and now it's time to spend your time and efforts elsewhere. If you want to consider yesterday an omen of sorts, by all means do so, but you had already indicated a desire to renounce those duties."

Holmes thought he knew Jennie Merrill fairly well, but her next comment stopped him cold.

"Why should you care, Mr. Holmes?"

He shrugged, buying time while he fumbled for an answer. Although he had never considered her on such terms, he couldn't help wondering if she was coquetting. After all, Jennie Merrill was a lovely, charming young woman who had no trouble attracting men. He thought of the night they'd dined at Delmonico's, when Charles Dana Gibson had brashly approached their table and pursued her from the restaurant right onto the sidewalk. Gibson was a man with exacting standards of beauty, yet, as far as Holmes was concerned, Jennie was oddly sexless. Any man who captured her, he thought, would have to be an unusual amalgam of strength and submission, a bill he himself most assuredly did not fit. He weighed telling her as much but did not. There were more genteel ways.

"Because I see a friend who is momentarily adrift and needs a helping hand," he said finally. "You've thought of others so long, you've forgotten how to think of yourself."

Jennie rolled her eyes. "My brothers and sisters would certainly argue that point."

Holmes took a gamble. "Because they see you as willful and spoiled and self-absorbed?"

To his surprise she did not challenge him.

"None of them ever knew me well, Mr. Holmes. Only my father and, to a certain extent, yourself." She paused, thinking of Duncan. "Perhaps one other person."

"I'm honored."

She went to the window and contemplated the hubbub of Washington Square. "You've influenced me more than you know, sir. Had you not taken me to Longwood I might never have been inspired to come here and do charitable things. I might even have gone back to Europe and been forever swallowed up in an endless social whirl. Ha, ha!"

Jennie's sudden cackle unnerved Holmes. He had heard her soft, gentle laughter before, but this laugh seemed tinged with hysteria.

"That's why I wasn't upset when you called me those un-pleasant names a moment ago.

"You're quite right. My father spoiled me terribly." She shrugged and returned to the couch. "In any case, thanks to you I've had another...oh, I forget the word."

"Epiphany?"

"Yes. A strange sort of epiphany. It happened last night. Early this morning to be exact, when I realized that by coming to New York I wasn't running *to* anything but running *away* from something. It's time to go back to where I started and res-cue something dear I almost lost forever. I'm going home to Natchez, Mr. Holmes."

"If you'll forgive my frankness, does this rescue involve the young man I met the day I whisked you off to Longwood?"

Jennie's eyes widened. "I'm surprised you remember him."

Holmes realized he had struck a nerve. "Reporters recall pe-culiar things, Miss Merrill. I also recall that he was quite angry when we left. You were upset, too, although you did your best to hide it."

"I now realize he would have been angry at anyone taking me out of his sight," she conceded. "And, yes, he is the main reason I am returning to Elms Court."

"Again."

"Again and for the last time, I think. Like Father." Jennie thanked and dismissed Maggie after she delivered a silver tea service. She unwrapped a basket of fragrant sweets and made a face of mock disappointment. "So sorry, Mr. Holmes. There is no mice candy."

"You have a good memory, too," he smiled, helping himself to a chocolate cookie. "It's kind of you to remember."

Jennie poured tea and passed him a steaming cup. "When I first began work for the King's Daughters, our founder told me something I've never forgotten." Holmes leaned closer as she extended another rare confidence. "She said, 'Memory en-riches life but forgetfulness makes it possible.' After yesterday's terrible events and my thoughts in the aftermath, I have realized the truth in that." She nodded, satisfied. "Our paths will diverge again in a few days, Mr. Holmes. I must confess I will miss your company."

"The sentiment is indeed mutual." This time Holmes knew there was no mistaking her intent and welcomed the pleasant revelation. He watched her unclasp a chain around her neck, remove something tucked behind the collar of her robe and press it in his hand. "What's this?"

"My St. Christopher medal. I want you to have it."

"That's much too personal a gift," he protested.

"Nevertheless, please keep it. In gratitude for saving my life yesterday, and so that St. Christopher may protect you on your many journeys. My traveling days will soon be over."

"Thank you." Holmes was genuinely touched as he leaned forward so Jennie might hang the medal around his neck. "I hope we'll see each other again, Miss Merrill. It's certainly possible with my mother and sister constantly after me to come home."

"Then please come calling at Elms Court." She shrugged and laughed softly. "Who knows? Maybe some day I'll even give you that interview I promised."

In the shadows of Holmes's mind, the word "interview" screamed like a banshee, and he grabbed his watch so fast he nearly tore the chain from his waistcoat.

"Great Scott! In all the excitement I almost forgot I'm to conduct an interview this very afternoon. One that's taken me weeks to arrange." He got to his feet. "You'll please excuse me, but I must rush off."

"Of course." Jennie trailed him to the front door, newspaper in hand. "Although I can't imagine anything more important than going to your office and waiting for the public's reaction when this issue of the *Sun* hits the streets."

"Oh, it's important alright," Holmes replied. Deciding there was no time to wait for Maggie, he grabbed his hat from the coat tree. "I'm speaking to some gentlemen who are putting together America's first expedition to the Antarctic. Such intrepid adventures are always exciting, of course, but this one has a special angle."

"And what is that, sir?"

"A woman is going along to keep their journals, and, if all goes well, she will be the first female to set foot on Antarctica."

"How wonderful!" Jennie reconsidered. "Although I personally could never brave such a climate."

"She struck me as the type of woman who could brave most any storm. Very self-confident and quite remarkable, really."

"You've already met her?"

"We've only spoken on the telephone. She finalized the details for the interview."

"Is she famous?"

"Not yet," Holmes said, hastily slipping into hat and coat. "But you'll want to remember her name."

Jennie cocked her head as she opened the front door. "Oh?"

"Miss Octavia Dockery."

PART TWO

1892–1932

*T*he situation bred idiosyncrasies — the dreamers out of touch with any reality. Years earlier, newcomers noticed that the Natchez plantation people were a small, tight group which grew smaller, tighter with the generations. Fifteen or twenty names, and the circle was complete. Intermarriage had begun early; the same names still merged. Now oddities developed.

Harnett Kane
Natchez on the Mississippi

9

ITH CALEB, THELMA and Eugene in tow, Jennie made a final inspection of the house and praised each one until they beamed. The flowers, food and drink were all in order, but most crucial were the lights creating Elms Court's celebrated "ball of a thousand candles." Ensuring all the tapers were lit and situated was a daunting task, but Jennie was, as always, thorough in her attention to detail and she swept through each room to check every chandelier, candlestick and candelabrum. Then it was on to the gallery to scrutinize grillwork intertwined with roses and vines cut from the villa's abundant gardens. She took a deep breath and grew pleasantly woozy from the fragrance. How she wished her beloved father and mother were alive to share the moment. She looked up and whispered to a dark Mississippi sky lustrous with stars.

"It's all for you."

Jennie had good reason to believe her parents would be pleased. Tonight was the culmination of months of preparation involving some genteel subterfuge with the *crème de la crème* of the town's younger set. Since returning to Natchez, she had curried their favor with small dinner parties and soirées and never squandered a moment on anyone begrudging her family's Union sympathies. When it was time to revive the famous ball, Jennie was confident her invitations would prove irresistible, but for extra insurance she secured Richard Dana as guest of honor when she learned he would be visiting Natchez. During this last year, he had carved an illustrious mark as a concert pianist and was even approaching the level of his celebrated cousin Charles Dana Gibson as one of New York's rising cultural stars. His presence was a special social coup for Southerners because his late father, Charles Backus Dana, had been Episcopal rector at Christ Church in Alexandria, Virginia—a church whose parishioners had included Robert E. Lee. All Natchez knew that the Lee family had generously gifted Father Dana with furniture, including the cradle that had rocked the famed future general himself. That Baby Richard had also occupied it was a fact awarding him a star in the rarefied Confederate galaxy. So, while the Old Guard fumed at home, their more curious sons and daughters could not resist the double temptation to meet Richard and experience the fabled Ball of a Thousand Candles.

"All for you," she whispered again.

Even as she spoke the words, Jennie knew her pledge wasn't altogether true. There was someone else for whom she was creating this night of nights. These days Duncan Minor was as much a part of her life as Elms Court itself, and since her return almost a year ago their mutual love had so deepened that he had become her shadow. Jennie, as was her nature, took charge, beguiling Duncan with daring dimensions for their new liaison. Despite welcoming her infinite surprises, however, he had not been prepared for what had recently transpired in the playhouse where they'd become friends as children. At Jennie's request, Eugene had cleaned and repainted the toy building and secreted it in the park surrounding Elms Court. She was giddy in her eagerness to show Duncan this latest inspiration, high spirits prompting her to don a provocative afternoon dress and rush to greet him while he was still tethering his horse.

"I have a surprise for you, dearest."

"It seems you have a new one every time I visit," he said with a smile.

"But this one's special," she insisted, taking his hand. "Very, very special."

Duncan indulged Jennie as usual, happily following her along a path winding deep into the heavily wooded grounds. Her excitement was contagious, and by the time they reached a sunny glen thick with blue Louisiana iris, Duncan felt almost euphoric.

"What's this?" he asked, squinting in the bright light.

"My old playhouse. Remember?"

"Dearest Jennie," he teased. "Do you really think I could forget my first moments alone with you?"

"You'd better not!" she said with mock petulance. "Well? What do you think?"

"I think it's charming." Duncan leaned down for a closer inspection. "Was it your idea to paint it to look like Elms Court?"

"Of course." Jennie tugged his hand. "Let's go inside."

Duncan demurred. "Can we both fit in there?"

"It's much roomier than you think," Jennie declared. "You'll see."

She opened the little door and ducked inside with a bold flurry of skirts and petticoats Duncan found as provocative as it was uncharacteristic. Once inside, she motioned him to follow, but his considerable height required him to bend almost double to gain entry. His awkward contortions made them both laugh, but their moods abruptly changed when he tumbled onto the soft ground beside her. She sighed and snuggled close enough for him to feel her body heat even through layers of clothing. Her gaze, guileless and troubling, set Duncan on his guard.

He frowned. "What is it, my dear?"

She brushed her lips against his ear and murmured, "I have another surprise."

Duncan watched as Jennie leaned away, unpinned the cameo at her throat and tossed it aside before turning her attention to the row of pearl buttons down her bodice. They opened one by one until it gaped to the waist.

Duncan was stunned. "Jennie! What—"

"It's time, my love."

Duncan swallowed hard. "Do you know what you're saying?"

"Absolutely," she replied airily. "I certainly should. I've rehearsed it often enough."

"But...but why here of all places?"

"Why not?" Jennie shrugged the dress from her shoulders to reveal an immodest glimpse of flesh. "Frankly, I see no reason to wait any longer."

"I don't know what to say."

"The less said the better." Her dark eyes narrowed when Duncan made no move. "You're not having doubts, are you?" Before he could respond, Jennie dared caress his thigh, small fingers boldly sliding higher until she found her answer. "Good."

What followed was a revelation for Jennie. Duncan was an attentive lover, his knowledge of the female body suggesting that his frequent trips to New Orleans included buying more than racehorses. When his crisis peaked, Jennie found herself wanting more and clung to him with stunning tenacity well after the moment passed and they reluctantly separated. Things will work out in time, she assured herself, making a rare concession to compromise.

Jennie repeated this dispensation now as she paced Elms Court's vestibule, reminding herself it wasn't Duncan's fault that his favorite thoroughbred had fallen ill and needed his attention. The reality of his lateness, however, fueled her anxiety, especially with guests due any minute. She flew to the door at the crunch of hooves on the gravel drive, but instead of Duncan the first arrival was her cousin James Surget. A portly man old enough to be her father, Surget was nondescript excepting a saurian gaze and woolly sideburns always needing a trim. Jennie had never liked him and was immediately distrustful when he requested a few moments alone with her in the billiard room.

"I need to be here to greet my guests," she insisted.

"If you understood Natchezians better you'd know they're always late," he said, fleshy lips drawing into a thin line. He gestured toward the billiard room. "In there. I don't want the servants to overhear."

Further distressed by his curt tone and demeanor, Jennie tried one more feint. "But surely this can wait, Cousin James." She gestured toward the glorious glow of candlelight. "As you can see, everything is in place and I need to be here when..."

He was unmoved. "I'll be quick, Jennie. Now come along."

James Surget was, in fact, brutally brief. Minutes after he had lured her into intimacy and spoken his piece, Jennie reeled onto the gallery. She was so furious she feared howling into the night but regained control when Duncan emerged from the shadows and embraced her. After a moment, however, he, too, was pushed roughly away.

"Don't, Duncan!" she cried. "Not now!"

Duncan wisely retreated, knowing she had a temper that could explode without warning. Once, in the midst of just such an eruption, he teasingly called her his personal volcano, but Jennie was neither amused nor distracted. Now he knew to let her vent her rage and, once she calmed down, offered some soothing words. He stepped back, waiting for clues to this latest outburst.

"I just want to scream!" Jennie's face was a mask of rage as she paced the gallery. "If only you had been there, heard what that awful man said!"

She glared until Duncan took the bait.

"What *who* said, dearest?"

"Your Uncle James, that's who. Imagine talking to me like that. Right here in Elms Court, my own home, mind you! Why, if Father were still alive...!" She stopped and took a deep breath, cursing her corset as she fought for air. "That's it, Duncan! He's trying to replace Papa! Doesn't he know Father stopped trying to run my life long before he died?" Her mind sped, groping for a hook upon which to hang a rational explanation, but choices were few. "Why doesn't he pick on Ayres Junior? He's a complete fool when it comes to both business and family matters. Idiots! They're both idiots!"

Jennie's rage was verging on babble, and when she paused for breath again, Duncan tried to steer her back on course.

"Exactly what did Uncle James say?"

"You!" she said, springing on tiptoes as she spat the word. "It was all about you, Duncan. Why did he have to choose tonight to say that terrible thing?"

Duncan swallowed hard, well knowing what the "terrible thing" was and dreading her next words. It had been gestating from the day that he and Jennie met as children in the gardens of this house. Destiny had directed them down disparate avenues, but even after being separated by time and an entire ocean, they had found each other again at Elms Court only to have their reunion come under attack. This latest, harshest impediment came from home as their bloodlines were scrutinized and objections rose over something Natchez once elevated to a virtual art form — marriage between cousins. Whether to unite plantations, merge family fortunes or simply because a more suitable partner could not be found, it was an ancient solution society had only recently damned as unacceptable. Jennie and Duncan were unfortunately caught in the backlash.

Duncan tried once more, gently. "What exactly did he say?"

Jennie wanted to shout again but forced calm into her voice. "He said you were an unacceptable suitor because our grandfathers were brothers!" Her tears sent Duncan rooting for his handkerchief. "As if we didn't know," Jennie muttered, dabbing her eyes before thrusting the linen back at him. "As if everyone in Natchez didn't know. As if people in this town haven't been marrying their cousins for generations. *First* cousins, Duncan! And we're only second cousins!"

He rested his hands on Jennie's narrow shoulders, fingers quivering as he absorbed her impotent rage. He took a deep breath. "I don't know what to say, dearest."

"Well, all *I* can say is your uncle certainly picked a fine time to bring it up!" she snapped, anger re-igniting. "Tonight of all nights, when everyone important will be here and I must not be distracted from entertaining them!"

"Knowing Uncle James, that's probably why he chose the moment," Duncan lamented. "Solely to embarrass us. He's always had the tact of a runaway train."

"He's the one who'll be embarrassed by the time I'm finished. I should order him from this house, even if he is family! That's what father would have done."

"Uncle James isn't worthy of so much attention," Duncan said, racing to rein Jennie's temper when he heard the crunch and jangle of approaching carriages. "Forget about him."

"What would you suggest then? Running off to New York or Europe? Never! That would only be admitting defeat, admitting that there's something unnatural about our love. There's nothing wrong with it, Duncan. Nothing! And I intend to let everyone know it!"

He sighed and asked patiently, "What about Uncle James?"

"I'll let him know, too. No one tells me what to do, least of all here at Elms Court!" Jennie turned away, clenching and unclenching her fists. Anger made her careless now, drowning out voices of guests that called her name.

"Remember one thing," Duncan said, mindful that they were being watched and would soon be overheard. "I love you with all my heart."

Jennie stopped pacing and gave him a long look. "Thank you, my darling. I needed to hear that just now, more than anything in the world." She stood on tiptoes, chin tilted in invitation, oblivious when her name was called again.

"Your guests, dearest," Duncan whispered, nodding toward the drive.

"*Our* guests," Jennie amended. "Now give me a kiss."

Duncan hesitated. "In front of——"

"In front of everyone in town if I choose!" She glared as James Surget stepped onto the candlelit gallery, her eyes blazing defiance as she laced his name with vitriol. "Especially *you*, Cousin James!"

To no one's surprise, Jennie Merrill got what she wanted.

Moments later, Jennie welcomed Rosemary Kellogg and her escort Calvin Kingsley, and within the hour the villa overflowed with vivacious young people, dancing, laughing and partaking liberally of Elms Court's extravagant food and drink. A fortunate few were fashionably dressed, but most were in well-worn suits and twice-turned gowns with dated ruffles and frills. Jennie saw no reason to be a fashion martyr and dared criticism with a svelte gown by Worth of Paris. Matching the canary yellow roses in her dark hair, it was sumptuous satin trimmed in lace with a five-foot train and a glittering bodice of hand-embroidered metallic beads and diamanté. Stationed just inside the front door, Jennie dazzled her arriving guests while dispensing heartfelt hospitality in hopes everyone would have a good time.

Jennie easily reigned as the ball's most dazzling belle until a red-haired beauty appeared on Richard Dana's arm. The slim young man was, Jennie noted, as solemn and intense as ever, and although most people considered him too serious and not a little peculiar, she found his introspection oddly charming, even considered him attractive in an ascetic way. At the moment, however, she was more intrigued by his lady friend.

"Richard Dana!" she beamed. "Our guest of honor at last!"

"Good evening, Miss Jennie," Richard said, bowing stiffly. "I apologize for my tardiness. It's unforgivable."

"Nonsense. We New Yorkers know the importance of being fashionably late, don't we?" Jennie glanced at the woman and back again to Dana, her lifted eyebrows finally prompting introductions.

"Oh!" he said, blushing. "Please allow me to present Miss Octavia Dockery."

"Welcome to Elms Court, Miss Dockery."

Octavia smiled. "A pleasure to meet you, Miss Merrill. Richard has told me so much about this legendary house." She glanced across the generous gallery swarming with candlelight and the scent of fresh-cut roses. "It's absolutely magical."

"Elms Court belongs to its guests."

When Jennie spoke the words for the first time, she felt her father and mother's presence as surely as the fragrant roses remembered from childhood.

"How charming," Octavia said.

The woman's smile was generous, but what struck Jennie most, aside from eyes blazing with some faraway fire, was her pale blue silk gown. Showcased by a perfect hourglass figure, the dress was much simpler than her own but so exquisitely cut and fitted that it made an equally elegant statement.

"Forgive my staring, but that gown is gorgeous."

"Thank you, my dear. It's my absolute favorite and was my father's favorite, too. In fact, he loved it so much he insisted I wear it when I sat for my formal portrait. You might say he wanted us both immortalized."

Jennie was dying to confirm that it was a Worth gown but was diverted by Richard's spate of information. "Octavia just moved here from New York to join her sister Nydia. Their father is Confederate General Thomas Dockery. He and your late father shared a very famous friend, you know."

Jennie's eyebrows rose again. "Oh?"

"I suspect he means our late President Grant," Octavia said, embarrassed by Richard's breathless recitation. "They became good friends after the war."

"General Dockery was asked to be a pallbearer at President Grant's funeral," Richard added, excited as though he had just shared a forbidden secret. "A remarkable honor for a former enemy, don't you think?"

"Indeed."

"He wasn't the only Confederate invited to be a pallbearer for Grant," Octavia reminded him. "General Loring was asked as well."

"There's need for modesty," Jennie chided gently. "I'm not ashamed to say Grant is a very distant relative, and although people here don't think it's anything to be proud of, he was a guest in this house during the occupation of Natchez. I was only a baby, of course, but I was around him on several occasions when we lived in New York. How strange and unfortunate that our paths never crossed, yours and mine."

"Oh, but they did," Richard said. "Well, almost."

"What do you mean?"

"It happened about a year ago. Octavia and I were dining at Delmonico's with my cousin Charles and—"

"Of course!" Octavia gave Richard a gentle reprimand. "Why didn't you tell me she was our hostess?"

"I...I guess I forgot," he said, retreating with embarrassment.

Octavia squeezed his arm, assuring him he was forgiven. "You were way across the dining room, Jennie. Leaving with a young man, I believe. You were wearing a mauve gown trimmed with pale blue flowers. It was such an unusual combination, and I distinctly recall admiring it."

"How kind of you to remember."

Octavia conjured the remainder of the memory. "Did Charles ever catch up with you? Charles Dana Gibson?" When Jennie looked blank, she added, "The famous artist who paints the..."

"The Gibson girls!" Jennie finished, amused by the recollection. "Of course!"

"So you remember?

"Oh, my, yes! Mr. Gibson introduced himself and followed us all the way to the sidewalk where I ran into my dear friend Lola Jacobs. She is the most fetching little strawberry blonde you've ever seen, and once I introduced them he promptly forgot all about me." She shrugged. "That was the last I ever saw of him, walking off with Lola, back into Delmonico's."

"I never saw him again either, something of a surprise after he absolutely begged me to give him a sitting." Octavia rolled her eyes with mock drama. "Our chances to be immortalized as Gibson girls forever dashed!"

They swapped conspiratorial glances as Jennie took Octavia's arm and ushered her toward the parlor. "Are you and your sister living alone?"

"Nydia is married to Richard Forman." Octavia had no intention of explaining that her sister and brother-in-law were virtually penniless and that her failure to earn a living in New York had forced her to move in with them. Nor could Octavia speak of her celebrated father's recent destitution. "Mr. Forman was a planter in Fayette, but...well, times have not been kind to him. It's nothing we need talk about."

"I'm so sorry," Jennie said, grateful that she wouldn't have to endure another hard luck litany. Natchez overflowed with them these days. "Forman, you say? The name is so familiar."

"He has people here."

Jennie was surprised when Octavia volunteered no further family information. Such omission was anathema to Southerners. "Perhaps I know them," she prompted.

"He's cousin to the Howells."

With her casual mention of that name, Octavia revealed her lofty social credentials. Varina Howell was the Natchez bride of Jefferson Davis. Links to the Confederacy's sole President, no matter how circuitous, catapulted one into the stratosphere of Dixie aristocracy and were almost the equivalent of being rocked in Robert E. Lee's cradle. Octavia seemed embarrassed by the connection and tried to shrug it away.

"I'm quite certain there are more interesting things to discuss than my family."

"Nonsense," Jennie insisted. "Why, genealogy is the favorite local pastime."

"Along with our glorious Lost Cause, of course. I suspect it's the same everywhere else in the South." Octavia scanned a room vibrant with young people. "Actually, I'm more interested in writing."

Jennie was further intrigued. She had few lady friends who read, much less wrote anything except letters and shopping lists. "Oh?"

"Several of Octavia's poems have been published in the *New York World*," Richard interjected softly, reminding them of his shy presence. "She's also been published in the *New Orleans Picayune*, and there's interest in her work here as well."

"I'm fortunate to count Mr. Julius Lemkowitz among my champions," Octavia said, referring to the publisher of the former *Natchez Evening News*.

"Tell Miss Jennie about your new poem," Richard urged.

Octavia laughed good-naturedly. "Really, Richard. You must quit prompting me as though I am an actress who's forgotten her lines."

"A poetess! How enchanting!" Jennie smiled. "Natchez can certainly use someone like yourself, although I'm afraid you'll find us a backwater after New York."

"As I'm afraid you'll find me a bluestocking."

"I assure you I don't find that revelation off-putting."

"Then I must say I welcome my move to Natchez," Octavia confessed. "New York is stimulating, but, as you no doubt know, it can also be overwhelming. By the same token, whenever I come back to the South I find myself ignoring books and spending too much time at balls and barbecues." She hastily apologized when she misread her hostess's quixotic look. "Please don't think me rude, Jennie. Tonight is lovely."

"I don't think you're rude at all, my dear. The truth is I feel as if I'm missing something by not reading more." She wondered if Octavia realized she was offering a rare confidence. "If only opportunities for us females weren't so limited. I mean, what else can we do but this?" She gestured at her guests, wondering now why she had been so eager to court their approval. In Octavia's stellar presence, they suddenly seemed lackluster. "But I mustn't be dreary. May I offer you a glass of champagne?"

Octavia beamed. "You may indeed, Jennie. Thank you."

Moments later, Jennie returned to the front door, leaving Richard and Octavia to bask in the hospitality of Elms Court. As guest of honor, Richard found himself on the receiving end of a gaggle of childhood friends. Never one to relish the spotlight offstage, he repeatedly shifted attention to the more gregarious Octavia and was content to remain behind when she was swept onto the dance floor time and again. Only when talk turned to music or when he was asked to play the piano did Richard come to life. Such was the case when Jennie asked if he would honor her guests with a few favorite selections. The moment Richard touched the keyboard, his face radiated euphoria and a sparkle of joy rescued his dark, melancholy eyes. He seemed to physically change, growing larger than life as his rapturous etudes seduced everyone in the ballroom.

While Richard played, Octavia scanned the crowd, smiling at new acquaintances and nodding politely when she caught a stranger's eye. More than once she noticed a tall, mustachioed gentleman who, despite smashing good looks, seemed to float apart from everyone except Jennie. The two reminded Octavia of magnets, attracting one moment, repelling the next. Curiosity stoked, she turned to the plain, rather plump girl whom she had just met. Her name was Rosemary Kellogg.

"Do you know the gentlemen by the door?" Octavia gestured discreetly with her closed fan. "The tall one there."

"Why, that's Duncan Minor," Rosemary replied. Remembering Octavia was a newcomer, she added, "The Minors are one of Natchez's oldest families."

"He looks like a riverboat gambler," Octavia laughed. "At least what I imagine one looks like."

Rosemary didn't laugh. "He lives at Oakland with his mother and sister. They're not here, of course."

Sensing scandal, Octavia trod more lightly. "What is his line of business?"

"My dear, the Minors are famous for their victories at Pharsalia."

The only *Pharsalia* Octavia knew was the Roman war epic by Lucan. "Pardon?"

"The race track here in Natchez. Duncan Minor breeds thoroughbreds." Rosemary discreetly lowered her voice as Richard's music grew softer and more delicate. "Although some might say his main occupation is keeping company with Miss Jennie."

Octavia frowned. "They certainly don't seem very comfortable with each other."

"Perhaps because they're being watched," Rosemary whispered. "Not that it matters since everyone knows they're absolutely devoted to one another."

"Who's watching them?"

"Their relatives, of course. Neither side approves of the courtship. In fact, I hear Mrs. Minor has threatened all sorts of things if Duncan tries to marry Jennie."

"But why? You just said he comes from an old family."

"Well," Rosemary confided, "no one says as much, but I think it's because both the Merrills and Minors want to make certain their family fortunes are increased by any *new* marriages. Not just merged, you understand."

"I'm not certain I do."

"They're *all* Surgets." When Octavia looked blank, she added, "Jennie and Duncan are related. Of course, most everyone in Natchez is kin one way or another. Quite a few of our older couples even share the same grandparents."

Octavia's eyes widened as the plot unfurled. "Oh?"

"Jennie's maternal grandfather was Frank Surget. His brother James Surget is Duncan's maternal grandfather."

"So Duncan and Jennie are—"

"Second cousins," Rosemary finished.

"Well, it's high time these families learned marrying outside their clan is preferable to the genetic perils of consanguinity," Octavia said a bit too loudly. "Some may consider Darwin's findings controversial, but to me the dangers of inbreeding are all too obvious." Seeing Rosemary's blank stare, she added, "One need only consider the Hapsburgs."

"The Hapsburgs?" Math and history were mental quicksand for Rosemary, who had not benefited from Octavia's education at New York's exclusive Comstock School for Girls. "I don't believe I know them."

"The Hapsburgs were one of Europe's great royal houses," Octavia explained patiently. She leaned closer as though whispering a naughty secret. "Their intermarrying resulted in the most hideous physical and mental abnormalities. One poor soul had a jaw so distended he could hardly eat. Others were incapable of reproduction, which I suppose is nature's way of ending such unnatural mistakes."

"Really?" Rosemary foundered before Octavia's frankness about sexual matters but was disappointed when offered nothing more. "Well, we certainly could've learned something from those folks, couldn't we? Now that I think about it, one hears awful stories about how...oh, my mother would die if she heard me discussing such things!"

"My dear, I lived in New York many years. I assure you I'm not easily shocked."

Rosemary snapped open her fan and whispered behind it. "If you stay here long enough, you'll discover half the families have someone who is, well, not quite right. Mine included. Why, we have to keep our grandmother locked in the attic whenever a gentleman comes calling in a dark blue suit. No other color upsets her. Only dark blue."

"Perhaps she thinks the Yankees are invading again," Octavia ventured.

"You're exactly right!" Rosemary confessed with an irreverent giggle. "One time she managed to get Grandfather's old rifle and took a potshot at some poor traveling salesman. Not only that, but she uses the kind of language...well, we've never figured out where she learned such awful words. The point is that everyone in Natchez knows about Grandma, but we're not supposed to talk about her." When Octavia stifled a laugh, Rosemary wondered if she had been tricked into such a personal revelation. "I shouldn't have told you that."

Octavia hurriedly reassured the girl. "I promise there's no harm done. Beside, as you said, everyone already knows."

"I suppose," Rosemary sighed, apparently mollified.

Octavia was a little disappointed when Richard completed a Chopin etude and applause made further conversation impossible. Ever curious, she was about to plumb Rosemary for more local gossip when he waved away applause and hurried over to suggest retreating to the gallery for a breath of fresh air. Without Rosemary to quiz, Octavia pressed Richard for information about Duncan Minor. She wasn't quite sure why she was so intrigued, although she admitted to herself that the man was devilishly handsome.

"Someone was telling me that Miss Jennie's family doesn't approve of her romance with Duncan Minor."

"I don't know about those things," Richard said, leaning against the coolness of the iron grillwork. He quickly retreated when he realized it was damp with dew. "People in this town are too fond of gossip."

"New Yorkers love gossip, too," Octavia reminded him.

"I suppose so, but it's different in such a big city. Here it seems that kind of talk always hurts someone. My father died when I was three so I learned fast what it was like for people to feel sorry for you. They were always clucking with sympathy and patting me on the head like a dog. 'Poor little

Richard!' they said, over and over again. I think it's probably worse when you're a minister's child. There was an entire congregation saying the same thing, like a choir singing
a hymn off-key. Oh, Octavia! How I hated it!" Suddenly agitated, Richard downed his champagne and stifled a belch
with only partial success. He glanced around, terrified someone had overheard, and shook his head, as though dislodg-
ing mental cobwebs. "I don't really remember my father, so
how could I miss him? That's probably a terrible thing to
say, but it's true."

Moved to comfort him, Octavia rested a hand lightly on
Richard's arm. "You're very introspective this evening."

"I always feel strangely lucid after I sing or play the piano," he
confessed. "Such times make me feel more alive, more like myself. The world seems clearer and I see things that other people
don't. Hmmm." He paused. "It can also be very upsetting."

Richard gnawed his lower lip, a nervous tic when conversation grew uncomfortable or confusing. Octavia recognized a
red flag and provoked the demon in hopes of slaying it.

"Why is that, dear?"

He gazed deeply into her eyes, as though seeking something,
and then just as quickly looked away. "It makes me feel...sort of
outside the circle."

"What circle do you mean?"

"Oh, you know, Octavia." He nodded toward the tall windows, at the colorful whirl of dancers beneath the flickering
chandeliers and candelabra. His voice rose. "That! There!"

"Nonsense." Octavia squeezed his arm, purposely letting her
hand linger longer than necessary. "If anything, they're outside
our circle, and the loss is theirs."

"I'd certainly like to think so," Richard said, "but my circle
has dwindled terribly since you left New York. I don't know
what I'll do without you. Oh, Octavia, can't you please come
north again and—"

"We've been over all that before, dearest friend, and you

must understand that I have no other options. My finances are such that I can't continue living in New York. Father's not well and he's lost almost everything in the bond market. My only recourse is Nydia."

"I have a little money," he insisted, "and, if things continue well with my career, I'd be happy to —"

"That's very generous, Richard, but you know I can't accept charity. I'm sorry, but that's the harsh reality."

"But I don't want reality."

"You have no choice, my dear," Octavia said, weighing his odd observation. "It's as real as your sweet Amelia. She's all you need, you know, and once the two of you are married, you'll have room for no one else."

Not for the first time, Octavia watched something rise to Richard's lips without surfacing. He was momentarily lost in thought, then inexplicably giggled, a familiar nervous laugh that always disconcerted her. She knew not to ask what he found amusing because she wouldn't get a straight answer.

When Richard drifted deep into his private world, he was best left alone.

10

W ITH HER DEAR friend Richard gone back to New
York to pursue his dual music career, Octavia suffered a deeply personal void. It didn't help that most of her
days were spent helping her sister Nydia around the house,
leaving her little time to write poetry or research articles des-
tined for magazines and newspapers. Relief came from a most
unexpected source when Jennie Merrill invited her to tea at
Elms Court. After an afternoon's conversation, to the great
surprise of both, the two young women discovered important
common interests, primarily a passion for privacy and wariness of female friendships. There was also a shared fondness
for New York. Reminiscences of that city sometimes led to
discoveries of mutual acquaintances, none more startling than
Stephen Holmes. Jennie revealed the connection as Eugene
drove them out Liberty Road to visit some distant cousins.

"It's been plaguing me ever since we met," she said. "Your

name sounded so familiar, but it didn't dawn on me until just this morning. Stephen Holmes!"

It was Octavia's turn to be puzzled. "Who?"

"He's originally from here but now a reporter for the *New York Sun*. The last time I saw him, right before I left the city, he had scheduled an interview with you about a trip to Antarctica."

Recognition glowed in Octavia's eyes. "Of course! Mr. Holmes won several journalism awards for that article about that poor Irish immigrant who went mad and killed his family. He and I met the very afternoon that terrible story broke. Such a *cause célèbre*!"

"Indeed it was."

"I remember him very well," Octavia continued. "Handsome if a bit on the portly side. Wonderful walrus moustache... and he was so pleasant and charming it was hard to believe he witnessed such savagery."

Jennie waded cautiously deeper. "How much of his story do you recall?"

"Just that he happened to be at the scene of the crime and was almost killed, too. And that he said luck was often the key to getting a great story."

Jennie grew mischievous when she realized Octavia had not made the deeper connection.

"He got the story because a woman took him there with plans to do a story on the baby farms."

"Oh, yes. It's coming back now. Some lady who did charity work. I believe she saved one of the babies. She belonged to the King's...oh, what was it called?"

"The King's Daughters." Jennie faced her friend, unable to maintain the peculiar charade. "I was that woman."

Octavia's eyes widened. "No!"

Jennie chuckled, but her knavery evaporated as brutal memories of The Bend careened back. "Even after all this time it's difficult to talk or think about."

"I don't blame you." Octavia patted Jennie's gloved hand. "I'm sure I would have had terrible nightmares."

"More insomnia than nightmares. It certainly gave me new respect for what soldiers see daily on the battlefields." She shuddered inside, grateful when the memory passed. "Now. Please tell me about Antarctica."

"I'm afraid there isn't much to tell."

Octavia was accustomed to Jennie's penchant for abruptly changing the subject. It could be frustrating and annoying, but she accepted it as requisite for cultivating this burgeoning friendship. She had also learned there were certain subjects best avoided, namely Duncan Minor. Jennie's studied silence about their relationship warned Octavia to tread with care.

"I was to keep the official log and be the first woman on America's first Antarctic expedition. Unfortunately, after a lot of overblown publicity I found rather embarrassing, they were unable to secure the financing. Oh, I suppose it could still happen. I recently received a letter from one of the men putting the expedition together. He assures me they'll find the money, so I try to be optimistic. Frankly, it was my greatest disappointment because it came when I was having no luck getting published. The expedition would have been a godsend. Not only would I have been well compensated, but the resulting notoriety would surely have boosted my career."

"If you had survived the trip."

Octavia weighed the comment. "You know what, Jennie? That's something I never even considered. I would have been famous whether I came back or not, and if I had failed to return, at least I wouldn't constantly be plagued by financial woes."

"How morbid!"

"Oh, I know it's impolite to discuss it and I'm sure you find it distasteful, but it's an inescapable fact of my life, and I wish it would go away."

"You could always marry a rich man," Jennie offered. "Surely with your looks and intelligence and background..."

Octavia sniffed. "Oh, you know as well as I do that marriage is less and less a possibility. You've told me how many proposals you've turned down, and I totally empathize with your decision. I think I'd rather starve alone than be rich in a loveless marriage." Certainly Octavia did not mention that Jennie's wealth had been her liberation until Duncan Minor became part of her life. Or that marriage to him, should it ever transpire, would be anything but loveless. "We women inherit a strange lot, do we not?" When Jennie did not respond, Octavia said, "Lately I've been working on a new story that will probably bring me more criticism than fame and fortune."

"Oh?"

"A piece I'm doing for the *Picayune*, comparing antebellum Natchez to King Arthur's Camelot. Complete with dragon."

Jennie only half-heard when the carriage rocked hard as Eugene negotiated a steadily deteriorating road. "Did you say *dragon?*"

"The saga began when cotton planters discovered the incredibly rich topsoil over in Louisiana was fifteen feet deep in places, thanks to regular floods from the river. Profits were so phenomenal some of their plantations were larger than German principalities and produced larger revenues as well. Eventually they built big houses here in Natchez."

"Father used to say it was so they could be 'rich together,'" Jennie observed.

"Hmmm. I may steal that remark." Octavia smiled and made a mental note. "Anyway, the Natchez bluffs provided the perfect setting for these gallant knights to build castles in the sky for their ladies fair, and they developed their own strict code of chivalry. They had medieval costume balls and even jousts on occasion, so it was hardly a surprise that *Ivanhoe* was wildly popular when it was published."

"It was Mother's favorite book," Jennie said wistfully.

"I'm sure it was all very glamorous and graceful, but in the meantime, the fire-breathing dragon lurked just across the big moat in Louisiana. Metaphorically speaking, of course."

Since Jennie dealt with things at face value, subtlety usually eluded her. "What on earth are you talking about?"

"When I started researching my story, I learned some alarming facts. Did you know the Natchez planters almost never visited their estates?"

"What's alarming about that?"

"In Concordia Parish, just across the river here, the population in eighteen-sixty was something over fourteen thousand. Nearly thirteen thousand of those were slaves and the rest were overseers and their families. That was the dragon, Jennie. The planters knew their white overseers were hopelessly outnumbered and could easily have been slaughtered in their beds. In fact, it almost happened in sixty-one when a slave rebellion was aborted right here on Second Creek. The coloreds planned to kill all the white people who—"

"Octavia!" Jennie jerked her head toward Eugene, who was hanging on Octavia's every word.

"Sorry, my dear, but I'm sure your driver has heard all about it. Besides, I believe certain things should be talked about and not swept under the carpet."

"Even that?"

"Especially that, my dear. It's history after all, and we should learn from it, not hush it up." Jennie huffed, but Octavia continued, undeterred. "Imagine an entire world of wealth and privilege hanging by such a hazardous thread and ending tragically just like Camelot. It's nothing new, of course, an unimaginably elitist society undoing itself, but presented properly it can still make for an impressive cautionary tale. Don't you think so?"

"Oh, I suppose," Jennie said wearily, "but, to be honest, I've stopped caring about social issues. If I don't see things, they don't affect me."

"How like an ostrich!" Octavia exclaimed, wondering if they were having their first friendly disagreement.

"I can't help it, Octavia. My charitable instincts are gone, too. Lost, I should say, like when someone loses religious faith, I suppose. But unlike faith, I don't want it back." Jennie felt feverish as she remembered Clara Flanagan, those pitiful babies, Paddy O'Brien, odious sights and smells branded so deep they could never be exorcised. "Any of it."

"I'm sorry."

"I'm not." Jennie's tone warned Octavia to add this to the list of taboo topics. They fell silent until the carriage lurched hard left to avoid an axle-breaking pothole. "Good heavens, Eugene! Are you sure this is the road to Cedar Grove?"

"It's how Mr. Duncan told me to go," the coachman replied with a nod.

"This must be a terrible inconvenience for your relatives." Octavia seized the door handle as the carriage plunged and jerked again, wrenching both passengers and driver. "Good heavens!"

"Duncan says they rarely venture off their land," Jennie said, "which is why I'm paying this call."

"What exactly is your connection to these people?"

"They're Surgets," Jennie replied. "Three distant old-maid cousins I didn't know existed until Duncan found out. It seems they had a horse he was interested in, apparently the last item of value they had to sell and, well, one thing led to another and he found out we were related. When he told me how destitute they were, I thought I might help. I know this seems to contradict what I just said about charitable deeds, but these old ladies are family, after all." She smiled and touched Octavia's hand. "And you're very sweet to keep me company, especially since I have no idea what we'll find."

Octavia smiled back. "We'll just consider it an adventure, eh?"

She decided her words were well chosen when the coach lurched onto a deeply rutted drive lined with a double row of cedars in various stages of decline and death. The decrepit *allée* was an appropriate prelude to what lay at the other end. Cedar Grove was a modest farmhouse built in 1808 and haphazardly expanded over the years. It became even more of a rambling oddity when four columns were tacked on during the Greek-Revival craze later in the century. Now in a state of advanced desuetude, the pillars had wrenched from the house, tilting at odd angles and threatening to dislodge chunks of the facade. The place had not been painted in decades, and a slab of chimney lay alongside the sagging front steps. Despite looking like one of Natchez's notorious windstorms would shred the place like straw, it was home to three elderly ladies Duncan mysteriously dubbed the "alphabet sisters." When Jennie asked for an explanation, he promised it would be more fun to find out for herself.

Once the carriage had jolted to a halt, Jennie swung to the ground and surveyed the decay. "Oh, dear! How do you suppose we go about knocking on that door?"

At first glance the veranda looked collapsed, but as Jennie and Octavia mounted the steps they found two narrow planks leading to the front door. Good balance was essential because eight feet below lurked a pile of jagged timbers and rusted nails.

Octavia hiked her skirts, stepped onto the board and extended a hand. "It will be easier if we do it together."

Jennie looked skeptical. "I think I'd rather accompany you to Antarctica!"

"I promise no polar bears!" Octavia laughed. "Now come along."

Emboldened by such bravado, Jennie took her friend's hand and trailed her cautiously across the sagging planks. At the door, they huddled for mutual support when they heard muffled voices and strange, scurrying sounds. Before Jennie could knock, the door creaked open to reveal an old-fashioned silhouette with exaggerated sleeves and a hoopskirt bristling with crinolines. The smell of ancient pomade rushed forth as the woman leaned forward.

"Yes?"

"I'm Jennie Merrill of Elms Court, and this is Miss Octavia Dockery. My cousin Duncan Minor purchased your horse two weeks ago."

The old lady considered for a long moment before nodding. "All right then. I'm your cousin Emily Surget Price, but everyone calls me Miss Em." She stepped back and swept an arm wide. "Won't you please come in?"

Jennie and Octavia were relieved by the relative safety of the central hall but reconsidered when rotting floorboards sagged and groaned alarmingly as they followed their hostess. They inhaled the powerful under-odor of forgotten times as they passed a series of closed doors, made a forty-five degree turn and entered the oddest room either had ever seen. Stacked to the right and left were cedar trees, felled long ago but still fragrant. Against the far wall, elaborately carved Belter settees and chairs were jammed into a tight row, gold velvet seats ravished by rusty springs. In the center of the room, six mismatched chairs hugged an exquisite rosewood table. Watching the fine bronze clock at its center were two more women dressed and coiffed from bygone eras. Octavia was reminded of three shriveled cotton bolls.

"My sisters," Miss Em explained. "The one on the left is Beatrice. We call her Miss Bea, of course, and the one to the right is Deanna. You may call her Miss Dee." She turned to her sisters and announced, "This is our cousin Jennie Merrill of Elms Court and her friend Miss Octavia Dockery."

Bea, Dee and Em, Jennie thought, getting Duncan's little alphabet joke as she and Octavia murmured pleasantries and took their seats. The women nodded but said nothing as Miss Em turned the clock in her direction. Addressing her sisters, she announced, "I'll begin now."

The formidable Miss Em then launched into a rambling, thoroughly one-sided conversation about the weather, the deaths of two other sisters and deprivations endured since

Appomattox. Although nearly three decades had passed since Lee's surrender, the old woman spoke as though it were yesterday, and when boredom led Jennie's gaze to the stack of cedar trees, the hawk-eyed Miss Em waved a dismissive hand.

"That part of the house is under construction."

Miss Em resumed her monologue before Jennie could respond and was in mid-sentence when Miss Bea suddenly seized the clock, aimed it toward herself and deftly continued the conversation while Miss Em fell silent. The subject continued until her time expired and Miss Dee took her turn. The procedure was repeated with each sister speaking in ten-minute intervals until an hour had elapsed. At that point, Miss Bea produced a single die which each rolled in turn. Miss Dee scored the highest number, a five, and stood.

"Would you like to see my clay collection now? It's quite unique."

Jennie's mouth was dry from not speaking. "Why, yes!" she croaked.

Miss Dee signaled them to follow and left her sisters behind. As they passed closer, Jennie and Octavia realized that the trees formed a makeshift interior wall and that the fine Belter furniture prevented the unwary from falling through a piano-sized hole. They entered a parlor, now the repository for Miss Dee's handicrafts.

"On one of my morning strolls, I was drawn to the different colors of clay in the ravines riddling our land. I spied a chunk shaped like a church, steeple and all, so I brought it home, fetched my sewing box and used my scissors to enhance the resemblance. I later discovered a file did a better job and have subsequently devoted myself to my art." She gestured with pride at the misshapen clay heads, trees and animals swarming across mantles, shelves and windowsills, tucked in corners and glutting curio cabinets. Then, apparently satisfied that her guests had drunk their fill, she whirled in a flurry of crinolines and made a loud announcement.

"Time for plum-dumb!"

Jennie and Octavia followed her back to the table where a gleaming cut-glass punch bowl had appeared along with, inexplicably, six cups. Miss Dee seated herself while Miss Bea, with exaggerated theatrics, ladled a cloudy liquid and Miss Em resumed as speaker.

"Proceed with caution, my dears," she warned dourly. "My plum wine is quite potent, and too much will strike you plumb dumb!"

Taking small sips, neither Jennie nor Octavia detected the slightest trace of spirits.

The sisters' monologues continued as before with Miss Dee eventually holding forth on family genealogy. Finding this more numbing than the interminable Biblical "begats," Jennie wondered how much more she could endure when Miss Bea suddenly leapt to her feet with alarming agility. Face blazing beneath the rice powder, eyes squinting with revelation, she leveled a finger and broke taboo by interrupting a sister's dissertation.

"You! Why, you're Jennie Merrill!"

"I told you that when I arrived," Jennie replied, mystified by the accusatory tone.

"Ayres Merrill was your father?"

"Yes, he was." Jennie's look of distress was lost on Octavia, who was riveted by Miss Bea's outburst.

"Out!" Miss Bea shouted, sweeping past in a flurry of musty skirts and storming for the front door. "Out of this house!"

As Jennie hurried after her cousin, she grasped what had happened. The wizened sisters, residing deep in their fantasy world, were so delusional it had taken them the better part of two hours to decipher their visitor's identity. When her sister's genealogical diatribe triggered recognition, Miss Bea was alarmed enough to upset their strict, self-imposed etiquette and order the intruder off their property.

"Please listen, Miss Bea!" Jennie cried. "I came here to help!"

"We don't want your help!" the woman growled. "Yankee sympathizers!"

"I'm not responsible for my father's deeds!" Jennie protested. "And I wasn't even born until the last year of the war!"

She may as well have been pleading to the moon. Beatrice Surget Price was so angry she shook. "Get out of this house!" she screamed. "And never show yourself here again!"

"Jennie!" Octavia cried. "What on earth—"

"Come along, Octavia!"

Jennie lifted her skirts, grabbed Octavia's hand and dragged her across the rickety planks in four deft strides. By then the other sisters had joined Miss Bea and stood in the derelict doorway shrieking like harpies. Their screams roused Eugene, dozing in the carriage. Rushing to investigate, he chuckled at the sight of Jennie and Octavia driven away, it seemed, by three screeching old women.

"Get out! Get out! Get out!"

As they climbed into the carriage, Octavia caught her breath and chuckled. "What a mad little tea party, my dear. What in the world was all that about?"

"They finally figured out who I was," Jennie explained, heart still racing. "Family or not, they were not happy to discover the daughter of a Union sympathizer in their bosom."

"Loony old crones!" When Octavia saw Jennie's pained expression, she hastily added, "I'm sorry, Jennie. That was unkind."

Jennie's pain came not from hurt but anger. "You needn't apologize," she said in steely tones. "Obviously they're crazy as bedbugs."

"Well, we both know this inbred old town is full of them," Octavia shrugged. "Just last week Nydia introduced me to an old couple who speaks their own peculiar language. They've become a single unit with their two personalities more or less fused."

Jennie recalled the quotation from Monsignor Squillace:

"Their individuality is so blended that they are each the counterpart of the other." Now instead of comforting, it drove a
sharp chill through her chest.

"The French even have a name for it," Octavia continued.
"It's called *folie à deux*. The pure form is a rare disorder wherein
two intimately-related persons, such as a husband and wife,
two sisters or brothers and so forth, share identical delusions.
It usually occurs when they spend a great deal of time alone together. In the most common cases, the dominant half transfers
his delusions to the more submissive half. Perhaps your cousins have a sort of *folie à trois*."

Jennie remained fixated on the word "inbred" because it
dominated the heart of her most private nightmares. They
rode in silence quite a while before she stirred back to life. "You
know what I keep thinking, Octavia?"

"What?"

"Those old women are the issue of second cousins." Octavia
frowned as Jennie broached a taboo subject. "The madness is
not of their making."

"The madness comes from other things as well," Octavia offered sympathetically. "Look at that pitiful old house. The way
they're isolated in the middle of nowhere, little contact with
the outside world. Living hand to mouth, stuck forever in the
past. It's no wonder they're batty."

"You and I both know the real reasons."

Slender eyebrows rose. "Oh?"

Jennie bristled. "I'm not a fool. Octavia. I've done a little
reading and I know something about the perils of inbreeding."

Octavia was stunned not only that Jennie had explored such
a contentious subject, but that she admitted it. Obviously it
had taken the shock of the demented cousins to trigger this
dual confidence, and she was spellbound as Jennie revealed her
secret findings.

"When I lived in Europe, there was a lot of gossip about intermarriage. Talk about hemophilia, too. Half the royal houses

of Europe are afflicted, including Queen Victoria's family, and someone named Nasse believes it passes through the mother. I'm also familiar, not overly so, mind you, with the findings of Gregor Mendel. Do you know who he is? Of course you do."

"He wrote about the principles of heredity," Octavia said. "Back in sixty-five."

"I tried to read it but quickly got lost," Jennie confessed. "But I understood enough to know that...well..."

"That what?" Octavia urged when Jennie faltered.

"Oh, some people should just never have children. That's all." The door closed as swiftly as it opened.

11

THREE YEARS HAD passed since Jennie's distressing encounter with the women of Cedar Grove. The brutal lesson about the dangers of inbreeding made her secretly vow never to have children with Duncan, but, aside from that precaution, their status quo remained unchanged. When their private liaison drew public criticism, Jennie ignored the gossip and, some whispered, seized every opportunity to flaunt affiliation with her cousin. Carriage rides down Main Street became her preferred form of reprisal. One February afternoon, Jennie and Duncan took a drive through Clifton Heights, a new residential area atop the bluffs north of downtown. Despite raw, blustery weather, Jennie insisted on seeing what the new money of Natchez was building. She knew Victorian-style houses were all the rage but was thoroughly unimpressed by what she saw.

"For heaven's sake, slow down." Jennie gripped Duncan's forearm until he reined the horse to a walk. "Just look at that monstrosity. No grace at all."

"What about that one across the street?" He gestured toward a large brick home getting final touches from a small army of workmen. "I rather like the turrets and towers."

"I'm not surprised. It looks like a giant playhouse for little boys."

Duncan chuckled. "Don't forget, I have a special affinity for playhouses."

"I should hope so." Jennie smiled and snuggled close as she recalled seducing him in her playhouse, and the many forbidden trysts that had followed. Most proper women would have blushed at the recollection, but not Jennie. Instead she brushed Duncan's cheek with a kiss and relished the scrutiny of workmen as the carriage clip-clopped past. "That little playhouse holds my favorite memories."

"Mine, too."

Jennie frowned in disgust at another Victorian extravaganza embellished to a fare-thee-well with gables and gingerbread. Suddenly bored, she changed the subject.

"I saw Octavia Dockery yesterday. I was walking past the Natchez Hotel when she came galloping down Pearl Street like a house afire. I couldn't have been more surprised."

"I'm sure. How long has she been gone?"

"Almost three years. It was certainly a surprise to see her, but that's only part of the story. She was riding astride, just like a man and, as if that wasn't bad enough, she's cut off all that beautiful red hair. I suppose she's still pretty in a boyish way, but I find it scandalous."

"Did you talk to her?"

"I could hardly help it." Jennie sniffed. "Why, she yelled and waved and reined her horse so hard and fast I nearly choked on the dust."

"Has she moved back to town?"

"She's just here visiting Richard Dana over at Glenwood. She said he's down from New York for a few days and that she's giving a reading there this Saturday afternoon, from her articles on some of our older Natchez homes. She asked if we'd like to come."

"Shall we go then?"

"I told her I was busy."

"But I thought you liked her."

After some consideration, Jennie said, "I did at first, but I was just getting to know her when her brother-in-law died and her sister got the fever. Nursing Nydia consumed all Octavia's time, and after Nydia died Octavia moved in with some people in Mobile." She shook her head. "After seeing her today, I don't suppose we could ever have become true confidantes."

"Why do you say that?"

"Her cool, mannish airs for one thing. And her bluntness. It was as if she couldn't wait to tell me her father was frail and almost penniless."

Duncan was shocked. "Not the great General Thomas Dockery!"

Jennie nodded. "She also reported that she has no other family, no beaux, and no prospects and is poor as a church mouse."

"She didn't ask for money, did she?"

"Even Octavia isn't that bold, but she still upset me something terrible."

"But why?"

"Because she reminds me of things I want to forget, Duncan. Oh, I know Octavia isn't like those awful lost souls in the slums in New York, but I just can't abide any more charity cases."

"You did more than your share of benevolent works," he soothed.

"I know that, but I still…" Jennie frowned, unable to complete the thought as her mind drifted elsewhere. "Isn't it peculiar what we associate with unpleasant memories? There's a certain tobacco that reminds me of death because Dr. Henry was smoking it the night Father died. I smelled it on some man in church last week and thought of poor Papa. I miss him so."

"Shall we talk of something else, dearest?"

"Yes, let's do." Jennie looked toward the river. "And we'll walk along the bluff."

"But it's so windy," Duncan protested, attentive as always. "Aren't you cold?"

"Not in the slightest."

Weather was not Duncan's real worry. "Jennie, you know that place always disturbs you."

"It should disturb you, too. Frank Surget was your great-uncle after all."

"That was a long time ago. Besides, you're always saying that the war's over and that we shouldn't dwell on unpleasant..."

Jennie waved a hand, announcing an end to his argument. "You can park right over there, thank you."

"As you say, dear."

Duncan parked and helped Jennie from the coach, trailing a few paces behind as she followed a familiar path. Both grew lost in private thought as they considered the family tragedy that unfolded on this hallowed ground.

Clifton Heights had been carved from the remains of Fort McPherson, itself built on the site of Clifton, a neo-classic mansion built in 1820 and so huge it was visible for miles along the Mississippi. Jennie's maternal grandparents, Frank and Charlotte Surget, acquired Clifton shortly after their marriage and embellished the grounds with reflecting willow pools, secret grottos and parterre mazes adored by their children. A second conservatory was added and viewing benches installed at the lip of the bluff. With Frank's robust conviviality and Charlotte's graceful hand, Clifton's hospitality became legendary, but everything changed when he professed neutrality during the Civil War. Simultaneously damned as a coward and praised as a shrewd businessman, Frank insisted he wanted only to protect his home and, when the city was occupied by federal troops in 1863, he sought insurance by entertaining Union officers. Natchez's Confederates were as outraged as they had been by Ayres Merrill's invitation to General Grant, but they were not the only ones angered by Charlotte's guest lists. The morning after an especially elegant soirée, the Surgets received a U.S. Army order announcing that Clifton was to be replaced by a fort. Frank was incredulous since, with the entire Mississippi River now in Federal hands, new fortifications couldn't possibly be necessary. When he asked a close officer friend for help, Frank learned the cataclysmic truth.

The chief engineer was exacting revenge for not being invited to the previous night's dinner party, and the Surgets had precisely three days to evacuate their home!

The citizenry, some sympathetic, some gloating, gathered outside Clifton's iron fences to watch the sad spectacle. When repeated blasts barely rocked a house built to endure the ages, the enraged engineer ordered the mansion razed by hand. Clifton heroically resisted as soldiers swarmed over roofs, chimneys and walls, succumbing only after long hours of onslaught from picks, hammers, ropes and raw manpower. The Surgets kept silent vigil until their magnificent home was torn to dusty rubble and then sailed for France vowing never to return. Frank, heart as irretrievably broken as Clifton, died in mid-passage.

Nothing remained, not even the benches above the river, but Jennie paid frequent homage for reasons so intensely personal even Duncan could not fathom them. Clifton's demise had been a year before her birth, but she had heard the tragic tale often enough, and its memory invigorated something sacred in her soul. She tugged her collar higher and took Duncan's arm as they strolled the blustery bluffs. Black thunderheads swelled over Louisiana and roiled east like burgeoning nightmares. She pursed her lips and regarded the approaching storm.

"I'm not happy today, Duncan."

"Oh?" Knowing Jennie, this could mean anything, and her response iced his heart.

"Your mother's behavior yesterday at Mass was inexcusable. When I greeted you all outside the church, she looked at me as though I didn't exist. And she didn't even speak."

"She's been having those headaches again. I've told you they make her irritable. Why, as long as I can remember —"

"If your mother didn't feel well, she should've stayed at home, and I'm tired of your excuses. She's been giving me the cold shoulder since we started courting."

"I admit Mother can be difficult," Duncan conceded. He made a vain stab at humor. "Father often escaped her by locking himself in the library."

Jennie hadn't known that particular family secret but always heard that Katherine Minor's incessant nagging drove her husband to an early death, when Duncan was only seven. "We might as well face the truth, Duncan. She'll never approve our relationship, so why continue to curry her favor? Especially since we've agreed that any marriage would remain our secret."

"But, Jennie..."

"Frankly, I'm sick of playing cat-and-mouse."

"But these years have been the happiest of my life," he insisted. Duncan hoped to skirt confrontation, but Jennie was adamant.

"Listen to me, Duncan. The next time your mother is uncivil to me in public, I won't be held accountable for the consequences. You simply must say something to her or...or else."

Aghast at the ultimatum, Duncan gasped for breath, chilling his lungs with the storm-laden air. "I can't do that, Jennie. It would be like you going against your father."

That gave Jennie pause, but she said nothing.

"Nor can I force her to change her behavior. A good son is a respectful son."

"Only when the mother earns that respect," she countered.

"Jennie!"

"I'm sorry if this is painful, but I'm sure the reason for your mother's behavior is pure jealousy. She resents our happiness and that resentment has turned to hatred."

"I don't believe that."

"What else could it be?"

He sighed wearily. "I don't know."

It was the one lie Duncan ever told Jennie and it wracked him with guilt. How could he confess that his mother so despised Jennie's hold on her son that she not only condemned the relationship but promised disinheritance if he married her? Duncan told himself that his love for Jennie was all that mattered, but he was shamed by the inconceivable prospect of a marriage dependent on Jennie's money. It was a matter of honor he could not brook, so he buried his dark secret and prayed Jennie would never learn the truth. He also prayed that she would cease talk of a secret marriage. If such a thing was ever exposed, he doubted he could face the consequences.

"I don't know," he said again, as much to himself as to her.

Jennie was dubious but held her tongue. Duncan's mother was the greatest thorn in their two sides, and the one area where Jennie met defeat. She could beguile Duncan into dancing to her every whim, but when it came to Katherine Minor, Duncan became a sphinx. Like mother, like son, Jennie thought glumly.

"I see," she said at last.

Duncan feinted. "Since when do other people really matter?"

"We're talking about our family, Duncan, and I hate more dissension in the ranks. First your Uncle James, and now this. My brother and sisters have scattered to the four winds. Anna Maria is in Europe. I'm not even sure of Dunbar's whereabouts these days. Eustace, either. Anna Maria writes that Ayres Junior has done nothing more than squander his inheritance."

Duncan slipped an arm around her waist and pulled her close. "You mustn't upset yourself."

"I'm already upset, Duncan. Don't you see? This threatens us, and that means it threatens Elms Court, too. I swear I feel trouble in my bones. It's like that spring day back in eighty-two when we were watching the river and suddenly I knew Father was dying. I made you race home, and a few hours later he was gone."

Duncan started to remind Jennie she was with Stephen Holmes that awful day but kept still when he saw the determination in her eyes.

"Jennie? What is it?"

She wrenched away from him and turned her back to the mounting storm, a porcelain figurine against cobalt. Her usually light voice was low and determined as she gripped his arm and demanded an oath.

"Promise me, Duncan. Promise me that no matter what happens, you'll never leave me." Her grip tightened to the edge of pain. "Say it!"

"Of course I promise, but you already know that."

"I know nothing these days." Jennie released him and glared at the vulgar new houses encroaching upon her lost legacy. "Nothing at all," she murmured bitterly.

Duncan eased an arm back around her. Beneath the layers of heavy clothing a frightful trembling came from neither the cold nor the approaching storm. It signaled another of Jennie's dreaded mood shifts. They were as unpredictable as the river itself, deceptively serene one moment, viciously devouring the next. He watched her drink her fill of the familiar vista, then nodded toward the towering black clouds rushing toward the bluff.

"Come along, Jennie. You know how fast these winter storms can kick up."

"I like to feel its teeth!" Jennie shouted as the first needles of rain stung her face.

"Please, darling! Get in the carriage!"

Jennie reluctantly complied, but, as they raced ahead of the storm, she pretended they were pursued by furies masquerading as lightning and thunder. Her exhilaration vanished when they drew up before Elms Court and saw James Surget waiting on the gallery. She regarded him as great a nemesis as Katherine Minor.

Even Duncan felt apprehensive. "What's Uncle James doing here?"

"I told you something was afoot!" Jennie flared. "Obviously you weren't listening." She looked out at her cousin and nodded stiffly. "What brings you here?"

"I need to speak with you," Surget replied. There was no mistaking his emphasis on the last word.

Jennie bristled. "Are you suggesting I shouldn't invite Duncan in?"

Muscles twitched in Surget's left cheek, a tic she especially loathed. "Actually, I've come to discuss family matters."

"Since when is Duncan not family?

The fleshy lips tightened. "You know very well what I mean, Jennie."

Knowing it would infuriate Surget, Jennie kissed Duncan, smiled sweetly and thanked him for the afternoon. "Splendid as always, my darling."

She hurried up the steps and swept passed Surget, pointedly drawing her skirts aside as though he might sully them. She left the front door ajar, listening for any interchange between uncle and nephew as Caleb took her hat and coat. She heard only low voices and the crunch of hooves on gravel as Duncan drove away. Surget came inside.

"In the billiard room, please."

"Very well," she said icily.

Jennie recoiled the moment she entered, finding the room teeming with portent. Billiard balls scattered atop the pool table revealed a game in progress, and she was deeply unnerved by the other player's cocksure grin. This was the last person she wanted to see.

"Ayres Junior!"

"Hello, Jennie."

Although it had been thirteen years since she had seen her older brother, neither moved to embrace. "What are you doing here?"

"Business, of course."

Jennie was instantly on the defensive, more so when Ayres closed the door. "What kind of business?"

Surget gestured toward a chair. "Won't you have a seat?"

"I prefer to stand, thank you." Jennie moved toward the fire crackling in the hearth. The heat felt good but did not dispel the more pervasive chill of *déjà vu.*

"As you wish." Never celebrated for his tact, Surget said, "The family is deeply concerned about you, Jennie."

"Which family? My brother and sisters or you?"

"All of us."

"And what exactly are these deep concerns?"

"You're thirty-one. You ought to be married."

Jennie glared. "Since when is that anyone's business but my own?"

"Since it just doesn't look right." Her brother grunted. "You and Cousin Duncan—"

"Be still, Ayres! I told you to let me handle this!" Surget threw the younger man a sharp look. "Jennie, what your brother is trying to say is that you're a lovely, charming young woman who should make a choice among her many suitors instead of dismissing them."

"Ayres obviously doesn't have your way with words," she replied.

Surget ignored the gibe and continued. "People still talk about your marriage proposals from those three millionaires in Louisville. I happen to know that one of them, Rudolph O'Clary, still seeks a wife, and I'm quite certain if you gave him only the slightest bit of encouragement—"

"I'll do nothing of the sort!"

"Why in the world not?" James demanded. "Half the girls in the South would give anything to be in your shoes. With all you have to offer, your looks, your charm —"

"For heaven's sake stop this empty flattery!" Jennie snapped.

Surget seethed but held his temper. "You have everything you need to make a beneficial match, Jennie. If the Kentucky gentleman doesn't interest you, look elsewhere. A great many Southerners are marrying into Yankee wealth. The Wilsons up in Tennessee married their children to a Vanderbilt, an Astor *and* a British ambassador. Even Anna Marie married a count."

"I'm hardly my sister," Jennie shot back. She tugged off her gloves and warmed her hands by the fire. "But pray continue."

Surget knew she was toying with him and took a deep breath. "We're merely suggesting you consider someone else for a husband, someone more...appropriate." All knew he was skating on thin ice. "Your own mother chose a man not from Natchez, a man whose bloodlines were distinctly different from hers. As did Anna Marie. Men like that would be good for you, too. Someone to take you away from here and help you start a new life."

Jennie went on full offense. "I've no intention of leaving Elms Court, and I'm perfectly content with my life the way it is."

"You've made us well aware of that," Surget said with resolve. "In fact, you've made everyone in town aware of it. Your life is the subject of common gossip, the kind of talk unbefitting the Merrills, Surgets and Minors."

"Not *all* Minors! Did you ask Duncan if he finds my behavior 'unbefitting'?"

"We're not talking about my nephew. We're talking about you."

Jennie verged on explosion as she addressed the dancing flames. Her voice was low and controlled but bore a ferocious edge. "Why so circumspect, cousin dear, especially after a similar scene in this very room? Three years ago it was, the night I gave a ball. You chose that particular occasion to tell me my relationship with Duncan was inadvisable because we're cousins. Perhaps you don't recall my telling you what I did with my life was none of your business!"

"Jennie, I'm only trying to — "

She whirled, eyes narrowing as she vented her anger. "Trying to what, Cousin James? Condemn intermarriage or take over this branch of the family? Replace my father? Be the man my brother never was and never will be?"

"Jennie!" Ayres cried.

She would not be stopped. "You're all weaklings! Who took control when father got sick, brother dear? Who brought him home and held things together with half the town hating us? Who reopened Father's beloved Elms Court and worked like a fool to make it a showplace again? Who was with him when he died? None of you!" Her eyes blazed as she unleashed the final volley. "Good Lord, Ayres! You've never done an honest day's work in your life. You've never done anything except marry and have children and spend money."

"What's wrong with that?" Ayres shot back.

"What will you do when your inheritance runs out?" She shouted over thunder as the storm finally broke overhead. "Pray tell me how you'll educate your children and continue buying expensive gewgaws for that silly spoiled wife of yours!"

Jennie and her brother had sparred many times but never with gloves off. Ayres actually shook with anger, neck veins bulging grotesquely as he walked toward her. He didn't stop until his face was just inches away, and she recoiled from the smell of whiskey on his breath.

"I've already got the money!" he spat. "Plenty of it!"

Jennie backed away, suddenly frightened. Not by her brother's anger but the sinister implication. "What do you mean?"

"This house!" he shouted.

Jennie's insides churned. "What about this house? What have you done with Elms Court?"

Ayres smirked. "I mortgaged it!"

The fire crackled against the heaving storm, all sounds merging into a dull roar in Jennie's head. "You're lying!"

"No, he isn't," James Surget said. "The papers were signed last week."

For once in her life Jennie had difficulty focusing her thoughts. What these men had revealed was so monstrous, so utterly unbelievable that she didn't know how to react. She managed to mutter something about the house belonging to all the Merrill children before settling weakly onto the settee.

"As the only male, Ayres Junior has power of attorney," James explained. "It was his birthright and his decision to do with Elms Court as he pleased."

Jennie glared raw hatred while parsing the truth. "Not even Ayres would do something like this on his own. There's more to it!"

"Unfortunately, your brother has experienced some serious financial reversals on his plantations. You probably don't know that cotton prices are at an all-time low. Just last month it was selling for less than five cents a pound in New Orleans. Ayres really had no choice."

Jennie scarcely heard as her mind raced for a path free of the nightmare. She thought of her considerable inheritance, safely invested in stocks and bonds, and offered it without hesitation.

"I'll pay off the mortgage myself! Who holds it? I demand you tell me!"

Surget took a deep breath and expelled the answer with perverse satisfaction.

"I do."

He smiled, no longer concealing the loathing in his voice. Like Katherine Minor, he had always despised Jennie's willfulness and vanity, always resented her privileged upbringing and European airs. Now he would have his revenge.

"You!" Jennie gasped. "What do you care about Elms Court?"

Surget drew himself up and snarled back. "I care because I

intend to keep this house in the family, even if you Merrills cannot." Ayres started to protest the slur but instead retreated to a far corner where he poured more whiskey. "In fact, I intend to follow the tradition set by your grandfather Frank when he gave this house to his daughter and son-in-law as a wedding present."

"No!" Jennie cried.

"Oh, yes. I intend for my daughter Carlotta and her husband David McKittrick to have Elms Court as my gift."

Jennie struggled to make sense of the madness. "So this was all a charade, this feigned concern over my future, this insistence that I find a husband and move away. All you cared about was getting me out of Elms Court. At least be truthful about that, Cousin James!"

Surget shrugged, his manner arctic. "I would've had you out either way, but my concern about Duncan was never feigned. I condemn your relationship; always have, always will. I told you before that this business of marrying cousins is no longer acceptable."

"Duncan and I are not planning marriage!" she cried, desperate to ingratiate herself, frantic for anything to hold onto Elms Court.

Surget narrowed his gaze and countered savagely. "So you would continue this illicit relationship without the sanctity of marriage? There are ugly words for women who live in sin, Jennie Merrill, and you'd best be grateful I don't use them."

Jennie rose with difficulty, reeling with betrayal. Too outraged to look at her brother, she faced Surget squarely and summoned what dignity she could.

"I went to Clifton Heights this afternoon, Cousin James. I go there quite often because it was the site of my grandfather's home. You'll recall," she added pointedly, "that he was driven from a place he loved so much that he died when it was lost. I always felt a certain kinship with him, but I never, ever imagined it would be as strong as it is now."

"Your grandfather tried to play both sides of the fence," Surget growled. "Pretending to be neutral and then joining the enemy in a pathetic and obvious attempt to save his property." When Jennie gasped at this malignant betrayal of blood, Surget ventured into even more forbidden territory. "He was as duplicitous as your father!"

Jennie was speechless.

"Consorting and conniving with that crook of a president. I suppose it never occurred to you that not all your father's fortune came from respectable sources, that he was involved in business deals as corrupt as the Grant administration itself. It's high time you knew Ayres Merrill was no saint, Jennie dear, and charlatans have to pay the piper. Unfortunately your father didn't live long enough, but you have inherited his comeuppance along with his dirty money!"

"Lies!" Jennie screamed. "All lies!"

"Believe what you like, but there's one fact you cannot deny. As surely as your grandfather left Clifton, you must leave Elms Court."

"The sooner the better!" her brother spat.

Reeling with this new attack, Jennie fought mental paralysis and stared at the blazing hearth. Flames hissed and sizzled as rain gusted down the chimney, and another thunderclap rocked the house. Her dry throat ached as she intoned the unthinkable loss.

"My...Elms...Court...!"

Surget was unmoved. "What's done is done."

He and Ayres then witnessed a macabre metamorphosis as Jennie's subjugated anger erupted in a fury to match the storm. Her pretty features melded into something unrecognizable, skin turning ashen, eyes narrowing to slits. Her body was transformed, too, contorting as though an anaconda writhed and twisted inside her lush silks and velvets. She trembled terribly.

"Then may you be damned to hell, James Surget!" Jennie

snarled. She turned on her brother with equal venom. "And you with him, Ayres! You're no Merrill and no son of my father! Now both of you get out!" She seized a poker from the hearth and slashed the air with it. "Get out!!"

Drawn by the shouts, Caleb rushed to the billiard room but quickly retreated to open the front door as Jennie drove her enemies into the full fury of the storm. Terrible rage blazed and faded as she turned to a bewildered Caleb, poker clattering onto the veranda floor before she collapsed in his arms.

"It's lost, Caleb," she whimpered. "I'm lost, too."

"Miss Jennie...?"

"Lost."

12

As 1896 DREW to a close, New Yorkers anticipated the tenth day of December almost as eagerly as Christmas itself. For the last six years, their beloved Castle Clinton near the southern tip of Manhattan had undergone its latest and most unusual transformation yet. The onetime fort, restaurant, dance hall and immigration depot was reopening as the New York City Aquarium, and among the tens of thousands hoping for a first glimpse were Richard Dana and Amelia Cunningham.

"Isn't this splendid!" Richard gushed as they took their place in a long queue snaking along the waterfront. "I'm so excited I scarcely feel the cold."

"Me, too," Amelia said in a small voice. "I guess it helps that the sun's out and that there's no wind off the water."

"Indeed it does." He patted Amelia's small hand resting in the crook of his arm and nodded at the Statue of Liberty glowing deep green against the crystalline winter sky. "Just seeing that grand lady gives me a good feeling. She's beautiful, isn't she?"

"Yes, she is, but not as beautiful as your Mozart concert last night."

Amelia's small mouth crinkled with a smile, beguiling Richard as always and warming his heart. A few people in line noticed her big, liquid eyes, but most saw only a small, country girl in a threadbare coat and brave little hat. For Richard, however, this plain brown wren was a glorious bird of paradise whose presence over the past few years had become his *raison d'être*. He could barely remember life before Amelia, nor could he contemplate it without her; and he beamed as always under the weight of her praise.

"Did you have a favorite piece, my dear?"

"The Sonata Number Sixteen in C, I think."

"'The Sonata Facile'?" Richard said, humming a few bars while Amelia nodded approval.

"That's the one."

"I love it, too. It's such a joy to play."

"The critics loved it as well. Today's newspapers are full of glowing reviews, you know."

"Yes, I suppose they are," he sighed.

Richard's smile faded when the old anxiety caused trembles in his stomach. His self-confidence, personal as well as professional, had grown remarkably since meeting Amelia, but public scrutiny remained his *bête noir*. Although her mere presence before a performance meant nausea no longer came calling, Richard's insides still churned when he walked onstage or a curtain rose to reveal an ocean of eyes focused on him. Everything changed once his fingers found the keyboard or his rich tenor embraced a composer's notes and sent them soaring, but until that magical moment, even with Amelia's help, he endured a dark, very private hell.

"I especially enjoyed the review in the *Sun*," Amelia soothed, feeling the inside of his elbow tense beneath her fingers.

"Cousin Charles probably had something to do with that."

"Oh, you know that's not true, Richard. The other papers were just as enthusiastic and praiseworthy."

"You're right as always." Richard nodded, thin lips pursed. "Forgive me."

The enormous brown eyes danced with love and admiration. "There's nothing to forgive, dearest. I should be the one asking for forgiveness, abandoning you so often for New Hampshire."

"Your family needs you on the farm," Richard said. "I completely understand that, only..."

Amelia frowned. "Only?"

"Only I wish I could make enough to support you here in the city and send money to your folks to make up for your absence. Sometimes I think I should sell the house in Natchez and my other Mississippi properties and—"

Light as a hummingbird, her tiny, gloved finger touched his lips. "You mustn't say such things, sweetheart. Why, that's where you were born, and you may need those other things some day. You're only twenty-five, and if you continue to earn such fine notices, I've no doubt you'll find great success." Amelia stroked his cheek before withdrawing her touch. "I truly believe our separations will last only a few more years, and if you can bear it, so can I."

"Oh, Amelia," he sighed, not caring about a nearby couple watching him pull her into his arms and hold her tight. "If you only knew how much you mean to me."

"But I do know," she insisted. "I know only too well."

They held each other a long time, oblivious to the stares as they grew lost in their private reverie. They were barely aware when the long line at last began to move and they inched forward toward the domed brick building and a world as strange and fanciful as the one only they shared. Once they funneled through the front door, Richard and Amelia wandered through a series of splendid rooms more appropriate for a Fifth Avenue mansion than lowly fish. Colorful tile floors wove beneath arches supported by thick Romanesque columns, and there were enough potted palms to fill a dozen conservatories. Spaced at strategic intervals were enormous circular tanks rung by fanciful iron railings. The largest mirrored the great dome and contained a dazzling array of fish harvested from local lakes, rivers and seas. Richard warned Amelia before she peered into a tank writhing with lampreys.

"They look too much like snakes," he muttered, wrinkling his nose. "Don't like them."

"Then let's see what's over there," Amelia said, following the crowd to a pool filled with gracefully gliding Atlantic sturgeon over ten feet long. "Good heavens! Those things are bigger than our sheep!"

For the next hour, Richard and Amelia entertained and repulsed themselves as they observed needle-nosed gar, iridescent rainbow trout and an octopus tank that was clearly the aquarium's biggest draw. Richard felt immediate empathy for the shy sea creatures blending into the rocks and was oddly thrilled to see them explode with energy when an attendant heaved a bucket of scallops into their midst. The entire tank erupted with a flurry of tentacles as the octopi gorged themselves and, although he didn't know why, Richard was mesmerized by the defiant feeding frenzy. He was so captivated, in fact, that he didn't realize someone was talking to him.

"Excuse me, friend. How about letting somebody else have a look, huh?"

Jarred from his mystifying daydream, Richard turned to a man about his age with two wide-eyed children in tow. The father's look of annoyance announced he was tired of waiting for a look into the octopus tank.

"I'm so sorry," Richard said. "I didn't realize I was..."

"It's alright," the man's wife said in apologetic tone. "I guess we're just anxious to see the octopus like everybody else."

"I'm...I'm sorry," he said again.

Richard tipped his hat and backed away, eager to flee the

awkward moment. He turned to suggest to Amelia they look for the shark display, but she was nowhere to be seen. He scanned the throng before threading his way through them, battling a growing panic when he could not find her. He cupped a hand to his mouth and called out.

"Amelia! Where are you?"

When his anxious calls went unanswered, he repeated them until an attendant approached to offer help. Richard was explaining his dilemma when another man came over to ask if he was the concert pianist he heard last night.

"Absolutely not!" he insisted, voice shrill and mind numb with fear. "My name is R.S. Ament!"

Desperate to elude the nosy stranger, Richard fled into the crowd, shouting for Amelia at the top of his lungs. Acoustics in the aquarium were anything but ideal, making him almost impossible to hear above the heaving, noisy multitudes. Panic grew until Richard could barely breathe and dizziness drove him to find a bench. By then he was hoarse from yelling and on the verge of collapse, when the jostling masses parted enough for him to spot Amelia on the far side of the hall. Fighting rubbery legs, he lurched in her direction, his awkward wobble suggesting someone out of control. The concerned crowds parted as though making way for a drunkard.

"Amelia!"

"There you are!" she called back in a relieved voice. "Where have you been, Richard dear?"

He frowned and shook his head. "I…I was about to ask you the same thing."

"But I was right where I told you I'd be," she replied, confused. "Looking at those cute little sunfish."

"Sunfish?" he muttered.

"Why, yes. I told you I didn't care to watch the octopus feed and would meet you at the sunfish tank."

"You did?"

Concern grew on Amelia's small face. "Are you alright, my darling? You're very pale."

"Perhaps...perhaps I need some fresh air."

"Then come along," she said, taking a firm grip on his arm. "We'll go outside for a bit." Richard allowed himself to be led away like a child and steered to a bench overlooking the harbor. A wind was rising fast, stinging their faces with cold and rousing swarms of whitecaps at the base of the great statue. Richard felt a bit queasy, but he knew his discomfort didn't come from the heaving sea. Tears froze on his cheeks as he gathered Amelia into his arms and confessed his deepest fear.

"You don't understand, Amelia," he wailed. "I thought I'd lost you."

RICHARD'S SUCCESS PROVED as tenuous as Jennie's grip on Elms Court. For three more years, he sang and played at concert halls and churches all over Manhattan, even making a few forays to Brooklyn, but his salary never equaled his good notices. The resulting frustration, coupled with his other unattainable dream to marry and support Amelia, often crippled him with bouts of melancholy that kept him from performances. Adding to his misery were new family demands requiring Amelia to spend more time on the New Hampshire farm than in the city. It seemed the Cunninghams no sooner survived one crisis when another arose. First Amelia was summoned after her father was thrown by a horse. She'd scarcely nursed him back to health and returned to New York when she was called back to tend to her dying grandmother. She and Richard were more desperate than ever to be together when her mother developed scarlet fever, necessitating the cancellation of yet another reunion.

Despite such ongoing obstacles, Richard occasionally managed to summon his mental and emotional strength and deliver the sort of performance propelling audiences to their feet.

One such concert came in February of 1899, a success so great that the sound of applause thrummed in his ears long after he left the concert hall on Thirty-fourth Street and plunged into the snowy Manhattan night. Feeling unusually energetic and sure of himself onstage, he had dispatched Chopin's Opus "Winter Wind" with brilliance, fingers flying across the keyboard as though steered by the composer himself. He was so consumed that, halfway through the ambitious piece, he wondered if the old master's spirit had permeated his soul. It was, after all, not the first time he had been stirred by supernal notions.

The only blemish on the evening was Amelia's absence. Richard physically ached for her; she had scratched a wound on his heart that would not heal. She was so like him, this sweet, soft-spoken seraph who fathomed his moods in ways even his dear Octavia could not. Only Amelia, with just a faint touch to his brow, could vanquish the demons that often ravaged his mind. As he considered his good fortune in finding her, Richard whispered a prayer of purest urgency: "Please unite us soon, dear God."

Amelia waltzed in his thoughts as Richard strode up Sixth Avenue, so intoxicated by this soaring of spirits that he braced his lungs with cold air and floated through the snowflakes on a personal cloud. It didn't matter that he would be freezing by the time he walked the twenty-two blocks home. At this moment, his love for Amelia and his passion for the piano coalesced to provide powerful insulation against a cold, hostile world.

Richard was still exhilarated when he reached his apartment on Fifty-sixth Street. He sprang up the steps of the new brownstone and smiled when he encountered his landlady on the parlor floor. Signora Ambrosino was a kind-hearted busybody who knew all her tenants' business, but Richard didn't mind. She took special care of the ones she liked, and he was clearly her favorite.

He smiled broadly. "Good evening, Mrs. Ambrosino."

"Signor Dana!" She offered a contagious grin. "Your concert tonight. Was good?"

Richard glowed. "It went very well, thank you, and I wish you had been there."

She fussed with her keys, turning them over and over as though worrying a rosary. "Oh, I don't know. All that fancy music I don't understand."

"How do you know you won't understand until you hear it?" he challenged gently.

"Mmmm, maybe I come some time." Both knew it was a sweet lie. "Oh! I almost forget. I slip telegram under your door."

"A telegram?"

She nodded. "Just arrive. Maybe you pass telegram man on street."

"Thank you!" Richard flew up the stairs. "And good night!"

"*Buona sera!*"

Richard hurried into his apartment and scooped the telegram from the floor, hastily tearing it open to scan the address. Mr. Josiah Cunningham, Bartlett, New Hampshire. His eyes scanned the message, throat constricting upon seeing the terrible words.

"...sorrowful...duty...to report Amelia's death...."

A dull, painful rampage inside his head smothered his reasoning. He reread the telegram from Amelia's father, aloud this time as he tried to make sense of the strange words swimming on the page. He read silently a third time, lips moving very slowly, and then aloud again, working harder to comprehend the message. Then he counted the words. Ten. Ten simple words. Words that shimmered and blurred on the limp piece of paper, then floated off the page. They meant nothing until they reformed and focused into a sentence that would forever change his life.

"My sorrowful duty to report Amelia's death from scarlet fever."

Richard propped the telegram on the mantle. He lit an oil

lamp and turned up the wick, setting it alongside the telegram so it gleamed in the dimness. Then he drew up a chair
and stared at this incomprehensible message while pain pulsed
behind his eyes. The night was still until the snowstorm intensified, mixed with sleet now that pinged against the win-
dowpanes. Richard heard nothing except the incessant roar
inside his head, until faraway voices lured him from the flickering light and the telegram. He was drawn to the window, mesmerized by the melting snowflakes and grains of sleet tearing
against the panes. He pressed his cheek against the icy glass,
temples throbbing as he struggled to conjure Amelia's image. It materialized outside the window, a pale face sculpted in
lacy snowflakes. She was not smiling but neither did she look
pained.

She was just...there.

"Richard?"

He jumped back from the window as the howling inside his
head subsided and he heard Amelia's voice, clear and sweet. He
nodded toward this ethereal vision, puzzled because she spoke
without moving her lips. He remembered a ventriloquist he
had seen years ago at a carnival, but this was no trick. This was
real, very real.

"Richard?"

"Amelia?"

She moved her mouth closer to the glass and frosted the
pane with a ghostly breath.

"I love you, Richard."

He moved closer. "I...I love you, too, Amelia."

Their lips were only inches apart now, ghostly breaths
clouding the windowpane on both sides before trickling down
the glass. As he stared, more mesmerized than ever, Amelia's
image blurred and began to fade. Frantic at the prospect of losing her, Richard grabbed the window sash.

"Don't go!" he cried, rattling the heavy window high. "Amelia!"

Bitter wind whipped through the open window and stung

Richard's face with frigid pinpricks. He felt nothing but obsession for Amelia's fading visage. He straightened his left arm to push the sash as high as it would go, and then shoved his right hand into the storm, fingers extended in a frantic attempt to reach his beloved. He seized only the bite of sleet and howled piteously as Amelia drifted further and further away until she was swallowed by whirling whiteness. His frozen hand grew heavy and sagged onto the slippery sill, fingers splayed as though atop a piano keyboard.

"Amelia!"

Realizing she was gone, he let go of the window.

His scream propelled Mrs. Ambrosino from bed. It was raw and primeval, and there was no mistaking its origin. She rushed to Richard Dana's apartment, colliding with two other alarmed neighbors at the top of the stairs.

"Mrs. Ambrosino!"

"What on earth...?"

"Was that Mr. Dana?"

The landlady shoved them aside and pounded on the door. A second agonized scream prompted her to try the knob. In his haste to retrieve his telegram, Richard had left the apartment unlocked, allowing Mrs. Ambrosino and the other tenants to spill inside and gasp at the terrible sight before them.

Richard Dana's right hand was crushed between window and sill. He stared blankly, body gripped by spasms, an animal caught in a trap.

13

FOLLOWING HER FATHER's death in 1898, Octavia lingered aimlessly in Mobile, eking out a living as best she could. When all options ran out and her very survival was under siege, she turned to Richard Dana, her only real friend, but was further distressed when three letters to New York were returned to her, marked Address Unknown. Puzzled and alarmed, she wrote the rector at New York's Christ Episcopal Church who replied that Richard had moved back to Natchez following the death of his fiancée and an accident that had destroyed his career as pianist. After letters to Natchez also went unanswered, Octavia spent her last funds on a train ticket and arrived there in the summer of 1899.

When her knocking and calls went unanswered, she ventured inside Glenwood where she found someone in the parlor she scarcely knew, either physically or mentally. Richard was gaunt and ashen, eyes leaden as though he had sunk into himself, but that dramatic decline paled alongside the other.

Richard recognized her, but his conversation was rambling and disjointed with only an occasional flicker of real comprehension. Octavia was deeply unnerved by this new persona, bitter one moment and giddy the next before plunging into silences she could not break. The strangest moment involved an unseeing stare and seemed to reference some long-ago conversation with her sister Nydia, a confession.

"I promised her," he said.

"What did you promise?" Octavia asked.

"To help you if I could."

Beaten down by her misfortunes, Octavia scarcely dared wonder if she'd found safe haven at last. "Will you let me stay here a while?"

"Why, yes," he answered with a burst of lucidity. "You may stay as long as you like." Before Octavia could express her thanks, the strange creature went through another metamorphosis. "But remember that Richard Dana is no more. You must call me Dick now."

"Alright," Octavia said uneasily.

"Thank you." He bowed with exaggerated formality. "Come along, please. I'll show you to your room now."

That was Octavia's awakening to how far removed Richard was from reality. More warning signs quickly followed—clear evidence that the man she once knew and loved was lost forever. Still, she did not hesitate to accept his hospitality, partly to take care of an old troubled friend but mostly because she had no place else to go. The next few days, as she struggled to settle in to her strange new home, brought even more disturbing revelations. Although well acquainted with Dick's erratic moods, Octavia never anticipated his going into full retreat. One morning when he failed to come down for breakfast, she went upstairs and tapped on his door. Guttural moans prompted her inside, where he lay atop the bed, fully dressed, his back to the door. The shutters were tightly closed and the dark room was permeated by the sour smell of unchanged clothes.

"Dick? What is it? Are you ill?"

There was no response from the man on the bed.

"Dick? Please answer me. Do you need a doctor?"

His reply was almost inaudible. "No."

"Then what's wrong?" As she rounded the foot of the towering tester bed, Dick rolled away from her. She frowned and retraced her steps, only to have him turn away again. "Dick?"

"Please leave me alone," he whispered.

Octavia stood firm, alarmed but not intimidated. She spoke in low soothing tones, a mother comforting a frightened child. "I'm here to help you, Dick. Remember? You said you wanted me to stay at Glenwood and here I am." She took a deep breath and repeated herself more forcefully. "Remember?"

A moan and another long sigh before more silence.

Octavia dared rest a hand lightly on his shoulder. Dick's soft, damp flesh quivered beneath her touch, but he did not, she was relieved, pull away. They remained like that for a long time, silently observed through the open door by their only servant, a Negro woman named Myrtle who had known Dick since he was a child. She shook her head, a silent signal to Octavia that she had seen it all before, and walked away. When they were alone again, Dick slowly turned over and looked at Octavia. She had expected his face to be streaked with tears or contorted with fear. It was neither. What Octavia saw was a soul resigned to despair.

"Come here," she said.

Dick offered no resistance as Octavia perched on the edge of the high feather bed so she could gather him in her arms. Like a selfless Pietá, she cradled and comforted her old friend as best she could for the remainder of the morning. By noon Dick had wrenched free of his melancholia, but Octavia knew she would never again see him in the same light. Still, she continued to do her best to cheer him up, and, in the days that followed, he came to recognize her as a sympathetic confidante. Hearing him humming one morning, and anxious to keep his meandering mind focused, Octavia gently suggested his glorious tenor was a God-given talent he should not ignore.

"I find writing poetry most rewarding," she declared. "Surely you find equal satisfaction in your singing."

"Can't!" Dick refused, proclaiming his voice had vanished with the accident. "Gone."

After that bitter response, Octavia knew not to urge him toward the piano, but a few days later she and Myrtle heard the pathetic sound of missed notes and sour chords as Dick's crippled fingers sought music where none was possible. This latest disappointment propelled him into another bout of depression and a world where only Octavia was allowed entry. At his inexplicable insistence, Myrtle was let go, leaving Octavia the daunting task of running Glenwood alone. With no alternative battle plan, she soldiered on.

Octavia learned just how far south Dick's mind had migrated when they made a rare trip to town and encountered a number of old acquaintances. Octavia responded warmly to their friendly greetings, but Dick, to her horror, claimed to be someone else.

"Richard," he firmly insisted, "is in New York where he sings in the Christ Church choir and plays the piano at concerts. He hasn't been in Natchez for years."

Most shook their heads and walked away, wondering exactly what role Octavia now played in Glenwood's peculiar unfolding drama. Weeks later when she braved another trip to town, Dick loudly announced his name was R.S. Ament. She speculated about a connection between "Ament" and "Amelia" or even "amen", but it was an alias that forever remained his secret. Later that same day, Dick became so rambunctious and disoriented that Octavia hurried him back home, where his behavior would go unseen and unjudged. She prayed for his recovery, remembering people who painstakingly triumphed over the backwash of the Civil War. If they could survive the death of loved ones, poverty, hunger and a new world they neither created nor understood, surely Dick could get on with his shattered life. She was wrong. As more time passed, his self-imposed isolation only intensified and, despite her encouragement to receive old and trusted friends, he found every imaginable reason to avoid company. When callers came, Octavia answered the door only to make excuses for her elusive host until Dick's childhood friends finally stopped coming. His days of carousing with other young blades also died an awkward death, along with all interest in women. He wanted only to be left alone.

Octavia was also driven to social suicide, although her reasons were financial rather than mental. Reduced circumstances forced her to decline invitations because she had no hope of reciprocating, and because she now wore thrice-turned dresses and coats. As the daughter of a Confederate General, she provoked scandal by withdrawing from the United Daughters of the Confederacy and reaped stern disapproval from everyone but Rosemary Kellogg Pickett, the woman she'd met so many years before at the Ball of a Thousand Candles. Rosemary alone assured Octavia she understood her plight and asked how she might help.

"I ask only to be allowed to leave our esteemed organization with as much dignity as possible," Octavia replied.

"Consider it done," Rosemary said, promising to smooth the Daughters' ruffled feathers. "And please don't hesitate to call if I can do anything else."

"Thank you, my dear."

Octavia was sincere but doubted if the same was true of her last remaining friend. She knew very well that she had become an embarrassing inconvenience for Rosemary and everyone else she encountered; because the U.D.C. was her last social link, the day inevitably arrived when Glenwood had no callers at all. Octavia worked hard to adjust. She grew to share Dick's passion for solitude but prayed for a miracle to arrest his mental decline. Hopes for his recovery, however, were forever shattered by a bizarre incident revealing how fragile he really was.

One July night she was alone in her second-floor bedroom, struggling with a particularly elusive passage of poetry, when voices swelled outside her window. Situated deep in its vast forest acreage, Glenwood was silent after dusk except for chirruping insects and the occasional hoot owl or barking dog. Any other sounds were cause for alarm, and when Octavia went to the window to investigate, what she saw on the lawn below froze her soul.

A dozen or so of Dick's one-time cronies staggered about, torches in hand, shouting a bawdy tale about a girl named Jennifer and how Dick had compromised the poor girl's virtue. Knowing Dick would never respond to the lurid catcalls, Octavia decided to confront the young men herself. She was halfway down the staircase when she spied him in the vestibule, hand on the doorknob.

"Dick?" When she got no response, she called out again, knowing he sometimes responded to a firm, repetitive message. "Dick!"

He glanced over his shoulder at her; Octavia hoped she would never see such terror again. "Don't open the door, Dick! Don't open the door!"

Her heart sank when he looked away, threw the door wide and confronted the enemy. His appearance, in unlaundered shirt and dirty trousers, brought cheers and jeers from the drunken men outside the door. He said not a word as they repeated their taunts, accusations growing more obscene by the moment.

"Come out here, Dick!"

"You've got to marry her!"

"C'mon, Dick! C'mon!" The shouts metamorphosed into a vulgar chant staining the soft summer night. "C'mon, Dick! C'mon, Dick! C'mon, Dick!"

Dick stepped onto the porch, just enough to show his face

beneath the flickering torch light. A few men recoiled from what resembled a trapped animal more than a human being, while others were brutally fueled by the pitiful sight. When Dick slowly opened his mouth, the crowd hushed to hear what he had to say. There were no words, only chattering teeth and a feral whimper before he fled back inside, nearly toppling Octavia in his panicky flight upstairs. She heard his feet travel two flights and the slam of a trapdoor leading to the roof. Fury overcoming fear, she confronted the cruel rowdies.

"What kind of people are you?" she demanded, voice brimming with righteous rage. "Why have you come here to bully that poor, defenseless creature?" There was no response until Octavia took a step forward, emboldened when she recognized a few faces beneath the flickering torches. "Shame on you, Clarence Helgren! You too, Robert Bush! What would Reverend Searfoss say about your behavior?" When the accused parties slowly retreated, Octavia pressed her advantage and ventured to the veranda's edge. "Get out of here! All of you! Get out of here! Now!"

Octavia stood her ground until the grumbling crowd dispersed and melted back into the dark woods. Those sober enough to realize their mistake crept sheepishly home, while their more drunken cohorts headed for the saloons of Natchez-Under-the-Hill to relive and embellish their moment of triumph. Before the night was out, Dick Dana had acquired yet another name—the Wild Man of Natchez.

Alone again, Octavia hurried to the third-floor trapdoor. It was blocked from the other side, indicating to her that Dick was sitting on it. She banged and called his name anyway, but there was no response, nor would there be any the next morning as Dick remained isolated with neither food nor water. Worried that he might have hurt himself, Octavia wandered the lawn and scanned the rooftop. She called repeatedly as he skittered from one chimney to the next, eventually settling behind Glenwood's central pediment with only the top of his head showing. Deciding that Dick might interpret her pleas as more bullying, she went back inside.

The drama continued for another forty-eight hours, until sometime during the third night, Octavia heard footsteps. She sat up in bed and listened, ear cocked toward the sound of Dick creeping down the stairs. Instinct warned her to leave him alone as he closed his bedroom door and the house fell silent again. She awoke to find Dick at the kitchen table, staring into an empty coffee cup. Saying nothing about the incident, she made fresh coffee, filled his cup and chatted cheerily about her new poem while Dick sipped and smacked his lips. He lifted his eyes just once, and in that instant Octavia understood that he was forever lost.

Afterwards, Dick had what she observed as "here," "there," and "in between" days. The "here" days were when he was present physically as well as mentally. The "there" days were when he was neither. On "in between" days he might be physically present but mentally absent, which was most unnerving of all because it was like living with a stranger.

While Dick daydreamed and Octavia toiled, three years passed, each more exacting than the last. The worst crisis arrived in spring of 1902, a calamity she recognized as the unhealthiest they had lived through as she stood on the veranda and watched a fancy phaeton jangle away. How telling, she thought ruefully, that Glenwood's only visitors in so many years had been attorneys. Dick lurked behind her, mesmerized by puffs of dust riled by the wheels and hooves of the departing lawyers. She waited until the coach was gone and the dust had settled down, then steeled herself.

"Come along," she said, motioning Dick to follow. "You always feel better after a stroll."

"Oh, I don't know." He nodded toward the vanished carriage. "Those men seemed to know what they were talking about. Hmmm."

"Come along," she repeated firmly.

As they walked, Octavia weighed the bleak financial portrait painted by Dick's lawyers and, worse, the documentation they brought to prove it. Family investments bequeathed to Richard Dana had begun to decline in recent years. A few months ago, they had plummeted and now produced the most minimal of incomes. Dick's plantation lands were virtually worthless, fertility devoured by too many years of cotton. Even if he wanted to sell, there were no buyers. Nor was there a market for Glenwood, his 45-acre estate on the edge of town. Natchez's fabled wealth had come, dazzled, tarried and gone, leaving a backwash of crumbling grand mansions. Homes that had been a family's pride were now white elephants, a tragic surplus of splendor gone sour.

Octavia was grateful that Dick had been enjoying a "here" day when his attorneys called. At least he had some grasp of his desperate financial situation and therefore might understand what she planned to propose. She felt hopeful as she led him to one of his favorite spots, an iron picnic table Reverend Dana had installed before his son was born. From that charitable distance, under soft sunlight filtered through tall pines, the mansion glowed as glorious as the day it was finished in 1841, a capacious, columned affair with a two-storied veranda and graceful parapets. Glenwood looked so deceptively harmonious and peaceful it pained Octavia to look at it.

She gently took Dick's right hand. His flesh felt cadaverous, but Octavia resisted the urge to let go. "Perhaps this unpleasant news is a blessing in disguise, Dick." He stared a moment, then looked back at the house. "I haven't been able to sell my poetry for some time and think it's time I faced the truth."

"What truth?"

She shrugged. "That I'm not going to be America's great poetess. Oh, I can easily do without the recognition, but I can't do without the money I hoped it would generate. We must be realistic, Dick, while there's something left. We can't continue charging things at the butcher shop if we can't pay for them."

Dick watched a squirrel scamper up the side of a tall pine and execute a death-defying leap to a neighboring oak. He smiled vaguely at the animal's antics, making Octavia worry she was losing him. He surprised her.

"What shall we do then?"

Octavia squeezed his hand, hoping to infuse him with her enthusiasm. "Well, you know I was raised on a plantation and later stayed at my brother-in-law's plantation in Fayette."

"I remember."

"Good," she replied, pleased that he seemed to be following the conversation. "When I was little, I played with the colored children and sometimes helped with their chores. I enjoyed working with the livestock, especially the chickens."

"I like cats," Dick said.

Octavia nodded indulgently, hoping he would stay focused. "I'm thinking we should take what money we have left and invest it in livestock. Not just chickens but goats and pigs, too. I could also plant some vegetables behind the house. What I don't know about gardening I'm sure the men at the feed store will explain."

"I like chickens, too," Dick muttered. He jerked his head as the squirrel made another leap, this time with a friend in hot pursuit. They chased each other in a noisy spiral down the tree trunk before scampering into the woods. Dick smiled, vague and dreamy, and leaned to see them better. Octavia was losing him to a "there" day.

"Come along," she said. "It's lunch time." When Dick didn't respond, she said, "Shall I bring us something to eat out here? Shall we have a picnic?"

"I like picnics."

Octavia gingerly tugged her hand free and walked away. As she approached, the house loomed larger than ever, a monster demanding to be tamed. In her heart she had known for a long time that this moment would come, when the burden of Glenwood would descend fully onto her shoulders, and now that the day was here, she welcomed it. The wait was over. Abandoning her poetry may have been an admission of defeat, but it was also oddly liberating.

Octavia started for the kitchen but paused in the great hallway. She looked from the carved fanlights toward the parlor's exquisite marble mantle, the collection of Chippendale and Duncan Phyfe furnishings, fine rosewood and mahogany pieces once belonging to no less than the Lees of Virginia. In the dining room, she straightened a painting given to her family by Varina Howell, wife of Jefferson Davis, one of the few heirlooms she'd been able to hold on to, and in the library she admired black-walnut bookshelves lining all four walls. Dick told her that his father had collected over ten thousand volumes and she did not doubt it. Many, she knew, were priceless first editions with gilded pages and fine leather bindings, but, as with everything else, there would be no buyers in these trying times.

"Such richness amid such poverty," she muttered.

Tapestries, marble statuary, busts of famous authors and family portraits lined the walls of Reverend Dana's handsomely appointed study. Notes from his favorite sermons were tucked atop a Heppelwhite highboy, gathering dust where the old rector had left them decades ago. Octavia gravitated toward the far corner where her most prized possession reposed inside a glass display case—the uniform of her late father, Confederate General Thomas Dockery. She opened it just long enough to caress the epaulets and sash and murmur a silent prayer. At her touch, cherished memories danced free of the past. Octavia closed her eyes and invoked the pride on her father's face when he first saw the portrait of the daughter he so loved. She remembered the peerless excitement of dining with President Grant when she was only fourteen, the light touch of a young man's hand as he waltzed her around the dance floor. The thrill when her first piece of writing was published, the invitation, however hollow, by Charles Dana Gibson to be immortalized as a "Gibson Girl" and the heady honor of being the only woman invited on America's first Antarctic expedition. Finally, she recalled her father's death, still raw in her memory, ending misery and great loss as she brought the old warrior here to Natchez for burial. Whispered promises and half-remembered dreams. Octavia gently closed the glass case and walked away.

"Enough."

Knowing Dick had no concept of time, Octavia delayed lunch a while longer. She went upstairs and rifled through her collection of poetry for "Ignis Fatuus", published nine years ago, in 1893, the year her sister died. She had been twenty-nine then, still passionate about her craft. She sat by the window and read aloud when she found her favorite passage.

"Dancing on the stream of life, beauteous maiden in your boat." She took a deep breath and continued. "Hast thou thought of destination, whither bound?"

Octavia had worried the poem might make her weep. Instead, she smiled. Then, as she leaned back and felt the bright April sun on her face, she chuckled softly and proclaimed her destiny. It was the shortest, most heartfelt poem she had ever composed.

"From poetry to pigs."

14

FOR JENNIE, ESTRANGEMENT from family, hostility from Duncan's mother, and the loss of her beloved Elms Court and its staff proved to be a cataclysmic confluence. Dogged by an abiding anger, she cultivated bitterness and banished forever her once mighty compassion. A misanthropic shell began to form, thickening and toughening as the years passed. Although Jennie didn't notice it, others certainly did.

None more than Duncan.

A strange odyssey led Jennie through a string of old Natchez homes. First came Glenwood, leased while Dick Dana still pursued a musical career in New York. The desire for lavish entertaining had been snuffed out with the loss of Elms Court, but for a while she received a few close friends and gave an occasional tea and intimate supper. She occasionally ventured out, but eventually found repeated gatherings with the same people tiresome. When they became downright debilitating, Jennie stayed home and began ignoring invitations until, to Natchez's utter shock, she erased herself from the social scene altogether and embraced the life of a hermit. Like Octavia, whom she no longer saw, Jennie found her newfound privacy and isolation supremely liberating.

Her only daily caller was Duncan and, without disapproving relatives lurking about, the two spent endless days together and, defiantly, nights as well. She might have stayed at Glenwood forever had Dick's accident not forced his painful retreat to Natchez in 1898. Unnerved by this strange, disoriented creature appearing from nowhere to reclaim his home, Jennie relocated to nearby Gloucester, an enormous manse set among eighty acres on Lower Woodville Road. Once home to Winthrop Sargent, Mississippi's first territorial governor, the magnificent, pillared house had declined drastically in recent years. Jennie was appalled by the desuetude but welcomed its condition as a convenient excuse for continuing to refuse visitors. For five years she rattled around Gloucester, with only Duncan, her cook Effie and a small staff to keep her company. She might have stayed forever, but the summer of 1904 brought near-tornadic winds and rains that took further toll on the aging structure. Jennie complained to anyone who would listen but tolerated the stench of mold and mildew and sporadic leaks until creeping moisture brought down half the dining room ceiling, narrowly missing poor Effie while she served dinner. Wearied of rental property and wanting this move to be her last, Jennie seized the chance to buy a much smaller place she had admired for years.

Glenburnie Manor was a perfectly proportioned, one-story raised cottage with a generous, columned veranda: just the right amount of space for the aging lovebirds. The only drawback was that it faced Elms Court across Kingston Pike, but the vast, forested grounds made the estates invisible to one another, so Jennie decided she could live with it. The closest house was Glenwood, but with three hundred yards of woods, thickets and ravines separating them, Jennie never saw her famously reclusive neighbors either. She found this ideal since Dick and Octavia were links to a painful past she did not wish to resurrect. Indeed, the lights at the Ball of a Thousand Candles were eternally extinguished as Jennie embraced her shadowy new world.

Glenburnie also pleased Duncan since it was a bit closer to Oakland than Gloucester, making it more convenient for his nightly visits. It was now his habit to leave home at eight in the evening, after his mother and sister Mary Grace retired, and return at dawn before the household rose for breakfast. This idiosyncratic routine, which his family diligently ignored, became the stuff of local legend. Half of Natchez had seen Duncan on his nightly horseback rides, and the other half had certainly heard about them. He was a curious figure, indeed, ramrod straight in the saddle, always riding at a slow pace with an open umbrella even in dry weather. His oddball habits made him an even bigger target for local busybodies hotly condemning his liaison with the unmarried Jennie Merrill. The aristocracy was supposed to maintain high moral standards, they whispered, not drag them through the mire of flagrant fornication. And at their ages, too!

Now in their early forties, Duncan and Jennie had been gossiped about for over two decades, but it meant nothing since they had each other and had long ago stopped discussing marriage, secret or otherwise. As Jennie's passion for privacy became an obsession, she carefully fashioned a private world where, excepting the servants and some widely scattered estate tenants, she and Duncan were the only inhabitants. She thwarted visitors with an enormous NO ADMITTANCE sign at the entrance to Glenburnie; and when wayward travelers seeking Elms Court ignored the warning, she retaliated with a much larger, bolder sign: MERRILL. INQUIRE ELSEWHERE FOR PERSONS OF OTHER NAMES.

If that wasn't deterrent enough, Jennie had a gun. A woman living alone, she told Duncan, couldn't be too careful, and she made certain everyone knew she not only had a weapon but knew how to use it. Her servants soon grew accustomed to the sounds of gunfire as Miss Jennie took aim at everything from tin cans to bottles. If a squirrel or rabbit wandered into her sights, so much the better as it gave her cook Effie something extra to toss into the stew pot.

Jennie was targeting a row of cans one sunny summer afternoon when something moved in the woods toward Glenwood. She shaded her eyes from the bright glare and squinted until she spotted a bearded, ragged figure lurking among the trees.

"Another hungry hobo," she grunted. "Human vermin."

She watched the wretched soul slink through the shadows, darting from one pine tree to another, then into a clump of bushes. He peered over the leaves and cocked his head, inspecting her like a nervous bird. Then he scurried to another pine, closer now, and peeked again. The man was near enough for Jennie to discern details, and what she saw disgusted her. He was wild-eyed and unkempt, with tattered clothing and a beard halfway down his chest. When he stepped from the woods and started toward her, Jennie's reaction was lightning fast.

"Get off my land!" she yelled. When the intruder didn't respond, Jennie cocked the gun and took aim. "Are you deaf? I said git!"

"For God's sake, don't shoot, Jennie!"

Jennie started at the frantic plea, puzzled because it had come from behind her. She whirled around and strained to get her sights on a new target. "Who called my name?"

"It's me! Octavia Dockery!"

Jennie lowered the gun as a creature in a shapeless house-dress and ratty straw hat emerged from dark woods into blinding daylight. As Octavia drew closer, Jennie recognized her neighbor but with difficulty. The famously smooth skin was discolored with freckles and coarsened by the sun, and the hourglass figure had thickened in the middle. Octavia's wrinkled forehead was damp with sweat, and her feet were shoved into the sort of crude work boots worn by the wives of sharecroppers. Jennie knew Octavia had fallen on hard times, but this was beyond belief.

"Octavia Dockery!" she managed, so stunned she forgot the menacing hobo. "Can it really be you?"

"Hello, Jennie." Octavia extended a dirty hand, prompted to explain her appearance when Jennie hesitated to take it. "I'm sorry about the way I look, but...well, I'm not used to seeing anyone. We no longer receive at Glenwood." She frowned and wiped her hands on a bandanna. "Forgive me."

"No need to apologize," Jennie said. "It seems we have both taken reclusive roads."

Octavia smiled when they finally shook hands. "Goodness me. How long has it been?"

"Eleven years," Jennie answered, remembering easily because their last encounter was only a few days before she was evicted from Elms Court in 1895.

Octavia nodded. "And of course I remember meeting you at that lovely ball."

The mathematics took a bit longer before Jennie replied, "Fourteen years ago." She spun away when she heard more rustling in the bushes and remembered the bearded tramp. She cocked her gun again and took deadly aim. "I said get off my property!"

"Don't shoot, Jennie!" Octavia cried. "It's Dick, for heaven's sake! Dick Dana!"

Jennie lowered the gun again, bracing herself for the second shock of the day. "Can this be true? That pitiful creature is —"

"Dick Dana," Octavia repeated. She cupped a hand to her mouth and called out. "It's all right, Dick. I'm with a friend."

Jennie watched, incredulous, as the filthy figure made a jerky nod and slunk back into the murky forest. Was this all that remained of the New York piano prodigy with the golden voice?

"But how on earth..."

Octavia shrugged again. "Do you really want to hear the story?"

"Ordinarily, I'd say no," Jennie admitted, "but for some reason I do." She nodded toward the house. "Let's get out of this sun and have something cold, shall we?"

"Thank you." Octavia enjoyed the clean smell of grass as she followed Jennie across the freshly mown lawn. "I hope Dick didn't shock you too much. I'm afraid I'm quite used to his strange appearance."

"Really," Jennie mused, more intrigued than ever.

Jennie called Effie to bring some iced tea and steered Octavia into the parlor. They made a peculiar pair, indeed. Jennie trim in her crisp white blouse, jodhpurs and riding boots, her usual outfit for target practice, and Octavia, roughened and worn-out, the portrait of poverty.

"Well?" Jennie asked.

Octavia ignored the sharp tone. "It's nothing you haven't heard before, Jennie. My family has all passed on, and I'm left with nothing to support me except my wits. I'm afraid I'm very much like one of those poor souls who lost everything during the war." She gestured at her coarse clothing. "If you think Dick and I look bad, you should see Glenwood."

I'd rather remember it as it was, Jennie thought. "But what happened to your writing career? Didn't you do a story about Gloucester?"

Octavia brightened a bit, then her eyes flickered shut as she recited in a faraway voice. "Standing grim in the shade of handsome trees and past recollections, a veritable Bleak House with its air of mystery and secrets."

"And collapsing ceilings," Jennie added with unexpected humor. "I lived in Gloucester before coming here and always wondered how anyone could let such a great house deteriorate like that."

"People don't always have a choice," Octavia said. She took a long breath. "In any case, my writing career eventually dried up and I had no other means to support myself."

"What happened with that expedition to the Antarctic? Last time we spoke of it you were still optimistic."

"Why, that's so long ago I'd forgotten all about it," Octavia marveled. "What on earth made you think of that?"

"We talked about it the afternoon we drove out to Cedar Grove. Remember those ghastly alphabet sisters?"

Octavia nodded. "Whatever happened to them?"

"All gone now. When the last one was buried, that old house just laid down and died, too. It's nothing but a pile of rubble, just like their empty lives."

Octavia frowned at Jennie's callous dismissal and changed the subject. "Nothing ever came of the Antarctic expedition, and I long ago wrote it off as just another lost dream."

"And what about Dick? Good heavens, Octavia! He looks a fright."

"Yes, I suppose he does." She fell silent as Effie brought the tea and then left. Octavia retained enough of her upbringing to know personal matters were never discussed before servants. "Dick also had a series of personal and financial setbacks, all quite serious. Surely you know about the accident that broke two fingers. He can no longer play the piano."

Jennie nodded, recalling his bandaged hand when Dick had asked her to vacate Glenwood. "What about that beautiful voice?"

"I'm afraid he lost that, too, and, well… that and some other unfortunate factors have driven him a little mad."

"A *little* mad?"

Octavia stiffened at the condescending tone. "When one's mind is that rickety, proper etiquette and personal grooming aren't the priorities they once were." Octavia drove her point home by sipping the tea with exaggerated correctness before continuing. "I assure you Dick's quite harmless, happy even. Happiest when he's alone in the woods—sometimes he disappears for weeks at a time."

"But where does he go? How does he survive?"

"He manages." Octavia shrugged. "He muttered something once about eating roots and berries. He comes home when he wants something more substantial."

"Good heavens!" Jennie gasped. Although grateful for such private neighbors, she was suddenly consumed with questions. "And what about you, Octavia? How do you manage?"

Octavia drew herself up. "I've turned into a farmer," she announced with dignity. "I have a vegetable garden and some livestock."

"Livestock at Glenwood?" Jennie was shocked again. She could scarcely imagine farm animals fouling the gracious lawn and decided the distinguished Reverend Dana was surely spinning in his grave. "No!"

"Chickens," Octavia explained, unruffled. "Goats and pigs."

"And you sell them?"

"When we can. Usually we eat them. In fact, I've developed quite a taste for smoked goat meat."

Jennie frowned as Octavia's high-pitched cackle skittered across the room. "I'm afraid I can't imagine."

"I suspect you could imagine it quite vividly if it was all you had to eat, Miss Jennie."

The unmistakable combination of formality and sarcasm made Jennie wish she hadn't invited this strange woman into her house. "Indeed," she managed.

Octavia was also uncomfortable. She hurriedly finished her tea and stood. "I really must get back to my chores. I just wanted to make sure Dick didn't get himself into trouble. We hear your gun all the time, and when I saw him headed in this direction I got worried."

Jennie rose, too. "A good thing. I would never have recognized the poor fool and might have shot him if you hadn't told me who he was. Why on earth didn't he identify himself?"

"He's having a 'there' day," Octavia said, trying to smooth a soiled, hopelessly wrinkled skirt.

"I beg your pardon?"

"It's nothing I can explain." Octavia nodded toward the pitcher. "Thank you for the tea, and thanks for not shooting my poor, lost Richard Dana. He's not much, but he's all I have."

When Jennie's eyebrows rose, Octavia chuckled. "Oh, there's nothing romantic between us, my dear. Never has been. He's just been kind enough to put a roof over my head, and I'd hate to see any harm befall him. Dick's a gentle creature, hardly responsible for what's happened to him."

"No. Of course not."

Jennie followed Octavia onto the porch and said good-bye, watching her neighbor square her shoulders and head home to another day of endless drudgery. Despite the heat, a discomfiting frisson rippled down Jennie's spine when she remembered that she and Octavia had once moved in the same smart set, enjoyed privileged childhoods and educations, worn gowns by Worth of Paris, and even socialized with the same U.S. President. Despite so much in common, their lives had taken wildly divergent paths, but, as was her habit, Jennie buried all disturbing thoughts and called Effie to help remove her boots. Cozy and safe, she sipped the last of her tea, stretched out on the settee and welcomed her daily nap.

She never once thought to throw a lifeline to her drowning neighbors.

15

OAKLAND, THE HOME Duncan shared with his widowed mother, Katherine Surget Minor, and spinster sister Mary Grace, was a raised planter's cottage with handsome proportions making it appear far smaller than it was. A hipped roof and a deep gallery, sixty feet long, helped cool the house, as did acres of the namesake oaks where Duncan had played as a boy. The interior boasted sixteen-foot ceilings, mahogany doors with silver hardware, a brocade-walled drawing room and mantles of pink and black marble. The fine furnishings came from Duncan's great-grandfather, Steven Minor, Governor of Spanish Natchez. The marriage of his grandson John to Katherine Surget merged two of the South's greatest cotton empires and, although most of the family's fortune was lost during the dark days of war and Reconstruction, Duncan's mother remained a wealthy woman. With such impeccable provenance, Oakland should have been a dazzling showcase for one of Natchez's oldest, most patrician families.

Fate decreed otherwise.

The house was in full decline, with rotting columns, a front porch dangerously close to collapse, and a sagging roof riddled with holes. Although the Minors ignored the need for repairs, their staff did not. When heavy rains unleashed a leak in the kitchen ceiling, Sally, the long-suffering family cook, had endured enough.

"I got a chicken in that oven, Miz Katherine!" She pointed at the wet stovetop. "How you expect me to cook with water falling on my head?" Katherine Minor aimed a plump chin toward the ceiling as a drop fell to the stovetop. She waited a few seconds until another fell, and then another, but said nothing. "Well!"

"I suppose you'll have to use an umbrella."

"You crazy!" Sally exploded. "It ain't supposed to rain inside the house!"

"It will have to suffice for now," Katherine sniffed.

"How you think I can handle an umbrella and a heavy roasting pan at the same time? The good Lord only give me two hands!"

"Then get one of the other girls to help. I'll speak to Mr. Duncan about the leak."

"Fat lotta good that'll do," Sally grumbled, angry at yet another inconvenience grandly ignored by the Minors. She wondered how long it would be before she took the advice of friends and sought work in a sane household.

"What did you say?" Katherine demanded.

"Nothing," Sally muttered. Katherine turned away from the cook's exasperated glare, but the cook's voice chased her down the hall. "You better hear me right now, Miz Katherine! I ain't gonna be cooking under no umbrellas!"

Katherine ignored the parting volley and went looking for her son. She knew exactly where to find him, as sure as she knew what he would be doing this time of day. She paused outside the library door and listened. Yes, there it was. Audible during lulls of the howling rainstorm was the scratch of Duncan's worn-out pen against paper. Katherine heaved aside one of the pocket doors and found him hunched over the desk. She knew who he was writing but ignored the letter as usual. After all, Jennie Merrill's name had not been mentioned since Katherine forbade her son to marry the girl over twenty years before.

Katherine was a squat, plump woman but there was power in that package and she haughtily drew herself up as she competed with the storm. "There's a leak in the kitchen, Duncan!" She called out again when her announcement was drowned by a thunderclap shaking the entire house. "Duncan!"

"Mmmm." He didn't look up.

Katherine moved closer, but not enough to peer over Duncan's shoulder. She didn't care to see what sort of rubbish he wrote to that immoral temptress scheming to steal the Minor money. That would happen, Katherine vowed, only over her dead body.

"Are you listening to me?"

He finished a line and turned around. "Yes, Mother. A leak in the kitchen. I heard."

"Well?"

"That's hardly news." He gave her a thin smile. "There are leaks all over the house."

"This one's different."

Duncan was unfazed. "When the one in my bedroom got bad I moved my bed."

"Well, we can hardly move the stove!" Katherine snapped. "What's more, I'm afraid Sally will quit if it's not fixed. As it is, she'll have to use an umbrella."

Duncan rarely showed a sense of humor, especially around his mother, but he chuckled at the image of Sally cooking under an umbrella. Katherine was not amused.

"This is serious, son. Kindly tell me what you plan to do about it."

"Get it repaired, I suppose."

Duncan resumed writing, hoping to avoid one of his mother's trademark tirades. His sister had also been difficult that stormy day, and he was in no mood for further confrontation. He was not a man who liked ripples in his life, but his mother was not about to let him get off so lightly.

"And when might that be?"

"Surely you don't expect me to climb up on the roof in the middle of this storm."

"Don't be insolent!"

Duncan sighed heavily and withdrew. "I'm not being insolent, Mother. Now may I please finish what I'm doing?"

"Losing the family cook is far more important than that nonsense," Katherine insisted.

Knowingly or not, they both danced around the word "letter."

"Oh, don't waste your time, Mother," Mary Grace said from a far corner of the library. Katherine had not noticed her daughter until now, doubled up before the fireplace with a book propped against her knees. A pale, drawn woman of forty-six, Mary Grace Minor looked the quintessential spinster. A nasal, high-pitched voice corroborated the unfortunate image as she rose, smoothed her skirts and sailed toward her brother, girded for verbal battle. "Why try to goad Duncan to any sort of action? The whole town knows he doesn't care if the house comes down around our ears. For that matter, neither do you."

"I won't have you speaking to me in that tone," Katherine warned. "Someone might think you ill-bred."

"At least ill-bred people have enough sense to come in out of the rain."

Katherine was furious. "Mary Grace Minor!"

Mary Grace chuckled mischievously and moved behind Duncan, who was still writing away. As she expected, he slipped the wet page into a drawer and closed it. Like her mother, she ignored it and focused instead on other things.

"While we're on the subject of repairs, Mother dear, have you had a good look at the front porch? Those steps are so rickety someone could fall through and break their neck."

"When was the last time you used the front porch, Mary Grace?" Katherine countered. "When have any of us used it for that matter?"

"We could if it wasn't dangerous!" Mary Grace shot back.

Ignoring the claim, Katherine said, "I see no point in spending perfectly good money when we can manage quite well with the back door. Waste not, want not." She turned back to Duncan. "But it should be plain even to you that we can't manage without a cook and a kitchen."

"I already said I'd take care of it," Duncan muttered.

He wanted nothing more than to finish his letter to Jennie and flee to the haven of Glenburnie. He slipped a hand into his waistcoat pocket and retrieved his Spanish watch. It had belonged to his great-grandfather when he was governor, and Duncan always marveled at its considerable heft. The casing was pure gold, an ornate design with filigree around the face and rubies for numerals. A flick of his thumb popped it open and he checked the time. 4:28 PM. Over three hours before he could escape these worrisome, nagging mares. An ache shot down his back as his mother's voice rose again.

"I'd just like to see more action and less talk!"

"All right, Mother," he sighed. "I said I'd tend to it, didn't I?"

Duncan hoped that would end the discussion, but Katherine was more dogged than usual. "You'd better do something and do it soon. I don't know the first thing about talking to roofing people and neither does Mary Grace." Duncan seethed silently as his mother exchanged one familiar diatribe for another. "I just wish you'd start acting like the head of the household. I hated it when your father went off to New York after the war and left me to run the plantations. It was all I could do to hold on to Palo Alto and Carthage, what with you and your sister being sick all the time. I had to be father and mother to you both and it's absolutely worn me to the bone." Katherine couldn't imagine that her children were even wearier of the past than she. "Once you became a man I assumed you'd take over some of the burden, but these days I can't even drag you away from that old secretary."

When Duncan muttered something inaudible, Katherine demanded that he repeat himself, but before he could respond, Mary Grace grabbed the conversational gauntlet.

"There are other reasons for you to fix things," his sister insisted, shifting the topic to more tangible dilemmas. "I've been giving the situation some serious thought and decided I want to start entertaining again. In the spring, perhaps."

It was hardly the first time Duncan had heard that tired pretense tied to the argument over making repairs to Oakland. Both had been ongoing for years, arguments so belabored that they were numbing.

"Why, certainly, your highness!"

The sarcasm scraped his sister's patience. "Oh, for heaven's sake stop being such a milquetoast and do something! Mother's right. You're supposed to be head of the family and you're nothing but a lay-about. I've never known anyone with more excuses for procrastinating!"

"Or less spine!" added his mother.

Duncan abandoned hope of completing his letter and looked out the rain-specked window. How he wished these noisome women would find something else to argue about, or at least put a new twist to old complaints. He closed his eyes for a moment and took a deep breath before turning toward his sister with a rare show of spunk.

"Mother and I don't care anything about entertaining or having friends over. Why should you be any different?"

Thoroughly piqued, Mary Grace lashed back. "Of course you don't care about entertaining. You don't have any friends left because you ignored them and spent all your time playing with real estate and horses and…"

"And what?" Duncan pressed, fueled by his sister's rage.

"Oh, never mind." Although Mary Grace retreated, she longed to verbalize her loathing and address the unthinkable, yearned to accuse her brother of not caring if his bed had to be moved since he never slept in it. Just once she wanted to drag Jennie Merrill into the ongoing family feud, but a glance at her mother earned a sharp, mute warning. Katherine Minor missed nothing.

Mary Grace carefully regrouped. "I only want to see my friends again and have some fun. I want what any woman of my position deserves." She glared at her brother as she delivered a final poisonous volley. "Any respectable woman, that is."

If Duncan recognized the reference to Jennie, he revealed nothing. He cleared his throat and made another effort to end the discussion. "I'll go into town tomorrow and inquire about the cost of some new shingles."

The caterwauling ended when Sally angrily announced another leak in the kitchen ceiling. Duncan went to investigate and decided his best escape route from the harpies in the library was holding an umbrella while Sallie finished preparing supper. The meal was eaten in silence with Duncan glancing repeatedly at his watch and thinking eight o'clock would never arrive. He even welcomed the thought of riding to Glenburnie in the driving rain, but by the time he saddled his horse at 7:55, the storm had blown east toward Jackson and left a full moon in its wake. When he swung into the saddle at eight, the rain had ended altogether, but he protected himself from dripping branches with the ubiquitous umbrella. At his slow pace, the journey took exactly forty-five minutes, business as usual until Duncan rode up the gentle rise to Glenburnie Manor and saw Jennie pacing the gallery.

"Good evening, dearest!" he called. He folded his umbrella, dismounted and tossed the reins aside, knowing his old mare would not stray from the front lawn. He frowned when he met silence instead of his usual warm welcome. "Jennie? What is it?"

She pointed angrily at the lawn where a gray silhouette made an unnatural bump on the grass. "Just look at that!"

Duncan squinted in the dark, trying to make out the mysterious shape. "What in the world is that?"

"One of those Glenwood goats," Jennie snapped. "I already told Octavia I didn't want those beasts wandering over here, but about an hour ago I caught one chewing up my azaleas. Look, Duncan! Right by the porte-cochère! You know how much I've babied my azaleas to get them to grow in that tricky spot." Jennie was as fiercely protective of her beautiful gardens and manicured hedges as she was proud of them. "I tried to shoo the thing away and when it wouldn't budge, I shot it!"

Duncan chuckled. "Looks like all that target practice paid off."

"It most certainly did!" Jennie declared proudly. "I dropped the nasty thing with a single bullet to the head."

Duncan laughed again and pulled her close. "My own little Annie Oakley."

"Yes, indeed!" Jennie beamed. She looked toward the corpse and wrinkled her nose. "Goats are such vile things. That one stinks to high heavens."

Duncan frowned. "We can't leave it there all night."

"We have no choice, dear. That's caretaker's work, and Hatcher is away visiting relatives. He'll be back tomorrow and can deal with it then."

"I'm afraid all sorts of little critters will take a bite out of it before morning."

Jennie shrugged. "Well, there's nothing I can do about it now, so come along inside. Effie made some cookies this afternoon, and I could use one about now. We'll have some tea, too."

"That sounds wonderful."

Duncan chuckled again when he saw Jennie's pistol on the dining table, as permanent a fixture as the coal-oil lamp with the blue shade and a vase of freshly cut flowers. They had barely settled in the parlor when they heard an angry shout.

"Jennie Merrill!"

"Now what?" Jennie bustled into the dining room, grabbed her gun and headed outside with Duncan close behind. "Who's there?" she demanded, pointing the pistol toward the porte-cochère. "Identify yourself or I'll shoot!"

"Octavia Dockery!" came the sharp reply. Shaking with rage, Octavia stomped onto the veranda and jerked her head toward the moonlit corpse. "What the devil have you done to my poor goat?"

"What do you think I did?" Jennie answered coolly. "It ate my flowers so I shot it."

"Since when do you murder animals for doing what comes naturally?" Octavia demanded.

"When they turn into trespassers and destroy private property! I warned you about this, Octavia. Several times, in fact. And don't tell me you didn't get my letters."

"Oh, I got them alright," Octavia snorted, "but I told myself that no good Christian woman would harm one of God's helpless creatures."

"It certainly wasn't helpless when it devoured my azaleas!"

A querulous silence fell between the women, all pretense at manners and propriety disintegrating as both settled firmly into their roles as wronged parties. Thinking to act as mediator, Duncan stepped forward but held his tongue at the threat of Jennie's notorious temper. He'd felt its potent sting all too often, and, having had enough of quarrelsome women for one day, he retreated to the shadows where he silently watched and waited.

Jennie was almost as unnerved by Octavia's appearance as the brewing feud. Ten long years had passed since the afternoon she almost shot Dick Dana, ten long years of backbreaking work that had set Octavia's lips in a line of bitter resignation. Deep wrinkles wracked the once ravishing face, and the auburn hair was mostly gray. It was Octavia's hands that Jennie found the most shocking, their softness and grace destroyed by thick calluses and dirty, broken fingernails. The difference between then and now was wrenching, but an even harsher reality gripped Jennie. Both were fifty-two, but Octavia looked a decade older.

"All I can say is that this had better not happen again," Octavia declared, "or there will be hell to pay."

"Spoken like a true Christian woman!" Jennie shot back.

Octavia summoned a retort, reconsidered and attempted instead to reason. "Try to understand something, Jennie. You may consider it sport to shoot my goats, but these animals are all that stands between Dick and myself and starvation."

"And I'm telling you for the last time that you'd better keep your marauding livestock off my property or pay the consequences. That No Admittance sign at my front gate applies to animals as well as people. And that crazy Dick Dana, too!"

Octavia's dark eyes narrowed angrily. Jennie had seen the face of raw hatred before and was grateful for her gun.

"You haven't heard the last of this, Jennie Merrill," Octavia snarled. "Not by a long shot."

"We'll see," Jennie said cavalierly. "Now get off my land and stay off."

Octavia trembled with righteous rage. "Oh, I'll leave alright and I'll take my property with me!"

"What?!"

"You heard me!"

Jennie looked at Duncan. "Well, did you ever!"

Both watched Octavia stride defiantly across the lawn, seize the dead goat by its hind legs and drag it toward Glenwood. Long years of survival had made her surprisingly strong, and she maintained steady progress until she disappeared into the dark woods. Jennie shook her head.

"What a ghastly creature Octavia Dockery has become! And to think I once admired and respected her. I swear I'd just as soon shoot her as those infernal goats!" Duncan said nothing as Jennie steered him back inside to the dining table and smiled as though nothing untoward had happened. "Now then.

I've planned a special Halloween entertainment for us and I'm not letting anyone ruin it."

"Why, I'd completely forgotten it was Halloween," Duncan said, amazed as always by Jennie's capacity for glossing over unpleasantness.

"Well, I didn't. And as soon as we finish our tea and cookies, we'll go outside and..." She cocked her head at the crunch of gravel. "*Now* what does that harpy want!"

"I suppose it might be a trick-or-treater," Duncan offered.

"Just how large must I make those No Trespassing signs?" Jennie seethed, mood souring as she grabbed her gun again and headed back onto the porch. She peered into the moonlight, anticipating, even welcoming another confrontation with Octavia. Instead she saw a battered buggy rising up the drive. She lowered the gun to her side, not threatening but an obvious presence as the coach drew up and stopped.

"Good evening, Miss Merrill!"

The voice was vaguely familiar, but she could not identify it. "Do I know you, sir?"

"Stephen Holmes!" he called, stepping from the buggy, hat in hand.

Jennie squinted into the darkness beneath the porte-cochère. Her eyes were not what they once were, nor was her memory. "Who?"

"Your favorite newspaper reporter, I daresay, and partner in crime." Holmes reached the top step and emerged into the window glow. "Remember me?"

Jennie nodded as recognition dawned. "It's been a long time, Mr. Holmes."

"Twenty-four years to be exact," he grinned. "I'm here visiting my mother and tending to some family business. I tried to call but you have no telephone. I hope I've not come at an inconvenient time."

"I'm afraid you have," Jennie said coolly. "We've just had a most unpleasant incident with our next door neighbor."

Holmes jerked his head toward Glenwood. "Surely you don't mean Octavia Dockery?"

Jennie stiffened. "That's exactly who I mean."

"Why, if that poor soul is as helpless as I hear..."

"Her goats are hardly helpless, Mr. Holmes," Jennie said, waving the gun toward her ravaged azaleas. "Especially when they're hungry."

Hoping to lighten the moment, Holmes eyed the gun. "My goodness! Were they armed?"

Jennie ignored the joke and indicated Duncan looming behind her. "Perhaps you remember Mr. Minor."

"I do indeed," Holmes said, flashing a burlesque grin. "How are you, sir?"

Duncan muttered the most meager of pleasantries. Jennie was nearly as glacial, but Holmes wouldn't be frozen out so easily.

He nodded toward two rocking chairs. "Might we talk a few minutes, Miss Merrill?"

Her response was as blunt as it was swift. "I no longer receive callers, Mr. Holmes."

"Well, I saw that No Trespassing sign, but I figured it didn't matter since we were old friends." He grinned triumphantly when a German shepherd bounded across the yard and up the stairs to offer his furry head for scratching. "Your ferocious watchdog here doesn't seem to mind."

"Come here, Apollo!" Jennie snapped, infuriated when the dog ignored her command. "Apollo!"

Holmes gave the dog a good scratch before steering it away. Then, to jar Jennie's memory, he dropped his time bomb. "Miss Merrill, surely you haven't forgotten about our encounter with Paddy O'Brien."

Jennie grabbed Apollo's collar and shoved him toward Duncan. "Take him inside, Duncan. And fetch Mr. Holmes a cookie."

While Duncan did her bidding, Holmes eyed Jennie, seeking

vestiges of the young woman he remembered. It distressed him to come up lacking and receive such indifference from someone whose life he once saved.

"Thank you, Duncan," Jennie said when he delivered a single cookie. Her nod toward the door was one of dismissal, and Duncan quietly disappeared. Alone with Holmes, Jennie made a rare confidence. "Paddy O'Brien is the one memory I've never been able to vanquish. It troubles me to this day."

"Me, too," Holmes confessed. "That story launched me on the road to success, but we need not discuss it further."

Jennie eyed him cautiously, as though searching for a conversational thread with a shy stranger. "What would you speak of then?"

"Nothing in particular. I was just curious to see an old friend."

"I'm afraid your old friend doesn't exist any more." To her surprise, and his, Jennie descended the steps and leaned against his buggy. The horse snorted and shook his mane. "That poor girl disappeared back in ninety-five."

Holmes knew something of Jennie's history and notorious reclusiveness from his sister Margaret but played innocent. "I'm afraid I don't understand."

Jennie wasn't fooled. "If you know about Octavia Dockery's situation, I'm sure you know I was evicted from Elms Court by my own family. My soul had been badly bruised by what happened that terrible day in The Bend, Mr. Holmes, and this latest turn of events was almost more than I could bear."

He followed her down the steps. "Please call me Stephen."

She nodded and fell silent a moment before continuing. "I returned to Natchez to lick my wounds, as they say, and was just gaining strength when I was betrayed by my entire family. Were it not for Mr. Minor, I don't know where I would be." She looked toward the house, easily finding Duncan's watchful silhouette in the parlor window. "I wonder sometimes if I might have ended up like Julia Nutt. Remember her?"

"I do indeed."

"She died, you know, back in ninety-seven. She was still penniless and still living in that huge unfinished house." Jennie took a deep breath and released a ragged sigh. "But she fought to the end and I admire her for that. Deeply."

Holmes had a thousand questions but kept still lest he snap the fragile conversational web spinning between them. After a long pause, Jennie finally continued.

"I can guess what people are saying, Stephen. The same things they always say about people who secede from society and seek to live apart. At first it bothered me, but I long ago ceased caring. My world is Glenburnie now and there's room in it for only one other person." She pointed with her forehead. "That man watching us from the window there. He's all I need."

"I'm happy for you."

She considered the familiarity, frowned, then smiled just slightly. "Funny. That's something I never expected to hear again. A well-wishing."

"I meant it."

"I believe you." She paused again, rattling down cobwebbed corridors of memory. "The afternoon we said good-bye in New York I invited you to Elms Court, remember?"

"Very clearly."

"I also promised an interview. People may think I do strange things, but breaking promises is not one of them. Obviously, I can no longer invite you to Elms Court, but please consider this conversation to be your long-awaited interview. It's the best I can manage and certainly the most I've said to anyone besides Duncan in years." She sighed tiredly. "If I live to be a hundred, I'll never know why I didn't send you away tonight. Like I do everyone else."

"Perhaps you care about people more than you know," Holmes ventured. He recognized his error instantly as the mask that had ever so slightly dropped wrenched back into place.

"I meant what I said about that girl being dead, Mr. Holmes."

"A rather cruel fate," Holmes said.

Jennie's soft gaze steeled as she plumbed her memory. "How did Henry James put it? 'I know something about cruelty. I was taught by experts.'"

"*Washington Square?*"

She nodded. "I always identified with his poor heroine, and not just because we lived on the same famous square." Holmes pulled something from his pocket and extended his palm. The St. Christopher medal gleamed dully in the moonlight. "Goodness, I'd forgotten about that!"

"I've carried it since the day you gave it to me, and it's protected me well."

"I'm glad," Jennie said. Something rose to her lips but did not materialize. "And now I really must go inside."

Holmes followed her to the foot of the stairs. "I know I was an intruder tonight, and I apologize. I also have a confession to make."

She turned slowly. "Oh?"

"I came here tonight just to see if the rumors about you were true."

"I suspected as much," she said. "Were they?"

"Not for me. You'll always be that sweet, courageous woman leading me into the slums of New York." Holmes climbed into the carriage and blew her a kiss. "Goodnight, Miss Jennie."

Jennie lingered on the veranda, watching until darkness swallowed her visitor. Only when he was gone did she murmur to the night. "Goodbye, Stephen."

Duncan moved to the door the moment Holmes drove away, opening it so Apollo could race into the woods. He touched Jennie's arm.

"What did that reporter have to say?"

"Oh, nothing of consequence," Jennie said lightly. She surprised Duncan by standing on her tiptoes and giving him a kiss. "Now then. When I said no one was going to ruin my evening I meant it. But I'll need your help."

"Whatever you say, dearest."

Per her instructions, Duncan lit a series of single tapers and candelabra and stationed them strategically along the veranda and steps. Then he sat and waited. After almost half an hour, Jennie appeared in a costume saved from a ball she had attended as a belle, a reminder of her days at the Court of St. James. It was a diaphanous, Greek creation that blazed silver as she hummed sweetly and danced across the veranda and onto the moonlit lawn. A multitude of stars sparkled against a cobalt sky, and almost as many fireflies gleamed around her. Once again, as she had so many times before, Jennie created magic for Duncan and swept him into a world of private, slightly mad reverie obliterating everything except her. As he watched her dart and swoop through the rain-soaked grass, he wondered how much longer the illusion could last. They had been together twenty-four years, almost a quarter of a century.

Time was slipping away.

16

IT TOOK OCTAVIA the better part of an hour to drag the heavy billy goat through the woods and ravines dividing Glenburnie Manor from Glenwood and stash it in the shed where it would keep safely until morning. It seemed one chore always led to another, and a few minutes later she lugged the mattress from her four-poster bed and wearily shoved it in a corner. When she couldn't dislodge the much heavier bed-springs, she called down the hall.

"Please come in here, Dick! I need your help!"

The skittish, barefoot soul peeking into her bedroom would have terrified most people, but Octavia had long ago numbed herself to the shock. Dick's hair now reached his shoulders, matted and unkempt, and a bushy beard trailed across his scrawny chest. For reasons known only to his demons, he had taken to wearing a gunnysack, gouging holes for his head and arms. Personal hygiene had evaporated along with grooming,

and he reeked of stale sweat and worse. Octavia scarcely noticed as they dragged the bedsprings downstairs.

"We've got a lot of fresh goat meat to smoke and I need a
bigger grill," she explained. "Hear me?"

Dick nodded and helped her situate the springs on the
back porch. As they pushed and positioned them, the rotten
floor sagged hard with the added weight and one of the pillars
crackled and crashed free, narrowly missing one of Dick's nineteen cats. He and the cat screeched and fled into the house, but
Octavia merely ignored this latest calamity. She kicked the collapsed column off the porch, repositioned the springs and went
back inside. As she suspected, Dick had disappeared. These
days the slightest thing made him flee into the forests around
Glenwood and nearby Duncan Park. She repeatedly warned
him not to stray too far. Although he cut a frightening figure as
the "Wild Man of Natchez"—as she had earned notoriety as
the "Goat Woman"—it was best to stay close to home.

Working alone as usual, Octavia went about fashioning a
new bed. She fetched chairs and a small chest from downstairs
and arranged them to support her mattress. She was so thoroughly exhausted, as well as distressed by the slaughter of her
biggest goat, that she collapsed atop the improvised bed and
immediately fell asleep.

Outside her window, Dick began his nightly patrol of the
grounds. Consumed by nervous euphoria, he reveled in the
dither of insects and rustling animals as he ventured further
into the forest. He swooped down into the deep ravine dividing Glenwood from Glenburnie Manor, moving just close
enough to glimpse Jennie Merrill's neatly clipped hedgerows.
The moon was playing hide-and-seek, but Dick knew his territory so well he easily envisioned what he couldn't actually see.
Sometimes the two merged, fact and fancy, but he was no longer troubled by not knowing the difference.

He stared with fascination when he saw something so unusual it lured him into forbidden territory. He slithered onto

the ground and stealthily inched along, first behind the hedge-rows and then a thicket of azaleas. As he craned his neck for a better look, he dimly remembered one of Octavia's goats had been shot for eating these very bushes. Candles flickered across the lawn, throwing an eerie glow onto a figure weaving grace-fully among them, first in one direction, then another. It took him a few minutes to determine it was Miss Jennie in some kind of costume and that she was dancing. Another long look revealed Duncan Minor sitting on the porch, hypnotized by the performance.

For a few moments Dick was hypnotized, too. Then his mind cleared and he dared move close enough to hear Jennie's humming. It was a song he half-remembered, and he hummed along very softly as he struggled to conjure the lyrics. When they refused to come, his euphoria evaporated and he crawled back to his forest sanctuary, where he leapt to his feet and tore into the night. He always felt freest in flight and now he followed a vague trail through pine forests and oak groves and endless curtains of Spanish moss. He loved the ephemeral gray moss and had gathered enough of it to make himself a little mattress concealed in a bower where two massive live oaks merged into a natural dais. This mossy tree house was a private retreat from a world he no longer comprehended, one filled with half-remembered faces, for-gotten names and faded etudes. Memories of his poor, lost Amelia were the strongest, and whenever her snowy visage arose, Dick rushed here to the one refuge where he could sleep free of bad dreams.

He slowed to a trot before pausing to sniff the air as he ap-proached his secret sanctuary. He scratched his raggedy beard, eyes blinking with a wariness often characteristic of the barmy, until he found cause for alarm. The shadows at the feet of the great, moon-soaked oaks were unfamiliar, and as he got closer, almost close enough to touch them, the confusing chiaroscuro erupted.

"There he is, boys!"

"It's the Wild Man of Natchez!"

"Let's get him!"

Dick froze for just a moment before whirling and fleeing in terror. He tore back down the path, frantic to put distance between himself and his pursuers. Five men in dime-store Halloween costumes tried to catch up but fell behind as Dick desperately followed one of his invisible trails. For an emaciated man of forty-six, he led them a good chase until he cleared the dense forest and emerged onto the open grounds of Glenwood. There the pack closed in, bloodthirsty hounds after a defenseless deer.

Dick was some fifty yards from the house when he found his voice. The screech of raw fear bursting from his thin chest thrilled his tormentors and awoke Octavia. It was not the first time she had heard that primeval plea, and she hastily drew a wrapper around herself and slipped onto the second-floor gallery. She watched in horror as Dick zigzagged crazily across the lawn while masked men narrowed the gap. Thirty yards. Twenty. Ten. They were perhaps fifteen feet away when Dick realized he'd never make it to the house and did just what the gang wanted.

He climbed a tree!

"Look at that!" one of them cried. "Crazy old fruitcake climbs just like a monkey."

"Wonder how long he can stay up there?"

Another rowdy pulled a flask from his pocket, took a swig and passed it around to his drunken pals. "Let's hang around a while and find out."

"Go on up, Wild Man!"

Octavia watched helplessly as Dick scrambled higher, losing his grip and almost falling when the oak's weaker, more slender branches refused his weight. The townies whistled and cheered when he caught himself, but when they called for Dick to venture higher Octavia was galvanized to rip a chunk of wood from the rotten railing and wave it in the air. She shouted as loud as she could, praying her shadowy figure looked menacing in the moonlight.

"Get off our land or I'll shoot!"

"Jesus!" someone gasped. "It's the Goat Woman!"

"And she's got a gun!"

"Let's get the hell out of here!"

Octavia's bluff worked and she watched, relieved, as the drunken band hurriedly dispersed. Once they were gone, she rushed onto the lawn and begged Dick to come down. "It's all right!" she called. "They're gone!" She squinted into the dark tree but found him only by noise as he tripped from one branch to another. "Dick? Can you hear me? It's Octavia!"

After a long moment, Octavia heard a choked whisper. "You sure they're gone?"

"They're gone," she repeated again, and again. "Gone. Gone." Octavia employed a mantra of commands mixed with a tone of authority, often successful if Dick swooned deep into a "there" day. "Come on down now. Be careful. Be careful."

Another few minutes and the oak branches creaked and swayed as Dick began his slow descent. Octavia hovered at the foot of the tree, heart racing as he came into view. He swung from the last branch and dropped to the dewy ground with a light thud.

"Are you all right, Dick?"

He peered into the night, still wary. "They're gone?"

"They're gone. Now come on into the house and you'll be safe."

Octavia seldom touched Dick but now took his hand as one would a child, and led him onto the front veranda. He followed obediently, still trembling with fear. Octavia shook, too, not from fear but a hatred of human cruelty. She could no more understand men making sport of helpless creatures like Dick Dana than understand why Jennie Merrill could callously shoot a defenseless goat. The world grew more intolerable by the day, but she steadied herself one more time and steered her charge onto the porch. A dozing nanny goat bleated at the intrusion and clip-clopped off the porch, her newborn kid toddling after. Dick tenderly scooped it in his arms and carried it up to his bedroom, where Octavia hoped he might find peace. She wearily followed and told him goodnight before climbing back into her makeshift bed.

Dawn, as always, came much too soon.

OCTAVIA'S BONES ACHED miserably when she awoke, the result of her heavy late-night labor, Dick's crisis, and the uncomfortable new bed. She lay still for a moment, mentally weighing her list of things to do. After tending the animals, she would have to butcher and dress the dead billy goat, smoke what meat she could and salt away the rest. Then there would be the nearly three-mile walk out Kingston Pike for water at Duncan Park, followed by work in the vegetable garden. She desperately wished Dick could help, but these days she could not trust him with even the simplest chores. The last time she sent him for water, he didn't return for three days and had lost their precious tin.

It was two in the afternoon before Octavia found time to fetch water. She despised venturing from the haven of Glenwood because of the curious stares and occasional catcalls from people passing on the highway. Once in a while some sympathetic soul offered a ride, but most sped by, eager to tell someone they had actually seen the crazy old Goat Woman. Because she tried to remain as inconspicuous as possible, Octavia never looked up when a carriage or automobile approached and was always on guard if one slowed or stopped. On that particular afternoon, she had barely slipped through the ramshackle gates when she heard carriage wheels crunching to a halt and someone calling her name. Deciding the voice sounded harmless, she turned toward a plump man in his fifties, much too smartly dressed for his shabby buggy. He smiled and waved, but with tins in each hand Octavia could only nod and watch him approach.

"I'm sorry if I startled you, Miss Dockery." He doffed his derby. "It's Stephen Holmes."

"Do I know you, sir?" she asked warily.

"From our days in New York, I hope. I'm a newspaper reporter. I once did a story on the Warren Antarctica Expedition for the *New York Sun* and interviewed all its members." He smiled again. "You included."

"Oh?" Octavia frowned. She recalled the interview but not the man. "I'm afraid I don't remember you, sir."

"It doesn't matter," Holmes offered. "In any case, I was sorry to learn the expedition never materialized."

"So was I." She shrugged. "Obviously we wasted our time with that proposition."

Holmes took quick inventory of this poor creature, so radically different from the bright, vibrant woman he remembered from New York. He knew the less said about the old days the better. "You look as though you could use a lift."

"I'm going for water in Duncan Park." When his eyebrows rose, she added, "The cisterns at Glenwood collapsed years ago."

"The park is right on my way." Holmes popped the derby back on his head and climbed down from the buggy. He reached for the water tins. "May I?"

"Why, yes. Thank you." Octavia stepped aside while he tucked the tins away.

"There now." He moved a small yellow bouquet from the passenger's seat and brushed away some loose petals before offering his arm. "Shall we go?"

Octavia was flooded with emotion as he helped her into the buggy. She couldn't remember the last time she held a gentleman's arm, much less was treated like a lady. She appreciated the gesture but remained suspicious. "How did you know who I was, Mr. Holmes?"

"I grew up here in Natchez and came down last week to visit family and friends." He climbed in beside her, a little breathless as he flapped the reins and the buggy lurched forward. "It seems you're something of a local celebrity, so when I saw you at the gates of Glenwood..."

Octavia was instantly rankled. "So you've heard about the Goat Woman and the Wild Man, eh?"

"I sympathize with your difficult circumstances and assure you I mean no offense, Miss Dockery." She snorted and looked away. "You do believe me, don't you?"

Octavia considered his conciliatory tone and changed her mind. "Oddly enough I do. I only hope you're not looking to write some sort of horrid exposé."

"Absolutely not," Holmes assured her. "I'm just happy to be of service."

"You're very kind." Octavia cautiously reemerged from her shell. "Which is more than I can say about most people."

"You mean Jennie Merrill?"

"How on earth did you know who I meant?"

"I dropped by last night to pay a little social call. She mentioned some unpleasantness with you and Dick." Like all seasoned reporters, Holmes wanted both sides of the story.

"Only me. Dick had nothing to do with it."

"May I ask what it was?"

"She shot one of our goats after it wandered onto her property. When I confronted her, things turned unpleasant. She doesn't seem to care that those animals are the only things between us and starvation. If I have to fight for them, I will." Octavia grunted. "She's not the only one who can use a gun. My father the general took me hunting many times."

"I have to admit I was surprised by the No Trespassing sign. When I knew her some years ago, she was a sweet, charming little thing."

"I could say the same thing about myself... I'm afraid we've both changed," Octavia muttered. They rode in silence until one of her long dormant memories flickered and then blazed. "Wait a minute, Mr. Holmes! Didn't you write the story about Jennie and that poor Irishman who killed his whole family?"

Yes, I did," Holmes replied.

"Now I remember you."

"Favorably, I hope?"

Octavia nodded. "As I recall, it was an excellent story that reaped a great deal of worthy attention. As one who also aspired to good writing, I admire that."

"Thank you."

Encouraged by her improved spirits, Holmes was bursting with questions, but because Octavia struck an empathetic chord he shunned issues that might embarrass or discomfit her. There was, after all, just one exceptional thing about her story of reduced circumstances: Very few had fallen so far from such vertiginous heights.

As they approached Duncan Park, Holmes remembered the paper cone of chrysanthemums at his feet. He plucked a single blossom and held it out to Octavia. "Regardless of our changed circumstances, Miss Dockery, I believe it's still acceptable for a gentleman to offer a flower to a lady."

"Indeed, it is." The unforeseen gesture caused Octavia to blink away tears and muster a grateful smile. "And yellow is my favorite color."

"I'd give you the entire bouquet, but they're for my father's grave in Natchez Cemetery."

"How thoughtful."

"Today is All Saint's Day, and since I'm rarely in Natchez I thought I should take advantage of a day honoring the dead. My father was killed at Shiloh, you see, and— Is something wrong, Miss Dockery?"

Octavia looked anguished. "I'm about to ask you for a favor, Mr. Holmes. If it's inconvenient, please tell me so."

"What is it?"

"Might I ride to the cemetery with you? My father is buried

there, too, and I haven't visited his grave in many years. He was also in the war."

"I'd be honored." Holmes smiled and drew the coach up by one of Duncan Park's drinking fountains. "Let me fill your tins and we'll be off."

"Thank you."

Octavia's precious water sloshed in the tins as Holmes's coach bounced north along Cemetery Road to the stone walls and iron gates of Natchez Cemetery. Established in 1822, it was a lofty expanse with magnificent views of the Mississippi River and groves of mature live oaks, cedar and cypress and camellia bushes big as trees. Octavia pointed past an explosion of red and pink blossoms toward the site reserved for Confederate dead.

"Daddy's right over there." She frowned at the scattering of tree limbs and leaves. "It looks as if they haven't cleaned up after the last storm."

"That's what All Saint's Day is for." Holmes nodded at the dozen or so people weeding and sweeping and collecting wind-tossed debris. "Tending the dead."

He and Octavia joined in and soon tidied the gravesites of Jonathon Holmes and Thomas P. Dockery. Holmes's mother had given him a broom for the occasion, and, after Octavia worked so diligently, he insisted upon sharing his bouquet. He was pleased when she didn't refuse.

"I think our fathers would approve, don't you, Miss Dockery?"

"I do indeed," she said, after arranging flowers on both graves. She stepped back and nodded with satisfaction. "There!"

"I must admit I didn't recall your father was a general," he added, realizing her provenance was even grander than he thought. "I'm most impressed."

"But your father died in combat," she said, quickly shifting attention away from lost family glory. She drew her tattered sweater closer as skies clouded over and cool wind blasted up and over the bluff. "I'm afraid we're losing the sunshine, Mr. Holmes."

"And I've lost all track of time, as well," he apologized. "I'll try to get you home before it gets cold."

"You're most thoughtful," Octavia smiled, sorry to see the end of her first pleasure outing in over a decade. When she saw his solicitous look, she added, "Thank you, sir."

On the drive back, the two engaged in small talk, leading Holmes to mention the war in Europe. "Since the *Lusitania* was sunk, I don't see how the United States can stay out of the fray, especially after Germany announced unrestricted submarine action. As that will surely include American ships, I look for a declaration of war any day."

Octavia gave him a blank look. "I'm afraid I've been too pre-occupied with the situation at Glenwood to know much about war. Indeed, this is the first I've heard of it."

Such statements revealed the extent of Octavia's isolation, and once more Holmes felt pity. "It's nothing that need concern you. I was just making conversation."

Octavia shook her head. "Believe me, Mr. Holmes, there was a time when I loved discussing politics and the arts. Literature. Theater. Music. It was those passions that almost took me to Antarctica. These days, of course, my war for survival must take precedence over war overseas. I fear you're talking to a lady who no longer has opinions, and how sad is that?"

"Well, I..."

She waved an arm and pointed. "Over there, Mr. Holmes! The gates are so overgrown they're easily missed." Holmes reined the horse and jumped down to open the gates, but Octavia insisted, "I'll walk from here."

"Those tins are heavy, Miss Dockery. Please let me drive you to the house."

"I assure you I'm used to the weight, Mr. Holmes." Octavia climbed down, retrieved her water and slipped between the gates. "Besides, Glenwood has not entertained visitors in over fifteen years. I think it would be unwise to begin anew."

"Are you sure?" Holmes asked, more curious than ever about what lay beyond the dilapidated gates.

"Quite sure. Thank you for the trip to the cemetery and Duncan Park. It's been a special afternoon, Mr. Holmes, but even the poor old Goat Woman needs her privacy." She smiled. "Good afternoon, sir."

17

DUNCAN CHOSE DINNERTIME for a most unexpected announcement. "I've ordered new shingles for the house. They'll be delivered some time this week."

"Why, Duncan!" his mother gasped, assuming her request for repairs would go ignored like all the others. "That's wonderful."

Mary Grace was less than impressed. "It's only been two years since the emergency patchwork over the kitchen, brother dear. What's the rush?"

Duncan grandly ignored her usual sarcasm. "I told you I'd get around to it. I'm simply a man who enjoys taking his time."

"That's an understatement, if I ever heard one." Mary Grace snickered. "But it certainly explains why you took so long to sell that cotton."

Her barb earned Mary Grace a murderous glare as she referred to a recent incident that had infuriated her, bemused

Katherine and regaled the whole town. Some months ago, Duncan bought and stored a large amount of cotton and waited for the market to improve before reselling it. Such speculation was common enough, but Duncan's reaction to a declining market was not. He stubbornly ignored advice to sell and take a small loss, insisting prices would rise, despite strong indications to the contrary. He also dismissed mounting storage charges and fast deteriorating bale coverings. "I'll sell when I'm ready," he declared, clinging to his rotting cotton until the price plummeted from forty cents to five cents a pound. His infamous procrastination had cost him a fortune.

"That's none of your affair," Duncan sniffed.

Mary Grace glowered. "Since when is wasting family money none of my affair?"

"Managing money is man's work, sister dear."

Duncan's cavalier dismissal fueled her anger and turned her aim elsewhere. "Did you know there's a new leak in a corner of the drawing room? It's going to ruin the brocade walls and the paintings, too."

He shrugged. "I never really liked them much."

Katherine and Mary Grace traded looks over Duncan's latest curt remark. It was part of an aloof, unpleasant moodiness only one person could inspire.

Jennie Merrill.

"Not even the paintings of your grandfather's thoroughbreds?" Mary Grace asked. "With your love for horses I should think you'd be concerned."

"For heaven's sake, sister! Must I make all the decisions at Oakland? Just tell the servants to take the pictures down and store them somewhere."

"Where may I ask? In some closet that will develop leaks we don't know about?"

Duncan munched his fried chicken in silence.

His mother returned to the original issue. "When will the new roof go on?"

"Don't know yet. I have to find the right nails. They're very expensive."

"Plain roofing nails ought to be cheap enough." Further rankled, Mary Grace was sorely tempted to taunt her brother with his forbidden nickname, "Mississippi Miser."

"She's right," Katherine said, eagerly seizing the gauntlet of discord. "Even I know that."

Duncan picked up a wishbone and eyed it before taking a bite. "One thing at a time, Mother. I've got more important things to do."

More looks were exchanged between mother and daughter. "What's more important than the roof over our heads?"

Duncan took a deep breath and weighed his daring words. "Having a roof of my own."

His mother's eyebrows shot up. "What are you talking about, boy?"

"I'm buying a house, that's what." He broke apart a steaming biscuit and leisurely slathered it with chicken gravy before firing another volley. "I've got my eye on Glenwood if you must know."

"What?" the women chorused.

"It seems that Dick Dana can't pay his taxes. That means the house is coming available soon, and I want it."

"Why in the world would you want to waste money on that old wreck?" Katherine demanded. "Everyone knows Dick Dana and Octavia Dockery are poor as church mice and that Glenwood is coming apart at the seams."

Duncan studied the dripping biscuit. "One hears lots of things."

"Have you seen Glenwood lately?" his mother asked.

"Close enough to suit me."

Duncan's allusion to Glenwood's proximity to Glenburnie Manor was a shock since it remained an unspoken, unbroken rule that no reference, no matter how oblique, would be made to Jennie Merrill. It was so outrageous his mother was sucked into the dangerous current.

"You've other reasons for wanting Glenwood!" Katherine accused. "Admit it, Duncan Minor. You want Glenwood as some sort of...convenience."

Duncan remained fixed on his plate but there was a slight tremor in his left hand where it rested on the table. "I've no idea what you mean."

"Oh, you don't, eh?" his mother challenged, anger deepening. "Then suppose I remind you of a conversation you and I had many, many years ago." Still Duncan didn't look up. "I can still disinherit you."

"Do anything you like," Duncan said calmly. "I'm not exactly penniless these days."

"Neither is Jennie Merrill!" Katherine blazed, temper erupting as she addressed the unspeakable. "She's behind all this, isn't she?"

Something crawled up Duncan's back as his mother's voice rose higher and more shrill than usual. "Mother, please!"

"Answer me, boy! That awful woman is behind all this, isn't she?"

Duncan's arctic gaze shocked Mary Grace into further silence. While the women watched in horror, his skin grew taut across his cheekbones and his lips thinned to a menacing line. His eyes glazed with something new and terrible as he delivered his first family ultimatum.

"The conversation to which you referred never happened," he said, rising slowly from the table. "Furthermore, neither did this one. And if I ever hear either of you mention her name again, I can only say that you will regret it. Deeply." Satisfied by the stunned silence, he dabbed a napkin against his mouth and moustache, tossed it onto the table and checked his watch. "Now, if you will excuse me, I shall say goodnight."

In the face of the unthinkable, Katherine and Mary Grace could not speak. They were further dumbfounded when Duncan enjoyed a smile of self-satisfaction, bowed formally and went to saddle his horse for the nightly ride to Glenburnie Manor.

In TRUTH, JENNIE was not part of any conspiracy and knew nothing of Duncan's plan to buy Glenwood, an act he hoped would please her and secure peace of mind for both. Her feuds with Octavia had intensified, and, directly or indirectly, he always inherited the remnants of her anger. Last spring, Jennie had nearly gone berserk when a herd of goats ravaged her precious tiger lilies. She'd grabbed her gun and killed two of the marauding animals before the rest fled to safety. Charges and counter-charges flew as Octavia accused her of wantonly slaughtering valuable livestock, while Jennie claimed she was merely protecting her property from the trespassing goats. Things simmered down and tempers cooled, only to flare again when Jennie slew a wayward sow, and left nine piglets motherless. That loss was more than Octavia could endure, and she filed suit in magistrate court demanding restitution. Natchez quickly took sides, the great majority choosing Glenwood's impoverished residents over the wealthy mistress of Glenburnie Manor. One wag even said Octavia would be performing a community service if she got a gun and shot that arrogant harridan named Jennie Merrill.

Duncan thought he had found the solution when he learned Glenwood was up for auction after Dick failed to pay twenty-eight dollars in delinquent taxes. Big Natchez estates remained a glut on the market, and Duncan knew one as ramshackle as Glenwood would draw few if any interested buyers. He quietly bought the house for a song and waited for the terms of sale to expire so he could evict Dick and Octavia. As he hoped, Jennie was thrilled to learn both human and animal enemies would be vacating the house next door.

Peace settled over Glenburnie Manor for the first time in months, but this newborn harmony hit a snag when Episcopal Reverend Joseph Kuehnle learned Glenwood was about to change hands. Kuehnle had been a close friend of Dick's parents and knew Mrs. Dana's will had stipulated that the house become church property upon her son's death. This was a highly appealing bequest, considering the vast acreage involved, so Reverend Kuehnle engaged attorney Lawrence T. Kennedy to represent the church. Nicknamed "Tiger Man" for his fearsome tenacity, Kennedy was the quintessential Mississippi lawyer, from his deep Southern drawl to a penchant for white linen suits, and a short conversation with Reverend Kuehnle told him all he needed to know. Kennedy promptly asked the minister to bring Octavia to his downtown offices.

"Why her and not Dick Dana?" Reverend Kuehnle asked. "It's his property we're talking about."

"He's useless," Kennedy grunted. "The woman's your only hope."

No stranger to skeptical clients, the redoubtable Kennedy put Octavia at ease with quiet tones and personal assurance that he and Reverend Kuehnle could help her beat eviction. He stationed the minister comfortingly at Octavia's side and asked her to describe life at Glenwood in her own words. He took copious notes from her description of Dick's increasingly aberrant behavior, her tales of the so-called Wild Man of Natchez. After learning about the Halloween rowdies, he posed an explosive question.

"My dear Miss Dockery. Have you ever considered having Dick declared incompetent?"

Octavia frowned, taken aback. "Certainly not, Mr. Kennedy. Most assuredly Dick has his peculiarities, but he's a harmless soul who has generously allowed me to live..."

The old lawyer shook his head. "Excuse me for interrupting, ma'am, but I'm afraid we need to put fancy manners aside here and talk about survival. To put it plainly, it's time to declare Dick Dana incompetent and name you as his guardian."

"Wouldn't that mean putting him in some kind of institution?" Octavia asked, uneasy with the prospect of living alone. Dick might be slightly mad, but she preferred his company to none at all. She also believed his fanciful reputation kept away intruders.

"Not at all," Kennedy assured her. "You would both continue living at Glenwood as long as you like. I know a legal technicality to make it possible."

This gained Octavia's full attention. "Please continue, Mr. Kennedy."

"Mississippi law plainly states that infants and persons judged insane cannot be deprived of their property for failure to pay taxes. Since you have unofficially held the position of guardian for many years, it's a simple matter of making the situation legal."

"Would Dick need to participate?"

Kuehnle patted her hand. "Dick need know nothing about our little meeting, dear lady."

Octavia was relieved, since the likelihood of Dick's cooperation was nil. Some months ago, he had plunged so far into his private realm that his "here" days were few and far between.

"So you're absolutely certain," she said slowly, "that Duncan Minor won't be able to buy the place and throw us off?"

"No one will," the Tiger Man grinned. "Absolutely no one."

A smile creased Octavia's worn face as she felt in control for the first time in decades, along with sweet victory over her cruel and belligerent neighbors. Even the veteran Kennedy was moved when this poor, shabbily dressed soul dredged deep from her genteel past and spoke with authority.

"Please draw up the necessary papers, Mr. Kennedy. The sooner the better."

News of Octavia's amazing coup raced through the little town — Glenwood had been saved! Although Duncan was merely disappointed by Kennedy's clever maneuver, Jennie was outraged. Far from being vanquished, the Merrill/Dockery feud escalated to new heights, and Duncan took the brunt of Jennie's fury. Things also worsened at Oakland when the promised shingles arrived, only to lay untouched in the side yard. When his mother demanded to hear an excuse for his latest procrastination, Duncan blithely replied that the nails were too expensive and he was waiting for their price to go down.

Helpless, Katherine and her daughter watched and waited as other things succumbed to the deadly coalition of time and the elements. More leaks developed, existing ones worsened, two of the house's six columns actually teetered in a good wind, and the front steps collapsed as Mary Grace predicted. One morning the yard boy was swallowed alive when the steps splintered beneath him and gouged him bloody while he screamed for help. Duncan's solution was to position a ladder across the collapsed steps to provide entry from the lawn. Mary Grace ridiculed her brother's slapdash solution, but her laughter died under a murderous glare from Duncan.

Life at Oakland drifted on, as rickety as the house itself.

18

THINGS WERE NO less anomalous at Glenburnie Manor. Like most aging souls, Jennie did not appreciate change, but unlike them she took disdain to extremes. When telephones were introduced to Natchez in 1881, everyone rushed to have one installed, and the same was true when electricity arrived not long afterwards. Jennie was thoroughly disinterested in both newfangled conveniences, preferring life by gaslight and oil lamps, with no telephone calls to disturb her cherished quiet. Not until 1919, shortly after turning fifty-five, was she finally captivated by something new. She and Duncan were enjoying dusk on the veranda when she revealed her secret fascination.

"I want an automobile."

Duncan was aghast. "You can't be serious!"

"Oh, I am indeed. In fact, I know just the one I want." She leaned forward in her rocking chair and pulled a copy of *Collier's* from behind her back. "Look here."

Duncan scanned the advertisement for a Model T-Ford and shook his head. "But you don't know how to drive."

"I'll learn," Jennie announced. "In fact, we'll both learn. I've already made some inquiries and the car salesman said he'd arrange everything. He's in Baton Rouge."

Vexed that she had made such an important decision without him, Duncan tossed the magazine aside and retreated to a glider at the far end of the veranda. Apollo quickly bounded after him, tail a blur as he begged attention. While Duncan scratched the dog's ruff, Jennie mulled over his behavior.

"You don't seem very pleased, dearest."

The term of endearment he always cherished now grated on him. "You might have consulted me first."

"What for?" Jennie asked, as if the notion never occurred to her. "I'd already made up my mind."

"That's just it," Duncan said, more to the dog than Jennie. "You always make up your mind and never ask my opinion."

"Why should I when I never really think of us having two minds?" When he didn't reply, Jennie said, "Don't you remember those newspaper clippings you sent me when I was in New York?"

"I sent a lot of things," he muttered. "And I've always been disappointed that you never received the St. Christopher medal I sent you in Brussels."

Determined that Duncan not learn she had gifted Stephen Holmes with the medal, Jennie galloped quickly over the digression. "The articles were about marriage, taken from an address made by some monsignor in New Orleans. I memorized part of it." She closed her eyes and spoke slowly as the words came back. "'Their individuality is so blended that they are each the counterpart of the other.' Isn't that lovely?"

"I suppose."

"And doesn't it make you think of us?"

Again, slowly, "I suppose."

Jennie joined him and sparked another tail wagging when she bent to pet Apollo. "I'm sorry, my darling. I honestly didn't think my choice of motorcars mattered. After all, I never in-terfere in your business decisions." When he gave no response, she pressed harder. "Isn't that true?"

"Only because you don't know anything about cotton or horses."

Duncan's criticism, uncharacteristic as it was unexpected, ignited Jennie's mercurial temper.

"Is that so?" she snapped. "Well, dearest, the fact is that if you had asked my advice about that cotton speculating, you would've avoided that financial fiasco. Just how much did that little escapade cost?"

Dear God, Duncan moaned to himself. Will these damned women never stop throwing that in my face?

"That was thoughtless, Jennie."

"You're the one who's being thoughtless, behaving like a lit-tle boy who didn't get invited out to play." She pushed Apollo roughly away and stood. "What difference would it have made if I had asked your opinion about automobiles? The fact remains that I want a motorcar, and I shall have one. It's my money, and I need no one's permission to spend it." She stormed back to the rocker and retrieved the magazine where Duncan had tossed it. She opened to the advertisement and thumped it with her fore-finger. "You may as well know I've already placed the order. The man will deliver it a week from Thursday."

Duncan approached slowly. "Then you don't really need me for anything, do you? You have your own money and make your own decisions. You have your own house and now you'll have your own automobile."

"Duncan, don't —"

He rolled his eyes. "Good Lord! Why should I be surprised you didn't tell me about the car when you never mentioned the plantation you just sold over in Louisiana for a profit of eight thousand dollars?"

She frowned and shoved hands against her hips. "Who told you about that?"

"I deal in real estate, too, Jennie dear, and transactions of that size are always news." He shook his head. "I shouldn't be surprised if you're loaded with secrets."

His petulance stoked her temper. "I've never been ashamed of my successes, Duncan. Nor will I apologize for them."

"But must you flaunt them?"

"You brought them up, not I."

"But it's what you were thinking. As you just said, we're virtually one person, so I'm supposed to know exactly what's inside that pretty little head."

"Then I wouldn't look too closely, if I were you. You might not like what you see!"

"You're absolutely right. In fact, I don't like it at all."

"Don't make me angry," she warned.

"Why not? I'm angry."

"You? Angry?"

He glowered. "Careful, Jennie."

"Careful of what? I've kept company with you almost thirty years and I've never seen you show any spine."

Her last words were especially infuriating because Duncan heard them so often at home. His retaliatory rage was such that he lashed out hard, aiming to inflict the most pain.

"You sound just like Mother!"

The accusation triggered an even more trenchant response. "If you ever say anything like that to me again, Duncan Minor, I'll cut you out of my will and throw you out of this house forever." The brown eyes turned into menacing slits. "Don't think I won't do it!"

Numbed by rage, Duncan stalked off the veranda and continued across the lawn until he was well away from the house. Jennie's blistering ultimatum tolled in his brain, but he ignored it along with her plaintive cry.

"Come back, Duncan! Duncan! Please! I didn't mean that!" He walked further away. "Please, dearest!"

This time, he thought, this *one* time, she must come to me.

"Please!"

Jennie's tone was so pitiful Duncan turned slowly around and took a step toward her tiny figure, but no more. His feet were as firmly rooted as the ancient elms creaking nearby. Enough, he thought. Enough!

The slight movement in her direction signaled surrender to Jennie. She flew off the veranda and raced through a galaxy of lightning bugs. Duncan embraced her, though not altogether willingly.

"It isn't true, Duncan," she cried tearfully. "I would never throw you out of the house, any more than I would cut you out of my will."

Duncan looked puzzled. "Jennie, I didn't even know I was in your will."

"Of course you are. Who else?"

"You really are full of surprises tonight, aren't you?" He hoped his chuckle would end their argument, but Jennie remained upset.

"It's not funny, Duncan. What happened just now scared me half to death, and we must never allow it to happen again." She tugged a handkerchief from his waistcoat and dabbed her eyes. "Hold me, dearest! Hold me!"

"Shhh. It's all right now. Let's go back inside."

Duncan draped a protective arm around Jennie and steered her through the harmless inferno of fireflies. By the time they reached the house, she had stopped crying and tucked the handkerchief back into his vest. She turned at the top step and put her hands on his shoulders to hold him so they were face to face.

"Everything's all right now, isn't it?" she asked with a faint pout.

"Yes, dearest."

She kissed him lightly. "Then you don't mind if I get the automobile?"

"Of course not."

"Oh, thank you, darling!"

Jennie hugged him and, as she hurried back to the magazine, Duncan knew she had gotten her way yet again. Nothing had changed after all.

Or had it?

19

Jennie's Model-T provoked Natchez far more than it provoked Duncan. She was impossibly impatient with Mr. Yancey, the Louisiana car salesman who unwisely promised driving lessons to cinch the deal. While Duncan was a quick study behind the wheel, Jennie wouldn't listen long enough to master the basics. She insisted on grinding gears and brakes like toys played with by her rules. The beleaguered Model-T reacted by choking and lurching crazily down a country road, the tormented Yancey fearful for his life. Duncan finally took pity and offered to continue the difficult task himself. Waving a grateful Yancey off to Baton Rouge, Duncan suspected it was the most regrettable deal the poor salesman ever made.

After two weeks of continued lessons produced only bitter arguments, Duncan was so exasperated he told Jennie she was hopeless. He pleaded with her to abandon the dangerous folly, but she chose to prove him wrong by testing her questionable skills in traffic. Jennie's yard boy Willie Boyd peeled off the protective burlap wrapping she insisted upon when the Model-T was parked, and she chugged off toward town. Duncan could only watch helplessly as his private worries went public.

Jennie's unfortunate foray, her first of many, taught Natchezians that she was as arrogant as she was reclusive. Pedestrians and other drivers scrambled clear as she adjudged stop signs to be nonexistent or, more likely, not applicable to her. When several outraged people complained to the police after a brush with calamity, a pair of rookie cops dared confront her. Jennie coolly announced that she had more money and paid more taxes than anyone in town and, if they valued their jobs, they would be wise to protect rather than harass her. Reporting the outrageous threat to Police Chief Ryan, whom Jennie had also warned, they were ordered to steer clear and pray she didn't kill anybody.

Jennie's immunity from the law fueled growing public resentment, as did other flagrant misbehavior. Whenever she came to town, she rarely got out of her shiny new toy, ignoring No Parking zones on Main Street and blowing her horn until a shopkeeper came to investigate. She then explained what she wanted to see and demanded it be brought out for her perusal. While passers-by gawked at such audacity, Jennie casually browsed merchandise from her car, inspecting everything from shoes to gloves. One especially torpid August afternoon, she ordered clerks to fetch bolt after bolt of drapery fabric and stand in the fierce heat while she deliberated. Nor were bank employees exempt. Tormented tellers learned the only way to quell Jennie's relentless honking was to go outside and cash her personal checks, always in the amount of three dollars. Tourists and visitors naive enough to ask her for directions were simply not acknowledged.

The one place where her honking did no good was the Adams County Court House, but her behavior inside was no less abrasive. On the advice of her attorneys, and deliberately ignoring Duncan's disapproval, Jennie continued dabbling in real estate and soon proved she had inherited her father's business acumen. Her investments prospered as she acquired new properties in and around town and expanded old holdings across the river in Louisiana. Keeping tabs on her small empire was one of her greatest pleasures and took her to the courthouse with regularity to check records, search titles and tend to other business matters. If a line of people waited, Jennie simply marched to the front, pounded on the counter and imperiously announced her demands.

"Bring me Miss Merrill's taxes, please."

If anyone dared remind her others were waiting, they were fixed with a steely glare and ignored. If the person persisted, they received a high-handed dismissal. "I do not know you, sir!" was Jennie's favorite rebuff. Such hauteur was as much about self-defense as protocol since her long years of isolation meant she remembered few people from her past. She was forced to confront it one day when she exited the courthouse and was addressed by a well-dressed lady her own age.

"Why, Jennie Merrill! How nice to see you out and about."

Jennie fixed the stranger with a cold stare. "I do not believe we are acquainted, madam."

"Of course we are," the woman insisted. "I'm Rosemary Pickett."

"Never heard of you."

"Rosemary Kellogg. I used to attend your lovely balls at Elms Court. I married Randolph Pickett. We live out at Halcyon."

Jennie squinted in the harsh sunlight as she struggled to organize those facts. They danced a moment in her clouded memory before congealing. "Oh."

Such behavior made Rosemary wonder if everything she had heard was true. For years, the town had teemed with rumors about Jennie's solitary existence, and how no one but Duncan Minor visited since she bought Glenburnie Manor sixteen years earlier. Rosemary took a quick inventory of the smooth skin and shiny brown hair untouched by gray. Time hadn't quite stood still, but Jennie Merrill seemed to be holding it at bay, especially dressed in the leg o'mutton blouse, long skirts and beribboned sailor hat that had gone out of style two decades ago. It was even possible, Rosemary thought, considering Jennie's Creole heritage, that she darkened her hair with coffee grounds. It wouldn't have surprised her.

"You're certainly looking well," Rosemary offered.

"And you," Jennie muttered.

"Are things well at Glenburnie?"

"They are."

"I've heard you've done wonderful things with the place."

Jennie's gaze cooled. "From whom?" she demanded.

Rosemary had only been making polite conversation and was disconcerted by the abrupt interrogation. Heat rose in her cheeks. "Well, I...I don't remember exactly," she stammered. When it became clear Jennie was not going to pick up the conversational thread, Rosemary said, "Randolph and I would love to see the house some time."

"I no longer receive," Jennie said curtly.

Rosemary recklessly waded deeper. "Then perhaps you'd like to come to Halcyon. We're having a little soirée this coming Saturday and we'd love for you to—"

"I don't receive and I don't pay social calls, Mrs. Pickett." Jennie's version of a polite nod was in fact a rude jerk of the chin. "Good day."

Rosemary was thoroughly abashed as Jennie flounced into her car and drove away in a hot cloud of dust. She was dabbing her eyes with a handkerchief when she was joined by Caroline Dunbar, who had observed the peculiar drama from a safe distance.

"Good morning, Rosemary. Looks like you just got the full Merrill treatment."

Rosemary looked shaken as she greeted her friend. "I'm not certain *what* I got."

"It's really very simple, my dear. Jennie Merrill was unforgivably rude, that's all. I had the same experience last week at the bank. I was coming out just as she pulled up in that horrible car, and when I said hello she looked at me as if I had the black plague. I reminded her that we had gone to parties together—"

"So did I!" Rosemary cried, still smarting.

"It made no difference. She just kept honking that awful horn until one of the tellers came running out to see what she wanted. She gave him a check and then looked at me and said, 'That was a long time ago.'" Caroline shrugged. "Then she turned away and acted as if I didn't exist, while waiting for that poor man to come back with her money."

"Good Lord!" Rosemary watched the Model-T careen down Wall Street, honking incessantly and scattering pedestrians before veering left onto State Street and vanishing with a loud screech of tires. "I'd heard all sorts of talk, but nothing prepared me for this."

"Quite a change from the sweet young belle we used to know, isn't she?"

Rosemary was still at a loss. "How could such a thing happen?"

"I always thought the trouble began when her family threw her out of Elms Court," Caroline said. "When I called on her at Glenwood, she was as sweet and sociable as ever. When she moved to Gloucester, she began to change and started claiming she couldn't entertain because the house was in such miserable shape. With her money, Jennie Merrill could certainly have afforded to fix things up, but, well, after she bought Glenburnie Manor, she stopped making excuses and slammed her door in everyone's face. She even put up some sort of No Trespassing sign and turned into a complete hermit."

"Except where Duncan Minor is concerned."

"Exactly." Caroline took Rosemary's arm as they strolled up Wall Street. "And I suppose you've heard about that nasty business with Richard Dana and Octavia Dockery. How Duncan tried to buy Glenwood and get them evicted. Everyone says it was so he and Miss Jennie could merge those two properties and build the biggest house in town and openly live together in sin. Not that they don't do that already. Isn't it disgraceful the way they rub everyone's noses in their tawdry little affair?"

"Oh, I don't know." Rosemary didn't appreciate Caroline's gossip any more than she had Jennie's rudeness. "That's really their business, isn't it?"

Caroline jerked away as if she'd touched a hot iron. "Rosemary Pickett! How can a fine Christian woman say such a thing after the way Jennie Merrill treated you?"

"Maybe I'm just trying to do the Christian thing and forgive her," Rosemary said softly. "And perhaps try to understand her behavior."

"Well, you're certainly more forgiving than I am. Carrying on with that loony Duncan Minor and treating everyone as if they were her servants, expected to bow and scrape every time she prances into town like the Queen of Sheba." Caroline sniffed. "I suppose that's the kind of behavior she learned from living up North."

Rosemary wearied of the conversation as the sun popped trickles of sweat on the back of her neck. "I really must go, Caroline. If I don't hurry, I'll be late for choir practice. I'll expect you and James Saturday evening."

She broke away and bustled toward the Jefferson Street Methodist Church, forgetting about Jennie Merrill and hoping it wasn't blasphemous to pray for divine help in hitting the high notes in *How Great Thou Art*.

THE VERBAL JOUSTING between Rosemary and Caroline typified Jennie Merrill's opposing camps. Her dwindling defenders insisted she had been unfairly victimized by her own family and sought escape by losing herself in an era forever gone. What else, they asked, explained why she disdained electricity and telephones and dressed as though still in the nineteenth century? Especially since everyone knew she had an immense fortune.

A larger, much more vociferous group declared Jennie's conceit was thoroughly calculated, a vengeful reaction to a town that despised her father's politics and refused to accept her liaison with Duncan Minor. Still others disliked her more for her bad behavior than her incestuous relationship, regarded Duncan as her equal in condescension and dismissed the eccentric cousins as deserving one another. Almost everyone agreed, however, that somewhere along the line, Jennie Merrill had changed from generous, gregarious belle to irascible, demanding harridan, and that was where she made her fatal mistake. Natchezians could forgive a great deal but never a breach of Southern hospitality.

Jennie's list of enemies was steadily growing.

20

KATHERINE SURGET MINOR died in 1926, but even after her passing she continued to sow discord between her son and Jennie Merrill. On the night she died, for the first time in many years, Duncan spent the night at Oakland instead of making the usual trek to Glenburnie, and although Jennie understood his need to tend to family matters, her sympathy waned when his absence stretched into a week. Aggravating the separation was Duncan's inaccessibility, his lack of response to her notes, and his utter silence while he mourned a woman Jennie had loathed. She sought to alleviate her frustration with books, hours of target practice, and long drives through the country. When that didn't work, she patrolled Glenburnie like a drill sergeant and berated her servants for the slightest infraction. One Sunday evening she was fuming over a cobweb in the parlor gasolier when she heard noise outside. She grabbed her gun and squinted across the veranda as a familiar figure emerged from the shadows. Duncan, tall and straight in the saddle, umbrella in hand, was returning to Glenburnie.

He waved and called to the menacing silhouette at the window. "'Tis I, dearest!"

Jennie's initial elation evaporated as she went outside and watched her absentee lover draw closer. When Duncan dismounted and leaned down for an embrace, she slapped him hard across the cheek. Before he could react, she grabbed his neck and kissed him with a passion as overwhelming as it was startling.

"Jennie!" he gasped. "Good Lord!"

"Welcome home," she smiled.

The peculiar incident was never mentioned, buried forever beneath the far more consequential interchange that followed when they were alone in the parlor. While Jennie watched in disbelief, Duncan slipped to his knees, took her hands and asked her to marry him. Her response was unhesitating.

"No."

"What?"

"I said no."

"But why?"

"Think back, my dear. Back to the time we first seriously discussed marriage. It was at Elms Court, on this very couch, when I proposed an elopement we would forever keep secret. Although you never asked why, it was simply because I wanted to keep our lives private. When you announced there would either be a public marriage or none at all, I thought you noble, but as time wore on I discovered the regrettable truth."

"I...I don't understand."

"You didn't want a public marriage simply because your mother opposed it and you were afraid to confront her."

"Jennie! How can you say such a..."

"We both know it's true," she continued, unmoved. "Just as we know it was all very convenient for you. But now that she's gone I must refuse more strongly than ever."

"But why?"

"Because marriage now would acknowledge her disapproval, along with that awful hold she had over you. By continuing as we are, we're saying her blessing meant nothing to us. That now, as always, we need each other and no one else."

Jennie's logic totally eluded Duncan. "Please don't do this," he begged. "Not today, when I desperately want to hear you say—"

"You're never going to hear me say I'll marry you, Duncan. You refused my proposal and terms and now I'm refusing yours. Now get off the floor before you wrinkle your trousers." He rose slowly and rubbed his left knee before sliding onto the couch, lost in confusion. When he continued staring, Jennie unknowingly conjured the one criticism he most despised and slashed him to the quick.

"You're a day late and a dollar short, my boy."

"Mother," he muttered.

"What about her?"

"That's what she always said when I disappointed her." Before Jennie could comment, his ultimatum came, swift and fierce. "Never, *ever* say that to me again."

Now, six years later, that unpleasant interchange returned to haunt Jennie. As they were undressing for bed, Duncan shocked her with another marriage proposal, and, certain he was teasing, Jennie playfully pushed him away. When he insisted he was serious and even suggested a European honeymoon, she laughed and blurted the damning phrase.

"You're a day late and a dollar short, my boy."

Duncan's resentment was as keen as ever. "I told you never to say that to me again!" He climbed into bed and turned his back to her, something he had never done.

Realizing her error, Jennie hastened to apologize. "I'm sorry, Duncan, but surely you didn't think I'd take you seriously. I'm sixty-two years old, for heaven's sake, and I certainly don't need you to make an honest woman of me this late in life." When there was no response, they lay in silence until Duncan's snoring closed the issue and left Jennie oddly adrift.

The next morning after Duncan left for Oakland, the awful moment plagued Jennie as she stretched out on the parlor settee and tried to bury the memory with a slender volume of romance poetry Duncan had given her for her fiftieth birthday. The words blurred as she dozed fitfully, repeatedly yanked awake by her own nodding head. Her mind was cluttered with malignant dreams of Katherine Minor, in church, on the street, the first time she met the woman at Elms Court. Even from beyond the grave, she thought, Duncan's mother continues to torment me.

The heat hardly helped. The summer of 1932 verged on the apocalyptic. The damp, sweaty couch cushion annoyed her, and she was contemplating a bath when she heard something under the porte-cochère. She sat up and listened closely, counting as sluggish footsteps mounted the veranda steps, one-two-three-four-and-five. As the sound grew closer, she wondered if the front door was locked and glanced toward the dining room where her gun commanded its usual place on the table. She heard loud knocks.

"Effie!" she called. "There's someone at the door." Silence reverberated in the heavy heat, and Jennie grimaced as sweat trickled down her sides. "Effie!"

Then she remembered it was Monday. Effie would be outside hanging the wash and she was in the house alone. She rose at another series of insistent knocks and wondered if those heavy shoes belonged to Octavia Dockery. She half-hoped they did, deciding a confrontation might be just what she needed to pass the torrid day, but the shadow thrown across the foyer belonged to someone else. A few feet away, just on the other side of the flimsy screen door was a Negro man, features indistinct because of the intense glare of the sun behind him.

"Afternoon, ma'am." His voice was low and gravelly.

"What do you want?" Jennie noted with unconcealed

annoyance that he did not remove his hat when addressing her. She shoved both hands on her hips. "Well?"

"Work, ma'am." He shifted his weight from one foot to another. "I do all kinds of odd jobs and I work for almost nothing."

"I already have help."

He stepped a little closer to the screen and gave her a lopsided grin. "Don't you remember me, Miss Jennie? I done work for you some years back. Name's Lawrence Williams."

"I don't remember you," she replied tartly.

"Sure enough I did some work along that bayou over there." Williams pointed toward the ravine separating Glenburnie from Glenwood. "Dug up a bunch of bushes and did some weedin' and you told me I done a mighty fine job." Jennie was silent. "You sure you can't find nothin' for me to do 'round this big place?"

"I told you I don't have anything. Now run along."

Williams hung his head a moment, then looked up and, it seemed to Jennie, peered past her and into the house as though searching for something. The gesture unnerved her, and she silently cursed Apollo for being off chasing squirrels when he should be guarding the house against intruders.

"Don't reckon you got any tobacco, do you?"

"Certainly not!" Jennie huffed, appalled by such impertinence. If she had her way, uppity Negroes like this would stay in Colored Town where they belonged.

Williams stepped closer. For a moment Jennie thought he was going to reach for the door latch, but his hands remained at his side. "Then maybe you could give me somethin' to eat. I ain't had nothin' since day before yesterday. That's what I really need, somethin' to eat."

"Why didn't you say so in the first place?"

"Didn't mean to be rude, Miss Jennie. Guess I was just hopin' you'd remember me and give me some work."

"Go around back," Jennie ordered, tired of his whining. "My girl will get you something. Go on now."

When Williams didn't stir, Jennie swiftly shut the front door, relieved by the loud click of the lock. She retrieved her gun and watched, heart racing, until the man's silhouette slowly retreated and disappeared toward the porte-cochère. Then she hurried to the back porch, where she saw Effie hanging sheets and pillow slips in the still, heavy air.

"Effie!"

The housekeeper peered around the sheets. "Yes, ma'am?"

"What have we got to eat?"

"Got a peach pie in the oven!" Effie called. Jennie didn't know why she hadn't noticed that delicious aroma until now. She had certainly noticed the hot kitchen. "Ought to be ready in 'bout ten more minutes."

"What else?" Jennie asked, having no intention of sharing that pie with anyone but Duncan. Before Effie could answer, she added, "There's a colored man wanting some food. He's coming around the side of the house."

Effie shaded her eyes and looked toward the driveway. "Don't see nobody."

Brandishing her gun, Jennie left the back porch and went to see for herself. She skirted the house until she reached the veranda, then looked down the drive. There was no sign of Lawrence Williams.

"Where on earth did that black fool go?" she muttered to herself.

"You find him?" Effie shouted.

"No," Jennie called back. "Never mind."

She walked across the yard, scanning bushes and the periphery of the thick woods. Except for a few weary butterflies, nothing stirred in the dreadful heat. Jennie wasn't certain how, but Lawrence Williams had simply evaporated. She retreated to the house, turning around just once when she heard Apollo barking in the direction of Glenwood. Then she heard nothing.

"Worthless animal," Jennie grumbled, tiredly mounting the front porch steps. She started at the shriek of a blue jay and in one swift move cocked the gun, aimed and fired. The resultant explosion of feathers was her only satisfaction in an otherwise wretched afternoon.

JENNIE FORGOT ABOUT Lawrence Williams until the following Thursday night when Duncan's talk about the relief crisis in New York prompted her to interrupt and recount the incident, and she got angry all over again.

"I don't understand what's wrong with people these days. I mean the very notion that this Negro could be so insolent! Why, he came right up to my front door like he was making a social call. As if that's not bad enough, he asked me for tobacco. Me!" She served up the last of Effie's peach pie and slid a piece across the kitchen table. "Can you imagine?"

"The Depression is making people desperate I suppose."

Jennie snorted. "Well, I can't help how colored people behave in the streets, but I'm certainly not having it here in my home." She turned down the lamp. Lately the light bothered her eyes. "How's your pie?"

"Delicious." Duncan glanced toward the door, where Apollo thumped his tail against the porch floor. "I think Apollo wants a piece, too."

"You know better than that," Jennie reprimanded. "Human food always makes him sick."

He forked another piece of pie and glanced at the dog. Apollo's tail went into action again. Duncan watched for a moment and became reflective.

"You know something, Jennie? It's a strange world when dogs have enough to eat and people don't."

"What on earth brought that on?"

"I was still thinking about the relief crisis. New York City has twenty-five thousand emergency cases on a waiting list. That's almost twice the population of Natchez."

"So?"

"They're separating families in Chicago and sending husbands and wives to different shelters. Philadelphia just ran out of relief funds altogether. State, private, city, everything, and they've cut aid to over fifty thousand families."

"Of course those places are in trouble. I saw it first-hand when I worked for the King's Daughters forty years ago. Obviously things are still a mess, which is why so many colored men come down South looking for work. Natchez seems to be taking care of its own. Why don't they do the same up North?"

"I think it's a matter of numbers. Their problems are so much greater than ours and—"

"It was a rhetorical question," she sighed.

Duncan's response to the familiar tone of dismissal was to bring up something to pique her interest as well as his. "Did you see the latest on the Smith Reynolds case? It looks like Libby Holman's going to be indicted for his murder."

Jennie shrugged. "Serves that family right for letting him marry a Yankee Jewish girl. You'd never see any self-respecting Southern white woman singing black songs for a living. I'll bet she had her eye on that tobacco money from the start."

"Interesting that it took the police a month to indict her," Duncan ventured. "I'll wager she gets off Scot-free. What do you think?"

Fueled by the heat, Jennie's temper ignited. "For heaven's sake, Duncan! All this talk is giving me a headache!"

"I was only making conversation."

"Well, it's much too hot to think tonight. Who cares about people starving in New York or that silly murder case?"

"I was just—"

"Oh, fiddlesticks!"

Dessert was finished in silence. Afterwards, Jennie rinsed the dishes and left them in the sink for Effie to wash in the morning. She went out to the gallery, seeking a breeze to relieve the ponderous heat. Duncan followed, kneeling to scratch

Apollo behind his ears while Jennie leaned against the railing. Finding the night air just as stifling, Jennie went back inside and hummed to herself as she roamed about the house doing nothing in particular. Duncan stayed on the porch where he and Apollo enjoyed a quiet moment until the dog smelled some wild creature and tore into the night. Loud barks disappeared toward Glenwood and then abruptly stopped, suggesting the dog had either lost or caught his prey.

As he often did, Duncan lost all track of time until Jennie announced she was going to bed. That surprised him because her chronic insomnia often drove her to pace until the wee hours, purposely exhausting herself before retiring. That night he was the one who couldn't sleep, tossing and turning in the miserable heat until his pajamas were sour with sweat. Twice he got up to pace the dark house, and went back to bed only to be awakened by Apollo's distant barking.

"Must be another tramp," he muttered. He watched Jennie sleep until light glowed through the windows, then read his watch on the nightstand and silently mouthed the hour. 5:40 AM. He coughed and sat up. Jennie stirred beside him, then rolled over.

"What time...?" she yawned.

"Time for me to go." Duncan slipped from bed and dressed by the light of the growing dawn. Jennie watched sleepily, then closed her eyes as he leaned down to kiss her. "I'll see you tonight, dearest."

"Mmmm."

Duncan stood for a few moments, waiting until light snoring signaled Jennie had fallen back asleep. He touched her shoulder and coughed softly. "Goodbye."

As he climbed into the saddle and popped open his umbrella, Duncan was swallowed by a silence broken only by the slow clip-clop of the mare's hooves and birds waking for the day. He reveled in the early hour as though he had never experienced it before.

"Hundreds of dawns," he muttered. Then thought, "Not hundreds. Thousands."

Duncan was still too groggy to calculate how many mornings and nights had passed during thirty-six years of riding to see Jennie, first to Glenwood, then Gloucester and finally, Glenburnie Manor. He was now seventy, Jennie two years younger. Who could have known the ride would last so long?

Suddenly, Duncan wanted to put distance between himself and Glenburnie Manor. For the first time in all those years, he furled his umbrella and urged the horse into a gallop. When he arrived at Oakland, almost as lathered as his horse, he reached for his watch and came up empty-handed, then remembered leaving it on Jennie's beside table. He hurried inside to check the grandfather clock in the hallway.

"Twenty-seven minutes instead of forty-five." He sighed. "That adds up to a lot of wasted time over the years."

21

J ENNIE LEANED CLOSER to the mirror, shook out a clean lace
handkerchief and dabbed a moist upper lip. She turned her
head, this way and that, critiquing her reflection beneath the
pale lamp light. Her face revealed few wrinkles, just as her dark
hair remained remarkably free of gray. It pleased her, but was
scarcely enough to merit a smile. Instead she fussed with the
jeweled head combs securing the long hair away from her face.
She usually wore it off her neck, especially in the heat, but because she knew it would please Duncan, it hung loose in mute
apology for last night's harsh words due to her headache.

"It was the heat's fault," she murmured.

Jennie also chose his favorite perfume, the ancient lemon
verbena, as forgotten as Natchez itself, and dabbed it lightly
behind her ears. She was frugal because this was her last bottle and the manufacturer had ceased production decades ago.
As she rose from her dressing table, the scent mingled with
perspiration trickling down the small of her back. The sweat

felt oddly cool against an ongoing torpor settling hard into her old bones, robbing her strength and making her skittish. The floor-level windows to the veranda were thrown high in search of a breeze, but none stirred, only more scorched air sucking at the very breath of life.

Jennie grudgingly considered the relief an electric fan might bring from summers that seemed to worsen as she grew older. She had no idea how much it would cost to wire the house for electricity or what a power bill might run, although neither expense would have mattered. What *did* matter was that it fatigued her to think about it, so she tucked it in the back of her brain alongside other petty vexations. No, she decided. She had done without electricity this long and was too old to change. In defiance, she picked up an ancient palmetto fan and riled the thick air as she drifted beneath the glow of oil lamps. Moving from room to room, she checked and rechecked to ensure everything was in its proper place. Despite a staff strictly trained over the years, she found an untrimmed wick and had no choice but to fix it herself. Effie and the gardener had left for the day, and Willie Boyd, her yard boy, had finished supper in the kitchen and no doubt wandered off somewhere by this point in the evening. M.W. Hatcher, the elderly caretaker, was away on an another extended visit with his ailing son, and Apollo had chased off to the woods again. Except for tenants on the far fringes of her property, Jennie was completely alone amid Glenburnie's forty acres of forest, ravines and lazy creeks.

She looked toward the hall as the grandfather clock pinged once. 7:15 PM. Duncan would be there in exactly one hour and a half, and her solitude would end as it always did at 8:45 PM. Certainly she was used to waiting for him, but tonight's anticipation was exasperating. She dabbed her upper lip again and again.

"Lord, I can barely breathe!"

Frowning and waving the fan a bit faster, Jennie wandered onto the rear veranda. A pale crescent moon — an angel's eyelash her mother called it — and a dusting of stars struggled for dominance with high-flying clouds haloed by humidity. With only a few vague shapes of trees and bushes emerging against dark skies, it looked as though heaven and earth had been melded by summer's inferno. The usual thrum of insects was absent, as though they were too heat-fatigued to scrape legs and wings and chat with one another.

Jennie lifted her head when the sluggish stillness was interrupted by the passing of a train, the Mississippi Central Railroad, which ran along the northern corner of her property a quarter mile away. She used to relish the sound because it stirred dusty recollections of childhood travel and other, happier times, but these days the trains discharged an endless stream of tramps. As the Great Depression worsened, a growing sea of desperate souls washed across her land, begging for work or, more often, a handout. With a convoluted charity only she understood, Jennie instructed Effie to send no hobo away hungry, while steadfastly refusing to help her indigent neighbors at Glenwood.

When the train horn faded, Jennie went back inside. She fussed with the sleeves of her pink silk dressing gown and checked the time again. Still too early for Duncan. She hummed to break the stillness and patrolled the house again. Inspection of a bookshelf tempted her to swap a Chinese vase for an Old Paris figurine that had belonged to her grandmother, but she resisted, as always, the temptation of change. She scanned the row of familiar books and considered rereading a favorite before deciding she was too irritable to concentrate. She hummed louder, determined to vanquish ennui that weighed as heavy as the heat. Then she grew bored with her own music.

"Fiddlesticks!"

She went into the dining room and sat at the great mahogany table where her gun reposed as always. She studied her moist hands as they folded and fidgeted in front of her and spotted a tiny fleck of leaf beneath the nail of her little finger left hand, a reminder that she had arranged a bowlful of roses late that afternoon. She flicked away the offending mote and gazed around the room, oil lamp to floor, wall to unlit gasolier and back again until she grew woozy.

"Good heavens!"

Jennie picked up her gun, but the metal felt unpleasantly warm, so she put it back where it belonged. She closed her eyes, waiting for the ping of the clock to announce seven-thirty. Duncan was as punctual as that clock, and she pictured him in half an hour, fussing about the stables at Oakland, saddling his horse for the two-and-a-half mile ride to Glenburnie Manor.

A scraping sound shredded the heavy stillness.

"What...?"

Had Jennie heard something or was her mind playing tricks in the dreadful heat? No. There it was again, more pronounced this time, closer and accompanied by the stink of must and stale sweat. It reminded her of old clothes, or maybe goats. One of Glenwood's marauding goats could have wandered over again. Jennie chuckled at the notion of blowing one of those infernal beasts to kingdom come, but recoiled when the odor grew so strong she wondered if one had dared climb onto the veranda. She rose to investigate, but when she turned toward the open windows, she learned too late the source of the stench.

"What do *you* want?"

The figure moved closer, enveloping Jennie in the fetor of a heavy overcoat. She gasped when she spotted a glint of metal in the folds of the man's coat and whirled around, lunging across the dining table in a frantic grab for her gun. Crippled by terror and haste, she knocked it clattering onto the floor and watched helplessly as it spun out of reach. She faced the intruder again, drawing herself up with as much nerve as she could muster, but when the intruder's gun came into full view, aimed directly at her heart, Jennie knew there was no negotiating.

She screamed.

"Don't!"

WILLIE BOYD WAS about two hundred yards from the manor, heading for town, when he heard the first howl, high-pitched and shrill. He froze. Had that awful cry come from the big house? He heard a gunshot and another scream. A second shot and the chilling silence that followed galvanized the black youth into action, but not toward the terrifying noises. Instead he bolted for Kingston Pike, wanting only to distance himself from danger, but not before he heard a final cry merge with a third gunshot.

"Help!"

Then silence.

Willie raced north alongside the darkened highway until his aching lungs slowed him to a walk. He ambled aimlessly for an hour or so while trying to decide what to do. Several cars passed, but he hugged the shadowy woods and made no request for help. Mississippi Negroes well knew to steer clear of white folks' business, and, although he was only an uneducated colored boy, Willie knew better than to go to the police. If there had been foul play, they'd be all too quick to consider him their prime suspect. Finally he stopped his frenetic rambling and sat by the side of the road, trying again to sort his addled thoughts. His heart raced when he heard horse's hooves on the macadam road. Only one person in Natchez would be riding a horse down Kingston Pike at this hour and, thank the Lord, it was the one white man who might help. Duncan Minor was heading for his nightly assignation with Miss Jennie.

It was 8:30 PM.

"Mr. Duncan!" Willie cried, leaping to his feet and waving frantically in the hot night air. "Mr. Duncan!"

"Who is it?" Duncan called, squinting into the darkness. It took him a few moments to identify the figure dancing in the middle of the road. "Willie Boyd? Is that you?"

"Yessir, Mr. Duncan! It's me! You got to hurry, Mr. Duncan!"

"Calm down, boy," Duncan ordered. He reined his horse,

straightened in the saddle and peered down at the wild-eyed youth. "Now tell me what's got you so excited."

"It's Miss Jennie, sir! It's Miss Jennie!"

Duncan frowned and cocked his head. "What about her?"

Willie was burning to tell someone what he'd heard, but when the moment arrived his story spewed in a torrent of hysterical babbling. After repeatedly telling Willie to slow down, Duncan deciphered enough key phrases to understand.

"Gunshots in the big house!" and "A lotta screaming!"

"Jennie!"

Duncan urged his mare into a gallop while Willie, ranting senselessly, chased after them. When Duncan turned into the drive and approached the manor house, he found total blackness, no welcoming light as always and no familiar, comforting sound of Jennie's humming as he reached the porte-cochère. He cupped a hand to his mouth and called into the night.

"Jennie!"

No answer.

"Jennie! It's Duncan!"

He slipped to the ground, dropped the reins and crept up the porch steps. He never thought to worry that an intruder might still be on the premises; concern for Jennie propelled him into the house. He even dared shout again as he entered the dark hall and groped toward the dining room.

"Jennie? Where are you? Answer me!"

The silence was unnerving enough, but far more ominous signs loomed ahead. He fumbled in his coat pocket for matches and struck one. As the match blazed bright, Duncan spotted something amiss on the dining room floor. A blanket lay crumpled at the foot of the big mahogany table and it stank abominably. Duncan shook his head. The slightest disorder at Glenburnie Manor was cause for concern, as was the oil lamp missing from the dining table. He struck another match and leaned toward a dark splotch on the floor.

Blood.

"Dear God!" He backed out of the house just as Willie loped up the drive. "Willie! Come in here!" Still shaking, the youth paused to catch his breath before slowly making his way onto the porch, where he froze again until Duncan raised his voice. "Get in here, boy! I need you!"

While Willie cowered behind, Duncan grabbed an oil lamp and lit the wick. He turned it high as he followed a trail of blood leading through the conservatory and into the bedroom. Things worsened with every step.

"Oh, my God!"

Jennie's normally pristine bedroom was a shambles. Her feather mattress had been torn from the four-poster bed and lay on the floor. Drawers were yanked from a dresser and rifled, more telltale signs of burglary. Duncan explored the chaos further and found one of Jennie's bedroom slippers splattered with blood. The crimson path continued across the floor-level sill of the French windows and onto the rear veranda. Lamp in hand, Duncan followed it to the porte-cochère, where still more blood screamed silently from the walls.

"Jennie!" he cried, voice hollow in the torpid night. "Jennie! Where are you!"

Ordering Willie to wait on the front steps, Duncan ventured onto the dark lawn until he lost the trail, all the while yelling until his throat ached. When his hoarse cries remained unanswered, he made a final search of house. Finding nothing, he swung back into the saddle and went looking for a telephone.

It was a few minutes before 10 PM when he rang the sheriff's office from a neighbor's house. Laurin Farris, the night jailor, took the call and was instantly on the alert when the caller identified himself. He knew Duncan Minor belonged to one of the town's oldest families, a descendant of an early Governor of Natchez, if he remembered correctly. It would, Farris knew, take something dire indeed for this aristocratic old bachelor to call the sheriff.

"What can I do for you, Mr. Minor?"

"I'm afraid something has happened to Miss Jane Surget Merrill," Duncan reported with crisp formality. "Something terrible."

"Yes, sir?" Farris urged.

"I've just come from Glenburnie Manor, and she's not to be found anywhere. The house has been ransacked."

"Go on, Mr. Minor."

The words hung briefly in Duncan's throat before he expelled them with a determined breath.

"I found blood on the floor, sir."

PART THREE
August, 1932

*H*orrendous fights took place all over town, Under-the-Hill of course (where they often went unrecorded), but also in hotel bars, in the streets, even on the steps of the courthouse. Lawyers were not above biting and gouging, whipping and shooting, in the wake of incautious words exchanged in the courtroom...The level of violence was not regarded as unusually high. Yet for a town of that size, there was (by today's standards) a great deal of mayhem.

Winthrop D. Jordan, *Tumult & Silence at Second Creek*

22

Like most of his counterparts across the South, Sheriff C. P. "Book" Roberts's office in the Adams County Jail was often an all-male social center. On Thursday evening, August 4, 1932, he and night jailor, Laurin Farris, had been joined by former sheriff W. P. Abbott, Deputy Sheriff Pat Mulvihill and two other cronies with nothing more to do than swap local yarns and complain about the infernal heat. The sheriff was heading into the hall for a fresh cup of coffee when Farris took Duncan Minor's urgent telephone call around 10 PM. Years on the job told Roberts a call at that hour meant a prowler or wayward husband, but when he heard the caller's prominent name he leaned through the door to eavesdrop on Farris's conversation.

"Duncan Minor? What can I do for you, sir?" The office hushed as Duncan's voice crackled over the wire. "Yes, sir." Then, after a pause, "Go on, Mr. Minor." Another pause, longer this time, as Farris scribbled away. "Sure, Mr. Minor. I'll send someone out right away. Yes, sir. Good night, sir."

Roberts stepped back inside his office. "What's up with Duncan Minor?" While the others crowded behind him, Farris repeated the scant details. The sheriff made a quick assessment and barked orders. "Okay, Laurin. You and Mulvihill get on out to Glenburnie and see what the devil's going on. I'll be along directly." He wiped sweat from a generous forehead and tucked away the handkerchief before phoning his chief deputy, Joseph M. Stone, and highway patrolman Joe Serio. Within minutes the three were speeding down Kingston Pike in Serio's car.

"We're not going to Glenburnie Manor, gentlemen," Roberts announced. "Not yet anyway."

"Where to, Book?" Stone and Serio knew Roberts was a no-nonsense lawman and they seldom tried to second-guess him.

"I'm playing a hunch that may buy us some time. If Miss Jennie Merrill's really in trouble, I know who might have some answers." He sucked his teeth before delivering his surprise. "Boys, we're gonna pay a little call on the Wild Man of Natchez."

Stone peered over the rims of his spectacles. "Whoa!"

Serio muttered something under his breath. "Better give me some directions, sheriff. That old place is so damned overgrown, I'll never find it in the dark."

"Just keep a sharp lookout to the left as soon as we pass Glenburnie." Roberts was pleased when Police Chief Ryan's speeding car approached from the opposite direction and turned into Jennie's driveway. That meant his men were on the ball. "If I remember correctly, Glenwood's gates are just beyond where Ryan turned." He squinted into the night. "On the left...there it is, Joe. Pull over!"

Serio braked hard. As they bounced off the highway and parked, headlights picked out a wooden gate so dilapidated and overgrown it was invisible to anyone not searching for it. The men got out and slowly edged along a winding private drive corrupted into a rutted nightmare of weeds and tangled briars. Through great trees swarming with Spanish moss they caught occasional glimpses of Glenwood. Washed in weak moonlight, it looked dreamy, but harsh reality focused as the lawmen closed the distance.

"Good Lord," Stone muttered. "Look there!"

The great pillars were cracked and flaked, some leaning crazily as though weary of bearing their load. Two columns supporting the second floor gallery and chunks of the balustrade had crumbled away, giving the façade a snaggle-toothed appearance. If ever a house looked haunted, the men thought, this was it.

"Damn!"

Roberts expected the elderly residents to be asleep, but faint light flickered from a second story window. "Looks like the tenants of Glenwood are still awake."

"Wonder why," Stone hissed.

"Maybe they've had a busy night," the sheriff ventured. The men moved closer, ears pricked in the hot, heavy stillness. As they slowly mounted the front steps, the sheriff banged his knee and groaned in agony.

"You all right, Book?"

"Yeah. Just give me a minute."

Roberts had stumbled against an old marble mounting-block, the kind ladies used to access stirrups in the forgotten days of riding sidesaddle. When the noise triggered scuffling inside the house, he and the others braced for shouts or even a hail of bullets, but the rustling stopped as suddenly as it started. Roberts eased onto the wide veranda and groped his way across spongy planks, mindful of holes and chunks of the six-inch oak flooring that looked completely rotten. He lifted the heavy bronze knocker, but before he let it drop, the front door creaked free and swung slowly back.

"What the heck—"

All three peered inside, but as the door floated open a stench with teeth smothered the lawmen and drove them back.

"Good God!"

Serio grabbed a handkerchief and covered his nose. There was more rustling before a pair of eyes glowed in the dimness. Roberts reached for his gun, but Stone's chuckle stopped him.

"Easy, sheriff! It's just the goats. Look!"

The deputy's flashlight washed over a plump billy goat that bleated with annoyance and clattered to the staircase, where his harem of nanny goats huddled in fear. Further inspection revealed a sizable herd coming and going freely through a porch window open from the floor. It was a putrid introduction to the spectacular waste lurking beyond, but the men forced themselves to venture into the house itself. In the east wing, they found a library containing countless rare books, most mildewed beyond repair, others half-devoured by goats. Also on the shelves were cooking utensils and filthy tins of desiccated meat. In the parlor, vines sprouted through broken windows and trailed up walls to strangle chandeliers, their tendrils leached white from lack of sunlight. Chickens nested in furniture that once belonged to the Lees of Virginia, and pig droppings fouled floors where Mississippi's most aristocratic feet once waltzed away soft Southern nights.

"Dear Lord!"

The men shook their heads and moved on.

"Damn!" Serio clenched his handkerchief tighter. "Nobody's gonna believe this!"

"Or this." Roberts aimed his flashlight dead ahead. "Over there!"

The late Reverend Dana's study was another horror, now a makeshift kitchen with an ancient oil drum employed as both stove and heater. Goat meat had been roasted over flames fueled with Chippendale sofa legs and the arms of Heppelwhite chairs. Curtains were devoured as high as the goats could reach, family portraits were strewn across rotting tapestries, and notes for a sermon delivered sixty years ago lay black with soot. Strangest of all, General Thomas P. Dockery's uniform had escaped when its glass case crashed to the floor, arms locked in a macabre death grip with a toppled marble statue of Mercury.

"Dear God!" Roberts gasped.

Combined with stinking mold, the filth and pong of goats, chickens and pigs were overpowering. Dust smothered everything, rendering the dead air nearly unbreathable. Roberts coughed and announced they'd done enough exploring.

"Time to find the Wild Man, boys." He led his men back to the entrance hall and boomed up the stairs. "Richard Dana!"

After a few moments, a crisp tenor drifted down the staircase. "Who is it, please?"

"It's Sheriff Roberts, Mr. Dana. I want to talk to you."

"I'm afraid I have retired for the night," came the polite reply.

"And I'm afraid that doesn't matter, sir."

Silence followed. Then another voice sailed down, this one female and confrontational. "What do you want with Mr. Dana?"

"It's the Goat Woman, boys!" Roberts hissed, mustering his companions. "Come on!"

He edged up the broad staircase with Serio and Stone close behind. Three dusty flashlight beams danced ahead, merging when a figure in nightgown and wrapper sprang from the darkness to block their path. Octavia's blue eyes flashed defiance.

"What do you want here?" she demanded.

Before Sheriff Roberts could respond, a second figure materialized like a will-o'-the-wisp. Wild-eyed and bearded to his waist, Dick Dana brimmed with infantile curiosity as he lurked behind his protector and eyed Glenwood's first visitors in decades. He wore a filthy linen suit, sagging and torn at the knees with all the buttons missing, and was as nervous, disheveled and unwashed as Octavia was not.

Roberts ignored her and inched closer. "I'd like a few words with you, Mr. Dana."

Octavia directed her charge toward his bedroom. "Go back to bed, Dick."

He retreated a few steps and blurted, "I don't know anything about that murder!"

Stone lowered his voice. "Hear that, Book? That crazy old
fool just hung himself!"

"What murder?" Roberts pressed, hoping his hunch might
indeed pay off. So far as he knew, there was no corpse and the
public remained unaware of any crime.

"Over at Glenburnie," Dick replied, retreating further while
Octavia glowered.

Roberts brushed by Octavia and followed Dick into his
bedroom, a nightmare of filth glowing beneath smoky gaslight. Chickens nested everywhere, and something unseen
rustled beneath heaps of debris in a far corner. The lawmen
cringed as they speculated whether it was a rodent or something reptilian. In the midst of the chaos soared the sort of bed
popular with wealthy Southerners a century earlier, ten-foot
posters supporting a stained and torn silk canopy. Its fine rosewood carving was badly scarred, and the mattress was missing.
A malodorous pallet of filthy rags and pillows served as Dick
Dana's bed.

Roberts eyed Dick closely. He couldn't help feeling sorry for
any human being who had sunk to this sorry state of affairs,
but he still had to get at the truth. "Tell me, Mr. Dana," he said
lightly, as though inquiring about the weather. "Why do you
think there was a murder next door?"

Octavia sprang to life. "I'll answer that, sheriff. We were
talking on that balcony out there and there were some loud
screams and some shots. We both heard them."

"From what direction?" Roberts asked.

"Glenburnie Manor, of course." She shrugged. "That woman
is our only neighbor."

"You heard Jennie Merrill's screams?"

"Possibly." Octavia spoke so slowly the lawmen wondered if
she was spinning a tale.

"Who else could it have been?"

"One of her colored tenants. I'm afraid he beats his wife on a regular basis."

"How many shots did you hear?"

"Three."

"Why didn't you call us?" Serio asked.

"Look around, gentlemen." Octavia gestured grandly. "It should be readily apparent that we cannot afford the luxury of a telephone."

The sheriff turned his attention back to Dick. "What did you do when you heard the shots, Mr. Dana?"

Dick answered, now unexpectedly articulate. "Well, when I heard the commotion, I first thought to notify the proper authorities via a public pay telephone in Duncan Park. That would be the closest one, you see, but Miss Dockery dissuaded me. She was terribly frightened by the shots and did not wish to be left alone."

What a twisted irony, Roberts thought. Half the people in town feared this man, yet Octavia saw him as her genteel protector. Richard Dana may have looked like the half-crazed hermit he was, but his words were both cultivated and cogent. It all made a sort of maddening sense, an outlandish juxtaposition of demeanor and dementia. The sheriff wanted a better look and shined his flashlight on the suspect, noticing for the first time that Dick wore a freshly laundered shirt incongruous with the rest of his filthy clothing. He made a mental note.

"I'm afraid I'll have to ask you to ride downtown with us," he said, speaking softly so as not to frighten this unmoored soul. "Please."

To Roberts's relief, Dick was cooperative, almost humble. "As you wish, sheriff, but I assure you I have broken no laws."

Octavia loudly challenged the sheriff. "You've no right to do this!" she snapped. "You can plainly see Mr. Dana is not capable of any violent actions."

Roberts ignored her hostility. "Appearances can be deceiving, ma'am."

"But as his legal guardian—"

"I'm afraid that carries no weight at present, Miss Dockery," Roberts said, gently shepherding Dick down the dusty stairs. "But I will give you some advice."

"Oh?"

"If either of you keeps a gun, you'd better let us see it now. If you try to conceal it, you'll only make matters worse later."

"We have no firearms at Glenwood. Regardless of what you may have heard."

"You're quite sure?"

Octavia tugged the wrapper more tightly and drew herself up. "Don't question me, sheriff!"

"I only meant that—"

"There are no guns here, gentlemen," Dick interrupted gently. His next words unnerved the lawmen with their simple sincerity. "I have no weapon except my faith."

SECRET DETOUR COMPLETE, Sheriff Roberts hurried next door to Glenburnie Manor for a progress report from Deputy Mulvihill. As the car swept up the drive, he had an unsettling sense of déjà vu. Like Glenwood, this house belonged to a forgotten age, with residents who had withdrawn from society and fashioned a world off-limits to the public. That night, however, Roberts was stunned to discover a virtual invasion underway. Word of the tragedy had obviously spread throughout Natchez because almost a hundred volunteers had joined his small posse in the search for Jennie Merrill. They massed beneath the great oaks, their torches creating flickering apparitions in the hanging moss, lanterns twinkling like giant fireflies as they swarmed through the woods, along the hedgerows and down by the deep ravine.

Angry that locks had been broken to access outbuildings and fearing the loss of crucial evidence, Roberts ordered his men to control the overzealous volunteers. That done, he went looking for Duncan Minor. It wasn't difficult to spot the tall, distinguished gentleman with white hair, trim moustache and slender build. He stood beside the front door, a lone unmoving figure in an ocean of chaos. Roberts respectfully introduced himself before taking his usual inventory. He registered a man struggling for composure, eyes brimming with an uncomfortable mix of loss and vigilance, someone waiting to be told what to do. Roberts would soon add "soft-spoken" to his tally of character traits.

"I know this is a difficult time, Mr. Minor, but would you kindly describe everything that happened before you made the phone call?"

"I will try my best, sir," Duncan replied, nodding politely as he began. "I was riding my horse along the Kingston road, coming from town, when I saw Willie Boyd."

"Willie Boyd?"

"Miss Merrill's yard boy, the one standing over there with your men. He was in an extremely agitated state and reported that he heard three shots and some terrible screams as he was leaving Glenburnie about twilight."

"He's certain that it was Miss Merrill?" Roberts glanced in Willie's direction and decided the kid still looked pretty upset.

"So he said."

"Do you know what time that might have been?"

"Miss Jennie feeds her staff promptly at seven, right after she eats supper, so I suspect Willie would've heard the shots around seven-thirty or so."

"And when did you encounter Willie Boyd?"

"Eight-thirty," Duncan replied. "I know that road very well, and that particular spot is about fifteen minutes' ride from Glenburnie."

Roberts didn't doubt those calculations. Everyone in town knew Duncan had traveled that route every night for decades. "So there's roughly an hour between the time Willie Boyd said he heard those gunshots and the time you encountered him on the Kingston road."

"So it would appear."

The sheriff decided the rest of Duncan's story could wait. "Mr. Minor, if you'll excuse me, I'd like to discuss the time factor with Willie Boyd."

Duncan turned toward a destructive crackle as a clump of searchers waded through Jennie's precious azaleas. He sighed helplessly and looked away. "Very well."

The terrified yard boy corroborated Duncan's report, adding that the other servants had also left and that Hatcher, the caretaker, was out of town. Roberts was curious about that last detail. "Is Hatcher often gone?"

"Oh, no, sir," Willie answered breathlessly. "He don't never go nowhere 'cause he's real old."

"So Miss Jennie was completely alone when you left?"

"Yes, sir. When I left right after supper, she was all by herself."

"What did you do when you heard the shots?"

"I run as fast as I could!" Willie blurted. "I was mighty scared, sheriff, and I didn't know where those shots was comin' from or who was doin' the shootin.'"

"What did you do during the hour between the time you heard the shots and the time you encountered Mr. Minor?"

"Nothin'!" Willie cried. "Didn't do nothin'. Just kept runnin' up the highway, I guess."

"For the entire hour?"

"Yes, sir!"

"Didn't you see anybody you could've stopped for help?"

"I wasn't lookin' for nobody until I saw Mr. Minor."

"What do you mean?"

"'Cause I knew he'd wanna help, sir. I knew he and Miss Jennie was good friends."

The sheriff easily read Willie's fear and knew the boy was anxious to distance himself from white people's business. Although he didn't consider him a serious suspect, Roberts nevertheless booked the terrified Willie and, preliminary in-terrogation finished, turned him over to Mulvihill. Then he re-sumed his conversation with Duncan.

"What did you do after hearing Willie Boyd's story?"

Duncan took a breath and continued. "I immediately hur-ried over here while Willie ran after me. I must confess I was frightened when I saw the place so dark, because there is al-ways a light in the dining room. As I rode up the drive, I called for Miss Merrill several times but got no response."

"Then you entered the house?"

"Yes, sir."

"Was Willie with you?"

"He caught up a few minutes later."

"So you went into the house alone?"

Duncan replied so softly that Roberts asked him to repeat himself. "Yes, sir."

"Would you please show me where you went and what you saw?"

"Certainly." When Duncan finished leading Roberts through the house, he said, "I've touched nothing, Sheriff Roberts. What you see is exactly what I found."

Roberts duly noted the ransacked bedroom and blood-splattered slipper. He returned to the dining room for a closer look at the blanket on the floor and discovered it was a man's heavy wool overcoat. It was filthy. Duncan wrinkled his nose and stepped back.

"Something wrong, Mr. Minor?"

"Such a disgusting thing doesn't belong here."

"That so?"

"Glenburnie Manor is immaculately kept," Duncan an-swered. Judging from the undisturbed areas of the house, Roberts didn't doubt that was true.

"What else did you find?"

Duncan took a lantern from the buffet and led Roberts to the bloody trail outside. They followed until it disappeared near a down-sloping path, into a grove of trees separating Glenburnie Manor from Glenwood. The amount of blood certainly suggested Jennie had been murdered, but Roberts wondered if the feisty old recluse had managed to fight off her captors and escape. He also wondered why her trail led toward Glenwood. Back in the house, Duncan looked haggard and tense under the gaslight, and although Sheriff Roberts respected the long relationship that had existed between the elderly cousins, he needed answers to some urgent questions. Most important, he wanted to know why over an hour had elapsed between Duncan's arrival at Glenburnie and the time he called the police.

Duncan cooperated, but his voice was strained.

"When I first encountered Willie and made some sense of his story, I naturally hoped that the shots had not come from here. After all, the boy was hysterical when he flagged me down, so I didn't know what to believe. I realized the terrible truth when I saw things for myself. At that point I could think of nothing but looking for Miss Jennie." He swallowed hard and shook his head. "How could such a horrible thing happen? I just don't understand."

"Please answer my question, Mr. Minor. Why did you take so long to call the police?"

"I'm sorry, sheriff. When I arrived at Glenburnie, my first thought was to find Miss Jennie, to help if she were injured. A delay to phone the police might have added to her harm, and I couldn't risk that possibility. If I had not done everything in my power to help her, I should not have been able to live with myself."

For the first time, Roberts doubted Duncan's story. "You couldn't take a few minutes to make a phone call?"

"There is no telephone at Glenburnie Manor," Duncan replied. "And I didn't want to waste precious time until I realized there was nothing I could do. As it was, I had to ride halfway into town to make the call."

The explanation sounded reasonable, so the sheriff took a different tack and asked if Duncan recalled anything unusual happening in or around Glenburnie within the last week. He specifically asked if Jennie might have quarreled with her servants.

"They have all been with Miss Jennie for years," Duncan said, glossing over the recent, frequent spats between mistress and servants. "None of them would wish her any harm."

"So you found nothing out of the ordinary?"

"Only Apollo, Miss Jennie's German shepherd."

"What about him?"

"He was locked up."

"Who locked him up?"

"I've no idea. Perhaps Willie Boyd might have an answer to that."

"Is the dog trusting of strangers?"

"No. He's a very good watchdog. I released him for help in hunting for Miss Jennie but locked him up again when I knew the authorities were coming."

Roberts frowned. "Anything else?"

Duncan considered for a long moment. "Miss Jennie said a Negro came to her front door Monday afternoon asking for a handout. She'd been frightened by his coarse manners, and as she continued her story I recalled that I had encountered the same man."

"Do you know his name?"

"I believe his last name was Williams."

Roberts wondered if he'd found his first real lead.

"When did he approach you?"

"A few nights ago. On the way to Glenburnie."

Chief Deputy Stone had joined them and was listening closely. "What exactly happened, Mr. Minor?"

"Well, I was riding over here when he came out of the woods so suddenly that he frightened my horse. He called me by name and claimed he had worked for me some years ago. I was shocked by his insolence, and when I told him I didn't have any work and suggested he try the cardboard box plant, he got uppity. He said he'd already been there and seen so many other colored men waiting around that he decided it useless to apply. That suggested to me that he wasn't too serious about finding work."

"What do you think he was looking for?" Stone asked. "Someone to rob?"

"It certainly crossed my mind, sir. People can't be too careful who they hire these days."

Roberts remembered the absentee servants and told Stone to round them up, along with any tenants on the vast estate. He then picked up the mysterious brown coat for a closer examination. It was far too heavy for such a sultry night, but, when he recalled that the Mississippi Central was nearby, he theorized it might belong to one of the hobos that traipsed through Natchez by the hundreds. Then again, he decided, the coat could have been a disguise. Or perhaps it was intended to muffle screams, something it obviously failed to do.

Stone returned to report that seven servants and tenants had already been rounded up and were in jail waiting questioning. "Counting Dana, that brings our total to eight," Roberts said.

"Right, sir."

"Good work." The sheriff headed for the dining room, asking his chief deputy for help with clues. "Be careful, Stone. We don't want to destroy any evidence or lose any fingerprints."

Stone carefully checked the windows and whistled. "Look at this!" He indicated a pistol ball buried in the window frame. "Looks like a thirty-two-twenty, eh, sheriff?"

Roberts investigated. "I'm no ballistics expert, but that's definitely recent."

With Duncan quietly following, they moved into the adjacent bedroom where another whistle announced Stone's eagle eye had found a second bullet. This one was imbedded at shoulder level in the paneled wall. "It's right in line with the dining room," the deputy noted. "Most likely it was fired from there."

"Willie Boyd said he heard three shots," Roberts said. "Let's keep looking."

A thorough search turned up no more bullets, but it was enough for Roberts to begin reconstructing the crime. He theorized that the intruder surprised Jennie Merrill in the dining room and fired when she stood and screamed. The bullet passed through her frail body and buried itself in the window frame. She then fled into the bedroom, seeking escape through French windows opening onto the veranda. The killer shot again but missed. Because its path had been unobstructed, the second bullet was more deeply imbedded. The third bullet might be anywhere, perhaps lodged in its human target.

Roberts and Stone followed the bloody path outside, Duncan a few steps behind. They found another large stain on the rear porch banister. Continuing onto the grounds, the trail became erratic, making Roberts wonder if Jennie had bumped her head on the railing when she tried to flee and zigzagged in a daze. He also theorized the path could have been made by someone struggling with Jennie's weight. That theory strengthened when he factored in a red smear five feet high beneath the porte-cochère. Jennie was barely that tall.

About twenty feet from the house, Special Deputy Ed Evans found a second bedroom slipper. Another few yards produced a jeweled head comb smeared with blood, making Roberts speculate Jennie might have been carried upside down by her assailant. The trail continued fifty feet to a hedgerow south of the house before ending in a thick pool of drying blood. At that point, the sheriff stopped the search and conferred with his men. Ex-sheriff Abbott suggested sending for George Allen, a rich Louisiana sportsman owning the finest pack of bloodhounds in the region. Abbot believed if the dogs couldn't track the killer they could at least help find Jennie, and

Roberts agreed. He dispatched a minion to call Allen and request a trainer and his two best hounds. The man was also ordered to phone fingerprint expert J. E. Chancellor in Jackson, the state capital a hundred miles away.

"We're gonna need all the help we can get on this one, boys," Roberts muttered.

The search continued into the early morning hours. At 2 AM Roberts heard the deep baying of excited hounds as Allen's car chugged up the drive. The dogs leapt from the car and briefly sniffed the veranda before taking off, straining at their leashes as they followed the trail east toward the dead end that had baffled the sheriff. When they reached the blood-stained ground near the hedgerow, the dogs took off for the house again. After circling it twice, they headed west, away from the trail, leading Roberts and his posse through a mile of thickets, pecan groves and open fields before emerging onto a gravel road. From there they headed directly to a small cottage facing the road. One of the volunteers recognized it as home to a logger named Odell Ferguson and told Roberts the man had a solid reputation and was a hard worker.

Ferguson staggered to the door, still sleepy and obviously unnerved by the baying hounds and menacing posse. "What's going on, Sheriff?"

"I'll be asking the questions," Roberts replied, aware that everyone was watching. "Where have you been these past few hours?"

"Right here," Ferguson asserted. "Ma can tell you I ain't been out of this place all night."

An old lady peered over his shoulder, voice riddled with fear. "That's right."

Ferguson draped an arm around his mother and pressed his case. "I'm a woodsman, sir. I go to bed early because I get up before dawn."

Roberts was inclined to believe Ferguson, but the dogs were making such a racket he overruled his instincts. "How about visitors? Who's been here besides you tonight?"

Ferguson answered quickly. "Bourke come by. I ain't sure, but I reckon it was sometime after seven."

"Bourke?"

"J. R. Bourke." Ferguson pointed into the night. "Our land-lord. Lives right over there."

Roberts reasoned it could be Bourke's trail driving the bloodhounds crazy. but he still wasn't taking any chances. "Get dressed, young man."

"I ain't your man!" Ferguson cried, stricken. "I'm telling you I been here since yesterday afternoon!"

"Maybe so, but you're still taking a ride downtown."

Roberts assigned two men to escort Ferguson and dis-patched two deputies to take Bourke into custody as well and hold him for questioning. When he observed the bloodhounds milling quietly about the yard, he ordered everyone back to the Merrill estate. Five hours had now elapsed since Duncan Minor's call. As Roberts walked toward the manor house, Farris and Mulvihill approached. Farris was carrying some-thing.

Roberts quickened his step. "What's that you got?

"Farris just found this lamp," Mulvihill answered.

"Let's take a look," Roberts muttered.

Farris was obviously excited as he lifted the lamp for the sheriff's inspection. "It's real old-fashioned, the kind that's got a fancy china shade and a silver bowl. Looks like a couple of others we saw in Miss Jennie's house."

"The shade was all broken up so we left it on the grass," Mulvihill added. "We were real careful not to ruin any finger-prints that might be on the bowl."

Roberts nodded. "Show me where you found it."

Farris continued talking as he led the men down a slope leading southeast. "We've been thinking maybe somebody used this lamp to get through the woods after they shot Miss Jennie. Why else would they take it from the house? Maybe the glass shade and chimney fell off and —"

"Or maybe he was carrying Miss Jennie and she knocked it off," Mulvihill suggested.

Roberts was skeptical. "It'd be pretty awkward carrying both Miss Jennie and the lamp. Of course, a big man might've managed since she was so small. Especially if she was dead and he threw her over his shoulder like a sack of meal."

Farris shined his light on the shattered lamp. "But why wouldn't a fleeing criminal use the cover of darkness? Why would he carry a heavy oil lamp?"

"Maybe he thought he'd get lost in these snaky woods without it," Mulvihill offered.

Roberts shook his head. "Somebody could have carried Miss Jennie while someone led their way with the lamp, and maybe everyone went their separate ways afterwards. That could've made those dogs run off in the wrong direction." He thought for a moment. "Then again, these could be false clues. Whoever carried this lamp could be trying to throw us off the scent, buying time while we look for a body. It makes no more sense than a heavy coat in this heat."

They walked further, supposing the path of the gunman until they reached the bank of a ravine. Farris shined his light on a high fence. "Reckon this is the property line." He pointed. "Glenwood is right up that rise."

"Reckon it is at that," Roberts muttered. "Come on, boys. We've got some unfinished business over there."

"What do you mean 'unfinished'?" Mulvihill sounded disappointed.

"We made a little stop on the way over here," Roberts explained. "The Wild Man of Natchez is cooling his heels in the brig. Now it's time to get the Goat Woman."

"You really think they shot Miss Jennie?" Farris asked.

"Somebody sure did something back over there. Now, c'mon. Oh, you boys better prepare yourself. That place is like nothing you've ever seen." He took a deep breath of fresh forest air. "Or smelled."

Despite Roberts's warning, Farris and Mulvihill were shocked by the abominable condition of Glenwood. Neither was disappointed when he told them to wait outside with Serio. Even there the stench was so strong Farris thought he might be sick.

"Damn! How can human beings live like this?" He put a hand over his nose.

"Just thinking that myself," Mulvihill said.

Roberts and Stone entered the house and, although a light still flickered on the upper floor, both found the old place even spookier. With the front door thrown wide and the goats and pigs gone, the house was quiet as a crypt.

"Miss Dockery probably herded the livestock into the night," Roberts said. "Let's see if she's disappeared, too."

They were halfway up the stairs when creaking floorboards above announced they had alerted Octavia to this second intrusion. The loud crack of a door being bolted was followed by an angry shout. "Who's there?"

Tired and sleepy, the sheriff was losing patience. "It's Sheriff Roberts and Deputy Stone, Miss Dockery. We need you to come with us, please."

"On what charges?" she demanded.

"No charges, ma'am. We just want to ask you a few questions."

"Ask me here!" she yelled through the door.

"I'm afraid we need to talk to you at my office."

"That's preposterous!" Octavia did not budge.

"Call it what you like," the sheriff said. "I want to treat you like a lady, Miss Dockery, and I'm asking you to come down peacefully."

The next pause seemed longer with the lawmen trapped in a vortex of heat and hideous odors. Both wanted a bath, and Stone was battling nausea.

"You'll just have to wait," Octavia answered finally. "I'm not properly dressed."

"We'll wait."

Octavia made one last attempt to be left alone and spoke in a softer, more conciliatory tone. "Sheriff, may I please remind you that I've already said I know nothing about any crime at that woman's house?"

Roberts was unmoved. "We're waiting, Miss Dockery."

Ten minutes later, her anger regenerated, Octavia grumbled loudly as they escorted her to the police car.

"I'll bet that woman won't be shooting any more of my livestock."

"What's that?"

"I believe you heard me, Sheriff Roberts."

"Why do you say that?"

"I meant what I said and I said what I meant!" Octavia jerked away when Serio gently took an elbow to help her into the car. "I don't need your assistance, sir. I assure you I am in complete control of my faculties, both physical and mental."

Serio shot Roberts a weary look as Octavia slid into the back seat and slammed the door. "Gonna be a long night, sheriff."

"Yep."

After depositing a newly subdued Octavia alongside eight other suspects, Roberts and his men returned to Glenburnie Manor. Duncan quietly but firmly insisted on joining in a search that dragged on another three hours. Dawn was just dispelling the forest gloom when a shout pierced the stillness. It came from a tall row of camellia bushes southeast of the house.

"Oh, Lordy! It's Miss Jennie over here! Oh, Lordy!" The posse turned as a young black man crashed through the bushes. Alonso Floyd, a neighbor and volunteer, pointed a trembling finger toward the ravine. "I found her down there, sheriff! She's..." Terror checked his words.

"She's what?" Roberts demanded.

"She's down there and she's..." Again he lost his voice.

"Take me there!" Roberts barked.

As everyone followed Floyd down the wooded slope, Roberts prayed Jennie Merrill might still be alive, that quick action might save her life. That hope disintegrated when he saw the body in the gnarled undergrowth of camellia bushes, head at the bottom of the slope. She lay face down, one arm flung wide, the other crushed beneath. Her frail body was splattered with brown blood, long since dried.

"Is she...dead?" someone asked softly.

The sheriff inspected a nasty neck wound before carefully turning the body over. A huge bloodstain had spread across the front of her lounging robe, and rigor mortis was settling in. He turned to the speaker.

"I'm very sorry, Mr. Minor."

Duncan moved closer, face draining of color as he leaned over Jennie's body. The men retreated and respectfully removed their hats as he looked at the remains of a woman he had loved all his life. No one spoke for a long time, until Duncan drifted back to the house alone. Roberts followed after telling a deputy to take Alonso Floyd downtown for routine questioning. Along with Archie Rutherford, a white neighbor who had been unable to account for his whereabouts, this brought the list of those in custody to eleven. After instructing Mulvihill to call the Foster Funeral Home, Roberts made notes while waiting for the ambulance. When the body had been taken away, the sheriff approached Duncan for a few words in private.

"Mr. Minor, again, I know this is difficult, but I still need your help. You knew Miss Jennie better than anybody and I'm hoping you can help me find a motive for her murder."

Duncan shook his head. "I'm afraid there's nothing else I can tell you, sheriff. I simply can't make sense of this awful thing."

Roberts was sympathetic but unsatisfied and knew he'd better handle the old gentlemen with kid gloves if he hoped to get anywhere. "I'm sorry if this sounds like prying, but I have no choice. Did Miss Jennie ever tell you her troubles, or perhaps confide that she was afraid of something? Did anyone ever threaten her, aside from those people over at Glenwood?" Duncan's mind was clearly elsewhere. "Mr. Minor?"

"Lawrence!" Duncan blurted. "That uppity Negro's name was Lawrence Williams." Roberts jotted down the unexpected information before steering him back on track. "Miss Merrill and I shared many confidences, and I can report that she was content with her life and not a timid soul. As for the people at Glenwood, everyone knows about their occasional disagreements, but she hadn't mentioned them in some time. To be frank, I do not consider them true enemies. Just poor, misguided souls."

"What about money?" When Duncan only stared, the sheriff said, "You may not know, Mr. Minor, but there have long been rumors that Miss Jennie hid a large amount of cash on the premises."

Duncan shook his head. "Never more than three dollars. When she needed funds, she drove into town and cashed a check for exactly that amount. I assure you everything else was in the bank."

"I see."

Duncan's voice rasped with fatigue. "Forgive me, sheriff. I really must get home."

"Alright," Roberts agreed. "Good night, Mr. Minor."

Duncan bowed formally and whispered goodnight. Roberts was disappointed, having no choice but to watch the man and his horse disappear in the growing dawn. He looked up as the sun began gilding the rotting roof and crumbling chimneys of Glenwood.

"Poor, misguided souls, eh?" The sheriff rubbed eyes burning with fatigue. "We'll just see about that."

24

ROBERTS AND ABBOTT were dog-tired when another scorcher dawned, but discipline and curiosity drove them back to the crowded jailhouse. The sheriff retreated to his office to devise a system for questioning his many witnesses and suspects. He'd managed to scribble only a few notes when Abbot interrupted.

"Got another logger out there, Book. Says his name's John Geiger and that he used to live at Skunk's Nest."

The sheriff perked up. Skunk's Nest was a tiny, ramshackle lodge on the fringe of Glenwood's sprawling acreage. "What's he want?"

"Says that overcoat we found at Glenburnie might be his."

"Word sure travels fast," Roberts grumbled. "Bring the man in and let's see if he can identify it."

Like Odell Ferguson, Joe Geiger was a young white man in his thirties with the pinched look of poverty stamped on his low brow. He shuffled nervously while inspecting the coat, apparently oblivious to the foul smell.

"Yeah, it's mine alright."

"How did it get to the Merrill house?" Roberts asked.

"Reckon it was stolen," Geiger replied.

"Who in hell would steal something like that, especially in this heat?" Abbott growled, the strain of a sleepless night rumbling to the surface. The sheriff shot him a sharp look. "Sorry, Book."

"You say you lived at Skunk's Nest?" Roberts pressed.

Geiger nodded. "Yes, sir. Leastwise I did 'til a couple of weeks ago. I moved out, but when I went back to get my stuff it was gone."

"What stuff?"

"This coat and a bed and some clothes. Some cooking things. Reckon they took it all."

"Who?"

"You know. That crazy old guy with the long beard." He coughed and cleared his throat. "Or maybe her."

"You were renting Skunk's Nest from Dick Dana and Octavia Dockery?"

Geiger nodded again. "She collected the rent. I only seen him once or twice maybe. Man, he always gave me the willies." He looked from Roberts to Abbott and back again. "Can I have my coat now?"

"Not until we know how it got to the crime scene."

Geiger paled. "I just told you I left everything behind when I moved out."

Roberts called his jailer. "Put Geiger in with the others, Farris. I'll question him later."

"We've got just about everybody now, don't we, Book?" Abbott asked after the loudly protesting Geiger was hustled off. "Everybody who's been anywhere near Glenburnie Manor for the past few days."

"Everybody except Lawrence Williams. And Duncan Minor, of course."

"Who's Lawrence Williams?" Roberts hastily recounted Duncan's strange tale about the colored man who asked him and Jennie for work. Abbot shook his head. "Probably just another drifter like Geiger, and probably long gone. You know how they are, sheriff. They hop freights the way fleas hop dogs."

Both looked up as someone knocked at the door. Roberts barely muttered, "Come in," when Stone and Mulvihill burst into the office. Since neither was especially excitable, the sheriff was eager for their news. "What've you got, boys?"

"Our best clue yet, sheriff." Stone beamed, laying a bundle of wrapping paper atop the desk. "Direct from Glenwood itself."

"Open it," Roberts ordered, leaning closer as his chief deputy unwrapped the package and held up a well-worn dress shirt. "Dana's?"

"Yeah," Stone said. "Still damp. And look at this!" He pointed to several dark splotches. "If this isn't blood, I miss my guess. The fact that it's just been washed tells me the Wild Man was mighty anxious to get rid of those spots."

Roberts studied the telltale stains then looked at Stone. "Remember when we first saw Dana? He was wearing a dirty white suit, but his shirt was clean."

"Looks like old Dick was doing his laundry last night," the deputy said with a lopsided grin. "Yes, indeed."

"That's not all," reported Mulvihill, gleefully laying a yellowed magazine on Roberts's desk. It was a long-defunct New Orleans musical journal with three fresh-looking stains on the cover. "Another bloody Glenwood souvenir."

"Well, looky here." Abbott was as amazed as the others. "It's blood, all right. No doubt about it."

Roberts allowed himself a tired smile. "Good work, boys. I'll have these stains analyzed later, but first Abbott and I are going to have a chat with the Wild Man. In the meantime, you two get back out to Glenwood and see what else you can find. Look everywhere, and I mean everywhere, no matter how disgusting it gets. And you'd better post somebody at the entrance to keep out the curiosity-seekers. That place is going to be a madhouse soon as this story breaks."

Within the hour, Roberts and Abbott faced Dick Dana. Both lawmen noted a strange serenity had come over their prime suspect. The faraway look in Dick's eyes had vanished and, except for the bad grooming and dirty clothes, he could have been any man off the street.

"Have a seat, Mr. Dana."

"Thank you, sir."

Dick nodded politely and glanced around the room, focusing on nothing in particular as he awaited further instructions. The sheriff watched for any reaction as Abbott produced the damp shirt. There was none. Dick remained cool as ever.

"Is this your shirt, Mr. Dana?"

Without hesitation he replied. "Yes, sir."

"It's damp," Roberts said. "Did you wash it last night?"

He nodded vigorously. "Oh, yes, sir. We did a washing last night."

The sheriff thought again of Dana's clean shirt and dirty suit. He pointed to the stains. "Do you know what these spots are?"

Again, no hesitation. "Blood."

Roberts shot Abbott a look. "You were trying to wash the blood out?"

"Dirt, too," Dick replied. He watched, unruffled, as Abbott produced the worn music journal, and responded without being asked. "That's mine, too."

Abbott pointed to the dark splotches. "Is this blood?"

"Yes, sir."

"Will you please tell me whose blood it is and how it got on your shirt and magazine?"

"Certainly, sir," Dick replied politely. "It's pig's blood."

"Pig's blood!"

"Yes, sir. We slaughtered a young pig yesterday afternoon."

Abbott didn't want to believe him. "You know, Mr. Dana, it's a very simple matter to test the blood and see whether it's human or animal."

"I'm quite sure it is."

Roberts waved Abbott to take the evidence for testing. "Let me ask you something else, Mr. Dana. About those three gunshots you said you heard last night."

"Yes, sir?"

"Where were you and what were you doing when you heard them?"

"Strolling the grounds. It's something I often do at twilight. Such a peaceful time."

"Go on."

"I was watching the sky and enjoying an enormous cloud bank swelling in the west. It reminded me of something."

"What's that?"

"The White Mountains of New Hampshire," Dick replied. There was a tinge of melancholy as he continued, the only emotion he had yet displayed. "I was there as a young man, and it summoned some rather poignant recollections. You see, in that particular part of New England — "

"So you were at Glenwood, eh?" Abbott interrupted, fearing Dick might careen into incoherent rambling.

"Yes, sir."

"But Miss Dockery said you two were talking on the balcony," the sheriff insisted.

Dick was unruffled as ever. "Miss Dockery was sitting on the balcony. I was in the yard below, easily within hearing range. We exchanged a few words of conversation. If you thought something else, I'm afraid you were mistaken."

Once again Roberts's line of questioning led nowhere. He tried another angle. "What was your relationship with Jennie Merrill?"

"We were friends in our youth," Dick answered. "She rented Glenwood from me at one time, but I haven't seen her since... Well, it's been a long time. Nineteen-fifteen, perhaps. Yes, that's when it was. I had a pig named Sandy Great. A red, white and blue pig. He unfortunately found his way to her grounds and I went to retrieve him. She warned me not to let it happen again."

"And what did you say?"

"Nothing. I got my pig home in a hurry!" Dick cackled, revealing a row of mostly missing teeth. "Everyone knows Miss Jennie's a crack shot with those guns of hers."

"Did you hate Miss Jennie after that?" Abbott asked.

"I don't hate anyone, sir. My father was Reverend Charles Backus Dana. I was brought up in a household that did not allow hate."

Abbott was exasperated. "Then exactly what were your feelings toward Miss Merrill?"

"We had some disagreements over the years, always involving our animals. I'm afraid Miss Jennie believed it was our intention to let them wander onto her property to do damage. Such was not the case, of course. It was always accidental. Our mutual property line is quite long, and you know animals have a habit of going where they like."

Roberts and Abbott immediately thought of Glenwood, of pigs and goats in the parlor and chickens roosting in the bedrooms.

"Go on."

"Well, sir, things seemed to have calmed down until Miss Jennie shot one of our sows and orphaned nine piglets. That's when we had to take her to court."

"How did you feel about her then?"

"I have no feelings one way or the other, but I'm sure sorry she killed my pig. I'm sorry someone killed her, too."

The interrogation continued for just over an hour, until both lawmen were out of questions. "That's it for now, Mr. Dana." Roberts sighed. "Thank you for your cooperation."

"You're welcome, sir."

After Farris took Dick away, Roberts turned to Abbott. "You know something, W. P.? That poor soul has been getting a bum rap all these years. He's eccentric all right, and he sure as hell needs a bath, but he's not as crazy as everybody thinks."

"Crazy like a fox maybe," Abbott offered, always the pessimist.

"I'm not saying he's innocent. I'm just saying that he stayed very cool. He's also sticking to his story like flypaper."

"So far, anyway."

"Well, let's see if Miss Dockery is that cool. Have Farris bring her in, will you?"

Unlike Dick, Octavia's mood had grown fouler since her incarceration. She fairly reeked of indignation when she was ushered into the sheriff's office. One look warned Roberts it was going to be an uphill battle.

"Miss Dockery, I'd like to ask you about something you said just before we brought you here." She glared. "What did you mean by saying that woman wouldn't be shooting any more of your livestock?"

"It's hardly a complicated comment."

"Just answer the question please."

"Dead women don't do much killing, do they, sheriff?"

"What made you think Miss Merrill was dead?"

"Well, she is, isn't she?"

Roberts wished she would stop responding with questions. "Please answer me."

Octavia merely snorted, muttered to herself and gave a look of reprimand to Farris, who was staring too hard for her comfort.

Stonewalled, Abbott took another tack. "We found a bloody shirt at Glenwood, Miss Dockery. Someone had been trying to wash out the stains. Dick Dana says it's one of his, but he can't explain where the stains came from. Nor can he explain the source of bloodstains on an old music magazine."

"Then he's having a 'there' day," Octavia said.

"I beg your pardon?"

"You've all seen how my pitiful ward is. I'm saying he's not 'all there' today. If he were he'd have told you we slaughtered a hog yesterday. That's the shirt he was wearing at the time. I washed it because it was bloody. I guess he got blood on that old journal, too. Lord knows why he's always leafing through it. He hasn't played a note in years."

Roberts and Abbott asked the same questions they had posed to Dick. One after another, Octavia not only corroborated his statements but supported them with confident responses. When Roberts decided to probe her past, she described a childhood of exceptional privilege, and her mood softened as she recalled happier times.

"When my father and sister died, I had no more family. My only recourse was Mr. Dana. He had been a close friend in better days and was kind enough to give me shelter after his accident. When I saw no future in my literary efforts, I sought to survive through farming, a small garden, and some livestock." Mistaking expressions of amazement for condemnation, Octavia grew indignant. "I had no other choice!"

"We meant no disrespect," Roberts apologized, touched by a fall from grace far greater than he suspected. "Please continue."

"Mr. Dana has a kind heart. You should know he's never tried to take advantage of my predicament as some men would. There has never been any sort of romantic attachment between us. I've been nothing more to him than a caretaker and housekeeper, and not a very good one at that." She brushed back a wisp of hair that had escaped her combs. "Perhaps you don't know that he wasn't always what you see today. Like me, he had a promising career in the arts and lost everything. I've stood by, helpless all these years, as his mind slipped away. He has faults, grievous faults, but none deserving of such consequences. I've watched him tormented by townspeople who call him the Wild Man, and me the Goat Woman. And our pitiful house Goat Castle. Oh, yes, gentlemen. I know what's said about us and I don't care. I can't care, you see, because I haven't the time or energy. I'm much too busy carrying water for miles

and trying to keep food on the table. Believe me, it was difficult enough without that woman next door killing our valuable livestock."

"Miss Dockery—"

"It's true I despised Miss Merrill," Octavia went on. "Perhaps
I hated her, more than anyone in this town. There's no point
in denying it. She and Duncan Minor tried to take Glenwood
away from us, and our feuds are a matter of public record. But
I assure you I did not kill the woman, and I will fight as hard
as I can to prove my innocence." Her voice rose along with her
temper, and she pounded her small fist on the desk like an em-
press hurling ultimatums. "I will not be punished for a crime I
did not commit!"

"Calm down, Miss Dockery," Roberts said. "No one has accused you of murder, but we need to ask some more questions.
Please."

"Very well," she sniffed, only slightly placated by his kindly
tone.

"Did you rent Skunk's Nest to a tenant named John Geiger?"

"I did, but I should never have trusted him. He not only let
his rent go several months in arrears but showed no inclination
of paying."

"So you evicted him?"

"I did, indeed."

"Did you take all his belongings?"

"I took a few pieces of old furniture and a feather bed." She
thought for a moment. "And some cooking utensils."

"Nothing more?" She shook her head as Roberts tried to get
her to mention the army overcoat. "No clothing?"

She looked disgusted by the prospect of taking Geiger's
clothes. "Only things that might have been some use to me. I
intended to hold them until he paid the back rent, but frankly,
that's money I never expect to see."

"So you took no clothing?"

"No, I did not."

Roberts looked at Abbott, then back to Octavia. "That's all for now, Miss Dockery."

"Am I free to go?"

"I'm afraid not," the sheriff replied. "There are still some missing pieces to the puzzle."

"But I've told you everything I know," she protested. When Roberts shook his head, she said, "Then please tell me who's watching our home. If people learn there's no one in the house, I'm afraid—"

"Some men were just sent out to secure the place, ma'am. The house is still being searched for clues."

"You're wasting your time, Sheriff Roberts," Octavia announced. "And I think you all know it."

By the end of the day, Roberts wasn't sure what he knew. One after another, he and Abbott grilled their suspects and one after another they were released with strong alibis or for lack of evidence. Roberts believed Odell Ferguson and J. R. Bourke and sent them home along with their neighbors, Archie Rutherford and T.W Carr. Willie Boyd, the black yard boy who reported the screams and gunshots to Duncan, was freed, as were Miss Jennie's other servants. Also released were Alonzo Floyd, the man who had found the body, his wife Lucille, and Albert Morrison, a drifter who had done some work in the area.

When Roberts finally drove home for some much-needed sleep, only three suspects remained at the Adams County Jail: Dick Dana, Octavia Dockery, and Joe Geiger.

25

T HE Natchez *Democrat* went to press in the wee
hours of Friday morning, August fifth, before Jennie's
body had been found. The third headline down, it nonetheless
leapt off the page.

WOMAN MYSTERIOUSLY MISSING; ATROCIOUS MURDER INDICATED.
INDICATED MISS JENNIE MERRILL
TRAGEDY VICTIM

Below, in much smaller type, "Screams in Night, Sound
of Shots and Blood Stained Home Indicate Murderous
Attack—Search for Body...OFFICERS AND POSSE ARE
SCOURING WOODS...Bloodhounds from Wisner to
be Placed on Trail—Army Overcoat May be Clue to the
Assailant."

The article concluded that "evidence of the apparent atrocious crime created intense excitement and high feeling," the entire report appropriately sandwiched between two other spectacular crimes at the extremes of the social spectrum. One reported the recapture of "Mrs. Bluebeard," an Idaho woman accused of poisoning four husbands and another male relative for insurance money. The other concerned Libby Holman, the New York torch singer whom Jennie and Duncan had argued about their last night together. Duncan's prediction that Holman wouldn't be convicted of murdering her husband, wealthy tobacco heir Smith Reynolds, proved true when the Reynolds family, skittish about scandal, dropped all charges. By the next day, however, August sixth, all other competing crimes were blown off the front page as the editors of the *Democrat* graduated Miss Jennie (née Jane) to top billing.

DEATH OF MISS JANE MERRILL REMAINS A MYSTERY

The story revealed that no less than eight people were being held for questioning in the "Most Brutal and Atrocious Crime in History of County." The overblown prose was appropriate during the anemic years of the Great Depression when poverty and desperation transfused America's bloodlust and generated mass adulation of folk heroes like Clyde Barrow and the Barker-Karpis Gang. Sensational crimes begot equally sensational journalism, and Jennie's murder was a dramatic plum with all the requisite trimmings: once-beautiful women, world famous players, great wealth, madness, illicit sex, incest and lives beyond the pale. Although she was so reclusive the *Democrat* dubbed Jennie Merrill "the woman whom nobody knew," old-line Natchezians knew her blood was the bluest of the blue and that her death would make headlines from New York to Brussels, along with every hamlet in Mississippi.

No one was more riveted than Stephen Holmes.

He was in his office at the *New York Sun* when the story hummed over the wires, horror supplanting incredulity as he registered the scant details. He promptly informed his boss that Jennie's death was big news because she had been a prominent New Yorker and was the daughter of a former Ambassador to Belgium. Reminded that Jennie had led Holmes to his award-winning story on Paddy O'Brien almost forty years before, the publisher told his prized journalist to catch the first train for Mississippi.

Other crime experts descended on Natchez as well. Over the weekend, J. E. Chancellor, the ballistics specialist from Jackson, turned his magnifying glass on Glenburnie Manor. Roberts was immediately put off by Chancellor's braggadocio and insinuation that he was doing the sheriff a favor by bringing big city expertise to such a small town. At the crime scene, Roberts retreated to his car when Chancellor's incessant self-promotion grew unbearable, and left the man on his own to dust with gray powder and brush for prints. But it wasn't long before the sheriff heard crowing and was summoned back inside.

"Fingerprints everywhere," Chancellor announced, gesturing dramatically around Jennie Merrill's bedroom. "I found twelve in the dining room, on the table, buffet and walls. There were three more in here that looked too small to belong to a man."

Roberts immediately thought of Octavia. Despite her arrogance, he had initially sympathized with her tragic plight and understood the immense chip on her shoulder. Now he saw her in a different light. If she was enterprising enough to endure all those desperate years, her survival instincts were obviously well honed and they could easily extend to defending her sole means of survival—the livestock. He was also still haunted by her remark about Miss Jennie not killing again, hours before death was confirmed.

"There were five prints on those French bedroom windows leading to the veranda, more on the dressing table and drawer handles. Got a total of thirty-two prints, sheriff, most good enough to be photographed and classified. After that, it's just a matter of matching the suspects."

"I hope it's that easy. What about the bullets?"

"I made microscopic photos of the woodwork before digging them out. They were both fired from the same thirty-two-twenty. The one in the bedroom wasn't buried like the first. It was protruding from the wall."

"We believe it was slowed down by passing through the victim's body." Roberts gestured toward Chancellor's camera. "How long before we can compare the fingerprints?"

"As soon as my photographs are developed. They're always good," Chancellor boasted, tilting his head down and peering over his glasses. "Surely you have fingerprints on all your suspects, including the ones you've already released?"

"Surely," Roberts grunted, affronted by the condescension.

Chancellor barely heard. "You'll need to create some sort of makeshift lab at the jail. That way we can stay in close contact and I can report my findings as they emerge."

"My men will help in any way we can," Roberts said, wandering back toward fresh air. "Let me know what you find."

"Sure thing, Sheriff Richards."

Roberts didn't bother to correct him.

Chancellor worked through Sunday night and into Monday. Roberts had had a serious disappointment when a lab report confirmed that the blood on Dick's shirt and magazine was indeed from swine, so he was definitely in the mood for good news when Chancellor strode triumphantly into his office late Monday afternoon to announce he'd matched a fingerprint.

Roberts almost leapt out of his chair. "Which one?"

"The left forefinger print on the post of Miss Merrill's bed belongs to Miss Dockery. And there's more!"

Roberts's heart raced. Had his hunch been right?

"Dick Dana?"

"I may have his prints on the silver bowl of the broken lamp, but I can't be certain. It's the right index finger, and your print of that finger is blurred."

"Because it's disfigured!" Roberts cried, excitement ballooning as another piece of the puzzle fell into place. "He slammed a window on his hand some years back. I noticed the deformity when we took his prints!"

Chancellor gave him a sly grin. "Then he's our man!"

"Take more fingerprints, Chancellor! We've got to be absolutely certain that your findings are correct. If so, I'll issue murder warrants for both Dockery and Dana."

When the investigator left, Roberts sent for the county attorney and explained the new development. "In view of Chancellor's findings," the attorney said, "we'll secure the arrest warrants from Judge Elizey right away. There's just one thing, Sheriff Roberts."

"Yes, sir?"

"You'd better hope to hell Chancellor knows what he's doing."

"What do you mean?"

The lawyer shook his head. "It wouldn't be the first time that man's gone off half-cocked."

A few hours later, Chancellor officially declared that the prints belonged to Dick Dana and Octavia Dockery, and by late afternoon they were formally charged with the murder of Jennie Merrill. The *Democrat's* headlines screamed the news.

MURDER CHARGES FILED
AGAINST DANA-DOCKERY
FINGERPRINTS OF TWO FOUND
CAUSE FOR THE CHARGES
Jackson Expert Says He Has Positive
Print of Miss Dockery,
Believed He Also Has Prints of Dana

Natchez, however, wasn't so sure. It was common knowledge that the eccentric old couple feuded with the murder victim, but few saw that as sufficient motive to kill her. Many believed the shy Wild Man and fiercely reclusive Goat Woman incapable of such a hideous crime. Others simply felt sorry for Octavia and Dick. Thousands were suffering beneath the crush of the Great Depression, but few had sunk to their pitiful depths. "There but for the grace of God go I," was a commonly heard sentiment. Old Civil War wounds were even reopened as people stood behind Octavia, daughter of a distinguished Confederate general, and loudly condemned Jennie for her family's pro-Union sympathies.

Aside from personal prejudices, the public considered the evidence flimsy. How authentic were the fingerprints found at Glenburnie Manor? What proof was there that Dick and Octavia left their property the night of the crime? Where was the murder weapon? How and why would that elderly couple carry Jennie's body such a distance and hurl it into a ravine? Rumors began flying that his doubt about Chancellor's findings had prompted Sheriff Roberts to summon one of the nation's foremost criminologists for help. Attention now focused on the arrival of Maurice B. O'Neill of the Bureau of Identification, New Orleans Police Department, and former President of the International Association for Identification.

Reverend Kuehnle publicly voiced his sympathy, and a number of people sent flowers, baskets of fruit and cheery notes of encouragement to the prisoners. Adelaide Merriwether, one of the wealthiest women in Mississippi, had her chauffeur personally deliver a huge box of American Beauty roses to Octavia, while a few local ladies, recalling her from decades past, attempted to pay social calls. Octavia refused to see everyone, politely telling Laurin Farris, "Thank you, but Miss Dockery is not receiving."

Octavia also shunned all interviews until one morning when Farris handed her the one calling card she could not ignore. For the first time since her arrest, Octavia smiled and told the jailor to show this new visitor to her cell. There was a glow beneath the hard-won freckles when she saw Stephen Holmes.

"Miss Dockery," he said, pleased by her healthy radiance. "How good of you to see me."

"I've not forgotten your kindness the day you took me to the cemetery, Mr. Holmes," Octavia explained as he was ushered into her cell. "There have been so many untruths printed about me. I'm hoping if there is anyone who might tell my side of things it would be you."

"I'll do my best," Holmes promised.

"Then please sit down and ask me anything you wish."

"Suppose you just tell me how you got here," Holmes said as he extracted his pad and pen. "If you'll forgive my presumptuousness, perhaps as you would tell a friend."

Octavia smiled. "I don't consider that presumptuous at all."

Her story rushed in staccato bursts as she revealed a terrible burden she had shouldered alone for years. Holmes's pen could barely keep pace. Twice, he asked her to slow down.

"I was born in eighteen-sixty-four on Lamartine plantation in southern Arkansas. My great-grandfather was Cato West, Territorial Governor of Mississippi. My father was Brigadier General Thomas Pleasant Dockery, C.S.A., Commander of the Nineteenth Arkansas Infantry. After the war, we moved to Houston, Texas, where my father worked to ease that city's bonded debts, and when I was twelve, he took us to New York, where I attended the Comstock School for Girls on Forty-second Street. I made my debut in a Worth of Paris gown and, believe it or not, was considered part of the city's smart, young set." She tucked away strands of greasy hair that had escaped her battered sun bonnet." I began writing poetry and achieved a certain amount of local fame for my efforts. When my mother died and my only sister Nydia married a planter in Fayette, Mr. Richard Forman, I divided my time between New York and Fayette and became the proverbial social butterfly without a care in the world. I did nothing but attend balls and house parties in Vicksburg and New Orleans."

Anyone else, Holmes noted, might have allowed herself

a moment of blissful escape in recounting palmier days, but Octavia Dockery's swiftly delineated past was a litany of indulgences gone and best forgotten. He suspected it was as much an unburdening as a plea for the truth.

"Eventually I tired of such frivolity and began writing again. My poetry and special articles were well-received for their freshness and originality, and I was given high praise from Mrs. Nicholson, editress and owner of the *New Orleans Picayune*, and Mr. Julius... Oh, what was his name? Ah! Julius Lemkowitz, publisher of the *Natchez Evening News*. With their support, I hoped to achieve enough fame and fortune to sustain myself. It was about that time that I was invited to be a member of the Warren Antarctica Expedition you wrote about. Ah..."

Octavia took a deep breath, as though filling her lungs might rejuvenate her foundering spirit. "Would you like a glass of water?" Holmes asked.

"In a moment, perhaps," she replied. Another deep breath as she clasped her hands tight. "Then, one after another, things collapsed like a house of cards. My sister Nydia died along with her husband, and my father followed some years afterwards. I don't know where I might have gone had it not been for the kindness of Richard Dana. Fortune had stopped smiling on him as well. You may recall he had a promising career in New York as both singer and classical pianist until an accident crushed his hand. When he returned here, he took me in like the proverbial Good Samaritan. We managed until financial reverses overwhelmed him and put us in the same drifting boat."

"So that's when you began raising chickens and goats."

"And pigs," Octavia added, absently studying her gnarled, calloused hands once sheathed by satin gloves. "It was either that or starve. As Richard grew more withdrawn, it fell upon me to run Glenwood alone. There was nothing but ceaseless drudgery to fill my days, and I was worked almost to death. No one knows better than I that the beautiful place fell into horrible ruin, but I had no time for housekeeping and certainly no funds for repairs and upkeep." She looked up, composure betrayed by an uncontrollable quiver in her voice. "I implore you to ask your readers what they might have done under similar circumstances."

"I most certainly will," Holmes assured her.

"Can you wonder that Dick chose to shun the world, when people can be so heartless and cruel?" she asked, patience eroding as she addressed the present. "I've read in the newspaper that ghouls in human form are taking away some of our more intimate personal possessions. While we are behind the bars of a prison for a crime of which, as God is my hearer, we are innocent, vandals prowl through our home. True, it is just a pitiful place now, but it's all we have. Is there no law, no justice that will protect our property rights?" She gestured tiredly at the walls of her cell. "Is everyone outside devoid of human feeling?"

"I'm so sorry to hear this, Miss Dockery. What a truly awful thing."

"Indeed! And I beg you as a famous newspaperman to please tell the world the truth. Tell them, too, that I did not kill Miss Merrill. God knows I did not kill her. It's true, she was no friend, but had I known her life was threatened on the night that I heard screams and gunshots at her home, I would have offered my assistance. Yes, if I hadn't been so decimated by my labors during the day, I would have helped anyone in distress, even gone to her rescue through that black, snaky forest."

Octavia's mood was swiftly darkening. "Even though I have no money, I intend to prove my innocence. I still have a few friends in the North, friends from my days as a Southern belle, and I hope they will help me fight my arrest." She coughed and took another deep breath. "I'd like that water now, Mr. Holmes."

It was clear that Octavia was thoroughly drained of energy and the will to continue, and Holmes was grateful that his fast writing had captured her incredible tale. Once he secured the water from Farris, he said, "I will do my best to serve justice to your story, Miss Dockery, and I thank you again for talking to me."

She gratefully drained the glass and set it aside. "I remember enough about journalism to know the importance of an 'exclusive,' Mr. Holmes. In your capable hands it should have special impact."

"I hope so."

He rose to go, but Octavia gripped his forearm with surprising strength. He couldn't know this was her first physical contact with another human being in years.

"What is it, Miss Dockery?"

"There's another reason I'm trusting you, Mr. Holmes," she said. "The day you left me at Glenwood with those tins of water, I found something most unexpected when I got to the house. You had tucked a twenty-dollar bill into the pocket of my old sweater. I've never forgotten because it was the last act of human kindness anyone showed me." Octavia squeezed gently before dropping her hand and triggered a rush of emotion from the seasoned reporter as she whispered, "I thank you with all my heart."

HOLMES'S COMPASSIONATE STORY appeared in both the *Democrat* and the *Sun* on August tenth, rousing both sympathy and a flood of fascination for the grotesque crime. Because of the victim's aristocratic bloodlines, as well as those of Dick and Octavia, and the shocking squalor of Glenwood, reporters from all over the country descended upon sleepy Natchez. Money changed hands, not always quietly, as photos were acquired of the three principal players. There was Jennie as a baby and in her presentation gown at the Court of St. James. Before and after pictures of the tragic Octavia showed her in the Worth of Paris original and in prison garb. Dick was seen as a promising New York musical genius and, of course, as the

Wild Man of Natchez. They were instant celebrities as their faces and stories were splashed across newspapers and magazine covers from coast to coast.

Curiosity-seekers and those merely with a taste for the macabre joined the ever-growing army of reporters. They deluged the little town, overflowing the hotels and mobbing the jail in hopes of glimpsing the alleged murderers. They flocked to Glenburnie Manor and Glenwood, clamoring for a first-hand look at the crime scene. Sheriff Roberts placed additional guards at both houses and sealed the driveways to keep the swelling crowds at bay, but it was a losing battle as Octavia's so-called "ghouls" skulked about the vast grounds at night and helped themselves to souvenirs while the guards dozed.

Stirring equal controversy was Jennie's will. She was known to have inherited a substantial sum from her father and rumored to have scored high in the real estate market on her own in her later years. Exactly how great was her fortune and who would benefit from it? As a spinster without children, everyone assumed her considerable estate would remain within her family, and Sheriff Roberts was as curious as the next man when he learned Jennie had given her attorney, S. B. Laub, a strongbox some years ago. On Thursday, August eleventh, a week after the murder, Laub opened the strongbox in chancery court and revealed her last will and testament. It caused a sensation when he read aloud.

"I will to Duncan G. Minor all the realty, personal property, bonds and everything of which I am possessed at the time of my death, who knows my wishes and will execute them accordingly without giving bond, and who I do further appoint my sole and only executor." Laub handed the documents over for probate as he added, "It's signed Jane S. Merrill, February twenty-eighth, nineteen-twenty-five."

The public was stunned to learn Jennie's estate included not just the vast acreage of Glenburnie Manor but two productive plantations across the river in Concordia Parish, Louisiana, plus bonds and securities with estimated value exceeding a quarter of a million dollars! Her siblings up North and in Europe were totally excluded, as were a scattering of cousins in Mississippi. Local gossips had a field day, singing that she flaunted her illicit affair from beyond the grave, while reporters exploited this new angle of a spinster heiress spurning family to leave her fortune to a forbidden paramour. Correspondents came with entourages of photographers, staff artists and young female writers claiming to be experts on romance and crime. Columnists all over America went wild over Dixie's aged Romeo and Juliet and their feuding families. Old photographs of Jennie, Dick and Octavia would run yet again, but pictures of a fourth party were needed. Images of Duncan Minor became the most sought-after properties in town because early ones were unavailable to the press and new ones were impossible to acquire. Duncan belonged to the old school, believing women might allow their pictures to be published as brides, hostesses and garden clubbers, but men posed only for portraitists. Relatives and friends were harangued for help, but to no avail.

Duncan Minor had emerged as the mystery man in what the press was now calling the "Goat Castle Murder." Although the victim was slain next door, reporters knew the sensational label would sell plenty of newspapers. Indeed, the phenomenon snared the attention of more than news hounds, gossip-mongers and souvenir hunters. On Friday morning, August twelfth, a stranger strode unannounced into Sheriff Roberts's office. Wearing a severely tailored gray suit and minimal cosmetics, she was as business-like as her appearance. A bold, assertive voice reinforced the image and prompted Roberts to rise before he knew what he was doing.

"I'm Sophie Friedman," the stranger announced with a firm handshake. "We spoke earlier on the telephone."

"Oh, yes. You're here to represent Octavia Dockery."

"Correct."

"Please have a seat."

She did not sit. "Thank you, Sheriff Roberts, but I'd prefer to visit my client right away."

"I see." Roberts was not surprised by her brusqueness. Because she was one of the most famous female attorneys in the South, celebrated for championing the underdog and definitely a power to be reckoned with, he couldn't help being intrigued. "Is there anything I might help you with, Miss Friedman?"

"Thank you, no. You see my partner on the case is Lawrence T. Kennedy. He's quite familiar with Miss Dockery's unique situation, having worked with her before."

Roberts's weariness flooded back when he heard the notorious Tiger Man was involved again. "I recall the case."

"Mr. E. H. Ratliffe is also on our team, and you should know we intend to bring a habeas corpus proceeding on behalf of Miss Dockery and Mr. Dana. Given the evidence, we see no purpose in their being further detained."

"Fingerprints are pretty strong evidence."

Another smile, carefully controlled, played across Miss Friedman's lips. "I understand that you've sent for Maurice O'Neill."

"That's correct."

"Sir, the very fact that you would seek such a renowned criminologist suggests you are doubtful about Mr. Chancellor's findings."

"We want to be as thorough as possible in this investigation, Miss Friedman," he replied. Her superior attitude reminded him of Chancellor. "People's lives are involved here."

"Indeed they are, Sheriff Roberts," she said with a curt nod. For a moment, neither had anything else to say. "Then you'll kindly direct me to Miss Dockery?"

"I'll call the jailor," Roberts muttered, now anxious to be rid of this woman. His tolerance of smug, condescending out-of-towners had just about reached its limit.

26

ONDAY MORNING, AUGUST fifteenth, Sheriff
Roberts fought a vicious headache as he mulled
over the wild card in Jennie Merrill's murder—Lawrence
Williams. Until a few days ago, multiple suspects had consumed his investigative energies, but Roberts was a lawman who worked by the numbers and, once everyone except
Octavia and Dick had been excused, his mind returned to the
Negro who sought work from Duncan and Jennie on separate
occasions. He discovered that Williams was a local fellow who
had been raised by a man named Will Bailey. A visit to Bailey's
house led to Beaupreaux plantation outside town where
Williams's cousins said he occasionally did odd jobs. Roberts's
curiosity turned to suspicion when he learned Williams often carried a gun, had been arrested for possession of a firearm,
and sometimes went by an alias: Pinckney Williams. More
queries took the sheriff to a lady friend of Williams named
Katherine White, who lived five miles from Glenburnie. Miss

White said Williams left her house about 1:30 in the afternoon on August fourth, the day of the murder, and she hadn't heard from him since. At that point his trail went cold.

Roberts was weighing this dead end when Farris leaned into his office. "You've got a long distance call from Pine Bluff, Arkansas, sheriff."

Roberts massaged his throbbing temples. "Can't you take it, Laurin?"

"Better if you did, Book. The police chief up there says it's urgent. Something about the Merrill case."

Roberts grabbed the receiver. "Sheriff Roberts here."

"Hello, sheriff. This is W. D. Fiveash. I'm Chief of Police up here in Pine Bluff."

"Yes, sir?"

"Something happened here last night that may be of interest to you. Might be connected to that big murder case down there. The Merrill woman."

"Go on," Roberts urged.

"Well, one of my officers, Bob Henslee, was arresting a colored hobo for hopping a freight, and the man pulled a gun. Fortunately, Bob was faster on the trigger and shot first. Killed him. When we looked in the dead man's bag we found evidence that he's lamming it from Natchez."

"What's his name?"

"George Pearles." Fiveash spelled the last name for the sheriff.

"Never heard of him," Roberts said. "How did you know he was here?"

"A letter he was carrying. Mentioned him being in Natchez."

"What's his address?"

"There wasn't an envelope, sheriff, but the return address on the letter is Argo, Illinois."

"George Pearles, eh?" Roberts hoped the name might ring a bell if he said it aloud. It didn't. Nor had he ever heard of Argo, Illinois.

"Yeah. I know it's a long shot, sheriff, but the circumstances are suspicious no matter how you look at it. First, why would a tramp be carrying a gun? And, second, why would he be so quick to use it on a policeman unless he was in some kind of trouble? Big trouble. That Merrill woman's murder has been in the news so much lately, when I found a letter connecting this guy to Natchez I thought I better give you a call while he's still on ice up here."

"What kind of gun was it?"

"A thirty-eight."

Roberts's heart sank. The bullets that had killed Jennie Merrill were unquestionably from a .32.20.

"Don't think he's our man, chief, but I'll see what I can find out and call you back."

"I'd appreciate it."

Roberts hung up and tiredly tossed this new information into the mix. He now had a second mysterious black man to investigate, but that project shot to the back burner when Farris popped in again to announce Maurice O'Neill had arrived on the morning train from New Orleans and was ready to see him. Roberts was ready, too, eager to point the famed criminologist toward J. E. Chancellor and wait for some fireworks. He wasn't disappointed when the three were finally together and the no-nonsense O'Neill interrupted Chancellor's overblown account of his investigation and snapped orders.

"Get Duncan Minor's fingerprints!"

"You consider him a suspect?" Chancellor blurted.

O'Neill ignored the obvious answer. "I want prints of anyone who was in that house on a regular basis, servants included. That will separate them from any other prints you might find."

"I don't think we'll find more prints," Chancellor said, annoyed by the slight on his work. "You see, Mr. O'Neill, I —"

"I need to see the crime scene for myself." When Chancellor's jaw sagged, O'Neill barked, "Now!"

Roberts waited until O'Neill bullied Chancellor outside before releasing the chuckle he'd stifled since introducing the two.

The laughter felt good, and he was more relaxed as he followed up on his promise to the Arkansas sheriff. With Serio in tow, he combed Colored Town for information on either Lawrence "Pinckney" Williams or George Pearles. He turned up nothing. Knowing that Mississippi's Negro communities could be notoriously close-mouthed when questioned by white authorities, Roberts tracked down a man he described to Serio as "my most reliable customer, inside and outside the law." Tyrone Johnson was a petty thief always eager to supply information in exchange for a sympathetic ear after his inevitable next arrest. Johnson said he'd never heard of George Pearles but reported Pinckney Williams had been staying at an unnumbered cabin on St. Catherine Street.

"Keep your fingers crossed, Joe," Roberts whispered as they approached the decrepit shack. "This is our only lead so far, and if doesn't work we're cooked."

After a series of knocks, a thin black girl answered the door. As Roberts feared, she clammed up the minute she saw his uniform and wouldn't even give her name. After some gentle but insistent pressure, he learned she was Emily Burns and gained entrance to the cabin.

"Don't know no George Pearles but reckon I knew Pinckney Williams," Emily admitted, voice barely above a whisper. "He... he stayed here a while."

"What's 'a while'?"

"Few months."

"And when did he leave?"

"Couple of weeks ago, I guess."

"Do you know where he went from here?" Roberts pressed. The girl's reluctance was exasperating, but he knew patience was the key. "Please answer the question, Emily."

"Yes, sir."

"Did he leave any of his belongings here?"

"Oh, no, sir!"

Obviously eager for the white lawmen to leave, Emily shifted from one foot to the other, fidgeting with her unkempt hair and the pockets of a ragged housedress. Her eyes roamed everywhere, but neither Roberts nor Serio missed the anxious glance toward a battered trunk in the corner. Its awkward angling suggested it had been shoved there and left in a hurry. Emily yelped as Roberts pushed past her and nudged it with his foot.

"It's Williams's trunk, isn't it?" She frowned and looked away. The sheriff's patience was fraying. "Answer me, girl!"

"Yes, sir."

He leaned down to examine the padlock. "What's in it?"

"Don't know," Emily insisted. "But he said to don't let nobody see it 'til he sends for it."

"In that case, you and the trunk are coming downtown with us." Emily whimpered and shook terribly but didn't budge. Knowing she was terrified after being caught in a lie, Roberts gave her an avuncular smile. "You just come along quietly and there won't be any trouble."

He couldn't help thinking Emily Burns was the picture of pure terror.

BACK AT HIS office, Roberts's headache worsened when a routine meeting with O'Neill and Chancellor turned into a shouting match. "You're thoroughly unprofessional, Chancellor!" O'Neill thundered. "I've never seen such sloppy investigating and baseless conclusions!"

"If you doubt my findings, then double-check the damned fingerprints!" Chancellor shot back.

"I'll have nothing to do with your work!" O'Neill turned to Roberts. "Take my advice, sheriff, and do the same."

Roberts paled. "Are you saying Chancellor's findings are wrong?"

O'Neill ignored the question. "I'll work with the ballistics findings and look over any new prints. Nothing more. Good day, gentlemen!"

Roberts watched helplessly as the rivals stormed out, nearly colliding with Farris. One look at his jailor's face told him there was news. "What's up, Laurin?"

"The habeas corpus writ is in the works," Farris replied.

"Man, Friedman and Kennedy sure didn't waste any time," Roberts grumbled. "Those two are old pros and if they hire experts to check those fingerprints and find out Chancellor was wrong, we're in big trouble."

Farris shrugged. "Maybe the writ is a blessing in disguise, sheriff. With Dick and Octavia free, it'll take the pressure off you for a while. You wouldn't want to fight it anyway. That crazy old couple sure as hell isn't going on the lam."

Roberts nodded, annoyed that he'd let himself get so lathered up. The pressure and lack of sleep these last few days had shredded his nerves, and he wasn't thinking straight. "If we get new evidence or corroborate the existing evidence, we can always re-arrest them."

"Exactly."

"Alright then. Get a crowbar and let's look inside Williams's trunk."

The rusty lock popped without much effort, and Farris lifted the lid. The tray at the top was full of dirty laundry. He tossed it aside and pulled out overalls, an overcoat and a pair of heavy shoes. Stashed at the very bottom was a stack of letters tied with a string, all addressed to Williams c/o General Delivery, Natchez, Miss. Postmarks ranged from late May to August second, two days before the murder, and almost all were from women.

Farris shook his head and chuckled. "Son of a gun! This character must've been some ladies' man."

The letters came from all over Mississippi and Louisiana, one as far away as Texas. Some were addressed to "Pink" and "Pinkie" and included such salutations as "Lover Boy," "Papa Man" and "Honeybunch." Two were from married women fearful that their cuckolded husbands would learn about the virile

Williams. The Texas woman expressed concern that "George" might find out about them.

"Wonder if she's referring to George Pearles," Roberts muttered.

Farris was still sifting through clothes at the bottom of the trunk when he let out a whoop. "Maybe this is what we've been looking for, sheriff!" He handed over a soiled envelope. "It's empty, but check out the address."

"I'll be damned!" Roberts gasped at the address: George Pearles, 7727 Sixty-second Street, Argo, Illinois.

"The guy shot in Arkansas," Farris muttered. "You suppose those two knew each other?"

"Maybe." Roberts brightened. "And maybe George Pearles and Lawrence Pinckney Williams are one and the same!" He clapped his jailor on the back, happy for the first time since the case broke. "I'm calling Pine Bluff."

Chief Fiveash hung on Roberts's every word. Then he dropped a bomb of his own. "Remember that gun I told you Pearles was carrying?"

"Sure," Robert said. "The thirty-eight."

"Turns out there was another one."

"What?"

"Yeah. The guy at the morgue found it when they were stripping the corpse."

Roberts's heart was racing. "A thirty-two-twenty?"

"How'd you know?"

"That's what killed Jennie Merrill! You find anything else?"

"Nothing important. Less than a dollar in change. A pack of cigarettes and a fancy gold watch." Fiveash chuckled grimly. "And a rabbit's foot that sure as hell didn't bring this character good luck."

The gun was all that mattered and Roberts thought fast. "Reckon I'd better get up there and take a look at the gun and the body."

"Body's gone, sheriff. We found the guy's wife and shipped it to that Illinois address. You want the name of the undertaker?"

"Sure do, chief. Looks like I'm going to Chicago." Roberts wrote down the information, hung up and looked at Farris. "Time for another talk with Emily Burns."

Paralyzed with fear, the girl was more uncooperative and evasive than the first time they'd spoken with her, swearing repeatedly that she didn't know if Pinckney Williams had an alias. It took the sheriff over an hour to coax out the name Will Tulls, a colored neighbor Emily said knew Williams. Roberts promptly had Tulls brought in and checked his fingerprints, but they didn't match any found at the crime scene. The poor man was as terrified as Emily.

"What you want with me, Sheriff Roberts, sir?" Tulls asked over and over again. "I ain't done nothin'!"

"Calm down, Tulls. I just want to ask you about a friend of yours. Pinckney Williams."

"Yes, sir."

"How long have you known him?"

"'Bout fifteen years, I guess. Used to work together on the plantations 'fore he go up North."

"Did he ever work for Duncan Minor or Miss Jennie Merrill?"

"He worked some for Mr. Minor, but that was a long time ago."

"What about Miss Merrill?"

"Don't know," Tulls replied uneasily. "Uh, wasn't she the lady what was killed?"

Roberts nodded. "Did Williams ever go by the name George Pearles?"

"Not that I know of, sir."

"Would you be able to identify him if you saw him again?"

Tulls nodded rapidly. "Yes, sir."

Roberts stood and paced his office. "You ever been to Chicago, Will?"

"Why, no, sir. Ain't never been out of Mississippi."

"Well, you're about to get a free trip."

BEFORE BOARDING THE train for Chicago, Sheriff
Roberts met with District Attorney-General Clay
Tucker, who was representing the State of Mississippi at the
Dana-Dockery habeas corpus hearing. County Attorney
Brown was also present, and the three quickly agreed not to
fight the proceeding. All were concerned about the avalanche
of public sympathy for the defendants and the flimsy fingerprint evidence. They were also anxious to know what facts
Chicago might yield, none more than Roberts. His spirits were
good, and they soared even higher when he learned O'Neill
would accompany him and Will Tulls. His only real regret
was that he could not be in two places at once—the Dockery-
Dana hearing was the next day in chancery court.

Roberts's abrupt departure fueled the rumor mill and es-
calated the town's excitement. By early Tuesday morning,
August sixteenth, lines snaked around the Adams County
Courthouse, and the streets were jammed with traffic. It was

standing-room-only in the stifling courthouse as Dick and Octavia were ushered into the room, looking lost and subdued in their drab prison uniforms. Octavia turned once to scan the courtroom, comforted to find Stephen Holmes in the crowd. She visibly brightened when he came over to greet her and introduce himself to Dick.

"Judging from these crowds and the word about town," he said, "all of Natchez believes you're innocent."

"Let's pray the judge agrees," Octavia sighed.

"And how are you, Mr. Dana?" Holmes asked.

"Fine, thank you." Dick nodded politely then grinned when he saw the American flag beside the judge's bench. "Look, Octavia. Just like Sandy Great!"

Octavia rolled her eyes and turned to Holmes. "His red, white and blue pig," she explained.

Holmes smiled and patted her shoulder as Judge R. W. Cutrer entered the courtroom. "Good luck!"

The judge felt the tension in the air as he faced the biggest crowd in his career. He listened intently as defense attorney E. H. Ratliffe read a prepared brief proclaiming his clients' innocence, and, while the crowd muttered approval, he waited for the prosecution to respond. Attorney General Tucker rose to address the bench, his back against a wall of animosity.

"Your honor," he announced in a voice that carried to the rear of the courtroom, "the State of Mississippi does not have sufficient evidence to warrant or justify the murder charges filed against Richard Dana and Octavia Dockery. Nor does it wish to challenge the habeas corpus plea of the accused. I therefore move that they be released on their own recognizance."

The audience scarcely had time to digest the stunning recommendation before Judge Cutrer reacted.

"So ordered!"

The whack of Cutrer's gavel was lost as pandemonium erupted, along with cheers and applause unprecedented in the Adams County Courthouse. In an odd case of role reversal,

Octavia said nothing while Dick nodded and mouthed, "Thank you, Judge." They were then engulfed in a wave of well wishers offering all manner of aid as they inched their way to freedom and a much-needed breath of fresh air.

"Please let me offer you all a ride home."

"Would you like to stay with us a few days, Miss Dockery?"

"How about a free seat in my barber chair, Mr. Dana?"

"Will you write about your experiences, Octavia?"

Dick continued grinning, a bit idiotically some thought, but as many noted it was better than scurrying up a tree like a wild animal. Energized by the outpouring of support, Octavia finally spoke for the pair, raising a hand to silence the noisy, ebullient crowd. Everyone pressed forward, eager to hear words later printed verbatim in the *Democrat*.

"For the present our only desire is to remain undisturbed. Please do not think me ungrateful, but with the trying ordeal to which we have been unjustly subjected still so recent, I cannot think of future plans. I will say it is my intention to clean and renovate Glenwood, but first I must make an inventory of the possessions that remain to us after the depredations on our property during the period we were in jail." She waved at the crowd, pleased when Dick did likewise. "Thank you," she said, again and again. "Thank you."

Since Holmes was still driving a two-seat buggy, the couple gratefully accepted a ride in Rosemary Pickett's Model-T and led a peculiar caravan of cars and carriages carrying locals and visitors, young and old, all celebrating the judge's decision while hoping for a glimpse of Goat Castle. Like everyone else, Rosemary had shamefully ignored the situation at Glenwood and she hoped to alleviate her guilt by helping now. The result was a mood of nervous jubilation.

When Octavia and Dick arrived home, a few of the tamer goats bounded over to greet them, playfully rearing and butting whatever struck their fancy. Octavia asked everyone to wait while she and Dick went inside, high spirits plummeting when she noticed, as she'd feared, several family heirlooms were missing. She returned to the veranda to make her unhappy announcement.

"It's most distressing," she told the gathering. "My very first night in jail I asked Sheriff Roberts about protection for our home and was assured that a guard would be posted. I also gave an interview in which I publicly pleaded for protection for my property, but I see that those requests have been ignored."

"I'd think seriously about restitution if I were you," someone said.

"Yes!" called someone else. "Not only for your incarceration time but for stolen property. It's the sheriff's fault."

Octavia waved them away and phrased her response carefully. "As I said before, these vandals are ghouls in human form, and I choose not to dwell on their unholy deeds just now."

The crowd was disappointed when she didn't say if Sheriff Roberts was included in that category. Folks wondered if she would be so circumspect if she'd seen the newspaper article entitled "Dana Relics On Display." Published in the newspaper of a nearby Louisiana town, it described a number of articles and furnishings taken from Glenwood, including personal letters belonging to Dick's father, Reverend Charles Backus Dana, and even his parents' marriage certificate. The thieves were publicly advised to return everything or face legal action, but everyone knew if they were prosecuted the articles would only vanish and resurface at a later date.

Dick provided a welcome diversion when he rounded the corner with a basket of newborn kittens. "Look what I found, everyone!" he grinned. "They're glad to see us come home, too."

Rosemary ventured as far as the third porch step, dying to get inside the house but too polite to intrude. She whispered to Octavia, "There should be a pleasant surprise in the kitchen, my dear."

Octavia hurried into the wreck of a kitchen and clapped her hands when she saw stacks of boxes and bags. Anticipating their release, one of the local grocers had donated enough food to last a couple of weeks. Octavia was so moved by this unexpected generosity that she wept softly, while Dick went through the cache like a child overwhelmed by too many Christmas toys.

"Look at this!" he cried, waving a box of cookies in the air. He dropped it in favor of a can of creamed corn, then grabbed a tin of sardines. "And this!"

Octavia knew no one expected them to share their bounty but said nothing as Dick opened the sardines and went outside to offer them all around. Her tears of gratitude changed to laughter when he chose a jar of peanut butter for an accompaniment. Smiles were exchanged, but no comments were made about Dick's peculiar hors d'oeuvres, and the occasion grew more festive as additional well wishers arrived with flowers, clothing, more food, and, best of all, a fair amount of cash. Several people asked Dick to say a few words about his ordeal, but he shyly insisted he was too overwhelmed.

"But I'd be pleased to entertain suggestions for naming the new kittens," he exclaimed.

Seeing Dick so animated and relaxed brought a glow to Octavia's furrowed face. Happiness was a long extinct emotion, but this day delivered her closer to it than she had been in many years. She sat on the front porch, her knees nuzzled by a favorite goat, and thoroughly enjoyed herself until dusk signaled suppertime. When the last visitor had departed, Octavia seized the opportunity to catch Dick in a "here" day. He had been amazingly clear-headed since the night of their arrest, but she had no way of knowing when this fragile lucidity might snap. She spoke gently while he played with two of the mewing kittens.

"After all that has happened here today, Dick, I want to make a proposition."

"Yes?"

"While we were in jail, some friends contacted our attorney, Mr. Ratliffe, and consulted him about charging a fee for people interested in seeing Glenwood. It seemed a reasonable way to raise money while we were incarcerated, but when Ratliffe asked Reverend Kuehnle about the matter, the minister said he thought it might be perceived as capitalizing on the murder. But my old friend Stephen Holmes says to ignore him and make the most of the situation."

Dick's eyes narrowed a moment, blinked and then widened again. "We could charge admission?"

"Exactly," Octavia said, thrilled that he understood. "We could take this new money and get the place cleaned up a bit. Fix those fallen columns and cart off the debris in the yard. Perhaps I might even read a few of my old poems for our visitors."

For the first time since before his accident, Dick was way ahead of her. "We could sell souvenirs!"

Octavia chuckled at this unexpected enthusiasm. "What a wonderful idea! I'm sure there are plenty of things of little value to us that someone else might want to collect."

"Photographs!"

"You mean of the house?"

"Of the house and of us, too. And we could charge a fee for people to photograph us with the goats."

"Of course!" Again Octavia was astonished by Dick's canniness. "Why, I could pose right here in this chair with a kid on my lap. I see one of our nannies will be delivering any day now."

"We could sign autographs!" Dick gushed. "I'm going to get my hair cut. My beard, too. And maybe I'll get some store-bought teeth. I don't like smiling and showing my gums."

"A lady from the beauty parlor offered me a free appointment," Octavia remembered. She unpinned her loose bun and stroked her hair as it tumbled over her shoulders. "I noticed a lot of women are bobbing their hair these days. Perhaps I should cut mine short, too."

Octavia was simultaneously thinking what idiots people could be and relishing the bizarre gold mine she and Dick had suddenly found underfoot. If people considered them loony old eccentrics, so be it, but they'd damn well have to pay to experience this lunacy in person. She smiled at the delicious irony that the hateful shrew next door was responsible for their windfall. Now who had the last laugh?

The next morning brought more visitors and more opportunities. Octavia had been exhausted and skeptical the day before, but now she paid close attention to every offer of help. She was especially surprised when a representative of a local railroad came calling and proposed special trains bringing visitors to Goat Castle.

"You could charge admission," he beamed.

"My, what an interesting idea," she said, feigning surprise as she beamed back. "And what other ideas might you have, sir?"

"Why, this is just the tip of the iceberg, Miss Dockery. Just the very tip. I have a whole promotional campaign to propose."

"My goodness gracious! You don't say!"

Yes, Octavia thought. People could certainly be fools.

28

W HILE THE GOAT Castle circus was being orchestrated, the *Natchez Democrat* published a series of articles by Stephen Holmes focusing on Jennie Merrill. The last and most intriguing ran August sixteenth and included an interview with David L. McKittrick, husband of Carlotta Surget. Natchez remembered Jennie had been evicted from Elms Court thirty-seven years before, when her Cousin James, Carlotta's father, gave the estate to the newlywed McKittricks as a wedding present.

"Looking back," McKittrick said, "I can see Jennie Merrill when she was considered one of America's most beautiful women. Thick, dark hair with a satiny sheen cascaded in ringlets about her pale throat and framed a lovely face. She was olive-skinned like so many Southern belles with French ancestry, and I have never seen more beautiful eyes. They were a deep golden brown, radiant and compassionate. I remember she wore the coiffure and costume of the classic Greeks to dazzling effect. Jennie Merrill was not only a delight to see but also had rare intelligence and character. She fascinated everyone she met and acquired male admirers everywhere she ventured. She so charmed the gentlemen of Louisville, Kentucky, that three millionaires proposed marriage."

As Holmes fully intended, McKittrick's gushing portrait swayed no one who remembered Jennie as an arrogant, overbearing harridan. Indeed, the majority of readers considered his remarks nothing more than aristocracy closing ranks.

Less frothy information about Jennie appeared in that same issue as details about Roberts's investigation were made public. On page two, a large story headlined, "Officer Placed On The Trail By Tip Of Old Negro," reported on Lawrence Williams's telltale trunk and timely visit to Beaupreaux Plantation. According to Zula Curtis, one of his many landladies, "He said he went by Dick Dana's house where he saw Miss Dockery working in the library. He said the place was so filthy he knew they didn't have no money so he went across to Miss Merrill's place. She was rich, he said, but too stingy to give him any work. He said the same thing about Duncan Minor and talked about him for a long time, especially Mr. Minor's habit of riding a horse." A much smaller item on the same page entitled "Negro Wanted For Merrill Murder Has Been Killed" gave a brief account of the shooting of George Pearles alias Lawrence ("Pinckney") Williams.

The town was frenzied with these new revelations and anticipated more thrills when Sheriff Roberts returned from Chicago — and as O'Neill continued on to New Orleans with the .32.20 gun found on George Pearles's body and the type of bullets that killed Jennie Merrill. Hopes were high that there would be a ballistics match. While awaiting word from O'Neill, Roberts received a telegram from the Chicago Police Bureau of Identification. He smiled and showed it to Abbott: .32.20 Colt blue steel revolver cylinder Number 4-1-11-5-0-7 Letter 'I' sold to Lawrence Williams, Kiln, Miss., by Sears Roebuck & Company, May 16, 1916.

"Well," Abbott sighed. "Now we've got proof that the dead man purchased what may be the murder weapon. What next, Book?"

Roberts pressed the buzzer summoning Farris. "We'll talk to Emily Burns again."

"She hasn't told you much so far, has she?"

He shook his head. "That was before I knew for sure that Williams and Pearles were the same man. I've got a new line of questioning now, but getting her to talk won't be easy. She's either shrewd or completely stupid."

When the jailor appeared with Emily, the sheriff greeted her cordially and asked her to have a seat in his office. She obeyed but surprised them by asking the first question.

"You been up North, ain't you, Sheriff Roberts?"

"Why, yes, I have," he replied, hoping he had finally caught her in a garrulous mood. "How'd you know?"

Emily rolled her eyes. "People talk and I hear stuff, I reckon."

"What else did you hear?" When she shook her head and looked away, Roberts decided more polite coaxing was a waste of time and fired away with the blunt facts. "I guess if you know I was up North then you know your friend Pinckney Williams is dead. Stone cold dead, Emily!"

For a moment he thought he'd be ignored again; then very slowly, the corners of her mouth began twitching. Spotting a chink, Roberts aimed a finger in her direction and boomed his accusation.

"We not only know that Williams killed Miss Jennie Merrill but that you—"

Emily jumped to her feet, eyes dilated with fear. "No!" she cried. "I had nothing to do with that business!" She looked from Roberts to Abbott and back again. "I swear to God!"

"Be careful, Emily," Roberts warned. "We know you've been lying. You told me you didn't know George Pearles, and now we know that Williams and Pearles were the same man."

"I done told you and told you I didn't know that!" she cried.

"I swear to God Pinkie never told me nothin' about havin' two names!"

Roberts conceded that much could be true, but he was more interested in her use of the affectionate nickname. If Emily was one of Williams's girlfriends, it would give her plenty of reason to shield him.

"Were you in love with him, Emily?"

Her response caught both lawmen off guard. "Please!" she wailed. "Please let me go somewhere to pray."

Roberts was dumbfounded. "What?"

"I've just got to pray now! Please, Sheriff. Let me pray to the Lord!"

Abbott looked unwilling, but Roberts conceded. "All right then. Go back to your cell and pray as much as you like, but there's something you'd better be thinking about."

"What's...what's that, sir?"

"If you're a good Christian woman, you better tell me the truth about what happened at Miss Jennie's the night she was murdered." Emily bawled all the way to the women's quarters and Roberts groaned to Abbott, "All we can do now is wait."

The waiting game stretched through the night and into the next day. A little before noon, Roberts paid Emily a visit and pleaded gently for her to talk, but she insisted she wasn't through with her prayers. With no real evidence to pin on the girl, he was up against a wall, and, considering how Chancellor bungled the fingerprints, he was more cautious than ever. Adding to his unease was the public's demand that he find a killer.

A break came late that afternoon when Roberts returned to his office and found a telegram from Maurice O'Neill. It was precisely the confirmation he'd hoped for.

BULLETS FOUND IMBEDDED IN PANELED WALLS OF GLENBURNIE POSITIVELY IDENTIFIED AS FIRED FROM THIRTY-TWO-TWENTY COLT REVOLVER NUMBER 4-1-11-5-0-7 LETTER I AND OWNED BY WILLIAMS STOP CONGRATULATIONS STOP LEAVING FOR NATCHEZ TONIGHT.

When O'Neill arrived, he confirmed to Roberts that the key to all remaining mysteries seemed to be Emily Burns. He also told the sheriff he'd be wise to leave her alone with her prayers and possible guilt, and speculated that she'd come to him of her own volition—and that it wouldn't take long. That very thing happened on Sunday morning, August twenty-first, when Laurin Farris rushed into Robert's office.

"She's ready to talk, sheriff!"

"Get her up here fast," Roberts ordered. "Let's not give her time to change her mind."

While Farris retrieved Emily, Roberts called O'Neill, Abbott, Stone and County Attorney Brown. The four men hurried over, as eager as the sheriff to learn what she had to say. Emily arrived looking strangely peaceful, as though, Roberts hoped, she'd found serenity in her spiritual plea for guidance. He nodded politely and motioned her to the chair facing him, noticing she did not look at him but remained focused on the wall above his head.

"Are you ready to tell us the truth, Emily?"

"Yes, sir," she nodded.

"Good girl. Now tell me. Were you at Glenburnie Manor the night of the murder?"

No hesitation. "Yes, sir."

"What happened?"

"It was Pink...Pinckney Williams," she said slowly. She took a deep breath. "He was talkin' to me one night and said he needed money real bad and was gonna... gonna rob Miss Jennie. Said somebody done told him she hid a whole lotta money in her house."

"What was your reaction?"

"I was scared. Real scared." Her gaze flitted to the ceiling and back to the wall. "I was scared of Pinckney, too."

"Did he threaten you?"

"Well, he said I'd better do as he said if I knew what was good for me."

"So the two of you went over to Glenburnie?"

"They was somebody else there, too."

"Who else was there, Emily?"

She took a deep breath. "Edgar Newell."

The five men swapped excited glances. This could be the breakthrough they were waiting for.

"Who's Edgar Newell?"

"Just some colored man Pinckney knew, I guess."

"What part did he play?"

"Well, they said they was just gonna rob Miss Jennie, but while I was waitin' outside the house I heard gunshots and some screams. I was real scared and I wanted to run away, but then Pinckney come outside and tells me to carry this old lamp. He goes back inside, then him and Edgar Newell come out and they're...they're..."

"They're what, Emily?"

"They're carryin' Miss Jennie's body!" She sniffed. "And I had to go along with the lamp so they could see where they was goin.'"

"Where were they going?" Roberts pressed.

"Into the woods."

"Why?"

"So's they could leave the body, I guess."

"Do you know why they didn't leave it in the house?"

"No, sir."

"Did Williams or Newell have an army overcoat?"

"Pink...Pinckney did."

"Do you know where he got it?"

"No, sir."

When the sheriff pressed for more details, Emily clammed up and stared at the wall. Exasperated, he had her confession typed up and told her to sign it. She complied and was taken back to her cell while deputies were dispatched to find the mysterious Edgar Newell. He turned out to be an undertaker and was found at home just before dawn. Sleepy and bewildered, he was brought to police headquarters for questioning, all the time pleading innocent to any and all charges. While Newell acknowledged that he knew Pinckney Williams, he insisted their friendship went no further than a few card games and an occasional drink. His interrogation continued smoothly until he was told that Emily Burns claimed he was with her and Williams the night of the murder. The seemingly quiet mortician leapt to his feet and shouted loud enough to be heard well outside the station house.

"She's lying!" he bellowed. "That crazy fool is lying about me and she's doing it to protect somebody else!"

"Who do you think she's shielding?" Roberts asked.

"How should I know?" Newell bellowed. "Maybe a boyfriend. Maybe her mama. Maybe some white folks. I can only tell you I wasn't with them that night and didn't have nothin' to do with that damned murder!"

"If that's true," the sheriff said calmly, "then you'll be a free man again."

With Newell in custody, Roberts and his men paid a quick visit to Emily Burns's mother. The elderly woman convinced them she knew nothing about the crime but admitted that Emily and Williams left the house before dusk that night of the murder and didn't return until late.

When word leaked that Emily had made a confession and that a new murder suspect had been arrested, the press and public demanded the facts. Roberts refused to reveal anything and extracted promises from all his men to say nothing. He also decided to take Emily and Edgar to Jackson for safekeeping. These days, the lynching of colored men accused of killing whites was all too common in Mississippi, and Roberts didn't want to lose his key suspects to mob violence.

In Jackson, Emily and Newell were taken to the office of Sheriff Warren Ferguson where Emily was asked to identify Newell as the accomplice mentioned in her confession. Her terse response stunned everyone: "He ain't the man."

Ordered to tell the truth, she said only that Edgar Newell was not at the murder scene and that a couple named Percy Perry and Nellie Black were the real accomplices. Emily listened quietly as Roberts telephoned Natchez to have the couple brought in and then said she had something more to say. It proved to be a second version of what had happened on August fourth.

"Pinckney Williams asked me to go for a walk with him. I guess it was around five in the afternoon. We walked along Kingston Pike to the edge of town and then turned onto a path beside the railroad tracks. We were right behind Miss Jennie's house when we stopped and that's when he told me about his plan to rob Miss Jennie as soon as it got dark."

"Go on."

"While we was waitin' for it to get dark...well, that's when the others come along."

"Who were they?"

"Percy Perry and Nellie Black."

"Go on."

"Yes, sir. See, Pinckney had already told them what he was plannin' to do and that's why they was there to meet him."

"So there were four of you at Glenburnie Manor instead of three?"

"Yes, sir."

The rest was a rehashing of Emily's earlier confession. Roberts was understandably skeptical, given her abrupt recant involving Newell, and was not surprised when Abbott called from Natchez to report that the new suspects had airtight alibis. Emily had lied again. The sheriff tried a new tack and asked a Negro preacher named Charlie Anderson to counsel Emily in an effort to get the truth. Anderson's quiet time with the girl was apparently well spent because within the hour he said she was ready to talk again.

"I believe you'll get the truth this time," the minister said.

"I certainly hope so," Roberts replied. He thanked the

minister for his help and asked him to stay for the girl's next confession. "It might make her more comfortable."

Reverend Anderson agreed and everyone gathered again. Emily was brought in along with Edgar Newell, who sat quietly in a corner as she began. This time her story flowed freely, as though she wanted to unburden herself. "A little before sunset, I left home with Pinky Williams. He told me we was just goin' for a walk, but then he said we was headin' for Miss Merrill's house. He said she had a lot of money hidden there and that he was gonna get it. When he saw how scared I was, he threatened to kill me if I told anyone. I was so scared I guess I would've done anythin' he told me." She paused to fidget with the cuff of her sleeve. "So...um..."

"Go on, Emily."

"So we headed into the woods and waited for it to get dark. That's when Edgar Newell come along and he..."

"Goddamn liar!" Newell leapt to his feet. "I was nowhere near Glenburnie that night!"

"Sit down and let her continue," Roberts warned as two of Ferguson's deputies pressed Newell back into his chair. "We'll decide who's telling the truth."

"Well," Emily continued, "Pinky tells Edgar what he wants to do and he decides to help out. We all walked along the railroad track a little ways and then Pinky told us to wait while he went to Mr. Jack's house."

"Who's Mr. Jack?"

"The man who had the overcoat," she replied.

Roberts wondered if this was her nickname for John Geiger. "Why did he want an overcoat in that heat?"

"Pinky said he needed it for a disguise."

"Go on."

"When we got to Miss Jennie's house, Edgar and I waited outside while Pinky crawled underneath to figure out which room she was in. He wasn't under there very long and said he'd found her because he could hear her hummin'. Then I watched him go in first with Edgar right behind him."

"You lying bitch!" Newell lunged again, but the deputies kept him in his seat.

"Pinky was holdin' the coat in front of him so nobody could see who he was. Then I heard a gunshot and Miss Jennie started screamin'. There was a lot of noise inside the house like they was a struggle goin' on. I heard more shots and more screams and then it got real quiet. Edgar come back out and give me that lamp I done told you about. Then he went back in and the two of them come out carryin' Miss Jennie. She wasn't dead. She was moanin' and movin' around, and it was awful to see somethin' like that. Anyway, they told me to follow them into the woods and that's what I did. After they dumped Miss Jennie's body, I dropped the lamp and broke it."

"What did you do then?"

"We went back to the house so they could search for the money, but they didn't find none. I guess they was gettin' scared 'cause Pinky said we should go. Edgar went off, and Pinky and me took back roads along the railroad tracks so nobody would see us. When we got home, Pinky seen that he had blood all over him so he took off his clothes and soaked them with coal oil and burned them. He got dressed in another suit and at about eleven o'clock he told me he was goin' home to Chicago. That was the last time I ever saw him, but I got a letter from him a couple of days later. It was mailed from Pine Bluff."

"What did it say?"

"That he was safe and for me to not say nothin' to nobody 'bout Miss Jennie."

"Do you still have the letter?"

"No, sir. See, I was too scared to keep it, so I burned it right after I read it."

Roberts was at his wit's end. "Listen to me, Emily. Just yesterday you said Edgar Newell hadn't been with you. That it was Percy Perry and Nellie Black who had helped with the murder. Now you're saying that it was Newell again. We're all sick and tired of this double talk, so how about telling us the truth?"

Emily's answer came fast. "I'm tellin' you he was there, sheriff. He went into that house with Pinky and come out carryin' Miss Jennie. Now, I don't know what happened in the house, but I know what I seen when I was carryin' that lamp and I seen my cousin!"

"Your cousin?" Roberts gasped.

"Yes, sir. Edgar Newell's my cousin, and families got to tell the truth about each other and I'm tellin' the truth."

Newell didn't try to jump up again but screamed his innocence: "I was nowhere near that place, sheriff! I was in downtown Natchez when all that business was going on at Glenburnie Manor, and I can prove it!"

"How?" Roberts asked patiently.

"Sheriff Roberts, I been telling you all along that I got plenty of people, reputable people, who can vouch for me. They'll tell you where I was that night!" Newell was getting agitated again. "You got to believe me!"

Emily Burns had been lying so much that Roberts sympathized with the poor man pleading for his life. He took some names from Newell and called Abbott, urging him to check out the undertaker's alibi, and to get on the matter fast. When Abbott reported tempers had cooled and the town was quiet, Roberts formulated a new plan.

"We're going home, Emily," Roberts announced. "And on the way we're going to Glenburnie Manor and re-enact the crime."

"Oh, no!" she cried. "Please, God, no!"

"Oh, yes!" The sheriff's patience was dangerously close to evaporating. "Once and for all, you're going to tell us what really happened."

DUSK WAS APPROACHING as Deputy Stone drove Roberts, Brown and an agitated Emily to Glenburnie Manor. As they approached the house, a figure waited on the veranda. Duncan Minor stood straight and tall, hands clasped behind his back, very composed as the patrol car pulled under the porte-co-chère. Roberts waved a brief greeting before turning to Emily, whimpering in the back seat.

"We've run out of time for games, Emily. You're finally go-ing to tell us the truth about the night Jennie Merrill was mur-dered or I'm going to lock you up and throw away the key. Do you understand me, girl?"

Very softly Emily replied, "Yes, sir."

"Good. Now get out and show us what happened."

Emily was anything but eager to return to the crime scene and shook nearly uncontrollably as she led the men across the yard. When they were about a hundred yards from the house, she stopped and pointed into the growing darkness.

"That little house over there," she said. "That's where me and Pinky went first." All noted there was no mention of Edgar Newell.

Roberts followed her along a hedgerow and across a ravine to one of the many outbuildings scattered along Glenburnie's generous periphery. "Whose house is that?" he asked.

"Mr. and Mrs. Jack." Emily stopped a few yards shy of the house, as though afraid to venture closer. Stone ventured fur-ther, knocked on the door, then peeked through the windows and announced no one was home. Roberts turned back to Emily.

"Well?"

"Uh, they was on that front porch when we come by, and Mrs. Jack asked if we was ready, and when Pinky said yes, she went inside and got that overcoat I told you about before. Then we all went over to Glenburnie."

"Who's 'we'?" Roberts asked.

"Me and Pinky, and Mr. and Mrs. Jack."

Since there was still no mention of Edgar Newell, Roberts was prepared to rule him out as a suspect, figuring some kind of family feud had led Emily to implicate him in the killing. He had also decided the mysterious Mr. Jack was not John Geiger, the owner of the overcoat, and that Geiger could not have been involved. Obviously the killer stole the coat after Geiger left Skunk's Nest and before Octavia removed his property for safekeeping. But who were Mr. and Mrs. Jack, and why had they not been considered suspects?

"Let's go back to Glenburnie," he said.

Emily cowered as they approached the front veranda, clearly reluctant to go closer. "That's where Pinky told me to stay," she said. "They went into the house and I heard the gunshots and the screams. Mrs. Jack come runnin' back out and give me the lamp, and then Pinky and Mr. Jack come out carryin' Miss Jennie. They took her in that direction and dumped her in the woods. That's where I dropped the lamp."

"Show us."

Emily walked about twenty yards from the house and pointed. "Right here, sheriff."

"You're sure?"

"Oh, yes, sir."

It was two hundred yards short of the spot where the lamp was found.

Roberts sighed, frustrated as ever. "Then what?"

"We all went back to the house, but I never did go in. I stayed out here and I was cryin' 'cause I was so scared. Finally they come out, and Mr. and Mrs. Jack went to their house, and Pinky and I went to mine. I already told you, after that I didn't see him no more."

"You're absolutely sure this time?" Roberts pressed.

"Oh, yes, sir!" She looked at the house, eyes wide with fear. "Can we please go now?"

"All right," the sheriff said, his shoulders hunched with exhaustion. As they got back into the patrol car, however, he was suddenly aware of Duncan's shadowy presence. Duncan had not uttered a word the entire time they'd all been at the house, silently following and listening to Emily's strange tale as they wandered through the scene of the crime.

"Sorry for any inconvenience, Mr. Minor."

Duncan nodded, then vanished into the darkness of the veranda, still not speaking.

"That old guy gives me the creeps," Stone muttered. "Did you hear he hangs out here all the time now?"

Roberts ignored his chief deputy. "Let's go."

The four rode back to the jail where Emily was returned to her cell. Told by a deputy that Percy Perry, Nellie Black and Edgar Newell had reliable witnesses willing to vouch for their whereabouts on the night of August fourth, Roberts released them. He'd barely tended to that matter when a second deputy reported that the Jack couple also had solid alibis. When he learned that an infuriated Mr. Jack had bellowed that Emily Burns was flat-out crazy, Roberts was ready to concur. As a last resort, he contacted Dr. W. E. Clark, Assistant Superintendent of the Mississippi State Insane Asylum at Jackson and the state's foremost psychiatrist. Clark promptly drove to Natchez and submitted Emily to a battery of mental tests. He reported his findings a few days later.

"She's far from intelligent," Clark told Roberts, "but she's by no means insane."

Roberts shook his head. "I honestly don't know what to do with her."

"If I were you I'd turn the whole matter over to the grand jury," Clark advised. "Let them keep the girl until they convene in November."

Roberts agreed, simply because he didn't have a better alternative. He also realized it was time to talk to the press again. On August twenty-third, the *Natchez Democrat* blared headlines just shy of those reverently reserved for the Second Coming, and the paper also ran a photo of the alleged murderer.

CONFESSION IS MADE IN MERRILL CASE

NEGRO WOMAN GIVES DETAILS OF SLAYING OF MISS MERRILL,

Says George Pearles Fired Shots;
She Was With Pearles;
Robbery Was The Motive For Crime;
Emily Burns Spirited Away Immediately
After Confession To Deputies

THE OWNERS OF the *Democrat* surely adored Emily when she manufactured yet another version of the murder and dragged Dick and Octavia back into the convoluted fray. Headlines the next day were as dramatic and fast-selling as before:
RICHARD DANA—MISS DOCKERY IMPLICATED
Negress Says That Both At Merrill Home During Murder;
Says Dana Gave Pearles Coat To Be Used As Disguise;
Gave Details Of The Murder In Confession Yesterday;
Chancellor Says He Will Stand On Fingerprint Report
And Present It As Evidence in Circuit Court
Since the sensational story revealed that Sheriff Roberts had issued no official statement, Natchez wondered if Dick and Octavia would now be charged with conspiracy. Exhausted by yet another of Emily's convoluted confessions and acutely aware of local sentiment, Roberts thrilled Natchez by switching from persecutor to protector: the residents of Goat Castle, he declared—either in spite of or because of Emily's latest yarn—were to be left alone.

PART FOUR
September–November, 1932

I can truthfully declare that Natchez's problem is not too little but too much.

Nola Nance Oliver, *This Too Is Natchez*

29

As August played out and things at Glenwood assumed a macabre carnival air, life on the other side of the ravines and hedgerows could not have been more different. Glenburnie Manor was totally inaccessible, its secrets steadfastly shrouded by Duncan Minor, who refused all visitors, shunned interviews and, to everyone's astonishment, religiously continued his nightly horseback rides. Speculation was rampant about what he did by himself at the manor house. Some believed him in deep mourning, his stony silence in deference to Miss Jennie's memory, while others insisted the batty old soul engaged in rituals too bizarre to specify. Many thought he was hiding something critical to the murder.

Whatever the truth, he was more enigmatic than ever.

Only Mary Grace had access to Duncan's private world and she alone witnessed his reaction to the loss of the two most influential people in his life, Katherine Minor and Jennie Merrill. Duncan and his mother had clashed so bitterly in her final years that he abandoned his old weapon of silence for a venomous irascibility, prompting Mary Grace to assume that he, like herself, would be liberated by their mother's death. Instead, after the event finally transpired, she saw her brother consumed by an intense, bewildering melancholy. For the first time in decades, he had ignored Jennie and spent his nights at Oakland, taking prolonged strolls about the ruined grounds and conversing with the ghosts of lost childhood. His spiritual and mental retreat was so complete that Mary Grace wondered if he might be struggling to break from Jennie as well. She had long observed his perverse compulsion to balance the two governing forces in his life, to daily exchange maternal dominance for Jennie's equally demeaning, demanding regimen. Mary Grace even feared he might be losing his mind, but, exactly a week after their mother's funeral, Duncan's gloom evaporated and he resumed his nightly treks to Glenburnie Manor.

Duncan's reaction to Jennie's death, Mary Grace noted, was equally intense but even more irrational. He was, by turn, excitable, numb, reckless, and ultimately unbearable. Debilitated by his emotional seesawing, Mary Grace plotted peace. She ceased complaining about her brother's puny efforts to make repairs and even held her tongue when another porch pillar toppled and dry rot invaded the grand hall. When she made no comment about Jennie Merrill's stunning bequest, the town's current *cause célèbre*, her calculated silence forced Duncan to talk.

Late one afternoon while she sat beneath Oakland's great trees, immersed in Fanny Hurst's latest novel, *Back Street*, Duncan approached from the house. She looked up just long enough to notice an uncharacteristic lightness in his step before returning to her book. He stood nearby, scanning the grounds, glancing in her direction.

"Beautiful day, isn't it?"

"Yes, it is."

A long pause. "Still a little warm, though."

"I suppose."

"I'll be glad when summer is past."

"Mmmm."

After another long pause, Duncan said, "I've been thinking about buying a car."

That was truly shocking and, although her eyes remained on the page, Mary Grace was no longer reading.

"Oh?"

"I'm also thinking of doing some traveling." She cocked her head at another unexpected revelation. "I've never traveled much, you know."

Unless you tally the thousands of miles consumed between here and Glenburnie, Mary Grace thought. "Yes, I know."

"I can't decide where I want to go."

Beset by a curiosity as manifest as the humidity, Mary Grace closed her book and waded into the conversation. "Why not go wherever you like?"

She wanted to add that money was certainly not a problem but instead watched her brother venture a short distance and turn around. He studied the house for a while and began humming, something Mary Grace had never heard him do. Nor had she ever seen him in such high spirits. It was disarming but also a relief.

"Why not Europe?" she suggested. "Paris, perhaps, or London."

He pursed his lips and studied a pellucid sky as though searching for something. "Oh, I'm too old to be gallivanting abroad, Sister, but I might go up to Hot Springs for a while, or maybe The Greenbrier. And I've always wanted to go to the Kentucky Derby. I miss the races, you know."

Conversation about automobiles, travel and now horse races, Mary Grace mused, but not a word about Jennie Merrill. Well, one strange performance deserves another. "I know nothing of the sort, Duncan. In fact, I know very little about you." She smiled an overture. "You've never told me anything about yourself, not even when we were children. Tassie and the others say the same thing."

He frowned, as though trying to remember something about his siblings. "Perhaps you're right."

Registering his consternation, she added, "You needn't worry. I have no intention of trying to become friends. Not at our age."

"What a peculiar thing to say, Mary Grace."

"Nevertheless, it's true." She opened her book again.

Duncan walked away. From the corner of her eye, Mary Grace watched him inspect the stacks of shingles rotting for lack of roofing nails. He studied the fallen column and the ladder positioned across the collapsed front steps as if seeing them for the first time. He shook his head and returned to his sister.

"Did an invitation come to the Marshall's soirée?"

"It was in the morning mail," Mary Grace said, curiosity again escaping control. The day was surrendering surprises too rich to be ignored. "How did you know about the party?"

"I saw Douglas Oliver at the Court House yesterday. He asked if we might be coming. I told him I'd ask you."

The book closed again. "We haven't accepted party invitations in years, Duncan. I'm shocked that we even get them any more, and I'm even more shocked that you'd consider accepting one."

"Maybe it's time for a change."

Mary Grace laughed, but the sensation was a sour one. "Brother, dear! I absolutely cannot believe you would be interested in change of any sort. Cars. Travel. Parties. Horses. It's so unlike you."

"Is it?" He sniffed.

"Yes, indeed. You're the least adventurous, most regimented person on earth. Why, you haven't even stopped..." Despite a growing ease with her brother, she couldn't continue.

Now Duncan's curiosity was piqued. "Haven't stopped what?"

"Nothing," Mary Grace said, retreating. "I spoke in haste."

"Perhaps not. Please continue."

She looked up from her lap, squinting in the bright summer sunlight. "I don't think it's advisable."

"Suppose you let me decide."

"Very well. I was remembering something you said to Mother and me. Years ago. When you wanted to buy Glenwood."

"Go on."

"You're certain?"

"Absolutely."

Mary Grace took a deep breath before voicing the untenable. "Mother mentioned Jennie Merrill and you said we were never to speak her name again. Your entire demeanor changed that day, Duncan. There was a frightening sort of physical transformation and that awful ultimatum. I've never forgotten either of them."

Duncan frowned. "I'm truly sorry if I frightened you, Mary Grace, and I rescind the ultimatum."

Another shocker. "Really?"

"On one condition."

"Oh?"

"I want you to finish what you were going to say."

"Very well." She picked up the gauntlet. "I was going to say you haven't stopped going over to Glenburnie Manor."

"I thought so." He pursed his lips again. "Why should I? It's my property now."

Mary Grace risked a bit of frippery. "Hmmm. I seem to recall reading something about that in the newspaper."

"I apologize for not mentioning it," Duncan said, more sly than sheepish. "I had so much on my mind at the time."

"An apology doesn't mean much at this point." There was nothing accusative in her tone. It was merely a statement of fact.

"That's not all I'm sorry about."

"Oh?"

"I'm sorry I didn't say anything to you about Jennie's...well, about that terrible thing that happened at Glenburnie."

"It's your business, Duncan, and you'd warned me to steer clear. I see no reason to bring it up now since I'm sure her death won't affect me one way or the other."

"It might."

"How so?"

Duncan shrugged. "I was looking around this morning and thinking it might be nice to make a few repairs. You know... fix the place up a bit."

As if that subject had not been discussed ad infinitum, Mary Grace thought.

"I see," she managed after a moment, reeling from one unexpected disclosure after another. Was it possible that Jennie Merrill's considerable largesse would finally liberate Oakland from its curse of deprivation and decay? As long as Minor money wasn't involved, would Duncan's spending habits actually change?

"Do whatever you like. I don't much care one way or the other."

He brightened. "Then maybe you'd like to take a trip, too."

This is too much, Mary Grace thought. Her eyes narrowed as she blurted a bitter response. "Am I supposed to thank you for that?"

Duncan shoved hands into his pockets and looked away. His sister had confused him, like Jennie had so often done, making him worry he had said the wrong thing again.

"Well..."

"I can hardly be grateful after so many years of indifference, Duncan, and I'm afraid a trip to The Greenbrier hardly atones for those years of nightly disappearing acts. Much less for this..." Mary Grace encompassed Oakland's decrepitude with a sweep of her hand. "There's no house in Natchez in worse shape. Except," she added pointedly, "Goat Castle."

Duncan grimaced as reality struggled into focus. He didn't want to be unhappy again and gestured at the pile of shingles. "It's not really that bad, is it, Mary Grace?"

"Yes, Duncan, it *is* that bad," she shot back, resentment flaring. "And we both know we're not really talking about the house."

"We're not?"

"No," she said as long-repressed truth bubbled toward the surface. "We're not."

"I'm...I'm not sure I understand."

"I think there's a great deal you don't understand." Mary Grace sat up so suddenly that the book tumbled from her lap. She made no effort to retrieve it. "Your behavior over the years has been inexcusable, totally inconsiderate and not a little embarrassing. Did you really think that Mother and I didn't know where you were going every night?" He shook his head. "Everyone in town knew about you and Jennie Merrill. I can understand your wanting to retaliate against Mother— there were times when I wished I could have done so myself—but why did you punish me, too? When Oakland began to fall apart, my life, my hopes for happiness and marriage, everything went with it. It was all play-acting for Mother, badgering you about those stupid nails and shingles and leaks, but not for me. Asking you for help was like banging my head against the wall, Duncan. The only change at Oakland was that you hurt me more deeply every day."

Duncan turned away, unable to look at her. "I...I didn't know what else to do."

"I have to believe that's true or my hatred would know no bounds." Mary Grace felt her heart racing, years of rancor and resentment spewing forth. "As if Mother wasn't poisonous enough, that other woman got under your skin when you were a young man and never let go, never let you have a life of your own. Jennie Merrill stole your soul and—"

Duncan's face darkened. "You mustn't say such things, Sister."

Mary Grace dismissed his reproach. "I'm not sorry I said it, Duncan. I'm only sorry that it's true."

Duncan was quiet a long time. Then he looked toward an ancient oak, great moss-draped branches lifting and settling all of a piece as wind gusted across the grounds. He muttered as much to himself as to Mary Grace.

"Just like the Merrills and the Minors," he muttered.

"What?"

He shook his head in defeat. "Things might have been so different without all this terrible family feuding."

Mary Grace steeled her soul and broached another subject shunned for decades. Their mother was dead. She and Duncan were elderly. What did it matter if they finally dropped the masks?

"You mean if you and Jennie had been allowed to marry?"

"I didn't say that, Mary Grace."

"But it's what you meant, isn't it?"

Duncan's eyes glazed over, and he closed himself off as his sister had seen him do a thousand times.

"Something unspoken."

"What?"

"That's how I wish to regard everything that has happened between Jennie and me. Something unspoken."

Mary Grace told herself she should have known better than to open that forbidden door. Some things never change, nor perhaps should they. She retrieved her book and studied the hoary oaks, trying to judge the hour by shadows crawling across the lawn. "Is it time for supper?"

Duncan fished inside his vest and came up empty-handed. "I don't know."

"Where's your watch, Duncan?"

"I don't know," he said again.

"Surely you haven't lost great-grandfather's watch!"

He frowned and walked away without answering. One more new wrinkle, Mary Grace reflected. Since Duncan was given that watch as a young man, she had never seen him without it. She supposed it wouldn't be long before her brother sported a new, terribly expensive timepiece.

Purchased of course with Merrill money.

30

I N THE SPRING of 1931, the year before Jennie Merrill's death, the Mississippi State Federation of Garden Clubs held its annual meeting in Natchez. When a killer freeze wrecked the tender, barely blossoming gardens, frantic local ladies scrambled for something else to showcase and made the unprecedented decision to open their own homes to the delegates. Most Natchezians condemned charging admission to a private home as a grave social transgression, a violation of vaunted Southern hospitality. But when visitors swooned over a peek into the town's fabled past, criticism magically evaporated.

With proof that an unparalleled concentration of splendid antebellum houses could double as tourist attractions and pump much-needed dollars into a collapsed economy, the annual Natchez Pilgrimage was born. Its driving force was Katherine Grafton Miller, a petite dynamo whose outsized personality irked as many as it charmed. Determinedly criss-crossing the South by car, bus and rail, she was a one-woman crusade, intent on inviting the world through Natchez's historic doors. Shushing naysayers who insisted no one cared about these old homes, Mrs. Miller whipped local support into a genteel frenzy and, when April 1932 dawned, Natchez waited breathlessly to see if the lady's heroic efforts had paid off. A morning trickle of tourists swelled into a noontime flood, and by afternoon the town was inundated with visitors. Mrs. Miller had been right that the public hungered to view a living piece of Southern history; the first Pilgrimage was an unprecedented success. Natchez embraced a new and lucrative destiny as a tourist destination.

In September, only a few weeks after Jennie Merrill's death, to the absolute horror of the Garden Club ladies and the amusement of most everyone else, Octavia and Dick hopped on the tourist bandwagon and officially opened Glenwood to visitors. The Goat Castle Murder and its exotic cast of characters proved as potent a lure as antebellum history, and a fascinated public happily plunked down a quarter for an inside peek. To promote this ghoulish privilege, flyers with photos of the house sprouted everywhere, like posters for the Barnum & Bailey Circus, and their success proved Dick and Octavia were clever entrepreneurs.

HISTORIC GLENWOOD
Famous "Goat Castle"
Dana & Dockery Museum Open
to Pilgrimage Visitors
Piano Recitals

A second, larger flyer tantalized even more with a photo of Octavia holding a baby goat.

COME TO GOAT CASTLE
See The Famous Goats
Historic Papers. Antiques. Relics.
Piano Concerts & Lectures Every
Half Hour During The Week
By Richard H. C. ("Dick") Dana
Admission 25¢

A local committee volunteered to help Dick and Octavia with their outlandish enterprise, and a team of janitors made the place tolerable for tourists with sensitive noses. Roaches, rats and mice were routed as literally tons of garbage were carted off, the sagging galleries were shored up and the front porch replaced, but Octavia insisted on leaving the dilapidated gates and wildly overgrown grounds as they were. She knew if things were too manicured, Glenwood would be no different from the rest of Natchez's grand homes; she shrewdly groomed its creepy charisma as though dressing a stage set.

There were also changes for the stars of the Dana-Dockery show. Octavia finally accepted a complimentary visit to the beauty parlor and looked quite presentable with her chic bob, a touch of lip rouge and new blue dress and shoes. Dick was no slouch, shaving his beard, shearing his long locks and, with the help of a sympathetic local dentist, boasting a fine set of false teeth. He was quite the dandy in a new white suit and matching suede shoes, and Octavia marveled at the transformation in personality as well as appearance. It was as if celebrity had forever vanquished his shyness and a new Dick Dana emerged, joyfully reminiscent of the one she had known forty years ago. She was delighted to see him preen in his new role as "Colonel Dana" and enjoy long, refreshing stretches of "here" days.

"You look very nice, Dick," she said as they stationed themselves on the front porch that first day and prepared to greet their public. "Very nice, indeed."

"So do you," he smiled back. He turned toward the lawn as the first carload of tourists nosed warily up the driveway. "Oh, my! Look at Old Ball!"

To greet his guests, the herd patriarch rose on his hind legs and pranced down the driveway. The big goat's theatrics thrilled the crowd, a propitious moment as cars, trucks and a chartered bus discharged swarms of visitors that kept Dick and Octavia busy the entire day. Octavia was amazed by Dick's stamina as he gave endless tours of the house, played a few fractured tunes on his broken-down piano, posed for photographs, signed autographs and repeatedly coaxed Old Ball to perform his new trick. She was quite content to let Dick take center stage, quietly answering questions about the history of the house and showing her late father's Confederate uniform, cleaned and pressed in its new display case. At an Alabama woman's request, she read some of her early poetry and blushed helplessly at the round of applause from her new fans.

Tallying their take when they'd said goodbye to the last tourists, Dick and Octavia were thrilled to find over fifty dollars in their cigar box.

"My word!" Octavia laughed. "I guess it does pay to be crazy!"

The crowds swelled steadily as word spread about Natchez's most unique attraction. The railroad man made good on his offer, and on Sunday, September eleventh, the Mississippi Central Railroad operated a special train from Hattiesburg that brought six hundred passengers to Goat Castle. "Mississippi Day" was declared to herald their arrival and, a few days later, a second excursion train was inaugurated from New Orleans. For the first time in American history, public interest in a murder was strong enough to support trains from two railroads.

Goat Castle and its denizens, both human and hoofed, had become a bonafide tourist phenomenon, as well as a moneymaking proposition. There was talk of a concert tour and radio broadcasts for Dick, and a book on Octavia's tragic life. Naturally, such serendipitous success spawned no shortage of critics who denounced Dick and Octavia for profiting from Jennie's murder and accused their visitors of macabre taste, or, worse, a perverse need to feel superior to human beings sunk to pitiable levels. True or not, the public came in droves. Some wanted to see if this modern-day House of Usher could possibly have been as dire as described in the tabloids, while others simply wanted to shake the hand of someone accused of murder. Nobody was disappointed—Goat Castle offered all this and much more.

There seemed no end to it. Octavia and Dick rose daily to find the grounds inundated with sightseers and occasionally gave concerts in Duncan Park, one of Dick's preferred refuges during his Wild Man days as well as Octavia's one-time source for water. Despite his injured hand, Dick honed his musical skills with a combination of practice and a new piano with all its keys. Crowds were amused when the star pianist appeared onstage sporting two belts and, on a few occasions, two sets of suspenders as well.

"A man can never be too safe these days," he coyly advised his audience.

No one was surprised when a bite from the show business bug and its attendant financial rewards prompted the enterprising pair to take their show on the road. With Dick's full approval, Octavia expanded her role, reciting her poetry in nearby towns and giving colorful speeches on everything from the Old South to the serpentine route of her peculiar destiny. Among others, C.B. Coney, superintendent of Sicily Island High School, invited them to perform in the school auditorium. Dick gave a piano recital and lectured on antebellum architecture while Octavia poignantly expounded on her life and read a new poem written just for the occasion. These performances culminated in a booking at the Jackson auditorium, and eventually there was talk of venturing outside Mississippi, perhaps even a national tour, as long as Octavia and Dick could hold the public's fancy. They had finally found appreciative audiences for their life's work, and the grotesque circumstances thrusting them into the spotlight bothered them not at all. Nor did public opinion.

"They can say whatever they like," Octavia said, gleefully stashing eighty-seven dollars into one of her father's old cigar boxes.

"As long as they pay as well as say, eh?" Dick joked.

"Yes, indeed," Octavia chuckled. "Thanks to them, the Wild Man and the Goat Woman are doing just fine these days!"

31

W HILE THE GOAT Castle carnival flirted with national exposure, Natchez mostly forgot about their
famous odd couple and focused on more important issues. The
Democrat's headlines dutifully reported "Arrest In Lindbergh
Case" (September 4), "Jean Harlow Questioned About Death
Of Husband" (September 7), "Gandhi's Life-Threatening Fast"
(September 25) and "Roosevelt Defeats Hoover" (November
9). Then, on November 15, Miss Jennie's murder resurfaced in
a small item buried deep inside the newspaper:

INVESTIGATION OF MERRILL
CASE HOLDS INTEREST

Sheriff Roberts had finally announced enough evidence
for the indictment of a "number of persons" which he was
now prepared to present to the grand jury, and Natchez
caught Goat Castle fever all over again. By late November, the

Mississippi Grand Jury had examined evidence assembled by Roberts and Maurice O'Neill, as well as the Chicago Police Bureau of Investigation, and returned a first-degree murder indictment against Georges Pearles, alias Lawrence "Pinckney" Williams, for his role in the death of Jane Surget Merrill. The post-mortem indictment was recommended by the state Attorney-General to meet a peculiar legal technicality. Under Mississippi law, an accessory to a crime could not be indicted before a principal.

This opened the door to the indictment of Emily Burns.

Emily's trial, which commenced at 8:30 AM on November twenty-sixth, was the most exciting legal event since Octavia and Dick's habeas corpus hearing. Once again the courtroom was jammed as eager crowds waited to hear evidence brought against the accused, and once again there were several camps. There were those anxious to believe Miss Jennie's killer had a conspirator, while others suspected Sheriff Roberts had botched the investigation. A third, smaller faction believed there was a cover-up and that Emily was merely a scapegoat.

The state had subpoenaed some forty witnesses, but only twenty testified before Circuit Judge R. L. Corban and a jury. Emily's convoluted accounts of the crime were presented in affidavit form, a disturbingly erratic testimony convincing some and confusing others. Why did she keep changing her mind? Did she have a vendetta against her poor cousin, Edgar Newell, whose alibi was unshakable? Why had she accused the Jacks, who also had airtight proof of their innocence? Were her conflicting stories an effort to protect the real killer or some other accessory, or were they forced and/or false? Or was the poor woman simply crazy?

The prosecution was led by county attorney Joseph E. Brown and State District Attorney Clay Tucker, who asked for a guilty verdict carrying the death penalty. W. E. Logan and W. A. Geisenberger defended Emily with a plea of not guilty by reason of insanity.

In the opening arguments, the prosecution called John R. Junkin, president of the Board of Supervisors. Junkin had served as a special deputy sheriff in the investigation and testified that Emily had made three different confessions in his presence, implicating Pearles, Newell, Octavia and Dick. Junkin also swore that he had gone to Pine Bluff after Pearles was shot and returned with some clothing and a .32.20 pistol that Emily identified as belonging to the dead man. Cross-examined by the defense, Junkin said he had questioned Emily several times about the murder but denied using threats to coerce a confession.

Chancellor Clerk W. P. Abbott then testified that Emily had implicated several parties while they were en route to Jackson, the same night she made her confession to other officers at the Adams County Jail. Yet another confession, he said, came after Emily was taken to Glenburnie Manor where she re-enacted events at the scene of the murder. That time, Emily did not include Newell, Octavia or Dick in the crime. Abbott also testified that Emily's reenactment was done with no coaching or prompting from other parties present, including Sheriff Roberts. He said Emily showed them where she and Pearles hid under the steps of Glenburnie. She also indicated the bloody trail on the gallery and took them to the spot where the lamp was dropped and Miss Jennie's body was dumped in the thicket. All this information, Abbott insisted, merely corroborated publicly known facts about the crime.

Maurice O'Neill was up next, testifying that holistic tests made in his New Orleans laboratory confirmed that the bullets found at Glenburnie matched those fired from Pearles's gun. He proved his point with a demonstration using a small machine for comparing bullets and said there was no doubt Pearles's pistol had killed Miss Jennie. The jury also looked at photos of Pearles's corpse, made when O'Neill was in Chicago at the time the body was positively identified. O'Neill's powerful testimony was repeatedly challenged by attorneys for the defense, but Judge Corban overruled all objections. The strength of O'Neill's findings also overrode J. E. Chancellor's shoddy fingerprint work.

Other witnesses included Robert Henslee of Pine Bluff, the police officer who had shot Pearles to death. Henslee vividly described the critical moment when Pearles tried to kill him and he retaliated in self-defense. He also described taking a gun and bag of clothing from the dead man. More key testimony came when Sheriff Roberts stated that he had given the two bullets found in the Merrill home to O'Neill, and A. E. Sims, a postman, said that on August eighth he had delivered a letter to Emily from Pine Bluff.

The most damning evidence came from Herbert Kingsberry, a black trusty at the county jail, who testified Emily gave him a letter the day after she was brought in. She asked him to deliver it to Ben Johnson, who was in turn supposed to give it to one Annie Reed. Instead, Kingsberry passed it to Deputy Sheriff Farris and Special Deputy Sheriff Hyde Jenkins who both read it. In the letter, according to Kingsberry, Emily asked Annie to go to her house and retrieve a pistol, rifle, overcoat, hat and some letters from Pearles. He added that Emily urged her friend to either hide or destroy these items.

The prosecution then rested.

The defense called Sheriff Roberts back to the stand and questioned him about Emily's confession to Reverend Charlie Anderson. Roberts stated that he had been in the cell when the two were together but had heard nothing along those lines. Reverend Anderson testified that Emily had confessed to accompanying Pearles to Glenburnie Manor and related a story similar to those already given by the lawmen. Several jurors leaned forward as the soft-spoken minister said Emily told him Pearles went home with her after the murder and she tried to clean his bloody clothes with water and stain remover. There was more buzz in the courtroom when a Kingston Pike neighbor of Miss Jennie's testified that, on the scorching night of the murder, she witnessed the odd spectacle of a man wearing a black hat and overcoat heading toward Glenburnie. She could not say if he was Negro or white but swore he was alone and that Emily Burns was not in his company.

Throughout the proceedings, the court remained baffled by Emily's twisted testimony and the question of her sanity. The defense seized the final moments of the trial to address these critical issues, bringing to the stand Dr. A. W. Dumas, who testified that he had examined and treated Emily and believed she suffered from dementia praecox, a form of schizophrenia. His diagnosis was supported by eyewitnesses claiming the girl was prone to fits and spasms that caused her to foam at the mouth. Emily's mother corroborated, stating that her daughter had never been normal.

The prosecution quickly countered by recalling Junkin, Roberts and Chief Deputy Joseph Stone, with all three swearing that Emily had exhibited none of the behavior described by Dr. Dumas and the others while in their custody. While Emily's conflicting confessions were deeply frustrating, they were not enough to make the men doubt her sanity, at least not on a witness stand.

The tension was near unbearable when the defendant was finally called to testify. Emily Burns's lips barely moved as she whispered the oath, but her voice rang clear when she faced the jury and declared her innocence.

"Pinckney Williams left my house Monday morning before the murder and I never saw him again! I wasn't nowhere near Glenburnie Manor the night Miss Jennie was killed! I was at home all by myself!"

The courtroom erupted with rumbles of disbelief until Judge Corban pounded his gavel for silence. Order restored, Emily continued with a testimony that was no less stunning.

"Everything I said was based on what I'd read in the paper about the murder. I only said all that stuff 'cause I was scared. Soon's I got to the jail they started askin' me all kinds of questions. Sometimes they was two, three men askin' me things. Sometimes they was five, all yellin' at the same time. I got so confused, I didn't even know what I was sayin'."

The courtroom was especially interested in her comments about John Junkin: "He was the first one to ask me questions. He took me in a little room and I saw a whip on the table. Soon's I saw it, I knew he'd use it on me if I didn't do what he said. Then he says I got half an hour to tell the truth. I was so scared, I didn't know what to do and that's when I remembered what I'd read in the paper about Miss Jennie. I told Mr. Junkin I was there when it happened and so was Pinckney Williams. Then I recollected that Miss Octavia and Mr. Dick had been arrested, so I put 'em in there too."

"And Edgar Newell?"

"Seemed to me that those officers wanted him in it," she said, voice quavering. "I said he was there 'cause I was afraid not to do what they wanted. Like when they took me out to Glenburnie and told me to act out what happened that night. I was just doin' what I read in the paper, some of it anyway. Sheriff Roberts and Mr. Abbott kinda showed me where to go next. You know. Like where they found Miss Jennie's body and the lamp and things like that."

Chaos returned as more shouts and catcalls flew through the crowd. An angry Judge Corban threatened expulsion for anyone disrupting his courtroom again and instructed the prosecution and defense to make closing statements. When they finished, he dismissed the jury to deliberate. It was eleven o'clock in the morning. The trial had lasted two and a half hours.

The jury returned just thirty minutes later with a verdict of guilty.

There were a few rude whoops of approval, but most spectators remained quiet. Emily said nothing, not even when it was announced that she was to be remanded to the Adams County jail to await sentencing. All eyes followed her as she vanished from the courtroom as silently as she had appeared.

32

STEPHEN HOLMES WAS among those watching Emily disappear. He was relieved that Octavia and Dick were again exonerated but complained to Charles Ransdell, a fellow correspondent from the *Democrat*, that he was appalled by the trial.

"It was quite a good example of our judicial system *not* at work."

"And how an investigation can be botched," Ransdell added as they traded the stifling courthouse for the crisp autumn outdoors. "That business about the fingerprints, for example. We've both followed this crime, Mr. Holmes, and I just don't understand those early claims about Dick and Octavia's fingerprints being found at the scene. The investigation was so positive."

"I suppose they jumped to conclusions since Pearles had a disfigured right hand just like Dick, but Octavia's alleged prints were a botched job, plain and simple. Chancellor's going to have a rough time regaining his credibility after that fiasco. Frankly, I doubted the man the first time I talked to him. Arrogant and full of bluster."

"So Emily Burns's fingerprints were never found on the lamp?"

"Well, even the prosecution conceded fingerprinting isn't an exact science, but I wasn't surprised when they claimed they were rubbed off when someone else handled it, were you?"

"No. They didn't even talk much about the lamp and why Pearles might've carried it."

"Pearles was a man in a hurry," Holmes said. "The moon was playing hide-and-seek that night, and, with a body slung over his shoulder, he couldn't waste time getting lost in those thick woods. Duncan Minor was due to arrive at precisely eight forty-five."

Ransdell frowned. "You think Pearles knew that?"

"Pearles knew plenty," Holmes replied. "That's why he hid the body. He was buying time."

"What about Miss Jennie's dog being tied up? How come nobody got into that?"

"Pure incompetence."

Holmes suspected much more, but said nothing. It was good practice to let cub reporters formulate their own theories, and he was pleased when Ransdell took the bait.

"It's like the killer knew Miss Jennie's routine, like he knew when her servants would be gone and she would be absolutely alone. Even the caretaker was away that night."

"I believe the killer acted alone, too. He didn't need Emily Burns or anyone else for that matter. He sure as hell wasn't the kind of man to split the take, and Emily's defense should've been all over that." Holmes grunted, obviously rankled. "They didn't ask enough questions, and certainly not the *right* questions, but the point is they have a conviction and that's all they were really after. We've both seen this sort of thing before, especially in small towns." He winced as rheumatism gave his leg a vicious bite, prompting him to take Ransdell's arm as they walked down Pearl Street. "How about driving me out to Goat Castle and sharing the verdict with Dick and Octavia?"

"Capital idea!"

As they headed out Kingston Pike, Holmes massaged his aching thigh. "You know, I sneaked a peek at Glenwood while Dick and Octavia were in jail, but this rheumatism has kept me from another look. I've wanted to get back out there and see for myself what kind of show those two have put together. I hear they're charging two bits to see it."

"Unfortunately I didn't get this assignment until they'd cleaned the place up. Was it as bad as they say?"

Holmes grimaced at the memory. "Dear God! It was like the Augean stables, my friend. I've seen the worst slums in New York, and Goat Castle was right up there. It's hard to believe human beings can live that way, but we have to remember that Octavia was doing the best she could. It's one thing for an illiterate immigrant to be forced into dire circumstances, but quite another for a woman of privilege and intellect. I must say she's a remarkable and resourceful survivor. Lesser people would have simply been winnowed out."

"Some reporter I am," Ransdell chuckled. "I never even found out who nicknamed it Goat Castle."

"Ned Smith at the *Democrat*." Holmes chuckled irreverently. "When he first heard about conditions over there, he said the biggest question was how the goats could stand the place."

Ransdell's smile vanished. "Why didn't the locals do something about it?"

"Oh, I think people are the same everywhere, son. We're in the midst of the Great Depression and people these days have enough troubles of their own — "

Holmes's last words were obliterated by the blast of a horn as a large automobile roared by and rocked Ransdell's Model-T in a cloud of dust. "Well, don't that beat all!" Ransdell said, furiously pounding his horn in retaliation. "Who does that road hog think he is!"

"Duncan Minor, that's who," Holmes replied. "Seems like he's taking up where Miss Jennie left off. Great Scot! Will you look at that automobile!"

Ransdell squinted through the dust. "What kind is it?"

"Packard. A twenty-seventy-one Dietrich convertible Victoria. Right off the assembly line, too."

"What's something like that cost, Mr. Holmes?"

"Something in the neighborhood of sixty-eight hundred. I doubt if anybody in Mississippi drives a more expensive automobile. Even the Governor." He watched Duncan disappear around a curve in the highway and shook his head. "Well, I'd heard about it and now I've seen it for myself. First the parties and now that damned car."

"I imagine everyone in town knows Duncan Minor's a changed man."

"Maybe 'free' man is a better term." That gave Ransdell pause. "Douglas Oliver told me Minor is planning to take the waters at Hot Springs. Everyone knows the only traveling that man ever did while Jennie was alive was between Oakland and Glenburnie."

"I sure wonder what poor Miss Jennie would say about that!"

"Probably the same thing everyone else is saying."

"Which is what?"

"That old Duncan's too tight to spend his own cash, but he sure doesn't mind spreading the Merrill money around like manure. Something mighty peculiar about that."

"Oh, they're both queer ducks, Mr. Holmes. I always thought they deserved each other."

"Yeah." Holmes chuckled. "I hear Miss Jennie's family is furious about the will."

"No doubt. Imagine being cut off without a cent by your own flesh and blood."

"I suspect there was no love lost between Jennie and the rest of the Merrills. In fact, I doubt if she saw a single relative in the last thirty years."

"Except cousin Duncan, of course."

"I guess his undying loyalty paid off, eh?" Despite his pain, Holmes chuckled again as they turned into Glenwood's overgrown driveway. "Good Lord, man! Just look at all those cars!"

Ransdell found a parking place between a car from Ohio and a truck from Tennessee and took Holmes's arm again as they looked for Octavia. They found her in a rocking chair on the front porch, posing for the tourists. Cameras clicked and snapped as she was photographed with a bleating kid in her arms. She smiled and waved as Holmes approached.

"Hello there, Mr. Holmes!"

"Miss Dockery!" he called. "Have you heard the news?"

Octavia squinted in the bright sunlight and smoothed a wayward strand of hair when she saw Holmes's dapper tweed suit. "What news?"

"Emily Burns was just convicted."

She abruptly straightened. "Really? Were you there?"

"I'd say half the town was there." Holmes smiled. "Congratulations. You and Mr. Dana are completely exonerated."

"As well we should be," Octavia replied, a bit curtly. She stroked the little goat's head and smiled as it nuzzled in response, but her tone was strangely cold. "Will they execute her?"

"The verdict automatically carries a life sentence," Holmes explained. "They'll have to decide whether or not to give her the death penalty."

"I see."

"I doubt they will, though," Holmes continued. "I think the crowd pretty much got what they wanted."

"And what is that?"

"A conviction," he said a bit too loudly. When a clutch of eavesdropping tourists edged closer, the famous reporter lowered his voice. "It also means that the case is closed once and for all. We can go back to our routines and forget this unpleasantness."

"Speak for yourself, sir."

Holmes's face reddened. "I'm sorry, Miss Dockery. I didn't mean to suggest—"

"And I didn't mean to sound rude, Mr. Holmes. I only meant that things have not been resolved to my complete satisfaction." Octavia slid the kid gently onto the porch as she stood and scanned the driveway before revealing a shocker of her own. "Our new attorney is coming over tomorrow to discuss our lawsuit."

"What lawsuit?"

Octavia was surprised he hadn't second-guessed her. "Against the sheriff, of course. For false arrest, public humiliation and other personal damages. I should think you of all people would understand such action."

Far from understanding, Holmes was horrified. "You've already discussed it?"

"Certainly," Octavia replied. "One must stay on top of this sort of thing."

Holmes frowned. "I don't want to spoil your victory, Miss Dockery, but I'm not certain that's a wise idea. Sheriff Roberts isn't the kind of man to take that kind of..."

"These are for you and Colonel Dana, Miss Dockery!" A woman bustled between them and thrust a basket of cookies toward Octavia. "To celebrate your good fortune."

"Thank you, my dear," Octavia said grandly. "We'll share them as soon as he's finished his piano recital." She turned away from Holmes, forgetting him entirely when another group of tourists asked when she would give another poetry reading. "Fifteen minutes," she replied. "Each of you kindly give your fifty cents to the lady over there. Thank you for coming."

"Fifty cents!" Ransdell hissed. "They've doubled the admission!"

"Apparently nobody minds," Holmes observed as a dozen people hurried to pay Goat Castle's volunteer cashier. "Look at the line!"

"What about a photo, Miss Dockery?" someone called.

"Certainly," Octavia replied. She walked a few feet from the porch and flung an arm high, beaming when Old Ball trotted over and reared on cue. The cameras clicked again and again as she smiled for posterity.

HOLMES'S ASSESSMENT OF the sheriff's reaction was right on target. Roberts and his buddies were lounging around the jail when he was handed papers announcing the Dana/Dockery lawsuit. He snorted with disbelief. "What the devil is wrong with those people?"

"Reckon they've got themselves a wiseacre lawyer out to make a few bucks," Abbott offered. Roberts's face darkened as he perused the terms of the lawsuit. "What's it say, Book?"

"A *few* bucks? Those crazies want thirty thousand dollars in damages!" Roberts threw the papers across the room and fumed. "It'll be a cold day in hell before they get a penny out of me."

"What're you going to do?" Farris asked.

His response was swift. "I'll indict them for their part in Miss Jennie's death. Has everyone forgotten that George Pearles was at Goat Castle a few days before the murder? Just how much did they learn from his visit? How do we know they haven't been withholding information?"

"C'mon, Book," Abbot said. "You know those old fools wouldn't knowingly—"

"Those 'old fools' as you call them don't know what they're getting themselves into!" Roberts growled. "It's been my experience that if someone hands you a hot potato, you hand it right back to them!"

"Dear Lord in heaven," Abbott moaned. Like everyone else in the room, he was sick to death of the Merrill murder and its aftermath. "Is this damned thing ever going to end?"

"Oh, it'll end alright," Roberts said. "I'm the one who's going to end it."

ROBERTS WAS A man of his word. Dick and Octavia withdrew their lawsuit as soon as they heard about the sheriff's stunning counter-suit and hoped he would retreat as well. He did not, and they unhappily learned there would be a trial they had scant chance of winning. The news sent Dick careening deep into a "there" day, leaving Octavia to face the courtroom alone. Their lawyer insisted their best hope lay among the townspeople who would surely keep Natchez's most celebrated citizens from returning to jail, and he proved correct as hundreds rallied to the peculiar cause. No allies were more surprising or earnest than the Garden Club ladies, but their motives were hardly selfless. As averse to bad press as Octavia was to prison, they were horrified by the prospect of hoi polloi flocking to Goat Castle instead of quality folk admiring their grand antebellum mansions; they knew the less publicity about Dick and Octavia the better. On the day of jury selection, these graciously conniving souls flocked to the courthouse like everyone else.

This latest act in the ongoing Dana-Dockery sideshow promised more of the usual fireworks. The overflow crowd was so rambunctious that the judge likened it more to a county fair than a trial and ordered silence as the first potential jurors were called. Audience excitement escalated as one person after another was disqualified for obvious sympathies toward Dick and Octavia. Unable to shout their approval, the spectators nudged one another as the number approached one hundred and began chuckling and whistling as another hundred were dismissed. By the time three hundred people had been turned away, the crowd had grown rowdy again, and the disgusted judge decided to end the mockery and mayhem in his courtroom. He pounded his gavel until order was restored.

"It has become obvious that there is no one impartial enough to serve as a juror!" he thundered. "I am therefore declaring a mistrial!"

The Adams County Courthouse rang with cheers and applause as the town's favorite folk heroes were safe once again.

Sheriff Roberts had no official comment but was clearly pleased that his dealings with Goat Castle were finally over. Dick and Octavia thanked everyone for their support and made their way home, where Dick's mind miraculously unclouded and he went right back to playing Colonel Dana. When tourists arrived the next morning, they were welcomed by a lop-sided but freshly painted sign.

Visit The Nationally Famous Goat Castle!!

Save The Old Folks' Home!

To the dismay of the Garden Club ladies, publicity from the new trial produced a greater crush of tourists than ever. Cash in the cigar box was such that Dick and Octavia were able to hire an assistant to help with their enterprise and keep a lookout for light-fingered tourists. Things at Goat Castle couldn't have been better, except that Old Ball grew tired of performing and deserted the family circus. A good many of Octavia's precious herd followed the grumpy old billy goat to a new home alongside a distant ravine, but enough remained to keep visitors happy.

As the months slipped by, Octavia warmed to her life as an accidental celebrity and looked forward to answering questions and signing autographs. Dick blossomed, too, in ways that pleased and heartened her. As he acted and reacted with the crowd, there were more glimmers of the man she had known in New York, a man in love with poor, doomed Amelia and passionate about his music. Octavia occasionally blinked away tears when he missed piano notes while attempting sweet songs from times gone by, but she found peace in his contentment. While he played himself into blissful oblivion, she tapped her foot and applauded afterwards like everyone else. She was well aware that their freakish good fortune could not last forever and despaired whenever Dick's monologues unraveled, leaving a confused audience in their wake—and sometimes evoking heartless laughter. One afternoon a callous tourist addressed Octavia's bitterest fear.

"Hey, Colonel Dana!" the man called. "Think you might go wild again and take to the woods?"

"Oh, if the spirit moves me I just might," Dick replied, ignoring chuckles as he smiled benignly at the heckler. "Sometimes it's good to get away from mean folks. Right, Miss Octavia?"

"Why, yes," she replied, relieved when the laughter turned against the heckler and the ugly moment passed.

Even cocooned in fine lunacy, Dick had tilted lances and won a joust against human cruelty. It was a moment Octavia couldn't stop reliving as they strolled the grounds after everyone had left. She wrapped herself comfortably in the old familiar solitude descending over Glenwood and made a confidence.

"I've begun a new poem, Dick. My most ambitious yet."

"Why, that's wonderful! What's it about?"

"Us."

"You'll share it, won't you?"

"When it's finished…" She took his broken hand lightly, held it for a moment and then let it fall away. "I promise."

"Thank you."

"You're welcome, old friend."

Although fate had dealt Glenburnie Manor a devastating hand, it had ultimately taken pity on the people next door. As they walked through the woods toward home, Dick and Octavia were content to be swallowed by the deepening dusk and promise of something they long believed impossible—tomorrow.

33

WHAT DUNCAN RELISHED most about Glenburnie Manor was the solitude. He whiled away long hours in the parlor, lounging on the veranda and wandering the vast woods with only the whistle of a passing freight train or Apollo for company. It was a silence so perfect it was exhilarating, and, until early December, four months after Jennie's death, no intruders were allowed. He made an exception after receiving a letter from Stephen Holmes regarding "an article of Miss Merrill's I wish to return." He despised the nosy reporter more than ever, especially after his tear-jerking newspaper interview with Octavia Dockery. But since the letter indicated Holmes was leaving Natchez for good, Duncan acquiesced.

The meeting was set for ten in the morning, and a few minutes before the appointed hour Duncan unlocked the heavy chains guarding the gates to Glenburnie Manor. He retreated to the house and waited at the windows, a hollow pang in his chest as he watched for movement along the steep drive. At precisely ten o'clock, Charles Ransdell's Model-T chugged up the hill and discharged Holmes beneath the porte-cochère. Duncan couldn't identify his driver but was glad the reporter approached alone. He opened the door and watched with some satisfaction as his nemesis lumbered painfully toward the veranda.

"Morning, Mr. Minor!" Holmes called. "Beautiful day, isn't it?"

"Mr. Holmes." Duncan nodded crisply.

Holmes winced as he mounted the steps. "Afraid these old muscles don't work as well as they used to." He extended his hand. "Rheumatism."

Duncan gave him a limp handshake and stepped aside. "We'll sit in the parlor."

"Fine. Fine."

Holmes wheezed and eased his aching bulk into an over-stuffed chair. He took a moment to cast a keen reporter's eye around the chilly room, wondering if he might recognize something from Elms Court or Jennie's Washington Square apartment. The pair of Venetian blackamoors, he noted with some satisfaction, still stood guard.

Duncan perched on the edge of the settee, spine straight, lean face fixed on the reporter. His voice was riddled with airs. "You said you have something belonging to Miss Jennie?"

"I do, indeed." Holmes loathed the smug condescension and the absence of refreshments that indicated Duncan anticipated a brief meeting. "Before I get to that, however, I'd like to ask you a few questions."

Duncan's guard lofted higher. "Mr. Holmes, if you've come here thinking you'll coax out some sort of interview—"

"Calm yourself, Mr. Minor. Believe me I've already written far more about you than I care to." He jerked his head toward the murder scene. "I'm just as anxious to forget what happened back there as you are."

"Doubtful," Duncan sniffed.

Holmes ignored the rebuff. "Just between you and me, wouldn't you like to set the record straight?"

"I've no idea what you mean."

Holmes grinned, hoping to unnerve the sphinx. "Oh, I think you do."

"The record is already 'straight,' sir," Duncan replied. "A crime has been committed and solved. I've nothing more to say about something so personally painful, and surely even you can respect the wishes of a man who has lost the dearest thing in his life."

"Ordinarily, yes," Holmes granted, "but I don't think you're quite that man. Oh, I know you'd like the world to think you and Miss Merrill enjoyed something well beyond us mere mortals—"

"How dare you!" Duncan fumed.

"I told you to calm down." Holmes heaved his weight to get more comfortable. Excitement sometimes exacerbated his pain. "I want answers to only a few questions, and I guarantee they'll never leave this room."

Duncan was incredulous. "You expect me to believe that from a reporter? From you of all people!"

"I don't much care what you believe. I'd just like to get at the truth. We'll start by talking about your watch."

Duncan made a great show of thrusting fingers into his waistcoat pocket and coming up empty-handed. "I no longer carry a watch, sir. Time has no meaning since Miss Jennie was taken away."

Holmes groaned at the empty theatrics. "Suppose I tell you what I learned when I made a little trip up to Pine Bluff and chatted with Police Chief Fiveash. Seems the guys at the morgue found something besides a second gun on Pearles's body. An expensive gold watch to be precise."

Duncan said nothing.

"A Spanish watch with rubies for numerals. I did some checking around and learned that you had one just like it."

"Indeed," Duncan said icily. "Who said so?"

"Your sister."

Duncan's voice rose. "How dare you interrogate my family?"

Holmes snorted. "Miss Mary Grace is hardly sacrosanct, and neither are you. You might be surprised to know she had lots of interesting things to share. In fact, she was quite eager to talk to me. Relieved, even."

"I don't believe you."

"Sorry if the truth offends you, but let's get back to the watch. It belonged to your great-grandfather, Steven Minor, the Governor of Spanish Natchez."

Duncan shrugged airily. "Sheriff Roberts questioned me about the watch right after they found it. It was here in this house the night of the murder. Obviously Pearles stole it."

"A reasonable explanation," Holmes conceded. "So why were you so reluctant to talk about it?"

"That's none of your business."

"And where's the watch now?"

"I don't like these questions, Mr. Holmes!"

Holmes grunted. "Then you're really not going to like this one. Was the watch really stolen or was it partial payment for a job you engaged Mr. Pearles to perform?"

Duncan glowered. "You're opening yourself up to a slander suit, Mr. Holmes!"

"As long as no one else hears us, it's your word against mine, and I'm sure you don't want my queries to become public knowledge."

Duncan leaned back and laced long fingers together, as cool and composed as his enemy. "Just where do you think these questions will take you?"

"Where that idiotic judge and defense attorney never went!" Holmes snapped. "You've said Pearles approached you on Kingston Pike before Miss Jennie's murder. Looking for work, you said. You claimed you told him you didn't have any, but I think you told him lots more than that. I also think that wasn't your first encounter with the man. You'd talked to Pearles before, Minor, about Jennie Merrill and the fortune she supposedly stashed at Glenburnie. After all, you were the only person who knew if the rumors were true."

"As I told Sheriff Roberts, Miss Jennie never kept any money at home, and I don't intend to sit here and listen to..."

Holmes tore roughshod over Duncan's protest. "That's not what you told that desperate, gullible Negro! You fueled his fantasies of an easy robbery and quick lam out of town!" He shifted again and winced at the pain in his joints. "By all accounts Pearles was a simpleton. Someone set him on the trail to Glenburnie, pretending to ask for a handout while he was casing the joint before returning to commit the crime under the best possible conditions." He paused again before going for the jugular. "Aside from Miss Jennie, who else knew everyone, including the caretaker, would be away and that she would be totally alone the night she was murdered? Who chained Apollo in the woods? Who dangled gold and rubies under that desperado's nose and filled his Neanderthal brain with tales of more easy money, figuring he'd turn violent when he found no fortune? And who knew Miss Jennie kept a gun handy? Hell, man! Fireworks were almost guaranteed!"

Silence.

"I think you told Pearles all that and more, even offering to tie up the dog the morning of the murder. When Pearles arrived right on schedule, everything was in place and he did just as you hoped. When you got here, all that hysterical yelling and running around wasn't about Jennie. It was for Willie Boyd's benefit, something you knew damned well he'd recount for the sheriff."

"That's enough, Mr. Holmes!" Duncan leapt to his feet and strode briskly to the door. "You'd better leave."

"I'm going nowhere until I'm finished," Holmes called after him. "And if you're thinking about throwing me out, I'll remind you we're both old men and would look pretty ridiculous scrapping at our age. Besides, how would that appear to that hungry cub reporter from the *Democrat?*" He jerked his head toward the porte-cochère. "Young Ransdell came along only as my driver, but I guarantee he's dying to know what we're talking about and has absolutely no obligation to remain silent." When Duncan glared, Holmes added, "To reiterate, Mr. Minor, I have no intentions of going public. If I had, I would've done so right after that circus of a trial. Now sit down and relax."

"I prefer to stand."

Holmes clucked and shook his head. "I'll admit it took me a while to figure out why you would deliberately put Sheriff Roberts on the trail of the murderer when Pearles could implicate you as well. Hell, I'll bet you never gave it a second thought. I guess I've been up North too long to remember a Mississippi black man would never dare accuse a white man of a crime, much less be taken seriously if he did. Especially when he's a poor ignorant nigger with a criminal record and the white gentleman has an aristocratic pedigree as long as his arm. You wanted Pearles to kill Miss Jennie, but you also wanted him to be caught and punished. You wanted it all!"

Holmes watched something slowly coil behind Duncan's eyes, but the strike never came.

"You're a damned coward, Minor. A yellow-bellied coward who thinks he's above the law. You and all the rest of these white Christian hypocrites with sheriffs and judges in their pockets so they can lynch and imprison with impunity and attend church as though nothing happened." Holmes's neck burned as his temper rose and, despite the chilly parlor, sweat trickled down his back. "Worst of all is poor Emily Burns, an innocent bystander if ever there was one! I shudder to think how easy it was to intimidate and threaten that poor, simple-minded girl into signing a confession, just because she was in the wrong place at the wrong time! That worked out nicely for you, didn't it? Two convictions for the price of one. A little unexpected icing on the cake. Delicious, eh?"

Duncan drifted to the window and studied his new Packard gleaming beneath the porte-cochère. " I'm certainly not saying Sheriff Roberts or the cop who shot George Pearles were in ca-hoots with you," Holmes continued, "but how mighty conve-nient for you that the murderer never stood trial."

Duncan never flinched.

"Just as it was mighty convenient that you were the sole beneficiary to Miss Jennie's considerable estate." He chuckled grimly. "I don't suppose you know you're the talk of the town." When Duncan glowered, Holmes said, "Oh, my, yes! We poor local folks just can't understand your sudden spending sprees. After all, it's pretty uncharacteristic behavior for the notorious Mississippi Miser."

"It's my money to spend as I choose," Duncan muttered fi-nally. "I've done nothing wrong."

Holmes took a deep breath and expelled a suspicion that had haunted him since the moment he learned of Jennie Merrill's death.

"Except conspiring to commit murder."

Duncan turned slowly around, visage unwavering. "So you've finally said what you came here to say, eh? You brought nothing of Miss Jennie's, just false allegations."

"I have something to give you all right." Holmes patted his waistcoat pocket. "All in good time."

Duncan seemed unruffled by the audacious accusation. "I know you've won many distinguished journalism awards, Mr. Holmes, but this time your conclusions are preposterous. Why on earth would I wish to kill the one thing in the world I loved the most?" He held out his hands, palms up. "To be a murder, there has to be a motive."

"Aside from money?"

"I didn't need Jennie's money!" Duncan snapped.

"Then we'll examine another motive. Among the many things Mary Grace talked about was your mother. What a domineering, belittling, smothering shrew she was!"

Holmes struck pay dirt: "How dare you!" Duncan flared.

"How she ran Mary Grace's life and yours until you found escape with Jennie Merrill. Or thought you did. In the beginning, Miss Jennie was a pretty, sweet, compassionate young thing. I knew her then, too, remember? Temperamental and willful to be sure, but nothing like the harridan she became after her family evicted her. Somewhere along the line, you discovered you had merely traded one feminine hell for another, and that switching submission from your mother to Jennie was no bargain. That's when you began looking to get out. Old habits die hard, eh, Mr. Minor? Especially when they're almost forty years old!"

"You're insane!"

Holmes noticed the man did not try to hush him up. "Jennie's fortune only made escape more appealing. I wouldn't be surprised if you started looking for an escape hatch the day you learned you were sole beneficiary. Face it, Minor. That haughty, selfish bitch drove you crazy like she did everyone else."

Duncan's fingers closed into a fist and slowly reopened.

"Day after day, night after night, all those years of incessant nagging. Life with her must have been an unending nightmare. I saw how she treated you the night I came calling. 'Take Apollo inside! Fetch Mr. Holmes a cookie. Wait inside while we talk!' My God, man, she treated you like that damned dog! Talk about insane!"

Holmes mopped his damp forehead and studied Duncan closely, waiting for a telltale sign, a slip of any kind to confirm his suspicions. When Duncan remained as enigmatic and composed as ever, Holmes knew he would learn nothing more and struggled painfully to his feet. He pulled Jennie's St. Christopher medal from his pocket and tossed it onto the mantle.

"Here. Maybe this will help you find that peaceful journey you've sought all these years."

Duncan's dead eyes flashed to life and for once he moved swiftly, hurrying to identify

Jennie's keepsake. The mantel mirror reflected his gaunt face slumping with shock, a look not lost on Holmes.

"She gave this to *you?*"

"Before she left New York that last time. Before she came back to Natchez."

"I don't believe it!"

"Why not?"

A quiver edged Duncan's reply. "I sent it to Jennie before she left for Brussels, but she said she never received it."

"Really?" Holmes grinned, curiosity stoked.

"Why would she tell me that? And why would she give you something so personal?"

Holmes couldn't resist milking the serendipitous opportunity as he edged toward the front door. "I'm sure I don't know. Any more than I know why she told me it was a gift from the King's Daughters. She never even mentioned you at all." He savored the devastation on Duncan's face, the leaching of color and twitching cheek muscles. "In any case, it hardly matters now. You're the one she came back to after all."

"No," Duncan muttered. Then, loudly, "No!"

Holmes moved onto the veranda and negotiated the steps with difficulty. "You'll be happy to know I'm leaving."

"Wait!" Duncan said. "What did you mean *I'm* the one she came back to?"

"Just that." Holmes shrugged airily. "Nothing more." His calculated insouciance struck the desired chord.

Duncan leaned close enough for Holmes to smell his sour breath. "There was something between the two of you!" Silence. "*Wasn't there?*"

A crack in that stony facade at last, Holmes thought with great satisfaction. He shrugged again. "You have your personal inner sanctum, Mr. Minor, and I have mine."

"Damn you, Holmes!" Duncan snarled. "That's what really

brought you here, isn't it? To throw your affair in my face after all these years! Answer me!"

Holmes eased off the last step and gratefully accepted Ransdell's assistance into the car. Then he turned to confront Duncan's malignant gaze.

"Let's just say I wanted the satisfaction of telling you face to face that I don't buy your innocence, Minor. Never have. Never will."

"You bastard! You'll regret this!"

"To the contrary, sir. I've found our little visit very satisfying indeed." Holmes nodded with exaggerated politesse. "Good morning."

As the Model-T jounced down the hill, Ransdell studied the side mirror until Duncan and the pillars of Glenburnie Manor receded to nothing. "What in the devil was that all about, Mr. Holmes? Duncan Minor looked as if he wanted to kill you!"

"It's highly possible," Holmes chuckled

"But why?"

Holmes sighed contentedly as a cherished memory waltzed through his mind.

"Because half a century ago I saw a pretty girl standing at the rail of a Mississippi steamboat and couldn't resist striking up a conversation."

AFTERWORD

DUNCAN ENJOYED HIS uncharacteristic high life
for six years, following Jennie to the grave in 1939
at age seventy-seven. Owing to his legendary procrastination,
it was no surprise that he died intestate, but in a much-pub-
licized effort to clear her family name, Mary Grace Minor returned Jennie's bequest, along with Glenburnie Manor, to the
Merrills. A year later, the case had its final postscript when
newly-elected Mississippi governor Paul Johnson commuted
Emily Burns's life sentence. She lived another forty-three years,
a respected Natchez citizen fondly remembered as a favorite of
neighborhood children.

Pneumonia took Richard Dana in October 1947, also at age
seventy-seven. In an attempt to remain at Glenwood, her home
for nearly half a century, Octavia claimed to be Dick's common-
law wife. When failing health undermined her strength for
more legal battles, she was removed to a nursing home, where
she died six months later at eighty-four, feisty to the end.

With no one to tend them, Goat Castle's eponymous herd dispersed, and the fabled furnishings were auctioned off for a paltry thirteen thousand dollars. The property repeatedly changed hands until a developer proposed turning it into an orphanage, but his dreams were as doomed as those of Dick and Octavia. In 1952, hopelessly derelict and bereft of champions, the mansion was demolished and a suburban development called Glenwood carved from its vast acreage. Historians debate its exact site but concur that of all Natchez's grand town houses, it had surely suffered the longest, fallen furthest from grace, and died the most shameful death. The poor, unwelcome bastard had finally left the family reunion.

Although the principal players in the outlandish Goat Castle drama are long gone, with the exception of Glenwood, their grand stages endure. Jennie's beloved Elms Court remains in the family, Glenburnie Manor, Gloucester and Oakland are also privately owned, and Longwood is a house museum operated by the Pilgrimage Garden Club. All are handsomely restored and occasionally open to the public.

"Shadowy figures they remain."

NO DOUBT JENNIE Merrill made enemies, but did one or more of them abet George Pearles in extracting the ultimate revenge, or was her death simply the result of a botched burglary? Pearles, a brutish, small-time crook with several aliases, was undoubtedly dangerous, bold enough to accost a white man in a strictly segregated society where blacks knew and kept their place. Was it mere coincidence that he found Jennie alone on a vast estate usually populated by half a dozen others, or had someone supplied that crucial information? Did Emily Burns fail to name the real participants in her ever-changing list of suspects? What actually transpired when Pearles encountered Duncan alone on Kingston Pike?

Despite his abiding love for Jennie, Duncan's bizarre *folie à deux* may not have been ideal. Catherine Van Court, an early friend of the couple, observed the nature of their relationship in *This Old House*, published in 1950: "[Duncan and Jennie] had known each other since childhood and their love was of long standing. He was large of stature, she small and graceful with dark eyes and white skin. It was soon apparent that she would dominate him. Indeed, hers was a dominant personality."

After years of manipulation by Jennie and his mother Katherine, overbearing women by many accounts, Duncan's stability and indulgence could have easily eroded. We'll never know how Jennie treated him, but it's not unreasonable to assume the arrogance and acrimony she publicly flaunted also flared in her private life. Did Duncan contentedly remain a milquetoast for decades or did he secretly chafe at Jennie's strong reins? What raced through his famously stingy mind when she revealed he would inherit her vast fortune? The only certainty is that before her death he skimped on necessities and afterwards squandered Jennie's funds on luxuries and rekindled a social life dormant for decades. Surely this was the behavior of a liberated man, but did something else set Duncan's desire for emancipation in motion?

Despite Pearles's posthumous conviction, many Natchezians believed he did not act alone and that poor Emily was a tragic victim of time and place. Even Sheriff Roberts, who worked so doggedly to find Jennie's killer, did not consider the case satisfactorily closed. His doubts surfaced in "The Crimson Crime in Glenburnie Manor," a first-person account of his investigation serialized in *The Master Detective* a year after the murder.

"Who were the accessories to the crime whom Emily Burns shielded?" he asked. "None of us officially connected with the case really know. Shadowy figures they were, and shadowy figures they remain."

Author Harnett Kane voiced more direct suspicions in *Natchez on the Mississippi*, a bestseller in 1946. "Still, few

thought the real story told," Kane wrote. "Many became convinced that Emily Burns, the only person convicted, had received a raw deal, and petitioned state officers for her release.
But county officials, having gotten somebody into prison, were
quite satisfied... A newspaper expressed a common opinion by
declaring that though the man Pearles had seemingly been the
actual killer, 'the identity of the person who inspired the murder will never be officially known, or proved.'" The beginning
of Kane's next paragraph is abundantly telling: "A little before
then, death had come for Duncan Minor."

Michael Llewellyn
Natchez, Mississippi

About the Author

MICHAEL LLEWELLYN, the author of twenty published novels in a variety of genres, says *The Goat Castle Murder* was his most challenging book yet. "The details of the murder, trial and aftermath are as factual as I could make them, but with information on the private lives of Jennie Merrill and her circle often embellished or contradictory, the events leading up to that fateful August night in 1932 had to be fictionalized." Michael is married and lives in Fredericksburg, Virginia. He invites you to visit his website at *michael-llewellyn.net*.

+ The setting for most of Michael Llewellyn's novel is Natchez, Mississippi. Although a quintessentially Southern city, Natchez was divided in its loyalties to the Confederacy. Did you find this surprising? And how did those entangled loyalties impact the lives of Jennie Merrill, Duncan Minor, Octavia Dockery and Richard Dana?

+ The South is famous for colorful, eccentric characters and individualism. Discuss the ways in which Jennie, Duncan, Octavia and Dick reflect this tradition and how their quirks affected the outcome of *The Goat Castle Murder*.

+ Jennie Merrill was a very complex woman. Did you like her?

+ Octavia Dockery was on her way to a brilliant career until family circumstances pushed her onto a different path. How much did the time period affect the outcome of her life? How did her own eccentricities shape that outcome?

+ Duncan Minor loved Jennie from an early age. Discuss their relationship—which Llewellyn describes as a *folie à deux*. Have you witnessed or experienced a similar relationship?

+ Richard Dana might have become a concert pianist had an accident not intervened. How did his eccentricities shape his destiny? Do you understand his transition from Richard to Dick?

+ The main characters are real people with the notable exception of Stephen Holmes, the reporter. Discuss Holmes's role in the movement and impact of this story.

+ Various people were initially arrested for the murder of Jennie Merrill. Discuss the impact of race and class on the investigation and the trial.

+ Not everyone believed George Pearles acted alone in Jennie's murder. Who do you think might also have been involved?

+ Natchez is more than just a backdrop to this story. Were you intrigued or turned off by what you read about it? Would you like to visit?

Creole Son
by Michael Llewellyn
Published by Water
Street Press

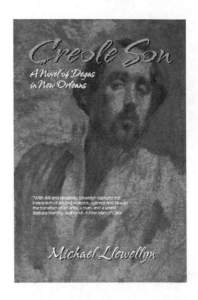

In 1872, French painter
Edgar Degas is disil-
lusioned by a lackluster
career and haunted by
the Prussian siege of
Paris and the blood-
bath of the Commune.
Seeking personal and
professional rebirth,
he journeys to New
Orleans, birthplace
of his Creole mother. He is horrified to learn he has
exchanged one city in crisis for another—post-Civil
War New Orleans is a corrupt town occupied by hostile
Union troops and suffering under the heavy hand of
Reconstruction. He is further shocked to find his family deeply involved in the violent struggle to reclaim
political power at all costs.

Despite the chaos swirling around him, Degas
sketches and paints with fervor and manages to
reinvent himself and transition his style from neoclas-
sical into the emerging world of Impressionism. He
ultimately became one of the masters of the new movement, but how did New Orleans empower Degas to
fulfill this destiny?

The answer may be found in the impeccably re-
searched, richly imagined historical novel, *Creole Son*.